Time 2 Die

BRENT LADD

T|ME 2 DIE

A CODI SANDERS THRILLER

NEW YORK

LONDON • NASHVILLE • MELBOURNE • VANCOUVER

Time 2 Die

A Codi Sanders Thriller

Published in New York, New York, by Morgan James Publishing. Morgan James is a trademark of Morgan James, LLC. www.MorganJamesPublishing.com

Proudly distributed by Ingram Publisher Services.

Morgan James BOGO™

A **FREE** ebook edition is available for you or a friend with the purchase of this print book.

CLEARLY SIGN YOUR NAME ABOVE

Instructions to claim your free ebook edition:
1. Visit MorganJamesBOGO.com
2. Sign your name CLEARLY in the space above
3. Complete the form and submit a photo of this entire page
4. You or your friend can download the ebook to your preferred device

ISBN 9781631958489 paperback
ISBN 9781631958496 ebook
Library of Congress Control Number:
2021951864

Cover & Interior Design by:
Christopher Kirk
www.GFSstudio.com

Morgan James PUBLISHING

Builds

with...

Habitat for Humanity®
Peninsula and
Greater Williamsburg

Morgan James is a proud partner of Habitat for Humanity Peninsula and Greater Williamsburg. Partners in building since 2006.

Get involved today! Visit MorganJamesPublishing.com/giving-back

Dedicated to my son Brady
—a true friend to others, willing to give even during the hardest times, no matter the costs. He will fight for what's right, consequences or not.

AUTHOR'S NOTE

This is a work of fiction. Any resemblance to persons living or dead, or actual events, is either coincidental or is used for fictive and storytelling purposes. Some elements of this story are inspired by true events; all aspects of the story are imaginary events inspired by conjecture. *Time 2 Die* was a true labor of love. Like life, the writing process is a journey, one meant to be savored, and to me, it's more about the pilgrimage itself than the destination. I learned a ton while writing this book, and I hope it's reflected in the story and the prose. Only you, the reader, can be the judge of the results. Drop me a line if you have feedback or just want to say hi.

Brent Ladd Loefke, 2019, Irvine CA

Chapter One

(Based on actual events)

LONG ISLAND, NY – JULY 2, 1906 – 4:23 P.M.

Charles Henry Warren spit on the worn floorboards as he slammed his beer stein back on the battered bar, spilling some of the murky brew. "What is this filth?" he said.

The demure barmaid dipped her head as she spoke. "Sorry, sir. I will pour you another." She wore a dingy apron with her curly brown hair tied up.

She turned and moved sheepishly toward the backroom where the good stuff was kept.

Charles was dressed in a brown custom herringbone suit with an ironed white collared shirt and matching tie. He flicked a piece of lint off his coat before pounding on the bar in an effort to speed up the barmaid. "Come now, woman!"

He had a nervous habit of tapping his middle finger on his father's gold pocket watch that he kept in his vest pocket, always making sure it was still there and situated securely away from any pickpockets. He surveyed his surroundings. The dark room seemed to be a haven for the less desirable of Long Island. There was a smashed and partially boarded-up window where sunlight leaked through the smeared remaining panes. It illuminated the stained, abused floor that had seen its share of blood and vomit.

A man with vile breath and rotted teeth stepped up next to Charles in hopes of starting a conversation with the wealthy patron and perhaps scoring a free drink. Charles gave the ragged man a stern glare that sent him down to the end of the bar out of smelling distance. In the back corner of the room were three hard-looking men that sat around a small weathered table speaking in hushed voices. They had a collection of empty glasses that now matched their pockets.

Charles had left his bank in New York three days ago to join his family at their summer beach house in Oyster Bay, along the north coast of Long Island. The sand and sun did little for him, and a household of children had finally driven him to this seedy sanctuary—Mollie's Tavern.

By the time the barmaid returned with a fresh brew, Charles was starting to feel over-heated. He pulled at his collar before guzzling the warm beer in a single lift. A final look around, and he stumbled out of the bar. The barmaid was surprised that just one beer would have such an effect on a grown man, but she pocketed the two bits and turned to the next patron. "What'll it be?"

Charles had walked twenty steps before he realized that the three men from the back of the bar had followed and surrounded him. He looked up with a dazed expression.

They were skittish, glancing around for a stray witness or policeman.

"We'll be takin' that watch and your wallet," the larger of the three spat out, as they closed in around him.

Their body odor was overwhelming and Charles's eyes started to water and burn.

One of the men palmed a small knife, making sure it was seen. Charles tried to speak, but an unexpected convulsion expelled most of his beer onto the cobbled street and all over the men's shoes. There was a moment that seemed like an eternity before the action registered.

"He's got the fever. Run!" The three thugs ran off, shaking their shoes in a strange tango, trying to flick off the beer-infused vomit that could be a death sentence.

Charles staggered in a crooked line past the gas lanterns and horse-drawn wagons that populated this section of town. He was oblivious to the shouts and calls for him to get out of the way. His vision was starting to blur as the fever spiked his core temperature to well above 106 degrees Fahrenheit. By the time he made it back to the beach house, he had crapped his pants and was shaking profusely. He reached for the door knocker, but it seemed unattainably high as he collapsed at his front door.

Within the week, the entire Charles Henry Warren family of eleven would be stricken, leaving three dead and four more fighting for their lives.

***

Mary Mallon closed the door behind her and started to unpack her sparse belongings. She laid them across the wood-framed bed in her tiny new quarters. Her last job with the Warren family had ended in tragedy, as part of the family had died off. Why she had not been affected was beyond her. New York City was caught up in a recent outbreak that was ravaging its occupants. It had left Mary out of work and back on the street at a time when most families were closing their doors to strangers. Luckily, there was a demand for good cooks, and she soon booked another job with a wealthy family in Brooklyn. She palmed a small gold Claddagh and let her fingers slide across the polished surface. The ring with the crowned heart represented love and loyalty, two things Mary struggled to feel these days. She held it close to her heart as tears welled and fell.

She thought back to her life in Ireland four years ago. The Boer War had started in South Africa, and nationalism was on the rise in Ireland. The economy was completely decimated due to an extended famine that had swept the normally verdant countryside. Catholic versus Church of England woes were at an all-time high and people were leaving their beloved emerald homeland in droves. Mary had watched her parents struggle to hold on to the family farm and their way of life while slowly succumbing to depression and starvation. She couldn't be a part of it any longer and left them behind for a chance at something better—anything.

Mary made her way to Dublin and found work at the Cat's Paw Inn. The pay was non-existent, but she was provided with a room and three meals a day. It was more than most people had and a lot more than she had hoped for. Her skill in the kitchen soon made her popular with the guests. Especially one in particular.

While working at the inn, she met a young man who won her heart—Miles O'Keeffe. He was a broad-shouldered, blue-eyed salesman who made her heart race and her burdens light. Miles sold her hook-line-and-sinker on a life together, but he had no dreams of staying in Dublin. America was where his dreams lie. He had saved enough for passage, and on a wet, stormy night, dropped to one knee to propose to Mary. It was not an average proposal.

"Mary, my love, I am going to America to start a new life, and I want you to be a part of it. I will work day and night and send you all I can so you can make the crossing. We will be together and start fresh in a new land, one that is full of promise. I will make for us a life that we can be proud of, a life with a family and a cozy home. But first, I must ask you to endure some hardships and time apart. I make this vow to you now, Mary. Do you accept, my love?"

Mary had paused, considering Miles's words carefully. It was everything she had hoped for. The time apart would be difficult, but she could cope. She had left her parents, and that had been the hardest thing she had ever done. This she could do.

"Yes, darling. I long to be your wife. I will do everything you ask to make this happen."

With a face full of adoration and hope, Miles placed a small gold Claddagh on her finger. The kiss that followed was filled with passion and young love. It was a dream come true.

The six months after Miles left for America had gone slowly for Mary, but hard work and a few side jobs helped pass the time in Dublin. She saved what little she made, along with the money Miles forwarded periodically, until she was finally able to pay for her ticket to New York. The tramp steamer would leave for America on the morrow, and the thought of seeing him again consumed her, especially since she had not received any letters from Miles in the last two months. That put her on edge with concern.

Before leaving her homeland, she borrowed a horse from a close friend and rode south away from the city. There was one last thing she needed to do before she left Ireland for good. She nearly missed the small road that led to her family's old farm. She pulled abruptly on the reins and turned the animal down the road.

The two wooden headstones had not been there when she left. The familiar names answered all her questions. Mary stepped down and paid respects to a mother and father that had given up. That was something she would never do. Deep in her heart, whatever guilt she had been carrying for leaving them, faded away, knowing that had she stayed, there would be three headstones.

Mary wiped away her tears and placed the gold Claddagh back in its hiding place in her bag. She shook the memories away and returned to organizing her clothes on a small shelf.

The Thompson home was a grand affair with a limestone façade and polished woods throughout. Mary came to replace the old cook who had displeased the master one too many times. Mary would not make the same mistake. During the interview, Mary had asked almost as many questions as the butler who was doing the hiring. Storing information gleaned about the picky eaters in the family, she would make sure not to fix anything that might upset them. Tonight, they were in for a treat, one of her specialties, fresh peach ice cream.

Mary was a slim five-foot-three woman with brunette hair that she wore pinned up. She had a round face with petite lips and large cocoa-colored eyes. As an Irish emigrant, she dreamed of one day overcoming the prejudice of her upbringing. She swept aside a single tear as her thoughts hung for a moment on the man she had held above all others, Miles O'Keeffe. The fever had taken him before Mary could reconnect, leaving behind a pauper's grave and her memories. There was, however, a promise that came with a ring—to make a better life here in America—and she was determined to fulfill that promise. After all, America was a land of opportunity, and she planned to take full advantage of it.

There was a soft knock on her door.

"Yes?"

"There is a gentleman to see you at the servant's entrance," the housemaid replied.

Mary turned from her thoughts and did a quick adjustment of her hair in her small hand mirror. She opened the back door to a short rotund gentleman in a beige tweed suit. His hair was a bit disheveled, and his small eyes were as black as midnight. He tried to clear his throat, but it turned into a cough.

"Can I help you?" Mary asked, curious who this stranger might be.

"Are you Mary Mallon?"

She nodded with a certain amount of skepticism. "Aye."

"I am George Sober with the city's sanitation department. I'm a sanitation engineer."

Mary gazed at the man without expression.

This innerved George, and he stammered a bit. "Anyway, what I mean is . . . the Warren family hired me to investigate the outbreak of typhoid that took Charles and two of the children. Would it be okay if I asked you some questions?"

"Sure enough," Mary said, as she stepped out onto the porch and closed the door behind her. "Terrible thing, that."

"I believe I have traced the source of their sickness to the freshwater clams the family had on the first of July. Did you, by chance, eat any of those clams?"

Mary tapped her finger on her chin as she thought back to the date in question. "Yes. I ate four or five, I believe."

"And you never had a fever or other symptoms?"

"No. I was just fine."

"Do you remember where you purchased them?"

"Not really. That was a month ago. Maybe the fish hut on Ships Point Lane. Was a real shame, that. I loved that family. Typhoid is a nasty bugger. Hope I never get it," Mary added.

George asked her several more questions and then thanked her for her time. He left more confused than he had been before the interview.

Mary closed the door and stepped back into the kitchen. The housemaid was hovering like a mother bird. Mary wiped her hands on her apron and started to prepare dinner for her new family.

"Who was that?" the housemaid asked.

"Some city engineer looking to blame the help for rich people's problems."

***

George Sober looked through the small window in the door. Bodies were lined up in six rows head-to-toe. The hospital was at maximum capacity. Each

metal-framed bed held a patient who was struggling with the most deadly outbreak of typhoid fever in American history. Nurses and doctors did what they
could for the dying and infirm. Those that succumbed to the vomiting, intense
cramps, diarrhea, and high fevers were stacked like cordwood in the basement,
waiting to be buried or burned. George was sure he had discovered the source of
Salmonella Typhi, but Mary Mallon had eaten the freshwater clams just like the
rest of the family, and she was fine. He would have to shift his investigation in
another direction.

He needed to discover the cause and put an end to the suffering that seemed
to be growing throughout the city. George knew that the toxin was spread through
contaminated water or the feces of infected patients. Even flies were suspected of
being able to spread it. Typhoid tended to assault the poorer sections of the city,
making the outbreak in a wealthy family's home highly unusual.

***

Three weeks later, two children were dead and everyone else was contaminated in the Thompson home. Mary left the house feeling only sorrow for her bad
luck. She lifted her head and reminded herself that adversity was part of life and
that it might take a few tries to get things working in her favor. The fever that was
spreading through the town was just one more hurdle for her to overcome. So far,
she had been unscathed. In fact, she felt great. That thought boosted her spirits,
and she strolled down the street with renewed purpose.

"Miss Mallon!"

Mary stopped and turned to see the man from the sanitation department that
had asked all those questions a month ago.

"It's George Sober from the sanitation department."

"I know who you are."

"Of course. I'm not sure how to put this, but . . ."

"Go on then; spit it out! I have things to do," Mary said.

"I think you might be a carrier for typhoid fever. You're the only common
denominator."

Mary crossed her arms at the insinuation.

"You are what I call a healthy carrier, but to prove it, I need a sample of your . . ." George fumbled with his eyes and mouth trying to get the words out, ". . . to test it."

"Sample of my *what?*" Mary demanded.

"Feces . . . your—"

Before he could finish, a fist struck him square on the nose. Blood gushed as he hit the ground.

Mary stepped over him in disgust. "Are you daft? I feel just fine—never had the fever. I am not responsible, ya bodach!"

She stormed off, leaving George on the ground, holding his damaged nose.

***

George paced as he waited for Inspector Roslyn to exit his office. His nose throbbed and both of his eyes had blackened. The New York Police Department Headquarters looked more like a church than a government building. It was a four-story monstrosity at Centre and Broome Streets built of carved limestone with crenelated columns, arched windows, and a tall central domed tower.

He could hear shouting and banging on the wall, as a man in the other room seemed to be angry with someone. After a long moment, a young patrolman scurried from the office, tears in his eyes. After a bit, the occupant, Inspector Roslyn emerged with purpose.

"George, I don't have time for you now," Roslyn said, as he tried to move past him.

"Inspector, you'd better make time. *I know how the fever is being spread.*"

The inspector stopped abruptly and turned back to the sanitation engineer, commonly referred to as the "shite meister" behind his back.

"It's a woman."

This made the inspector cock his head.

"She works as a cook and has infected everyone she has cooked for. She is what I call a healthy carrier."

The inspector looked skeptical. "George, I really don't have time for this."

"She gives but doesn't get."

This seemed to make sense to Roslyn, as he paused and processed the information. "So what do you need? And what happened to you?"

"I need help catching Mary Mallon and testing her as a carrier . . . and . . . she punched me."

"A wild one, eh?" he said, intrigued.

George gave a slight nod.

"Let me see if I've got this right. You want to use the New York City police force to catch a woman so we can collect and test her shite?"

"Exactly."

***

The cat and mouse chase extended over five hours throughout the city before the police finally surrounded and arrested Miss Mallon. She was fit to be tied and continued to struggle even after being placed in a cell. She pled her innocence and tried everything she could to disparage George Sober, but women's rights were many years away.

Mary managed to hold out for three days before the pain was too great, and she left a deposit in the provided bucket. She tried to toss the contents at the guards who barely managed to subdue her beforehand.

George had her feces tested quickly and was relieved when it came back positive for the bacteria *Salmonella Typhi*. News spread quickly that there was a healthy carrier dispersing typhoid all over the city—a woman and a veritable germ factory. Within the week, the prisoner had been given a name that would stand in infamy: "Typhoid Mary."

Based on George Sober's findings, the New York City Health Department imprisoned Mary under sections 1169 and 1170 of the Greater New York Charter. She was confined to a small bungalow on North Brother Island, just off the Bronx shoreline. It was part of the Riverside Hospital facility designed to isolate victims of contagious diseases like smallpox, typhoid fever, and tuberculosis.

Mary had lived in smaller rooms, but the thought of being a pariah to the civilized world did not sit well. She was allowed to venture only within fifty feet of her bungalow and had absolutely no contact with any persons. It was a prison without bars.

The exception came from the many doctors that prodded and probed her against her will. She was tested and experimented on for three years until she won her freedom in a controversial court decision. The new health commissioner, Ernst Lederle, agreed to release her with the promise that she would never cook again. It was a sacrifice for Mary to give up her true calling, but freedom was worth the price.

The smells and sounds of the city brought renewed joy to Mary. A joy she had almost forgotten living in seclusion as a guinea pig for uncaring scientists. As familiar sights and sounds filled her senses, it was like being born all over again.

The first order of the day was to put some distance between her and her now-famous moniker—Typhoid Mary. Her healthy distrust of men had grown tenfold. She needed to change her name and start over. Something easy to remember. As Mary Brown, she had a vastly improved chance to get work and start a new life. She picked up a paper and scanned it for hiring information.

After six weeks working at a laundry, Mary turned bitter. The pay was poor and the conditions harsh. She was practically homeless, and her meager two meals a day were making her too thin, and thin was not an attractive attribute for a woman. She needed to make a change, something to put her back on her feet. New York City was big enough to get lost in, and Mary Brown planned to do just that.

The Slone Maternity Hospital was looking for a cook. Mary dusted off her dress and applied. She had a natural way about her that made others feel at ease, and by nightfall, she had moved her belongings into her new housing. The hospital was a three-story building with room for up to thirty birthing moms and thirty recovering birth moms. Mary had never cooked for so many people before. She planned out her household menu and just multiplied it.

For her first night, she had something special planned—Shepard's pie and peach ice cream. She poured heavy cream into a ceramic bowl and added fresh peeled and diced peaches. After pouring in the sugar and egg yolks, she finished off with vanilla and cinnamon. It was her specialty and a surefire way to win the hearts and stomachs of her charges, just as it had in the past. She stirred it all up with a wooden spoon until it was frothy. A quick dip with her pointer finger told her all she needed to know—delicious. It was a simple recipe that never failed to please, and it required no cooking.

***

In May 1915, Manhattan's Sloane Maternity Hospital was struck with an outbreak of typhoid fever. Twenty-five workers and patients were infected, with two dead and several on the cusp. Mary had never understood the need to wash her hands, as she felt perfectly healthy. Surely, she did not pose a risk. It was a recurring thought that had perplexed her over the last few years. She packed her bags and left the infected hospital. Maybe it was time to try a new city. She had heard good things about Chicago.

The latest epidemic was traced back to the hospital's cook, and a simple description of her had the health department back on her case. They had lost track of Mary Mallon after her release and for some unknown reason, she had gone back to cooking.

A citywide search commenced for the most deadly woman in the city's history. To date, she was responsible for hundreds of infections and an estimated fifty fatalities.

As Mary moved through the crowded streets of New York, she could feel the net closing in around her. Throughout the crowds, policemen searched with tenacity, armed with a printed image of her. It seemed like they were coming from every direction. A quick turn down an alley had her unexpectedly trapped. She tried the door at the end, banging and pleading for it to open, but to no avail. Her shoulders slumped and tears flowed as her American dream came to an end.

Mary was once again quarantined to the Riverside Hospital on North Brother Island. She unpacked her belongings in the small bungalow, knowing this was her final destination. This small cottage separated her from others on an island isolated from the world. She slid the keepsake ring onto her finger. It would be its new resting place. She was left with nothing but time and memories. One in particular that had haunted her for many years was the memory of a young lover who had made her a sacred vow—Miles O'Keeffe. A man she had lost to the fever before she had even stepped off the boat in New York.

Mary spent the last twenty-three years of her life as a virtual prisoner in forced isolation, mostly due to the public opinion that had turned firmly against her after her failure to stay out of the kitchen. On November 11, 1938, Mary Mallon, alias Typhoid Mary, died. There was no autopsy performed, and she was buried at Saint Raymond's Cemetery in the Bronx.

Chapter Two

KOLKATA INDIA – 8:35 A.M.

T he state of West Bengal is characterized as one of the last British bastions in India. It stretches from a shared border with Bhutan in the Himalayas and runs along the neighboring country of Bangladesh. It finally ends at the Bay of Bengal where six major rivers end their journeys. Calcutta, renamed Kolkata in 2001, has a history as an East India trading post and is the state's largest city. Now, with a population, including suburbs, of just over fourteen million, it is an overcrowded city rich in history, wealth, and extreme poverty.

Prem rode in the second car of the electric tram. The seat cushion had worn away leaving a patinaed iron bench. He could feel every bump. The city was ripe with people, cars, and smells. Street vendors called out for customers, and on every corner, the aroma of curry and garlic competed with raw sewage. The heat and humidity were oppressive, like an overbearing mother-in-law.

The tram was overloaded, as usual, and the old electric motor could finally take no more. With a sudden *hiss*, it smoked and died, leaving the two-car street tram dead in the intersection. Within a few minutes, the entire roadway was clogged in every direction with horns honking and people shouting.

Just another day in India.

Prem followed his fellow passengers off the tram in search of another way forward. He was rail-thin with a full head of hair and a thick mustache. He wore a white collarless shirt, faded jeans, and an optimistic expression. He was about to start his new job for a medical company that was expanding in the area. He used the small signing bonus to travel up from Mumbai. The interviewer for the job had been somewhat cryptic about the new position, but Prem was not in a position to ask questions. He had recently lost his betrothed in a humiliating scandal. She had run off with another man three months before they were to be married. Prem spiraled downward and was released from his last job at a company he had worked very hard for before his implosion. This new opportunity was a rare chance at a fresh start in a new city away from the judgmental looks of friends and family.

Prem cut across three streets and hailed a cab, which was too expensive for his fellow tram riders. Within a few moments, he was back on his way.

The warehouse was an older steel structure with several pieces of siding rusted through. The back of the building had a large ramp with an access door for loading and unloading. Prem paid his cabbie, moved up the ramp, and ventured inside. It took his eyes a moment to adjust to the contrast in light. Eventually, he saw a cargo truck with several large barrels tied to the back.

An older man approached him. They greeted each other by giving *namaste,* each touching palms and bowing slightly.

"You're late," the man said. He was dressed in a dingy white lab coat and wore round-framed glasses that matched his face.

"India."

It was an excuse that seemed to satisfy his new boss, who gave a knowing nod. "Follow me."

Prem followed the man over to the older Ashok Leyland truck. The front cab looked like the head of a van, and the back half was a flatbed.

"You're going to relish this, Prem," the man said. He placed his hand on one of the barrels tied to the flatbed. "Inside each barrel are five hundred flies."

"Flies?" Prem asked, not relishing it at all.

"Yes, *Musca Domestica*. They are all females, and they are sterile. So what you are going to do is release them into the wild. Mr. *Musca Domestica* will come along and do his business but nothing will happen. Within three months the fly population will be cut by two-thirds. It's science at its best, my boy. And it will significantly reduce the spread of disease. Next month, we are going to do the same with mosquitoes."

He said the last part with a grand flourish of his arms. He placed his ever-present clipboard on the truck bed. "Here, let me show you what we need done."

The man gave Prem his instructions and handed him a cellphone and a map. They shook hands, and Prem drove away with a smile that reached both ears. He was feeling happy for the first time in a long time—this was going to be a *great* new job. He was going to help make his country a better place to live.

Prem followed the map that led him out to the suburbs and into an agricultural area beyond. He was always amazed at the infinite shades of green in the countryside. West Bengal was famous for its rice, potatoes, and jute production. The terrain had plenty of water and fertile soil. He let his mind wander with possibilities. He could now afford an apartment and a motorcycle. He would be a man about town, someone whom others would look up to.

The paved road turned to dirt and then mud as Prem drove out into the state's jungle heartland. The earthy smells were so foreign to the city life he was familiar with. After about an hour, he pulled over at kilometer marker 128, as instructed. The road was empty here. On the right side of the road were rice fields as far as the eye could see, and a small river flowed on the left. Beyond was raw jungle. Not a place you wanted to go.

Prem stepped out of the truck and stretched. He looked around but saw no cars or people. A rare sight. He followed his boss's instructions by grasping a small lever shown to him back at the warehouse. It was mounted next to the cab, just under the bed. He gave it a yank. The tops of the barrels slid open and a swarm of black flies filled the air. What would normally be a frightening sight was glorious to Prem. He watched as they filled the air and moved and spread like a possessed black cloud. He shielded the sun from his eyes with his palm as he watched the display. The swarm surged, swayed, and eventually dissipated until there were only a few flies left in the area.

He took out his cellphone, dialed a preprogrammed number, and stood next to the truck feeling a great sense of accomplishment. He couldn't wait to report in. As the phone rang he heard a small click under the bed of the truck. Prem looked down to see what it was.

The explosion was sudden and intense as the structure of the truck disintegrated and expanded outward. It moved through Prem as if he weren't even there, eviscerating him and taking out a chunk of the road as well. When it was over, there was little left that could be identified as a vehicle, just a hole in the road. And an unusual number of flies in the area.

***

She pulled herself through the water with ease. It required complete focus to maintain every element of the task. Breathing, body movement, direction, and form. As Codi neared the end of the pool, ready to flip and accelerate off the pool wall into her streamline form, out of the corner of her eye she saw her partner, Joel, standing at the pool's edge. Codi pulled up and looked at him curiously as she lifted her goggles to her cap, her breathing still labored but controlled.

"I think you're losing it, Joel," she said. "It's Sunday morning. Aren't you supposed to be in church?"

"I made the mistake of taking my phone with me."

"You didn't have to answer it."

Joel nodded, slightly embarrassed.

Codi sighed and climbed out of the pool. Joel averted his eyes, as her lean, well-formed figure clad only in a bathing suit, shed water. He watched his partner as she stepped over to a nearby bench and grabbed a towel, his eyes starting to water from the chlorine in the air.

"Give me a few. I'll meet you outside," Codi said.

Joel nodded eagerly and turned to leave, ready for some fresh air.

Working for the FBI's Special Projects division out of D.C. came with some unexpected moments, but that was all part of the job description. Codi had transferred there after a bout with the GSA (General Services Administration), where she and Joel cut their teeth on a high-profile case that launched them to celebrity status within the agency. The FBI recruited them, and it wasn't long before they had made a name for themselves there as well.

"So what's up?" Codi said as she slammed Joel's car door.

He flinched at the door's impact. Codi had always been a bit of a bull in a china shop, but Joel had mostly gotten used to it. He placed a few drops of Visine AC in both eyes and blinked rapidly as he spoke.

"I think I'm allergic to your gym."

"No, what's up with work?"

"Oh, boss called. He needs us to pop up to New York. Something about a stolen corpse." Joel started his Prius and put it in gear. "Here, I got this for you." He handed Codi a coffee cup that matched the one he was drinking.

"A stolen corpse is definitely not an FBI thing. Why us?" Codi asked.

"The city requested our assistance. It was some kind of celebrity. The New York office is slammed, so our boss gets a call from his boss and then asks us to look into it. It all rolls downhill," Joel said, as he pulled the car into traffic.

"You have given this a lot of thought, haven't you?" Codi said.

Joel had no answer. It was his nature to overanalyze and overthink things. Codi popped the cap off the cup and breathed in the aroma. Joel's predilection for great coffee was well known.

"So I guess we drew the short straw," she said after releasing the aroma with a satisfied sigh.

"That's all I have so far," Joel said.

Codi replaced the lid and took a sip. "This is good coffee. What is it?"

"Mandheling beans from Sumatra. They use a wet hulling process where, after they remove the skins, they ferment the beans overnight to break down the mucilage. That gets—" Joel realized he had gone too deep when Codi gave him a sideways glance that said *seriously?*

They drove on in silence for a bit, each sipping from their cups.

Codi broke the silence. "So tell me . . . what's going on with your Mountie?"

"She has a name," Joel replied.

"I know she has a name. I introduced her to you."

"You did? I don't remember that."

"Stop deflecting, Joel."

"We have date this Friday," he said sheepishly.

Shannon Poole of the Royal Canadian Mounted Police (RCMP) was stationed in D.C. as a liaison officer. She had teamed up with Joel and Codi on a particularly tough case involving terrorism, launched, in part, out of Canada. Joel just managed to hold his own against the brash street-smart operator. She had saved his life, and he had returned the favor twice. The seemingly odd couple had found common ground, and they were now making consistent time for each other in their lives.

Codi was happy for her partner who had struggled after the untimely death of his last companion. He had been powerless to save her, and she died in his arms, which put a real dent in his normally optimistic personality. But Codi could see the old Joel returning.

"I'm happy for you—for both of you," Codi said.

"Thanks," he said with a growing smile.

"New York, huh . . . I could go for some good pizza. Wake me up in four hours."

***

Pullin Ikaika stared in the full-length mirror. He loved the face that was staring back—the body, the mind, everything. At six-foot-three and 230 pounds, he was an imposing figure. As he buttoned up a starched white dress shirt, he glimpsed a tribal tattoo on his chest that told of his roots. A final inspection had him removing a micro-spec of lint on the lapel of his ten-thousand-dollar custom silk suit. It was tailored not for comfort, but to display his physique. To Pullin, appearance was a source of power that could be wielded as effectively as a gun. He was the very image of vanity wrapped in an ego that only extreme wealth could sustain. He was a ruthless man who delighted in using the backs of others to propel himself forward. Had he ever taken the time to see a therapist, the word *sociopath* would have come up, but Pullin had no time for such trivial pursuits.

He turned and collected his Richard Mille, Pablo Mac Donough watch with its double skeletonized baseplate and titanium bridges. It had a black bezel with a unique see-through crystal. Built to withstand the rigors of polo, but this watch had never seen a horse. Pullin opened a drawer and pocketed two of the day's burner phones. At fifty-two, he still had all of his dark brown hair. His olive-colored skin gave him the appearance of a permanent suntan, and his irises were so dark, they looked black. High cheekbones and a strong jawline made him attractive to both women and men alike, but he had little interest in emotional and physical connections. He wasn't gay, bi, or heterosexual; he was asexual. To Pullin, there was no one in the world more desirable than himself. Humanity was nothing more than a virus, and viruses left uncontrolled could be dangerous. Which reminded him. He hit the plunger on one of the many hand sanitizers stationed throughout the house. It was an unconscious act that was repeated often throughout the day. He rubbed his hands together until they were dry. He was now ready to begin.

The house was much more than a house; it was a compound with a sandstone façade and a gray slate roof. Set on five acres of lakefront property on the Nevada side of Lake Tahoe, it was one of the last homes built on the lake before the state park took over the shoreline. The main house was twenty-five thousand square feet. It had numerous bedrooms and plenty of room to entertain hundreds. But Pullin did little entertaining. This was his sanctuary, his place of respite.

A second building on the property was built to match the main house. It was a large rectangular two-story building covered in solar panels with several satellite dishes. There was a parking area behind it and a covered walkway between the two structures. This was where Pullin's businesses were run. He had satellite offices in several cities across the globe, but he kept his allies and best employees close. For example, Edgar Fallman on the financial side. The man was a wizard with numbers and accounts. He considered himself the Ivar Kreuger of modern times.

The thirty-something Welsh-born numbers man could cook the books and still make the IRS think they were getting the lion's share. He had been working for Pullin for just over three years now. Edgar was fastidious to a fault, always primping and mirror-checking his reflection—not a hair out of place. He had learned the behavior from his boss and was the ultimate suck-up. His attempt at being a "mini me" was not lost on Pullin, who showed complete indifference to his employee's actions. He was more concerned with results; that's what spoke the loudest to Pullin.

The office interiors looked like a cross between a luxury home and a Wall Street financial office. There was a mix of fine couches and chairs with natural woods used throughout. Standup desks blended with touches from local artists, all connected with the latest technology. It was the best of both worlds, and Pullin ran his companies like his own personal Monopoly game, but he collected at every turn.

The real surprise on the property was the underground structure. Just outside the office complex was a small stone building with a large set of glass double doors and a sophisticated entry system. It led to a foyer with a staircase leading downward and an elevator large enough to haul equipment. Two stories underground was one of the most sophisticated labs in the country. There, they could splice genes and repair or rebuild DNA and RNA. Viruses and bacteria could be grown, altered, and killed, and vaccines could be designed, replicated, and modified. It was the beginning of something much larger that was beginning to consume Pullin's thoughts and actions.

Pullin stepped into his favorite room in the house. It was bigger than some people's entire home and lavishly appointed with polished woods and handmade tiles. The back wall had four screens, each tuned to a different financial channel. News of an outbreak of a superbug strain of typhoid in India caught his attention. He pressed the volume button on a remote and listened carefully to the reporter.

"Over one hundred are now dead, as health officials battle a new superbug version of typhoid fever spreading across the state of West Bengal. Authorities have moved to quarantine the area. This particular superbug has proven to be resistant to all known antibiotics so far and is spreading unlike any previous outbreak here. Our hearts go out to the families of those—"

Pullin hit the mute button. He checked the Indian stock markets, the BSE, and the NSE. Both were in a free-fall. The small twinkle in his eyes was all that revealed his joy of the millions he would make over the next few weeks. Millions he could put to good use.

Chapter Three

T he gravestone was a solid chunk of gray granite that matched the darkening sky. It was carved with a curved top, lilies, and a simple cross. There was an empty hole in the ground in front of it about twice the size of an average coffin. Police tape, flapping in the wind, surrounded the scene, encompassing a fresh pile of dirt on the right side. Codi looked around. This was an old section of the cemetery with many unique headstones lined up head-to-toe, side-to-side, all leading toward a small hill. There were a few trees around, but otherwise, the place was eerily vacant.

"Mary Mallon, died November eleventh, 1938 . . . My Jesus mercy," Joel said, as he read the headstone's engraving.

"I thought there was a celebrity angle here. Who's Mary Mallon?" Codi asked no one in particular.

Joel took out his phone and started a Google search.

"Typhoid Mary." The voice from behind them startled Joel. He turned to see a thirtyish Black male with short-cropped hair and a dazzling smile. He was wearing jeans, a blue button-down, and an off-the-rack sport coat. The badge clipped to his belt introduced him before his mouth did.

"I'm Detective Jennings. You must be our FBI agents. Sorry no one was here when you showed up, but there is really nothing left to guard, and with our budget cuts, the office didn't see the point. Besides, hanging around in a cemetery seriously creeps me out."

They made introductions, and the detective gave them one last look of appraisal. "They sent two of you, huh?"

Codi disregarded his comment and knelt by the hole to inspect it. Joel raised his hand and then realized what he was doing and put it down. "Did you say Typhoid Mary, as in *the* Typhoid Mary?" he asked, afraid of the answer.

"That's right, Mary Mallon, *the* Typhoid Mary."

Joel's face turned white and he stepped back from the grave. The wind seemed to pick up.

"Though what someone would want with an old skeleton is beyond me," Jennings said. "Although, Halloween is coming up. I suppose it could just be some prank or a creepy satanic ritual. Maybe the bones are going into a giant cauldron."

Codi ignored his babble. "It looks like it was dug with hand shovels."

"That's our opinion as well," Jennings replied.

"Why do you think the FBI got called up on this?" Joel asked.

"New York has a lot of history. Not all of it good."

"9/11," Joel piped up.

"Sure. But Mary Mallon might be responsible for more deaths than any other individual in our history. The mayor asked for the FBI's help, not us. The last thing he needs is a bunch of conspiracy theorists spinning this into a public panic or another health crisis."

Codi stood and faced Jennings.

He said, "Frankly, I'm glad you're here. My plate's a little full, so let me know if I can be of any assistance. There's nothing more I got on this case—no surveillance footage, no real evidence, and no suspect. And right now, I got a real murder to attend to. Good luck." Jennings turned to go.

The wind picked up as the sky continued to darken. A storm was coming.

"Hey, detective!" Codi called out. "Do you know where we can get a good slice?"

"Try Louie and Ernie's down on Crosby."

Joel and Codi watched, somewhat stunned, as the detective effectively washed his hands of the case and left.

"Looks like we got ourselves another hit show," Codi said.

"One that is politically charged."

"Great. Well, at least we got the 411 on some good pizza." Codi smiled sarcastically. "Come on let's get out of here. This place is creepy."

***

The FBI office in New York City is located on Federal Plaza in Lower Manhattan. Codi and Joel were given a small back room on the thirty-seventh floor. The room had old carpet, one folding table, and three metal chairs. It was lit with vintage recessed fluorescents. There were no windows and only one door. The only decor was an extremely faded picture of J. Edgar Hoover and a sunrise photo of the Statue of Liberty.

They had sent a forensic team down to the cemetery in hopes of finding clues while Joel set up his laptop and started in. Codi sat next to him waiting for their next move. This was the hard part of her job, but one thing she had learned in the military was patience.

At five-foot-eight, Codi could hold her own with most men. She was an avid swimmer and took physical fitness seriously. She had even competed in college in both relay and as an individual. She had a lean, fit figure with long brown hair and intense brown eyes flecked with gold. Some would say that Codi was driven, but that would be selling her short. She used intelligence and tenacity to make her way forward without being afraid of good old-fashioned hard work. She knew that being a woman required more effort on her part and that was something she relished. But over time, Codi realized there was more to life than job success. She had found herself seeing a bigger picture and actually allowing an emotional relationship, something she had never had before.

After graduating college with top honors, Codi received several promising opportunities. But she left them all behind and joined the Marines as an enlisted soldier. She had something to prove to herself and to her dead father. After three arduous years, she was one of the very few females ever admitted to BUD/S training. Becoming a SEAL was her do-or-die goal. Nothing would stop her from achieving it. Nothing except a misogynist "boys club" that conspired against her. She was forced to tap out or DOR (drop on request) after a tragic injury left her ankle shattered, along with her dream. She would never forget the pain as she rang the brass ships' bell three times, signaling her exit.

Afterward, Codi spiraled down into a dark place that cast her out of the military and practically on the street. Eventually, she phoenixed from the ashes of despair and destructive behavior. The experience had changed her in many ways. She found there were some things more important than success. She found a softer side and married it to her driven side. It allowed her to appreciate others in a way she never had before.

She accepted a job as a GSA agent where she was responsible for tax and fraud cases, essentially a paper cop. Though she felt like she had let herself down, Codi put her best foot forward. She embraced the job with fervor and quickly got the attention of her superior, Director Ruth Anne Gables, a strong, politically connected leader who took Codi under her wing. She pushed Codi when needed and supported her when there was trouble.

Codi was assigned to work with Joel Strickman, a computer-savvy agent with a heart of gold. His wiry frame and unkempt blond hair framed his naturally positive curiosity for life. They had found success bringing justice to several individuals who had defrauded the US government. But it took a cold case from the 1940s to bring them into the light. It had started benign enough but quickly escalated to international implications and, ultimately, global terror. It pushed Codi to her breaking point and unleashed her full potential. She battled impossible odds to bring down a madman bent on world destruction.

It seemed the harder she was pressed, the harder she pushed back. It wasn't stubbornness but determination born of a confidence her father had instilled in her at a young age. In the end, she was credited with saving hundreds of thousands of lives.

The case got her noticed at the FBI, and now, she found herself in a position as Special Agent Sanders, assigned to the Special Projects division based in the D.C. field office. For Codi, her career was back on track, and even her personal life was finding its groove. It was a good time to be her.

She glanced at her phone, hoping for a text from Matt—Dr. Matt Campbell—the man with whom Codi had become involved. They had met on one of her first cases when they were nearly killed at the hands of a madman—twice. The resulting stress formed a bond that was stronger than either was willing to admit.

After the case, they spent nearly a month together convalescing. During that time, Codi and Matt had time to heal their physical wounds and discover a love neither was expecting. Eventually, work pulled them in different directions, stunting the growth of a relationship with little time for maintenance.

Recently, Matt had taken a job at a think tank in the D.C. area. At first, his close proximity put pressure on the relationship, but they re-found their stride and things were going very well. Codi and Matt had become a couple, and that was both strange and awesome. Now, she would do everything in her power to not mess things up. But fate always seemed to have its way.

"So what do you think?" Joel asked.

Codi leaned forward in her metal chair. "I think I'm going to have to cancel my dinner with Matt tonight, and this room smells like a mix of old air conditioning and carpet cleaner."

"Yeah, it's making my nose run," Joel said.

"Can't you access this information remotely?" Codi asked.

"Sure."

"Then let's get out of here. This place stinks."

"There's a highly rated coffee shop nearby I'd like to try."

"Perfect."

***

Dr. Erwin Mahl was getting a headache. He had been strenuously focusing on his microscope for over two hours. It was still his preferred method over viewing the HD screen illuminated right next to him. He pushed back in his chair and used his long bony fingers to rub the bridge of his narrow nose. He was a short gray-haired man of Bangladesh heritage. He was extremely thin and had never been able to put on weight. His large dark eyes seemed alien-like on a giant head that held prominent ears that stuck out like two satellite dishes on a redneck's trailer.

Nearly twenty-five years ago, Erwin's father nationalized the electrical grid across Bangladesh and took it over. It had made the family extremely wealthy, but money can be fleeting. His only son, Erwin, had come to America to study biology. He started out with a large house just off the UCLA campus in Brentwood and a nice Porsche 911s. Things were good, and he was looking forward to college life. Halfway through his matriculation, however, everything changed. Bangladesh authorities raided his family's business and reclaimed what they felt was rightfully the government's. The drama that ensued caused his father to succumb to a massive heart attack. His mother fled the country with only the clothes on her back.

Erwin picked her up at the airport. She was inconsolable for the next several days. He felt powerless. He made a vow that he would take care of her every need. He gladly sold his house and car and used the money to help them buy asylum in the States. It had been a struggle, but with a few student loans and a side job, Erwin eventually got his degree and graduated with honors. He made good on his promise to his mother. He slowly worked his way from a small apartment to a condo and eventually a beautiful home. Erwin's mother grew older and fell prey to influenza one winter. A simple but deadly flu stole the breath from her lungs. He was melancholy for a brief period and looked for someone to blame—too many people at the grocery store who didn't wash their hands or some idiot sneezing openly in a line. But he would never know.

An alert on his smartwatch pulled him from his thoughts. The expected delivery was here.

"Siri, open the loading door," he said into his watch. He grabbed a handful of peanuts and left the room.

Dr. Erwin Mahl stepped into the back loading area next to the elevator as the truck's driver and passenger carefully rolled the rotting coffin into the room. They placed it on a large stainless steel table with wheels.

"Any trouble?" Dr. Mahl asked.

"None whatsoever," the driver replied, as he dusted himself off.

"Good. You didn't open it did you?"

"No way, doc. Not in the job description." He gave Dr. Mahl a wry smile.

"I should have something more for you two in the next couple of days. So take some time off, but keep your phone on."

"Of course," the driver replied as the two men headed for the elevator, already planning their depravity for the night. They walked with a posture and gait that came from intense military training. *Special forces*, Dr. Mahl surmised. Though they had been nothing but professional, they still made him uneasy. His boss did the hiring and stratagems outside the lab. Dr. Mahl would have to trust his decisions.

He placed a mask over his face and pulled on safety goggles. He wheeled his new arrival back into the lab where he began to carefully remove and discard anything that wasn't human, including the scraps of clothing that remained on the body. The corpse was still intact with grayish rough skin sucked tight against the bones. The mouth was open in a never-ending scream from beyond and there was still some hair on the scalp. Dr. Mahl loaded the remains into a specialized grinder and hit the green button.

A sound reminiscent of a fork caught in a garbage disposal ensued. After a few minutes, Dr. Mahl removed just over three liters of a fine tannish-gray powder. He poured two liters into a large Pyrex jar and added one-and-a-half liters of a ten percent solution of sodium hypochlorite (NaOCL). He used a glass rod to stir the mixture until it resembled a runny pancake batter. The mixture was then drizzled across porous paper, eventually becoming a thick paste. He scraped off the paste and spread it across a pane of tempered glass. He then set the glass pane in a dryer and set the timer for twenty minutes.

Dr. Mahl removed his gloves; it was time for a snack. He had an extremely high metabolism and needed to eat every few hours or his body would literally start consuming itself. He chewed on some carrots dipped in chutney. He often thought that if he could isolate the defective gene that caused his metabolic problem, he could sell it as a weight-loss product.

"I see you have started without me," Dr. Kamba said as she entered the room. His colleague was a tall thirty-seven-year-old Kenyan woman with a broad forehead and tight cornrows in her hair. She had been working with Dr. Mahl for several years, and they had developed an efficient non-verbal communication system. They had met in a lab in South Africa a few years back, and she immediately impressed him with her attitude and aptitude. She was extremely bright and one of the best sounding boards he had ever worked with.

"You are welcome to finish what I have started," Dr. Erwin Mahl replied. "We have a large sample, and I feel confident that we will have our answer soon."

"That is very good news," she said as she moved over to the table where Dr. Mahl was standing.

"How's the chutney?" she asked.

"*Hmm* . . . mango chutney, and it is very good. I have a friend that shipped it to me."

A beep from the dryer told them it was time for the next step. Dr. Mahl watched as Dr. Kamba followed a procedure developed by Hochmeister and Budowle, placing the purified powder in equal parts of phenol-chloroform and isoamyl alcohol. This mixture was then covered and set aside to digest overnight.

"There we go. Now, we just have to wait," Dr. Kamba said as she set the sample on the shelf.

"Let's start a second batch so we have a backup," Dr. Mahl said. His mind spun with the task given him. It seemed impossible, but this new sample might just change everything.

***

The swanky little café was decorated in French country chic with old-world-style wooden tables and an eclectic collection of antique chairs. The bar had two red-and-chrome La Pavoni brewers and a good selection of beans. Joel did the ordering while Codi found a comfortable place for them to work with plenty of natural light. As they sipped their coffee, Joel opened his laptop and used a VPN to securely access a search engine. He would not be able to access FBINET this way, but he had a way around most computers. He adjusted his glasses and read from a page he had selected.

"Typhoid is a bacterial infection that can cause a high fever, diarrhea, and vomiting. It can be fatal and is from the bacteria *Salmonella Typhi*. The infection is often passed on through contaminated food and drinking water and is more prevalent in places where proper hygiene is not in place."

"People rarely washed their hands back at the turn of the century," Codi said.

Joel shuddered at the thought. "I could never have lived back then."

He continued, "Typhoid Mary was the first person identified as an asymptomatic carrier of typhoid. She never showed any signs of being infected and worked as a cook. She is credited with infecting hundreds of people and somewhere around fifty deaths."

Joel clicked his way through several more pages. "Although here, it says only six deaths for sure."

Codi leaned over to look. "I guess they had no real way of connecting the deaths back to her then," she said as she took a sip of her hot coffee.

"Probably. There have been other asymptomatic carriers, just not documented."

"That's the problem. You don't show any symptoms, so you're not on the radar. If Mary hadn't been a cook, they would never have found her."

"And she wouldn't have killed so many people," Joel replied.

"True."

The afternoon rolled on with limited useful information.

Codi's mind started to drift back to a recent trip she had taken.

Three months ago, she made a trip to San Diego to see some college friends and to reconnect with her estranged mother. Growing up just north of San Diego had been a fulfilling experience. Her father was a demolition diver for the Navy, or UDT, a job that sent him away for long periods of time. Conversely, when he was in town, he was very active in Codi's life. She took to the water at an early age, and her dad taught her to swim and surf almost before she could walk. He took her camping and taught her basic wilderness skills, including gun safety, maintenance, and shooting. Codi flourished and soon found that few people were faster than her in the water.

Her idyllic family dynamics came crashing down the day her father passed. The toll it took on her mother could never be quantified. Codi's mom spiraled into a psychological abyss. There were many days when her mother disappeared, and Codi was sure she would never come back. It forced her to grow up fast and trust in only one person—herself.

Codi used her dead father as a spirit guide, pushing herself to extremes to make him proud, competing at everything she did. She would never forget the look on her mom's face when she shared her plans to follow in her father's footsteps and join the military. It cracked open the widest fissure yet that had separated them. Codi found herself alone, with no support system, forcing her to succeed or fail on her own. Ultimately, it made her an overtly driven woman with something to prove.

Codi met her mom for lunch in a small café in San Diego. A brief hug was followed by a few awkward moments. Eventually, a conversation started and they found detente. Codi was not looking for an apology. Each had reacted to the death of a husband and father differently and that was how life often worked. They would never be close again, but at least they could be on speaking terms. The conversation seemed stilted and forced at times, but they muddled through with a promise to do it again.

Joel read from his browser, "It says here that, on average, two hundred thousand people die each year from typhoid."

Codi snapped from her thoughts. "Two hundred thousand? That's crazy. I've never heard anything about it in the news."

"That's because typhoid typically hits the poor areas of the world."

Joel scrolled down looking for something that might be relevant to their case.

"Do me a favor, will you?" Codi asked. "Check out the last two months in regards to anything new about typhoid fever."

Joel typed furiously and then paused as something seized his attention.

Codi looked over. "What?"

"There was an outbreak of a superbug strain of typhoid in India last month. . . . Something about it *spreading in an unusual way.*"

"Superbug?" Codi asked.

Joel adjusted his position in his chair. "Yeah. It's a strain of the toxin that's resistant to all known antibiotics. It's quite lethal. Hundreds of people have died so far."

"How is that even possible, this superbug?" Codi asked as she sipped on the dregs of her cold coffee.

"Well, each time a bacteria goes up against an antibiotic, a few versions of the disease survive. Natural mutations."

Joel turned, leaned toward Codi, and put his elbows on the table. "Imagine if you were to take those survivors and replicate them. Now, do it all over again with another antibiotic. Eventually, you would have a superbug that could not be killed by any known medicine. Scientists have been warning us for years that it was coming." He leaned back with a shiver. "It gives me the chills just to think about it."

Codi looked up for a second while she processed this scenario. "This isn't one of your late-night conspiracy theories, is it?"

"No, I saw it on the news. Plus, there was the Spanish flu. That was a superbug that killed nearly a hundred million people in 1918. The strange thing with that was the people it killed were usually the stronger, healthier ones. Their immune systems reacted to the flu virus by going into a sort of hyperactive mode. It was the uncontrolled immune reaction that damaged their lungs rather than the virus, and they filled with blood and other fluids, eventually drowning them."

"Ahh. Was the superbug in India man-made?" Codi asked.

"Not necessarily. Over time, nature can do the same thing. It's called cellular Darwinism. That's why I try to never take antibiotics. I want to keep my immune system at full strength," Joel said proudly.

"Okay . . . hypochondriac much?"

Joel's smile suddenly died.

Chapter Four

After collecting the DNA from his sample, Dr. Erwin Mahl placed it in a gene sequencer. He programmed his requirements and hit enter. A panel of lights blinked while tracking a predetermined course of action. He was hoping he and his colleague could isolate the flaw in the sample's genes or DNA that had allowed the famous Typhoid Mary to be asymptomatic to typhoid fever and effectively immune from the disease. He reached into his drawer for a quick protein bar. The tests would continue into the night.

"I'm right behind you with the second batch," Dr. Kamba said.

"I've been thinking . . . let's completely separate our efforts and see if we both come to the same conclusion."

"Excellent idea. I'll have an answer a couple of hours behind you. Right now, however, I'm beat. See you in the morning," Dr. Kamba said, as she headed for the door.

"Yes, the morning, Doctor. Thank you. I do need to get home and get some sleep myself."

Dr. Mahl stood. He felt sure he would get his answer. Now, all they had to do was find a way to alter a person's genetic code to make a vaccine. This was the cutting edge of science that he had trained for all his life.

He reached for the light switch and turned to look back at his desk with a hopeful, and at the same time, helpless feeling. Science had always required brave, open-minded professionals to break new ground and discover the unknown. Sometimes, it took several lifetimes; sometimes it came in leaps and bounds. Dr. Mahl was hoping for the latter.

***

The half-swing on his club sent the ball spiraling into the air with a ton of back spin. It hit six feet from the pin and practically stopped on a dime. Pullin wiped the grass from the top of his shoes with a small towel from his bag before doing the same to his clubhead and putting it back in the bag. The early morning air was dry and crisp. It would be a perfect autumn day. He had started his round at 6:00 a.m., as he did every Thursday when he was in town. Pullin had the whole place to himself. The course would delay opening until he was finished. Golf was one of the few sports where you could compete against yourself. He had no need for the camaraderie or competition of others. This was his time to reflect and focus, letting his mind go for a spell. It was when some of his greatest ideas had come—alone on the golf course. His head of security, a man named Crispin Gales, was the one man he allowed to tag along. Mostly because he would carry his clubs, but also because he knew how to remain silent while scanning the surrounding area for possible threats. The man was a model of efficiency—at times more robot-on-a-mission than human—but always professional.

Gales was a South African mercenary who had done much of the heavy lifting for Pullin over the years. A rare mix of Black and white from a time when his country was strictly segregated, his extremely short light-brown hair topped a face with a permanent scowl that he even took to bed with him.

Pullin lined up his putt and swung his arms pendulum-style through the ball with just enough force to send the ball toward the hole. He recalled growing up poor near the north shore of Oahu in Hawaii when he found an old rusty set of golf clubs that had been tossed inside a dumpster. Young Pullin took the set and cleaned it up. He then sneaked onto a local public course in nearby Kahuku after it closed just before sunset. The experience had been thrilling, but his game was a disaster. He had collected three range balls and lost them all after only two holes.

But young Pullin was not discouraged. He found more range balls, and after-hours golf soon became a regular endeavor. He smiled at the memory of his humble beginnings as he watched his ball circle the cup and ultimately drop. He had come so far from that elementary school kid with a set of rusty old clubs.

The memory of Kahuku pushed him to the time when, as a young man, he was involved with the HSM, Hawaiian Sovereignty Movement. The group was dedicated to putting Hawaii back into Hawaiian hands. His Polynesian brothers, after all, were not separated by land but were connected by water. Each of them had watched as Haoles (mainlanders) and Gigens (Chinese) raped and pillaged their homeland for nothing other than a dollar. Deforesting and clearing nature with little concern for the fragile ecosystem. He had seen it time and time again as he traveled and expanded his business. Man, by nature, was reckless and greedy with little regard for the future of our planet.

Back in the day, the locals had tried to fight back, but nothing they ever did was enough. Pullin convinced a select few that it would take violence to tear the outsiders from their profits. The group spent many nights planning the perfect attack on a local hotel in Waikiki, the hub of their hubris. On the night they were to initiate the operation, the Five-O (local slang for police) came down on them hard. It turned out that one of the brothers grew a conscience and ratted everyone out. Pullin managed to escape by hiding in a patch of bushes at Fort DeRussy. His dreams of a better Hawaii shattered with shaking fear. He was now a person of interest to the police. The next morning, he left his homeland, hoping to come back and start again one day. The fear was now something he had erased and managed, but his passion to make a difference had only grown.

Currently, things were very different. He could buy and sell an entire golf course just for the fun of it, and he could change not only his homeland, but soon, he would have the ability to change the entire world to better fit *his* design.

A buzzing in his pocket had him reaching for one of his phones. He flicked it open to see a thumbs-up emoji. Pullin checked his watch and waited a few moments while he opened a website in his browser. He hit a few keys and then dropped the phone and smashed it to pieces with his heel.

The next tee was a dogleg to the left. Crispin handed him the number one wood and watched as his boss placed the ball carefully on the tee exactly three-quarters of an inch above the grass and then stepped back. Everything in life required precision and perfection, and Pullin would not shortchange himself today. He addressed the ball, pulled back, and swung through, hitting it dead center, the text already forgotten.

***

Garrett Scott waited until he had a signal and then logged onto his VPN. He navigated to a twitcher site called Birdbrains. He scrolled down and found the drafts section of the message board. He checked the time and leaned back to wait the two minutes and thirty-eight seconds until the top of the hour.

He was a blond-haired, blue-eyed contractor who specialized in fixing problems—any problems—commonly known in the corporate world as a fixer. In his younger days, he had been part of Denmark's Jaeger Corps, their army's special forces division, where he had specialized in unconventional warfare. The teams had been cross-trained by some of the best in the world, including the SEALs, Recces, and SAS.

After two tours of duty, Scott left Jaeger Corps to take advantage of the money being poured into mercenary contract work. He had proven himself on many occasions and soon moved up the ranks of skill and clientele. At the age of forty-two, he had seen and done it all. In his current job as a fixer, it was like being a tiger among lambs. He so rarely came up against a worthy opponent, it was laughable. The world's corporate riff-raff was unprepared for violence, and it required very little on his part to bend the narrative in his bosses' favor.

At precisely 1:00 p.m., an *H* popped up. This was his cue. He typed a reply to the only person in the world that shared his ID on the site. *Watched the site, 2 F agents and 1 detective are all that are left on the case. Should lose steam within 2 weeks. Site already being covered back up.*

Garrett Scott watched as the words started to delete before his eyes. Then a new message began. *Take no chances. Clean up on aisle three.*

He nodded to himself and then deleted the words. He logged off, leaving an empty page behind. He knew what needed to be done—the removal of three government stooges. It seemed overkill to him, but he was the doer, not the planner. Good-doers did as they were instructed. And he was very good.

***

"Chicken made from plants? Interesting," Matt said through a mouthful of food. He seemed to be chewing much longer than usual. The two sat at Codi's small dining room table amid candlelight and soft jazz. The sun had set long ago and a full moon cast a blue glow on the room's sheer curtain.

"Yeah," she said. "It's supposed to be way healthier than real chicken. I got everything from this little health food store on D Street. The lady there helped me pick it all out. Figured we should try and eat more healthy with the schedules we keep and all." Codi said the last part while trying to chew the rubbery faux chicken herself.

Now that Codi was back from New York City, they had finally made time for dinner together. She convinced Matt that she would cook something special, not a side of her she had shown him before. He seemed very enthusiastic to be a part of her culinary world, but with every chew, that enthusiasm was waning.

Matt reached for his glass to wash down the food.

"What is this stuff?" Matt asked, smacking his lips and making a scrunched-up face. He was trying to place the flavor of the beverage.

"Kombucha. It's good for you. Filled with probiotics or something."

"Just not so good for your taste buds." He still tried to be grateful for Codi's attempt at making dinner.

They sat at the zinc-covered table in Codi's apartment. The lighting was low and there was even a small pumpkin spice votive candle. Codi's attempt at a romantic and healthy dinner was an incredible gesture, and she had gotten half of it right. Matt was determined to eat it all. He took another bite and began the prolonged chewing process required.

"So what's new with you and Joel?" he asked.

"Oh, you know, Special Projects, just trying to bring another dead case to life." Codi took another sip of her drink. "You're right; it isn't good. I think I have some wine left over in the fridge."

"Fridge wine's gotta be better than . . . what did you say this was?"

"Kombucha."

"Bless you." He smiled.

"Funny."

Codi opened her refrigerator and located the re-corked bottle of Chard.

Codi and Matt had found that comfortable rhythm couples have when every-thing is going well. They would try to get together two or three times a week and did their best to have actual conversations rather than just sitting around texting each other back and forth on their cellphones and sharing the occasional meme. Codi came to enjoy these moments, as they were a great way to unplug from the drama of being a special agent for the FBI.

She grabbed two glasses, poured from the half-empty bottle, and then sat back down. "Okay, where were we?"

"To us." Matt lifted his wineglass.

They clinked glasses and each took a sip hoping to remove the taste of the Kombucha from their palate.

"How long has this bottle been in your fridge?" Matt asked.

"Honestly, I have no idea." She started to laugh. Some of the wine dribbled out of her mouth. Matt soon followed, and they were lost in the moment. After a bit, the laughter died out. Matt leaned over the small table. Codi met him in the middle. It was a metaphor that matched their relationship, each giving equally. The kiss lasted only a few seconds, but the passion behind it lingered.

"Burger and a beer?" Matt said.

"That sounds wonderful."

They got up and left the apartment, leaving everything behind on the table.

***

Supervising Special Agent (SSA) Brian Fescue stepped into the conference room, carrying his laptop. Codi's boss had a casual way about him that hid the seriousness of his position and the cases he often oversaw. His Jamaican heri-tage was something he was proud of, but his accent he kept well-hidden until he became upset. Brian was about three inches shorter than Joel, but he was built like a tank. And his cappuccino-colored eyes seemed to get to the truth no matter how hard you tried to hide it. He was good to his agents and worked just as hard as they did. Codi, and even her partner Joel, had flourished under his tutelage.

It was not often that he had a chance to meet with all of his agents at once. Most days, they were off following up leads or buried in the enormous load of paperwork the government agency seemed to thrive on. Today's meeting, however, had been on the books for quite some time.

SSA Brian Fescue smiled as he padded across the gray carpet toward his seat. He was wearing a fitted blue suit with a white collared shirt and a magenta paisley tie with a matching pocket square. He loosened his coat button as he sat at the head of the rosewood veneer oval table, surrounded by black office chairs, each holding an agent from his team. Behind him were a whiteboard and a pull-down screen.

After a particularly intense case that Brian had first worked with Codi, he stepped away from the field and into an office job. His wife had given birth to their second child, Abigale, and he felt strongly that the field was no place for a good family man.

He was a committed husband and father. When the administration offered him his current position, he was happy to take it. A chance to blend the job he loved with the home life that was so important to him. He was now the driving force behind the FBI's Special Projects division based in the Washington D.C. field office. He had recruited Codi and Joel. Together they had solved several cold cases and had become two of the division's shining stars. Their results had gone a long way with the brass to confirm that Brian was the right man for the job.

"Thanks, all, for being here this morning," he said to the group. "I wanted to say you have been doing some solid work, and it has been noticed. So good job." Brian cleared his throat and continued. "We are currently closing more cases percentage-wise than Special Projects has ever closed, and I attribute that to you. So, kudos!"

Codi clapped her two pointer fingers together in a silent but sarcastic, *Yay!* Joel reached over and tried to pull her hands down. Brian ignored them and hit the remote that lowered the screen as he continued the briefing.

"As you know, from time to time, we are asked to help out with other departments' cases, depending on the nature of the case and how busy they or we are.

Today I come bearing gifts. We have been asked to help out the Cleveland office and the Denver office with two pressing cases. Both offices are overloaded."

Brian powered up his laptop and plugged it into an HDMI cable leading to a projector. The screen lit up showing his homepage. A happy family photo partially covered in icons popped up. The photo was taken three months ago during the Fescue's summer vacation. His wife, Leila, and their two children, Tristan and Abigale, could be seen smiling for the camera just before a giant wave was about to wipe them out.

The peanut gallery remarked on the kids taking after their mother and other silly comments before Brian could click over to the page he wanted. It left him with a proud smile as he read the list of cases to be distributed.

Each case was assigned to a team, and the e-files were sent to their corresponding emails. Brian always had agents in mind as he assigned cases, but he was willing to listen to their pushback.

"Now, I also have a few cold cases that have new leads that have come back to life. A couple of them have been haunting the FBI for decades."

"If it has anything to do with D.B. Cooper, I'm out," Codi said. "Been there, done that."

She and Joel had hit a dead end with the famous skyjacker cold case when a Washington teen found a wad of the missing ransom money along the Colombia River.

"Well, funny you should mention that." Brian turned his attention to Gordon Reyas. "There has been a team of retired investigators working the cold case, and they claim to have solved it. They identified D. B. Cooper as a former CIA man, Robert something-or-other. The main office wants us to take a look at their findings. Maybe you and Anna can finally put this one to bed?"

Gordon and his part-time partner Anna nodded their heads.

"Good luck," Codi said.

"And last, but not least . . . Tylenol. It's all yours, Codi and Joel."

Brian finished up the meeting and again thanked his team for their hard work. He ended with, "And remember, slow and steady wins the race. No unnecessary risks, please."

He left his agents and headed over to the main offices for a budget meeting with his higher-ups.

"Tylenol? What is he talking about?" asked Codi, as they walked back to their offices.

"I have no idea, but I could use a couple right now. I've had this headache all morning," Joel said while rubbing his temples.

"Probably a brain tumor. You should get checked."

"You might be right. I should call and set an appointment for an MRI."

"Joel, it's a headache. Relax, you'll live longer."

Joel nodded, realizing she was undoubtedly right. Codi just rolled her eyes as they entered his office. Busting her partner was one of her favorite pastimes, and anything along the hypochondriac scale was just too easy. Joel was the perfect partner for Codi. He was super book- and computer-smart with a streak of loyalty as long as they come. His tendencies, however, to go by the book and overthink things were both very fixable in her mind, and she had managed to move the needle somewhat in her direction.

Joel took out a bottle of Tylenol from his desk and chased two capsules with bottled water. He opened his computer and clicked on the file Brian had sent them and read the caption. "'The Tylenol Murders.' What?"

"I seem to remember something about this. Some nut case put sodium cyanide inside Tylenol capsules," Codi said.

Joel suddenly turned pale as he started to read the file. A light sweat beaded on his forehead as he fought the rising panic. He had just swallowed two Tylenol capsules!

Codi smiled to herself and played with the thought of how long she should wait to tell him. She decided to give him a break.

"It was back in the eighties; nothing to worry about now."

Joel calmed slightly as the two agents read through the file.

The week of September 29th 1982, seven people died from sodium cyanide poisoning within the Chicago area. The toxin was loaded inside Tylenol capsules. Once authorities realized the source, they worked with the media and manufacturer to warn people and recall all Tylenol from the market. Police drove through residential streets using bullhorns to warn people, "Don't take Tylenol!" They also went door-to-door, collecting bot-

tles. Announcements were made on school intercoms, radio, and TV. It cost Johnson & Johnson over $100 million in recalled product alone.

The FBI quickly realized that the tampered bottles came from various sources, so sabotage during production was ruled out. The culprit was most likely buying Tylenol from several stores around the Chicago area and then replacing the acetaminophen with cyanide inside the red and white capsules. They would then return to various stores and put the bottles on the shelf.

During the investigations, a man named James William Lewis sent a letter to Johnson & Johnson demanding $1 million to stop poisoning their product. Police were unable to tie him to the crimes, as he and his wife were living in New York City at the time. He was, however, convicted of extortion.

"Several suspects were investigated," Codi said. "But no one was ever officially charged. *Hmm.* So I guess we get another crack at it."

"That case was the reason we now have tamper-proof bottles today that none of us can open," Joel added as he read further.

In 2009, Illinois authorities renewed the investigation, and federal agents searched the home of Lewis. They seized a number of items, but nothing ever came of it.

"So he didn't do it. What's the new lead?" Joel asked.

Codi scrolled through the file to an addendum at the bottom and read the notation. "Prison confession. Looks like we're going to the Windy City. No, make that Tamms, Illinois. Wherever that is."

Chapter Five

C arlo Sandoval stood basking in the sun's rays. It was a rare treat. He was standing in the back corner of the walled-in recreation area. "Yard" had been called at 11:30. It was one of the few hours in the day that actual sunlight reached this part of his world. He was a rail-thin convicted murderer serving a life sentence at one of the nation's toughest supermax prisons—Tamms— located in the southwest corner of Illinois next to the small town of Tamms.

Conditions were harsh, with little to no contact from the outside world. Each prisoner spent just over twenty-three hours a day in solitary confinement. They were fed through a chuckhole in the cell door and carefully monitored at all times. It was a place where the bad go to die.

"Sandoval! You have a visitor," a guard yelled from across the yard.

This made all the others suddenly eye their fellow inmate with suspicion. Visitors were very seldom allowed. The general consensus among prisoners was if you had a visitor, you were snitching to the cops or feds. Carlo looked around fearfully as he moved toward the exit. Would this day be his last? He had developed an edgy twitch from so much time spent alone. He was already considered a pariah by the other inmates. It would only be a matter of time before he had an "accident."

43

The guard escorted Carlo to a small concrete room where he was strip-searched and told to put his orange jumpsuit back on and sit. He was chained to a concrete stool, and the guard took position by the exit door, never taking his eyes off the prisoner.

As soon as Carlo saw his two visitors on the other side of the glass, he knew he was a dead man walking. They looked government to him. Undoubtedly FBI.

"This is Special Agent Strickman, and I'm Special Agent Sanders from—"

"Yeah, the FBI. I get it. What do you want? I'm missing out on some quality sunshine time," he said without looking up.

The voice on the other side of the thick glass sounded tinny. The sitting man was small in stature. He had a shaved head and a prison tattoo of a Nazi dagger on his right cheek.

"Okay, Carlo, I'll get right down to it," Codi said. "I have the power to get you out of here, somewhere nicer with TVs, a cafeteria, books, and sunshine. What I need for you to get that is everything you know about the Tylenol murders."

"I see you got my message," he said, as he finally looked up with the hollow eyes of a killer. Joel took a reflexive step back even though there was thick glass between them.

"I know who did it and how," Carlo said. "But that information goes with me to the grave unless you can provide me proof of what you're sayin'."

"How do I know you're not lying to us for your own gain?" Codi asked.

"Yeah, how?" Joel piped up, now trying to act brave.

Codi glanced at her partner, slightly annoyed at the interruption.

"The tampering occurred after manufacturing but before the product was stocked," Carlo offered.

"And you know this, how?" Codi asked.

"Get me out of here, and I'll tell you everything I know."

Codi and Joel watched the prisoner for a beat. Joel was getting the creeps and was just about to break eye contact when Codi interrupted the moment. "Guard, make sure he is kept somewhere safe. We'll be back tomorrow."

The guard agreed, and the two agents watched as he unlocked the chain and hauled Carlo away.

Once outside the prison, Joel took in a gulp of fresh air and let out a large sigh.

Codi was on the phone with their boss trying to put things in motion. The wheels of justice moved slowly, and getting Carlo transferred to a lesser security prison was going to take effort.

They piled into their rental and headed for the hotel. The nearest town worth staying in was Urbandale, twenty minutes south along the Ohio River. Joel found the car had a strong tendency to pull to the left. The last driver had undoubtedly hit a curb at forty miles per hour and then just turned the car back in. Joel white-knuckled the steering wheel as it pulled and shimmied all the way to Urbandale. A nice bed-and-breakfast called the Bluebell Inn would be home until the paperwork came through.

Urbandale was Americana personified. A small town with classic 1950s brick buildings lined a main street with very few chain stores. This is where heartlanders lived and died.

The Bluebell Inn was a two-story gabled home with white grid windows and a baby blue paint job. It was clean and cozy. The woman at the desk was in her mid-thirties and extremely efficient.

Codi's room smelled of chemically manufactured wildflowers that seemed to match the wallpaper. There was an antique dresser and a small matching desk. She laid her head back on a fluffy over-stuffed pillow and closed her eyes, hearing nothing but the clanking of the room's old-school radiator. A vibration from her phone killed the solitary moment. She answered without looking.

"Sanders," she deadpanned.

"Who else would it be?" Matt asked.

Codi sat up as the corners of her lips reached for the ceiling. "I'm in a room covered in wildflower wallpaper and furnished with antiques."

"Let me guess. I'm not going to see you tonight, and you're in . . . Iowa?" he guessed.

"Yes, and close. You got the 'I' right—Illinois."

"Bummer. I was thinking of blue crabs and fritters. Followed by a little extra fritter on the side."

"Little?" Codi probed his failure on the euphemism.

Matt recognized his missed wording and tried to save himself. "I mean extra . . . *extra.*"

Codi started to laugh. Matt stopped trying to save his faux pas and joined in. They talked for almost an hour before Joel knocked on her door for dinner and Codi said goodbye. She felt suddenly reinvigorated.

***

Carlo had spent two days isolated in the medical clinic. There had been a guard on duty at all times. He was sure there would be some attempt to get at him, but as time went by, he suspected he was just being paranoid.

Once strip-searched and relocked back in the small concrete room, Carlo sat and looked at the two agents through the glass wall separating them. They gave him a legal document, and he perused it carefully. The only sound to disrupt the silence was a cough from the guard on duty by the door.

"This is real?" he asked.

"All legal and binding," Joel answered.

"But only if you tell us everything," Codi added. "If we find out you withheld anything, even the smallest detail, the deal's off."

He held the document like it was a precious commodity. "Okay."

***

A two-car convoy escorted Carlo Sandoval away from the supermax to the closest FBI field office in St. Louis. There were two additional armed policemen as security, each with their heads on a swivel.

They took him to an interrogation room on the first floor and cuffed him to the table. Codi and Joel walked into the room after letting him sit for over three hours. It was a simple but effective ruse against most criminals. But for a man who had been living in solitary confinement, it was just another day.

Codi sat in one of the steel chairs and Joel followed her lead. Across the stainless table sat their jittery witness. Codi hit the recording app on her phone and made introductions and explained the purpose of the meeting.

"Okay," she said. "How 'bout we start at the beginning."

Carlo cleared his throat and took a drink from a bottle of water he had been given. He deliberately set the water back on the table, adjusting it just so as he collected his thoughts. He was about to trade up his situation in life by being a stoolie. He had second thoughts, but the promise of a chance to stay at The Ritz rather than a metal box won out.

"Fishing. It all started with fishing."

Joel immediately looked confused.

"You see, we use strings pulled from our blankets to tie notes on the end and cast them to other cells within reach."

It felt good to get the words out. Carlo glanced back and forth at each agent. He wiped his nose on his sleeve.

"Solitary is incredibly lonely. We aren't even allowed to shake hands the one hour a day we get some exercise. I get no visitors, and talking is discouraged. I'm talkin', 'baton on the back of your head,' discouraged."

He demonstrated with his hands as best he could, considering the handcuffs.

"So we fished for friends. Someone, anyone that would respond."

He looked down at the table and paused for a second, remembering. Joel fingered a few notes into his phone.

"'Bout two years ago, I made contact with the cellmate right across from me."

"Name?" Codi asked.

"Allan."

Joel wrote it down.

"Allan what?"

"We just used first names. Anywho, he and I shared things. Old flames. Cities we'd lived in. Favorite foods, even favorite sports teams. Eventually, we started chatting about our crimes. You know, things like who, what, where, why—the basics. Turns out this guy was a fixer for big money."

"Big money?" Joel asked.

"Yeah, like those big companies that run the world."

Joel still seemed a bit confused. Codi leaned over to him. "A fixer is someone who does legal and illegal things to make a company run smoothly or to get an individual out of a jam."

"Got yourself a greenie there, have you?" Carlo said with a smirk.

Joel's face flushed red.

"Only on the outside." She changed the subject back. "So this fixer told you about the Tylenol murders?"

"He said he was working for one of them big aspirin companies. They was taking a beating in the market when Tylenol came along."

"Did he say which one?" Codi asked.

Carlo shook his head. He paused to take a sip from the plastic water bottle he was holding like a lost lover. "This water is so good. Anyway, so he single-handedly brought them to their knees. A few bottle swaps in the distribution center and his work was done. Three weeks later, aspirin was again the drug of choice, and Tylenol was literally off the shelves."

"That's quite brilliant," Joel said.

"I know, right?" Carlo said. "Allan was a real pal . . . one of the smart ones. Miss him, I do."

"What do you mean *was?*" Codi interrupted.

"One day, we was chattin', and the next day, he's gone. Never heard what happened. That's when I reached out with this bit of information to y'all."

"What else did he say?" Joel prodded.

Carlo remembered a few more details, but otherwise, nothing more. Codi and Joel stayed another two hours asking questions before they finally left. They had a solid lead.

***

Garrett Scott lowered the monocular and placed it on his lap. It was a palm-sized 8x20 Leica Monovid. He had a perfect viewing spot to watch his target. He watched as the first man on his list methodically walked back and forth, consumed by his job. The back alley was cordoned off by police tape and officers. It was a seedy part of town, the type of place tourists and locals alike avoided. The two bodies on the ground were covered in tarps. Scott knew how things would go from here, and it would be a long time before his target would be finished at the crime scene. He started his car and pulled away. *Time for plan B.*

The rain came out of nowhere chased by a strong northeast wind, and it was freezing. Detective Jennings had left his house that morning unprepared, his blue sport coat no match for the weather. He had the small collar turned up and his arms crisscrossed with fingers under his armpits. His short-cropped hair seemed unfazed by the weather. The grimace on his face revealed dazzling, white teeth set against his dark skin as he shivered.

He moved with a bowed torso trying to endure the three-block walk to his apartment on Glebe Avenue from the closest subway stop. The Bronx neighborhood was mostly three- and four-story brick buildings, some with classic New York stoops. It was much like the place where he had grown up with caring parents and two high-energy sisters.

He had moved to this community when his marriage nose-dived. It wasn't because of any one thing. His wife was an amazing woman; he was a great detective. They just drifted apart, each too focused on everything except making the marriage work. They had a very agreeable divorce, dividing things right down the middle. He insisted she keep their dog, Aggie, and she had just managed to keep the dog happy and alive. They still saw each other from time to time. Just two weeks ago, he had spent the night. But nothing more than the occasional tryst was all there would ever be between them now. He was forever grateful she had never wanted children. It would have been a burden that neither would have been able to carry now.

Jennings squinted through the horizontal rain, his shoulders raised to help protect his ears. He could see a couple of other fools out in the weather, but they were prepared with warm coats and umbrellas. As he passed a person standing on the curb consumed by his phone, he noticed the man was completely dry inside his angled umbrella. *Must be nice*, Jennings thought.

The man realized he was blocking the sidewalk and moved to the side to let Jennings by. "Sorry, mate," he said with an Australian accent.

"All good," Jennings replied, as an intense shot of pain surged through his body. He reached for his ribs and looked around. The man with the umbrella was nowhere to be seen. *What was that?* Jennings's hand came back with blood on it. He took two more steps, and then his legs seemed to betray him. The impact with the concrete was insignificant as his mind struggled over the pain to understand. A single word formed and then faded just as fast. *Camilla*—the wife he had failed. It was his last thought as his life force flowed out and mixed with the liquid sidewalk running for the gutter. The puncture wound, placed perfectly, pierced his lung and heart. His body twitched several times and then stilled, eyes open in confusion as raindrops bounced off his deep-brown irises.

Scott looked back at his handiwork from the protection of his parked car. He had been precise with his hand-forged Kunai knife. There would be no coming back for the thirty-eight-year-old detective. He put his car in drive and headed south.

Next stop, two FBI agents in Washington D.C.

***

It took Joel about fifteen minutes with a computer to track down the inmate that used to room across from Carlo.

"Allan Treharne. It says he's at a federal pen up in mid-state, south of Peoria," Joel read while looking at the man's booking mug shot with an uneasy expression.

"What did he get sent up for?" Codi asked.

Joel adjusted his glasses and read from the file. "Looks like he was convicted on two counts of murder and one of extortion. He's serving a twenty-five-to-life sentence."

"I guess he wasn't as smart as good ole Carlo said. Come on, I'll drive."

The three-and-a-half-hour road trip cut up through the heart of Illinois. Codi enjoyed this part of the country. Plus, mid-day traffic was light and the fall weather perfect.

"Says we should be in the prison parking lot by 4:32 p.m.," she said, breaking the silence in the car.

"Hmm."

"What are you thinking about?" Codi asked.

Joel closed his laptop and looked over at his partner. "This case. I was just perusing the files again. Did you know there were almost a hundred copycat cases throughout the eighties with multiple deaths? I was just wondering what's wrong with people."

"You're just now asking that? It's why we have a job, Joel. The world will always have people willing to harm their fellow man for some kind of gain or even sport. It's up to us to mitigate that sick mindset and catch the creeps."

"I'm not sure cold cases apply."

Codi drove on in silence while Joel's thoughts permeated the car. She couldn't disagree with his assessment, as they had tracked down more deceased suspects that had gotten away with it than alive. Cold cases were notoriously hard to close, and often, new information just led to new dead ends. It wasn't like they were stopping many active criminals.

As they walked into the federal correctional institution in Peoria, the sun disappeared behind dark brooding clouds that were growing on the horizon. Once through the security gauntlet, they were met by the assistant warden. He escorted them toward Allan Treharne's cell. A screeching alarm suddenly fired throughout the prison, followed by an impassionate voice. *"All inmates return to your cells now. This is not a drill."* It repeated every few seconds.

"Did someone escape?" Joel asked, his eyes glancing in all directions.

"Not likely," the assistant warden said. "More like a medical emergency, like a stabbing. We get a lot of those here."

The body lay on the concrete floor of the cell while two medical professionals tried to revive him. The assistant warden stepped next to one of the guards and conversed while Codi and Joel watched the macabre scene. It was obvious to them the man was dead. She took in the cell's setting and quickly surmised a blanket had been ripped and braided. It was then fashioned into a noose. Allan Treharne had hung himself . . . allegedly.

***

Pullin Ikaika walked around the figure before him. The small room was dank and smelled of rat feces, the portable lighting illuminating only the woman tied to the metal chair on the worn concrete floor. She was thirty-something with stringy brown hair and red sunken eyes. She looked like she had been taken from a boardroom and left tied to the chair for days without food or water—which she had.

Pullin wore a shimmering light-blue sharkskin silk suit that reflected the light whenever he strayed close to it. His custom handmade Duke+Dexter loafers clicked on the damp cement as he paced. Two other men stood nearby watching like vultures locked on fresh prey. One was his head of security, Crispin Gales, wearing tactical pants and a black Henley. The other man was his numbers man, Edgar Fallman. He was wearing pressed jeans with a collared chambray shirt and a white blazer. He wore tinted tortoise-shell glasses, even in the darkened room, his eyes following the action instead of his head.

Pullin circled the woman as he spoke. "I want to apologize. We had fairly good intel that linked directly to you." He picked at a piece of lint on his pant leg that captured his attention for a second.

The tilt-slab room had once been part of an old manufacturing warehouse. His voice echoed on the hard surfaces, creating a twin for every spoken word. "We were sure you were informing on us, but it turns out we had the whole thing flipped around."

"That's okay," Carmen croaked hoarsely.

"We typically don't make those kinds of errors. So I started thinking." He gestured to Crispin to untie Carmen with a wave of his hand. "Where did the intel come from? Who had the motive? I mean, it couldn't be for money. We are all doing quite well, am I right?" He looked around to the nods of all three in the room. "So it must be a philosophical problem. A change of heart?" Pullin placed his hands behind his back as he spoke. "Perhaps it's not what happened that really bothers me. It's more what happened afterward. I mean, we all make mistakes; no one is perfect. Perfection is reserved for the gods. I, above all, understand that. But each of us must own up to our actions. That's the thing."

He shook his head at the thought that one of his most trusted had not only betrayed him but was also too weak to own up to it. Pullin had spent considerable time and resources ferreting out the culprit. "I have worked so hard to help others and to build and protect what we all have here. And now we have a chance—a real chance to save our planet. We all know it is no longer a question of *if* anymore. Humanity's death is inevitable within just a few lifetimes if we continue the way we are going."

He paused, letting the words sink in before starting back up. "It is our sacred purpose to save those we can. All I'm doing is what nature and man have done throughout the ages. Man through breeding and wars. Nature through her own fickle ways. *We* all agreed on the plan . . ." He looked around at the exclusive group. "And *you* tried to destroy it."

He pulled a Galesi .22 pocket pistol from seemingly nowhere and pointed it at Edgar.

Edgar's expression shot up in confusion. The gun Pullin was holding was so tiny it could be concealed by just closing your fingers around it. It fired a bullet too small to be effective as a defensive or offensive weapon. It was more like a toy.

Edgar looked at the toy gun and started to laugh, thinking it was a joke or one of his boss's weird loyalty tests, but the look on Pullin's face doused his upturned lips. "What?" Edgar, stammered, suddenly shocked by the turn of events. "Have you gone mad? I would never betray you."

"And yet, here we are. You made just one small mistake. Senator Crandall is one of mine."

The subtle change on Edgar's face told Pullin all he needed to know. He pulled the trigger. The report was loud in the enclosed concrete room. A small .22-caliber short slug tore through the tinted lens and into the left eye of the man he had once trusted.

"Ahh!" Edgar leaned over holding his ruined eye, screaming.

Pullin watched, entertained by the traitor's misery. He pulled the trigger again and another small bullet entered Edgar's neck. The pain seemed less than the first bullet, but Edgar still jerked at the impact.

He was wailing and sobbing as spittle poured from his lips. He pleaded and protested his innocence. Pullin chuckled at the man's misery. Whoever said that using one big bullet and ending things in a flash was best had never tried this. It was incredible. He pulled the trigger again, sending a slug into Edgar's lungs. He fell to the floor writhing, and now, hacking was part of his death throes. This was more fun than Pullin had had in a long time. It was exhilarating.

He pulled the trigger again. This time into the man's leg. It seemed to invoke little reaction. *Probably should have started there. Next time.*

After a few more bullets and flopping, screaming, pleading, and even an attempt at crawling away, Pullin emptied the rest of his mag into Edgar's head.

"Wow! That felt good," Pullin said as adrenaline pumped through his body.

He took a big breath of air filled with cordite smoke and raised his hands in the air.

Carmen rubbed the blood back into her hands, her eyes stinging in the haze, and her ears now ringing. Seeing her boss dispatch her colleague in that way shot a full dose of reality up her spine. She would need to be very careful from here on out. A small curse word escaped through her dry lips.

"I know, right?" Pullin said as he put his gun back in his pocket.

A slightly shocked expression seemed frozen on Crispin's face, and he tried hard to remove it. He had seen and done many things in his life. A simple look into his eyes told you they had been hard things, but the way his boss reveled in Edgar's demise was something new. It lacked any efficiency or military style.

"That's what happens when you betray me," Pullin said to no one. "Apparently, he was not as on board with our plans as we are. I have to say, Edgar was very good at covering his tracks, pushing the blame elsewhere. It's what made him so valuable to me. Oh, well." He turned, looking at Carmen. "Once again, I apologize for the mistake."

She nodded her head solemnly, her eyes still watery and fixed on her dead co-worker.

"Crispin, get this taken care of."

The order was met with a curt nod.

Pullin let his eyes linger on the corpse. *Man, that was a rush.* "We will have to be very careful from here on out. No telling what damage Edgar has inflicted on us, but I will get to the bottom of it, rest assured."

He turned from the body and showed his teeth to Carmen. It was a forced smile at best, like a wolf before its dinner. "Carmen, there is something I want to show you. It's time you had the full picture." He extended his hand. "If you would be so kind."

She reached out tentatively and let him help her from the chair, her legs weak and a bit wobbly.

Crispin grabbed his phone and dialed a cleaning crew they had relied on in the past.

Pullin led Carmen down a set of steel steps to a basement storage area in the old abandoned warehouse. There was a narrow hallway lit with caged bulbs mounted every ten feet, revealing three metal doors with serious locks and manual latches. Pullin walked to the last one and yanked on the latch. It groaned with lack of use, and he had to pull hard to get the door to open.

"This door leads to a back entrance to one of my most secret projects. And it is time for you to be a part of it."

He hit the light switch and, once again, gestured for Carmen to go first. As she entered the room, Pullin shoved the door closed behind her and re-secured the latch. He could hear muffled screams from the other side.

"I'm sorry, my dear," he said, "but even though you were not at fault, I have lost my trust in you."

He flipped the switch off, sending the small metal prison cell into darkness. The door would not be opened again.

Pullin wiped his fingerprints off the light switch, the lock, and the handle with a handkerchief. He pulled a small vial of hand sanitizer from his pocket and squirted a dollop on his hands, rubbing away the germs and all thoughts of his two former employees. It was time to push his schedule forward.

Chapter Six

"Let me see if I have this right. With help from an inmate who traded information for a better cell, you tie the Tylenol murders to a fixer named Allan Treharne. But before you can find out which aspirin company is behind it—and if he really did it—he mysteriously hangs himself in his cell."

SSA Brian Fescue closed the file that was sitting on his desk. He looked up at his two agents, both seated across from him. They stared blankly back at him. Brian took a deep breath. "If I didn't know better, I'd say this Carlo fellow set the whole thing up. He makes up this story and then gets one of his buddies to off this Allan dude. There would be no way to prove anything, and Carlo gets a better life. What Carlo didn't know was that the governor of Illinois is shutting down the supermax prison systems. He would have been out of there in six months, tops." A small sigh escaped his lips. "Thoughts?" Brian said with outstretched hands.

"Joel?" Codi prodded.

"It fits," he said.

"What does?" Brian asked.

"The whole timeline. We did some serious digging into Allan Treharne's background. He was in Chicago during the murders. He owned a corporation called Greenbriar. It had no known function or product. He was known as a fixer."

"We confirmed that with multiple sources," Codi added.

"And a deposit of two hundred grand hit one of his accounts three weeks after the crime."

"Anything on which aspirin company he worked for or who sent the money?" Brian asked.

"Sorry, nothing there. The money came from a long-dead shell company."

Brian drummed his fingers on his desk.

"Alright. As you know, cold cases don't have the same burden of proof that a case with a trial does. Good work, you two. Close it out as solved."

Joel nodded eagerly.

"How is the stolen corpse case looking?" Brian asked.

"We got bupkis," Codi said. "No evidence at the site and the corpse hasn't shown up anywhere. I'm guessing she was sent to The Body Farm. Wanna go back there and take a look, Joel?"

"Never again," he blurted with dread.

Codi was referring to a previous case where a body in evidence had been shipped to the famous forensic anthropological site, a place where they lay decomposing corpses out in the open to record and track decay. Joel had tossed his cookies after only a few minutes hanging around the sights and smells of the rotting dead. The thought gave Codi a good smile but drained all the blood from Joel's face.

Brian put them back on track. "Okay, give it another couple of days, and if you don't find anything, send Joel to The Farm."

"Wait, *what!*" Joel stammered.

"Just kidding, Joel. Close the case. I'm off to a first-grade choir recital. Any takers?"

Joel was still trying to recover, so Codi answered for them both. "No, but give Abigale our love and take some pictures this time, Dad."

"Will do."

The meeting broke up and each went their own way.

Codi walked down the hallway to her office. A text popped up and she reflexively took a look. *Hey, coming out to Virginia for a conference next week. Would love to spend a couple of days together. Thoughts???*

It was her mom. Codi knew that they were on the mend after her visit to San Diego three months ago. Next week she was busy but still in town. There would be no escape, except for a lie. A thousand thoughts flashed through her mind, but two stood out the most. Should she introduce her mom to Matt, and should she get her a hotel room or ask her to stay with her? The answers would not come easy.

***

They had rented a warehouse for the week. It was a tall metal structure, with dusty skylights and a concrete floor. Matt and two of his colleagues supervised the crew that offloaded supplies and materials onto the floor. They set up their testing equipment on two folding tables as the four-man team began construction. Four thirty-foot-high walls, each twelve feet wide and each made of a different material. Glass, steel, wood, and concrete surfaces were planned, with further tests scheduled in three months. But today was their first milestone.

The Z-Man Program was a DARPA-inspired project designed to reduce the risks of taking the high ground in an urban environment. Historically, ladders or climbing equipment were the only options for vertical climbing to a higher position to give you an advantage over the soldiers on the ground. Today, Matt would hopefully see that change. He had been brought in late on the project to help refine the adhesive properties required.

The Z-Man Program had taken its cue from nature, the Tokay gecko to be specific, considered one of the climbing champions of the world. The trick was to recreate its ability to climb and transfer that to humans. A Tokay gecko weighs two hundred grams, whereas a human carrying gear could weigh two hundred, fifty pounds. It was a daunting task.

Matt had taken on the project with enthusiasm and had made several breakthroughs since starting the project. A gecko is able to climb a wall using physical bond interactions. It can literally hang by one toe. Each foot is covered with hundreds of stalk-like setae, and each seta has hundreds of terminal tips called spatulae. They branch out and make contact with the surface like an adhesive that only works in two directions—downward pull and left, right pressure. It allows the gecko to lift his foot with ease to release the bond.

For the human trials, Matt and his team had developed easily grip-able paddles using nanofabrication technology to recreate the result.

"Hey, anyone here named Dr. Matt Campbell?" A voice called out.

Matt turned to see a young man with a backpack striding with purpose in his direction. He had curly, moppish black hair with an angled face and lean build.

"I'm Dr. Campbell," Matt said, extending his hand.

"Kyle," he said, shaking Matt's hand vigorously.

"Yes, our climber. Good to meet you."

Kyle would be the man demonstrating their paddles. He would be required to climb the different walls with a mix of variables. A big part of their success or failure was in his hands.

Matt filled Kyle in on their current schedule, and they worked out a plan to go with it. Matt had always believed in letting the expert contribute his part to an operation, and Kyle's knowledge of all things climbing was extensive.

"If you don't mind, I'll go ahead and get things set up," Kyle said. "I got all the gear I need right here." He gestured to his backpack with a hooked thumb.

"Great. The walls should be ready to start testing in the next two days."

"Sounds good, Doc," Kyle said over his shoulder as he left.

***

Special Agents Gordon Reyas and Anna Green watched as a small television crew set up lights and cameras in their conference room. The film director, a man named Thomas, was bouncing about like a toddler on caffeine, telling everyone how he wanted things done. The conference table was moved to the side and two chairs were placed next to each other right in the sweet spot of the light. A man named Russ placed microphones on both agents while a young woman, Janice, powdered their faces. Gordon was a bundle of nerves. The thought of being on camera scared him, and he started to sweat through his makeup.

Joel noticed the commotion as he entered the office sipping his morning ritual.

"What's happening, Gordo?"

"Apparently, we are the final interview in a docu-feature on the D. B. Cooper case."

"They really solved it?" Joel asked, amazed, especially after the circle jerk he and Codi had gone through close to a year ago while chasing down a new lead on that same case.

"Yep. Case closed."

"Crazy. So who did it?" Joel asked.

"Watch the movie."

"Funny. Oh, Gordo, don't make us look bad and don't screw up, or you'll end up on the cutting room floor," Joel said as he left for his office.

Gordon went back to sweating.

"Can you believe that?" Joel burst out as he entered Codi's office.

"What?" Codi said as she turned her chair to face her partner.

"They're putting Gordo and Anna on camera."

"Good for them, Joel. We don't need that kind of publicity. It only makes our job harder."

"Apparently, the case is solved," Joel said, slightly bewildered.

"You mean the skyjacker case. Yeah, I read the file."

"What did it say?"

"Some filmmaker/author dude led the independent investigation into the cold case with like a forty-person team, mostly retired federal agents. The suspect's identity was hidden within some letters allegedly written by D. B. Cooper and sent to various newspapers right after the skyjacking. The guy was a former Special Forces paratrooper, explosives expert, and pilot with about twenty-two different aliases. He was a specialist in codes, and some think he worked for the CIA. A real narcissistic sociopath who never thought he would be caught. I guess he was trying to prove that he was smarter than everyone else."

Codi grabbed her phone and pulled up the files she had read. "Anyway, these letters contain coded messages that pointed directly to the hijacker's real identity."

"*I want out of the system and saw a way by skyjacking a jet plane,* was decoded in one letter."

"*I am 1ˢᵗ Lt. Robert Rackstraw. D.B. Cooper is not my real name,* was decoded in the second. Case closed."

"And Rackstraw?" Joel asked.

"Dead." Codi spun in her chair and went back to the report she was working on.

Joel stood there with his mouth open for a minute before shuffling back to his office. "Unbelievable."

***

It was more luck than science. The cells in Mary Mallon did something very unique. They created a protein that invaded the body's macrophages, the Pac-Man gobblers of foreign pathogens. The macrophages took the bacterium *Salmonella enterica serovar Typhi* and encapsulated it, turning the pathogen into a hospitable anti-inflammatory state, harmless to the body. There, it slowly withered and died.

Dr. Erwin Mahl pulled back from the screen. He had run the simulation many times, and the results seemed to be consistent. The gene responsible had been isolated. Though it wasn't a cure, it was a way to become immune to the symptoms. It was the breakthrough they had been searching for.

"Truly incredible," Dr. Kamba said.

"I know, right?"

The lab was small but efficient. It had everything needed for gene sequencing and DNA extraction. There were three long tables with black Chem-Res tops. They were neatly organized with equipment and samples. Dr. Mahl worked with three other lab professionals on a rotating basis. Dr. Kamba was his most trusted colleague. A young-looking Pakistani man named Kyber was a college graduate with a real head for procedure. He had been the surprise of the new hires. Everything he checked and followed through on was done first-rate. Kyber was in his mid-thirties but looked like he was nineteen with his messy hair and babyface. He wore octagon-shaped glasses that did little to help age him. His personality was perfectly suited to the scientific method.

The fourth member, Santos, was a twenty-five-year-old Cuban American with a neatly trimmed beard and a spiky haircut. He had graduated from the

University of Miami the previous spring with a degree in immunology and infectious disease. He was instrumental in several of their breakthroughs, as he had an affinity for taking risks. He pushed for human trials well before Dr. Mahl, Dr. Kamba, or Kyber.

Pullin had personally recruited him to help with the workload and the testing. As a team, they didn't work around the clock, but long hours ensued.

"Tell me what you think," Dr. Mahl asked Dr. Kamba.

His partner studied the results. She had followed *his* inspiration with inspiration of her own on the work they were doing and believed that the ends really did justify the means.

"It is remarkable. We've done it," Dr. Kamba said, never taking her eyes from the simulation.

"Well, the first step anyway. It's funny—there are many drugs and chemical compounds that are extremely effective in treating typhoid, but they turn out to be too costly to reproduce for the mass market."

Dr. Kamba pulled back to look at Dr. Mahl. The stress of the timeline they were on was showing on his face.

"Years ago, a very effective anti-cancer drug, Taxol, I believe was the name," said Dr. Mahl, "was discovered in the bark of the Pacific yew tree. Unfortunately, harvesting the compound killed the tree. It took millions of dollars and many trees, along with a host of chemists to finally synthesize it. By the time they did, something better had come along."

"But we can now make an injectable that will alter genes to produce the protein we need," Dr. Kamba said. "That should make it more cost-effective."

"And this time we are lucky. It is not so prohibitive," Dr. Mahl added. He tested a weary smile as he looked at his protégé.

"This is great news," Dr. Kamba said, matching his tired expression.

"Yes, it is. Looks like it might be time for you to start overseeing the transfer to the ships," Dr. Mahl said.

"I now know what we'll need and how to set up the labs."

"Good," he said, his trust for the woman's skill obvious. "I'll alert Pullin that we are moving to phase two and make sure the replication of the vaccine gets underway before you and I leave."

"We'll want to be vaccinated as soon as possible. This new strain we've developed spreads way too easy," she added.

"I concur." He turned to Kyber, who was taking down a reading in the back of the lab. "Kyber!"

"Yes, Dr. Mahl?" he answered as he crossed the lab.

"See if you can do a run of fifty on this compound. I want everyone injected. We are moving to phase two. That means you will need to make sure everyone here can run the procedure before we leave."

"Yes, Doctor. Right away." The words seemed to electrify Kyber. He took the sample and specs from Dr. Kamba and headed for the replicator, eager to start the procedure.

"Hey, Santos!"

"Yeah, Doc," Santos answered without looking up from the readings he was taking.

"We are moving to phase two. Call the Bug Boys and tell 'em it's time to move."

Suddenly consumed by the words he had heard, Santos looked like he had been hit with a high volt of electricity. "Seriously?"

***

Garrett Scott was running late. It was not part of his trained spycraft. Traffic on 95 had been brutal even though it was still dark outside. Eventually, he found the source. Three lanes had become one thanks to America's slowest working union, the MDOT, Maryland Department of Transportation. By 6:45 a.m., he had made it to his destination. Parking was non-existent, so he ended up jogging three blocks from a Starbucks parking lot to reach his destination. Pausing by a large tree, he waited to catch his breath while pretending to fiddle with his phone. His next target emerged from the building. Special Agent Codi Sanders.

She was carrying a gym bag and dressed in fitness attire. She moved with fluid ease—like a predator searching for prey. She had longish brown hair and a sexy athletic figure. This was a worthy opponent. Her file had revealed her accomplishments, but seeing her in person ratcheted up Scott's sixth sense. It screamed, *be careful with this one.* He regarded her for a few more seconds and then turned and moved away as if he had no cares in the world. Inside, his heart was pounding—finally, a quarry that would merit his best. Scott would spend the next several days tracking her movements while being extremely careful to avoid any security cameras. This had to be a smash and grab hit, and he knew just when and where it should happen.

Over the next three days, Garrett Scott watched from afar, careful not to be seen. On Tuesday, she had a male visitor spend the night. They looked to be in love, as they displayed an intimacy that results from two compatible souls. Scott had never experienced that kind of emotional connection with another human. He had bedded lots of women over the years, even a couple of guys when he was younger, but had never found a soul mate. He was sure that was a made-up word by some marketing firm selling roses, chocolates, or shiny baubles.

Agent Sanders had a somewhat predictable schedule, and he felt confident he could safely complete this mission and move on to her partner. According to his file, he would be the easier of the two. But he knew to never underestimate your opponent, even if they have no idea you are targeting them. It was a maxim that had kept him at the top of his game for many years.

Thursday evening, Scott parked his car down the block from Agent Sanders's building. He noticed that the lights were already on inside the third-story apartment. Apparently, she was less predictable than he had previously thought. He would need to wait until the time was perfect. Meanwhile, he watched as neighbors moved through their nightly routine, walking dogs and getting dinner. He was tempted to end one dog walker's life when he watched his pup leave a giant turd on the sidewalk and then just walked away. *What a prick.*

At just past 9:00 p.m., he reached down and pulled up an AK9 sealed in plastic. He donned gloves and removed it from the bag, double-checking the weapon and its magazine. The short-barreled compact rifle had a quick detachable suppressor and flameless tip. It used special subsonic 9x39 mm cartridges developed for the Russian Special Forces. The hi-tech Russian weapon would be extremely quiet against the ambient noise of the neighborhood. It would also leave authorities in a real quandary. He mounted a small black bag with preset clips to the side of the gun to catch the brass that was ejected during shooting.

The metropolitan area of D.C. employed a grid of listening towers across the city that could pinpoint the location of a single gunshot. The system was known as Shot Spotter, and it was directly connected to the police who could respond quickly to the location with an accuracy of less than twenty feet. A properly silenced weapon, though not completely silent, would never register.

Scott pulled a Nationals ball cap down over his head and opened his door. He exited the SUV and quickly hid the weapon in a large overcoat. He moved in a zigzag pattern to a preselected location. His movements avoided all known cameras mounted on the street or on homes that he had previously scouted. At best, they would capture the back of a person wearing black.

Once in position, Scott leaned against a large tree and watched the third-floor apartment from across the street. The building was a four-story red stone structure with white limestone headers across the windows and doors. It had a small staircase that led up to the main entrance, which gave access to all the apartments. There was an older-style cage elevator granting ingress to the upper floors. Two tower-like columns gave the façade a Romanesque style.

The street was currently empty, so he moved his weapon into a position where it was still slightly covered by his coat but ready to quickly aim and fire. Agent Sanders's living room window was lit up. It had a sheer curtain across it, barely disguising the contents.

Garrett Scott watched as his target's silhouette moved back and forth in the room. He waited until she moved up close to the window and stretched her arms wide to the sides to grab the solid curtains to close off the world outside for the night. This was what Scott had been waiting for. He quickly lowered himself to car height to make it look like a drive-by shooting and then fired a three-round burst into his target. He watched her shudder and drop, taking one of the curtains with her in a death grip. He then sprayed the building to make it feel more random, in accordance with the "drive-by" picture he was painting.

No weapon is truly silent. But the AK9 came close. With its subsonic rounds and specialized silencer, the noise sounded like a rusty bicycle chain on an old ten-speed. The bullet impacts across the street sounded like a hammer installing a picture in a neighbor's apartment. No one seemed to notice or care.

Once finished, Scott hid the weapon back in his coat and headed casually to his car, doing a reverse zigzag of his previous movements.

He drove to a back alley where he repacked the gun in its plastic, stripped off all his clothes, put them in a trash bag, and tossed them into a dumpster. He redressed and drove away. The next stop was a little place he had spotted along the Potomac River to dump the gun.

Two down, one to go.

Chapter Seven

1134 10th St. – WASHINGTON D.C. – 9:36 P.M.

A fog obscured clarity as she opened her eyes, trying to focus on her surroundings. The sounds around her were muted and dull. There was no coming back or changing the way things were. She shook off the destructive thoughts that had occupied her mind for the last half-hour and stepped out of the Uber. Codi thanked her driver and moved lethargically through the motions. First, up the stairs, and then toward her door. She had left her spare key under the mat, knowing work hours were unpredictable. Her after-work plans often needed to be fluid. Codi's mom had arrived in town sometime around 6:00 p.m., and Codi could just imagine her going through her apartment like a detective at a crime scene. The thought made her shudder. *It's just two days, Codi. You can do this.* After all that she had been through in her life—the Marines, BUD/S training, even being shot and tortured, this would surely be the death of her.

Codi decided to go against her instincts and have her mom stay at her apartment and meet Matt. It had taken some serious deliberation, but there was no turning back now. In typical "Codi fashion," she had jumped in with both feet. She paused at the door, took a big breath, forced a smile, and opened the door.

The first thing she noticed was the smell, coppery and sweet—blood. The next was the shattered front window and a body lying in her living room, covered in blood, gripping a curtain. Her first thought filled her with regret almost as soon as it materialized. Had her mom come here to heap guilt on Codi by offing herself in her apartment? It was rash and heartless. Codi instantly dismissed it. That act was not congruent with such a selfish person.

A closer look told the story. The bullets had come from outside. She knelt in the blood and checked for a pulse, trying to make sense of everything. Letting her training kick in, Codi called 9-1-1. She identified herself and her badge number to the operator and laid out the situation. Her mom was dead from an unknown shooter.

Codi hung up the phone and stepped back. She looked down at her lifeless mother. The woman who had raised her and in many ways made her the person she was today. Much of it by the things she *hadn't* done. Codi tried to bring back the good times. The times when they were a family doing normal family things. It all seemed too long ago to shed even a single tear.

"Oh, my gosh!"

Codi spun around, reaching for her gun. Matt was standing in the doorway with his mouth open in horror. She ran to him, just now remembering the night the three of them had planned.

The police, detectives, and EMTs all arrived within a few minutes of each other. The coroner was dispatched and Codi was questioned. It all seemed like a bad movie in a theatre with locked doors and arm restraints on the chairs, one you couldn't escape from or get out of your mind. After 11:30, Matt collected a few of Codi's belongings and took her to his place. It was going to be a rough night.

***

"Captain," the first mate said as a very tall and fit woman entered the bridge. Captain Charlotte Combs was in her early forties but looked ten years younger. She was six feet tall with broad shoulders and a crazy-good right hook. She had short blood-red hair that was artificially dyed and a spicy disposition to go with it. She had made a name for herself by outmaneuvering her competition with a firm but fair reputation. Consistently delivering her cargo on time and under budget, Captain Combs had a way of streamlining everything she did.

"Collins, report," she said with a clipped staccato.

"Repairs to the starboard anchor wench are complete," her first mate, Collins, replied. "We have managed a four percent savings on fuel consumption and should reach port in San Francisco by Tuesday, 4:10 p.m., give or take twenty minutes."

"Excellent. How are the modifications coming?"

"Still on schedule."

She gave him an appraising glance with one eyebrow raised. Collins held eye contact, confirming his appraisal.

"Okay. I'm going to have a look for myself. Good job," Charlotte said.

Collins gave her a short nod and turned back to his duties. He was a thirty-two-year-old navigator-turned-first-mate. He had distinguished himself over several successful years on a large container ship based out of his hometown. His efforts caught the eye of one of the most unique captains on the seven seas. She recruited him, and they quickly became a model of efficiency.

First Mate Collins Eynaut was an average-height man with short curly hair and impossibly dark skin. He had an alluring smile and a grateful disposition. He spoke French, English, and Creole and could read and write them as well.

Collins was always a straight shooter and a crew favorite. He was originally from Freetown, Sierra Leon, in West Africa, an overcrowded port town. As an orphan, he had little hope of escaping the crush of the area's poverty.

Left with his aunt after his parents had been killed during the bloody civil war that divided neighbors and families, Collins had given his struggling aunt a reason to survive. A post-war-era Sierra Leon had no regard for women or human rights. She ultimately was stabbed to death over a loaf of bread and a can of condensed milk, and Collins was forced to fend for himself on the streets.

As a young boy, he watched the ships come and go and dreamed of one day being taken away from his hardscrabble existence. He was bright and made the most out of a life on the streets, trading junk for pennies and pennies for food.

It was a warm spring day when fate dealt him a card. He jumped over the trash piled along the street, ignoring the rotting stench that would leave most people incapacitated. Collins had gone down to the docks to watch the ships and scavenge for anything worth selling. He had bumped into a well-dressed white man while rubbernecking at the huge cranes unloading containers. The man briefly regarded the street urchin. "You like the ships?" he asked.

"Oh, yes, sir," Collins replied.

The man paused at the boy's polite directness. He then asked for directions to an office on Ross Road. Collins was very precise with his response. The man looked him over for a second time with a surprised expression. A few additional inquiries ended the conversation with an offer to be a cabin boy. It was a once-in-a-lifetime chance and Collins jumped at it, never looking back, and happily severed all ties from his childhood. Not once did Collins leave the ship when it was docked at his hometown of Freetown Port. Soon, the sea was his real home. He used his position to learn everything he could, and over the years, it paid off. Collins was now a man of position and worth.

Captain Charlotte Combs moved with purpose below deck on *The Locust*. She was an older, smaller Panamax cargo ship, with 3,300 TEU. She was just under nine hundred feet in length with a raked bow and rounded stern. *The Locust* was made to work both large and smaller ports of call. By today's standards, with ULCVs at over twelve hundred feet in length plying the oceans, she was small and often overlooked. The owner had let her red hull and white superstructure fade and rust, giving her a neglected tarnish. But that is exactly what made her so valuable.

The hallway that led past the galley ended in a metal bulkhead with stairs going down to the right. Charlotte reached out and turned the fire extinguisher mounted on the wall in front of her. A hidden steel panel slid to the left, revealing a small empty room. She stepped inside and the door closed behind her. A quick palm scan resulted in a positive beep, and the wall beyond opened up. Thirty percent of the cargo space had been selected for a special project. They had hidden the space within the stacks of containers and limited its access with high-security measures and secrecy.

Charlotte stepped into the vast space to see a small group of workmen welding and grinding their way to completion. Sparks and flickering arc light filled the space as smoke drifted slowly to the exhaust fans. The fans were tied into the ship's main funnel, sending the smoke out along with the engine's exhaust to avoid suspicion.

Once completed, there would be two large labs, several offices, an autopsy room, crematorium, galley, and head. The starboard lab held four large growing tanks, each with specialized egress and piping. Everything you would need to run a very sophisticated offshore lab would decorate the main portside lab. All of it away from the prying eyes of any government. The entire secret facility could be sealed off and decontaminated with the push of a button. Should there be a dangerous parts-per-million, PPM, sensor alert, it could be destroyed. Mobile labs like these were growing in popularity, as they were impossible to regulate and were not bound by any country's laws as long as they practiced in international waters. It was a cloner's dream.

The carefully placed containers in the middle of the ship hid the workspaces while allowing the ship enough room to operate its cargo business of hauling containers for a small profit. The real money would be made in the laboratory.

***

Dr. Erwin Mahl nodded to himself as he focused on the specimen through the microscope for final confirmation. He was chewing absently on a mouthful of cashews. It was a big breakthrough and it happened much more quickly than he or any of his colleagues had expected. The initial trials on five sets of mice were showing promise, as the fuzzy critters seemed blissfully unaware of the toxin raging in their bodies. Mice are the only other mammals susceptible to typhoid fever, and they have long been used as test subjects for the disease. These mice had all been infected by just being in proximity to each other, as they were separated by two sets of mesh screens that never allowed them to touch. It started by infecting subject one, and the pathogen moved through the enclosures one by one until all five were infected. This was an unprecedented way for typhoid to spread. Any micro particulate could do it—a sneeze for example.

Dr. Mahl leaned back, almost giddy, an emotion foreign to him. Kyber and Dr. Kamba stared at him with expectant smiles.

"It is done," he said.

This triggered a nod from his coworkers and initiated an immediate action plan that would follow. It was time to close and move the lab.

Dr. Mahl opened a drawer that he rarely used and pulled out a flip phone with only one number programmed in it. His bony finger hit send, and he lifted the cell to his ear.

A curt "Yes" filled his ears.

"Time for the human element."

There was only a second of silence before a "Good" replied, and the line went dead. Dr. Mahl placed the phone on the table and smashed it to pieces with a small hammer. His assistants paid no attention, as they were busy disposing of nearly fifty mice in a small crematorium. It was time to start phase three—human trials.

***

"What are you doing here? You're supposed to be at Matt's, as in, not at work."

"I've been at Matt's for three days, and as much as I love him, I am going stir crazy. I need to do something, anything. *Please.*"

Codi had come to terms with her mother's death. Not that it wouldn't haunt her or always be a part of her consciousness. The vision of her bloody corpse was seared into her mind forever. Sitting on Matt's sofa, however, was not helping. She knew it wasn't her fault someone had tried to kill her and failed. Or that they killed the wrong person. None of it was her fault, but that didn't make it any easier. Focusing her mind on catching the killer was her best remedy for her guilt, and few people had the myopic focus of Codi Sanders. It was one of her defining qualities. Dogged to the finish line, no matter what.

Brian looked his agent over. He could tell she hadn't been sleeping. The look on her face was desperate. He tipped his head to the floor and processed the situation.

"Okay, half-days till you start sleeping. And you can have updates on your mom's case, but no involvement whatsoever. Agreed?" Brian gave her his most serious look.

"Sure. Thanks, Brian." Codi gave him a false smile and headed for her cubicle.

With sudden regret, Brian watched her leave.

Codi popped her head into Joel's workspace.

"Hey," Codi deadpanned.

"Oh, thank heavens you're here!"

It was not the reaction Codi was expecting.

"I think someone is targeting us. That alleged drive-by was no accident. It was meant for you."

Joel had a passion for late-night research, and one of his favorite topics was conspiracy theories. It wasn't always helpful to their cases, but his fringe skills and in-depth knowledge had been useful to the team in the past, so Codi decided to go with it.

"First of all," Codi said, "we are not allowed to work on this case. Second . . . what makes you think that?"

"The detective we met in New York?"

"At the gravesite?" Codi said, her forehead pinched, trying to remember him.

"Yeah. He was killed last week."

"Show me the file." Codi sat down next to her partner and perused the information.

"This could be anything, Joel. From a robbery gone bad to gang retaliation. What makes you think someone is targeting us?"

"Okay, one, there was nothing taken from Detective Jennings to indicate a robbery."

"That could still mean a lot of things, Joel."

"Just hear me out," he said, with his hand raised. "Two, the missing Typhoid Mary corpse never turned up. If it was a prank or something, they would have used it by now. Three, there was no evidence at the gravesite. That speaks *professional* to me. Four, the bullets found at your apartment are unique. They came from an AK9, a highly specialized Russian Special Forces rifle. You are not likely to find that here in the US. I think someone is messing with the cops. That was no drive-by. Five, your mom is not some kind of super-spy or anything from what I can tell. So that means it was you they were targeting. Six, I believe—"

"Okay, okay, enough with the counting. I get it. You have added one and one and come up with three. Luckily for you, your hypothesizing has proven to be more accurate than most I've heard. Let's go through everything carefully one more time to see what the evidence actually says."

Codi made herself comfortable as she and Joel covered every detail he had been compiling since her mom's shooting. He had spent hours collecting footage from her neighborhood and the detectives. The lack of evidence spoke volumes.

"No one is lucky enough to kill a detective on the street in New York City and leave zero evidence," Joel said. "Or shoot up a building at nine at night and, again, leave no evidence. There were thirty rounds fired and not a single shell casing was found. Plus, CSI says they fired on your mom first and then on your building to make it look like it was something it wasn't. The bullet pattern doesn't lie. Based on your window sheers being drawn and the fact that you live alone, he got the wrong Sanders."

Joel realized his blunder and wished he could take back his insensitive words. "Sorry . . . I didn't mean to . . ."

"It's okay, Joel." She placed her hand on his arm to reassure him. "This is all good stuff, but what's the motive?"

"*Ah,* I thought you would never ask," Joel answered, as he took a sip from his ever-present coffee cup. He cleared his throat. "Typhoid Mary. She's the key."

A beat of silence followed as Codi tried to form a mental picture of what he was saying.

"You're telling me that a hundred-year-old corpse—"

"Eighty-three."

"What?"

"It's an eighty-three-year-old corpse."

"Whatever, Joel. An eighty-three-year-old corpse is why someone killed Detective Jennings, my mom, and is targeting us?"

"Well, you see—"

"Joel," Codi said, interrupting. "Remember all those times I encouraged you to think out of the box and not be so by-the-book?"

"Sure, that's why—"

"*Well, stop it!*" Codi said as she turned and stood up. "You're ticking me off and wasting my time. Focus on the facts, not your manufactured idea of them." She abruptly left.

Joel looked up and watched her leave, hurt and confused.

***

The funeral in San Diego was small and surprisingly religious. The eulogy seemed heartfelt and the idea of heaven came across as hopeful. Codi sat and thought about how church had not played much of a role in her life. She remembered going as a family when she was very young, but it had died out by the time she was six. God was something to look forward to and put faith in, but without good works, he seemed like nothing more than a hollow mascot. Historically, organized religion had been responsible for more deaths than just about any other reason, but Codi had held on to her belief in God, as it seemed to keep her connected to her dad, and hopefully, now her mom.

Afterward, Codi endured so many "I'm sorry for your loss" comments, that she lost count. She had been stoic the entire time, trying to find some emotion inside her that just didn't exist. Had her mom's dive down a deep tunnel during Codi's youth been so destructive to their relationship? Codi knew she shouldn't judge others for how they grieved, but what about the ones left behind, especially a child? She shook the thoughts off as the last person left the room, leaving her alone.

A man approached with a silver urn and offered his condolences as he handed her the ashen remains. Codi thanked him for his kind words, although she was sure it had been a rubber stamp of many of his previous funerals—*insert name here.*

She drove her rental car out of the city and west to Torrey Pines Nature Preserve where she parked the car and grabbed the urn, stuffing it into her backpack. A quick hike took her to the cliff-side trail through the distinctive windswept pine trees that were the park's namesake. She looked out at the Pacific Ocean beyond. It was a blue, cloudless sky set against the deep blue water. Waves could be heard crashing below, and gulls were singing their high-pitched song. It was a favorite hiking path of her father's when she was a little girl. He would bring her up here to smell the air, said it was the best in the state.

Codi thought of the many funerals she had attended throughout her life. Death was a part of every life. Inevitable. No one could beat it. What mattered was what you did with your life. Sooner or later, death would take care of itself.

She poured the contents of the urn over the cliff's edge and then watched as the ashes floated wistfully on the air current. She tried to process her guilt that the bullets were meant for her. She reached for a small envelope in her pocket, which she had found tucked in her mother's suitcase. It had a single word on the front, *Coco*, a childhood pet name, and she had yet to open it. Codi used her finger to pry loose the flap and pull the contents free. A single piece of paper and a faded photograph appeared in her hand. She turned the paper over and let the words come to her.

Codi, if only I could turn back time, but the past is lost to us. What we build and become starts today, and I am willing to do the work necessary. I hope you will too... Please know that I love you, Mom

Codi held the picture. It was a vision of her as a young girl camping in the Sequoias with her parents. The memory flooded back. It was a perfect time in Codi's life. With her dad, she had caught a rainbow trout in a nearby creek. Mom was cooking it up, and Codi had a smile as big as her whole face.

The memory immersed her in the moment and erased all the bad. Codi knelt and said a short prayer, trying to process her emotions. A single tear dropped. It was followed by more tears, until she sobbed softly, finally grieving for the amazing mother she could now remember. All of the cruel memories washed away like a watercolor painting in the rain.

Codi stood and took a deep breath. Her dad was right; the air was good here. Her parents were in a better place and that gave her comfort. Though not particularly religious, she did believe that God had a better place for everyone. Without that, what was the point? She wiped the tears away and allowed herself to finally grieve. It was cleansing. Placing the empty urn back in her backpack, she put one strap over her shoulder and stood looking at the horizon. Now it was time to get the person responsible for killing her mom.

***

Joel entered the security checkpoint on the first floor of the FBI field office. He was running late and had missed most of his morning routine. He had just managed to find a clean white shirt and suit but had forgotten to wear a tie. The briefing was in ten minutes, and he needed to organize his thoughts. Since the blowup with Codi, he had not been himself. The drama had left him on edge and reliving their conversation over and over. He was at a loss as to what he had done wrong.

"Sorry about the other day."

Joel looked up to see his partner standing in the lobby waiting for him. It had been a week since he had last seen or heard from her.

"I brought you a peace offering," Codi said holding out a coffee cup in his direction. Joel instinctively reached for it.

"What is it?" he asked.

"Starbucks."

Joel recoiled as if the cup was a venomous snake. Then, realizing his actions, tried to cover them up by scratching his cheek in an awkward fashion.

"Just kidding. It's the good stuff. You'll like it."

He nodded and accepted the peace offering, smelling its aroma with elation.

"We have a briefing in ten," Codi said.

"How did you know?"

She gave him her best devilish smile and led the way to the elevators.

Once the doors closed to the sound of a ding, Codi turned to Joel. "We good?"

It wasn't much, but after all they'd been through, it was enough.

"Always," Joel said, letting go of the heavy weight he'd been carrying for the past week.

***

Matt set his laptop on the conference table. Several co-workers were already seated. His boss, who acted more like a camp counselor, pushed into the room, his happy expression leading the way. He was in his early sixties and seemed to be more up on the latest trends in science than anyone else in the building. His hair was buzzed to near stubble, and he had a perfectly white Van Dyke. Milky eyes saw everything in the room as he took the time to say hi to each of his employees before sitting down.

"Nice work on the Z-man trials, gents. Washington is very happy."

He always referred to the bosses as "Washington." It gave them both anonymity and status at the same time.

"I have a little something that has gone through testing and is almost ready for the field. So what they want us to do is find the faults. Where does it fail, under what conditions and situations? So put your heads together, and let's prove we are worthy of our moniker."

He stood and leaned forward. "They've given us two weeks."

He rapped on the table with his knuckles and left the room.

Back in his office, Matt pulled up the e-file on his laptop. EXACTO (Extreme Accuracy Tasked Ordnance) was written on the title page. He scrolled through the hundred-plus-page document to get a quick bird's eye view. It was a new kind of bullet that used a special optical sighting technology and a guidance system to adjust a .50-caliber bullet on the fly to its target. *Sweet!*

Matt started to read through the specs, but his mind wandered. He had made a decision, and now, he had to implement it.

"Hey, Jack," Matt said to his coworker, pausing his work.

Jack looked over. He was a balding middle-aged man with a narrow face and crazy bushy eyebrows.

"You're married, right?" Matt said.

"Sixteen years in December," he replied as he scratched the back of his neck.

"Have you ever regretted it?"

Jack turned his chair to face Matt as he considered the question as he would a scientific problem.

Matt immediately regretted his query.

"Yes, many times. But if I could go back in time, I would do it again. In the end, a shared life is a better life."

Matt nodded his head slowly. "Thanks."

The answer had actually been helpful. He pulled up a blank page and drew a line down the middle to create two columns. The left column was titled Codi, and the right one, Matt. He then started to fill in both columns with pros and cons, as he saw them. Once completed, he was again reminded of all the positives Codi brought into his life. It was a simple decision, but he was struggling with what came next. Did he leave things as they were or push them to the next level? And if he did that, would the relationship survive or blow to pieces?

It was too much to process. He went back to the simplicity of his current project, EXACTO.

***

Joel laid out his evidence in Brian's office. It had slightly improved since he and Codi had their falling-out. He made sure not to count this time. He and Codi waited for Brian's reaction.

The seemingly unrelated deaths under Joel's conspiracy theory actually did line up. The only unknown was motive. No matter how they tilted the facts, there was no clear, realistic motive. Brian drummed his fingers on his desk in thought and then stood up. He started to pace as he spoke.

"There are already two special agents working your mom's case, Codi, and we can't afford a messy crossover of the investigation or involvement from an agent who is related to the victim. That would undoubtedly result in a dismissal of any charges we might bring against the UNSUB." He said the last words looking directly at her. "But let's step back. Assuming you are right, Joel, what could I use Typhoid Mary's body for? A purpose sinister enough that I needed to kill Detective Jennings and the two of you just for being on the case?"

Codi and Joel watched their boss as he paced.

"Some science thing," Codi spouted. "Joel, you said there was an outbreak of a super typhoid bug in India recently, right?"

"Yeah, a superbug. It's killed hundreds of people with no known cure, and it seemed to spread just by contact. It took some serious quarantining by the government to stop it. Luckily, the outbreak had occurred in a rural location."

"Okay, so what if Typhoid Mary, who was immune to the disease, was being used to . . . I don't know," Brian said.

"To build or design a cure," Joel said, adding to Brian's thoughts. "She was asymptomatic. So I suppose you could use her DNA to find or design a cure . . . or at least a cure for the symptoms."

"What do you mean?" asked Brian.

"Asymptomatic people still get the disease; they're just not adversely affected by it," Joel replied.

The team let the words sink in.

"Why not just use an asymptomatic person who is living now?" Codi asked Joel.

"They are very hard to identify. They don't show symptoms, so they don't go to doctors and get diagnosed. Typhoid Mary was one of the few *known* asymptomatic persons. She was easy to track because she was a cook and the common denominator in several cases. This was back before they washed their hands." Joel visibly paled as he said the last sentence.

"I don't have to tell you," Brian said, "it's really thin, but it does make some sense. And with what's going on right now, it fits the facts."

He looked at both of his agents with a decision. "Okay, run with it and see if you can make it more solid, but anything you find on Codi's mother's death must be turned over to the team assigned to that investigation. Am I understood?" Brian leaned over his desk as he spoke the words.

Codi and Joel nodded in silence. Joel had finally convinced Brian and Codi that the deaths of Detective Jennings and Codi's mom were related. The killer would be coming for Joel next, and he had spoken the words with surprising bravado.

"Okay," Brian said as he sat back down. "Now, let's talk about how we are going to catch the person trying to kill you two."

"I have a plan," Codi replied, "but, Joel, you're not going to like it. Plus, you're going to have to reschedule your date."

Brian lifted one eyebrow. *A date?* It looked like his book-smart agent was gaining some street cred.

Joel listened to Codi's plan. It seemed reasonable, except for the part where he was the bait.

***

Garrett Scott sat on the edge of his hotel bed. He had screwed up. This was bad, and the only way he could make it right was to complete the mission. The news blurb told him all he needed to know. He had killed agent Sanders's mother. His mind spun with the dizzying quantum odds that put her in Codi's apartment at just the time he was targeting her daughter. He should stay away from Vegas for a while.

Now, he would have to take another run at her and be very careful, as the authorities were now on alert. It would need to look like an accident. But first things first. He had had Agent Strickman under surveillance for the last week, and he had a plan of attack already worked out. It was time to implement it.

Picking up his gear bag, Scott headed for the door. He would have no further use for the hotel room.

Chapter Eight

C arbon monoxide, CO, is a clear, colorless, odorless gas, but it does things that are most extraordinary. When inhaled, the body cannot distinguish it from the nitrogen and oxygen blend we normally breathe. It readily takes in the CO and combines it with hemoglobin to form carboxyhemoglobin. This prevents the body from carrying oxygen. A person can asphyxiate and die while breathing normally.

Garrett Scott had driven to the small town of Bowie, Maryland, off Highway 564. From the exit ramp, he pulled onto a crushed gravel driveway and parked his SUV. The small slump-block building was painted white with a large green sign, *AirGas - Gasses, Welding & Safety Supplies.*

Scott pushed through the double doors and made his way up to the counter. The shelves were filled with welders of every kind and all the supplies that go with them. An older man wearing welding coveralls over a white tee shirt exited a small office.

"Help you?"

Scott gave him a list of the things he was looking for.

"All of this is on the shelves behind you. Regulators aisle four and tubing on two. The tanks are all kept in the back. Pay for everything up here, then you can pull around, and I'll load you up."

"Sounds good," Scott replied as he headed to aisle four.

After paying, Scott pulled his vehicle around to the back. It was a small chain-linked yard with tanks stacked in organized piles. They loaded up two CO cylinders, and he left the yard with a quick wave.

While in town, he picked up a few additional supplies and a meatball sub from Rieve's Deli, a shop with good reviews.

***

As the neighborhood quieted down for the night, Scott watched the interior lights in the small home shut off, one-by-one. The home was a quaint 50s-style one-story cottage. It had a small front lawn and a driveway down the left side that led to a onc-car garage in the back. The clapboard exterior was painted Oxford gray with stark white windows, trim, and doors. There was a small front porch with a couple of weathered Adirondack chairs awaiting use.

Scott watched for another three hours until the neighborhood grew completely peaceful. He noticed a suspicious plumbing van parked on the corner's edge behind him. He had not seen it on the block during any of his previous scouting missions. Rolling down his window just an inch or so, Scott placed a small black tube outside and aimed it at the van. He hit a button and put in an earbud that was connected to it. The small device used an invisible laser to measure the vibrations off the glass of the front windshield. Vibrations from inside the van could be picked up and interpreted into audible words. He was rewarded with a conversation.

" . . . Jenny's wedding, yeah a real waste," one of the voices said.

"Wow, all the women were so standoffish," came the reply.

"I know! Maybe it's you. I should have gone on my own."

"Funny guy."

Scott removed the device and rolled up his window. He immediately knew it was a surveillance van. He hung his fingers on the steering wheel and contemplated his next move. Grabbing a few items from his kit, he stealthily exited the car.

***

Joel had done everything, just like they had planned, making his evening routine as normal as possible. He made a simple but healthy dinner, accompanied by a much-needed glass of white wine. His home was a mix of modern and traditional. Though his parents seldom interacted with him, they had set up a trust, which allowed him to live slightly better than his paycheck permitted. He was not a man given to greed or showiness, but a few things of value were important to him. He loved handmade shoes and tortoise-shell glasses. He kept a few higher-end computers in his home and demanded the best when it came to coffee makers. Otherwise, Joel was happy with who he was and what he had.

He sat on his couch wondering what to do next. It was weird knowing you were being watched. It made everything you did different, even if you were trying to not let it. You had better manners at the table, better posture when you moved, even better thoughts.

Joel imagined that if everyone lived their life as if they were being watched, the world would be a better place. His eyes moved over to the small camera mounted in the room. He casually extended his middle finger and scratched at an unknown itch. He realized this was an act he would have never done before being teamed up with Codi, but it felt good. And it made him have to exert effort not to smile.

He turned on his laptop and did some searching on the internet to try to keep his mind occupied, but he felt like a stranger in another man's skin. He couldn't get comfortable. A quick trip to the fridge and he returned with the wine bottle. Before long, he had downed his third glass of wine and was starting to feel more relaxed. Joel wasn't a big drinker, but tonight was an exception. He was scared and needed a bit of liquid courage. He found himself yawning, so he retired to his bedroom. A quick shower, followed by his nightly routine, had him in bed by 11:50 p.m. He glanced up at the camera aimed at the room. He felt like a guinea pig. He tried to do some reading and finally gave up, not remembering a word. The third glass of wine did the trick, and Joel's heavy lids closed.

***

Scott stayed low and slipped underneath the van, avoiding cameras mounted on the outside. He slithered to the back where he leaned out and up to place a heavy-duty zip-tie through the double handles of the van's back doors. Back under the van, he slid over to the driver's side door. He reached up, pressed the tip of a tube into the door lock, and squeezed half the contents into the mechanism. He repeated the operation on the passenger door. Staying low, he slid out and placed a small black box on the side of the van. He stood and walked back to his car as if he had lived there all his life. He knew his actions wouldn't last, but he would now have enough time to accomplish his mission and still make a clean getaway.

The black box was something special that one of his buddies in R&D had cooked up. It emitted a cycling signal that would jam all frequencies in an intermittent way. Just enough to make people think things were still working but not enough to let them know they were being jammed. Surveillance video would go in and out of focus, and communications would dial and send just a fraction of a word per attempted call. It would drive them crazy.

Agents Rowe and Ricks, commonly referred to as the "R Brothers" back at the office, sat in the rear of the van. There was a small bench loaded with electronics and a few fast-food wrappers. A rack wall behind them held more serious firepower than the two .40-caliber Glock 22s they each carried.

The lighting was low and controlled. A barrier wall separated the front driving area from the back operations. To the casual passerby, it looked like any other service van. Inside, it was built for surveillance. Ricks watched the monitor feeds that showed the front and back of Joel's house, along with three views from the inside. Camera three could see Joel sleeping in his room. All was well.

"Tell me how this is fair. He gets to sleep like a baby while we're out here working our butts off."

"Let's hope it stays that way," Agent Rowe said.

Ricks nodded at the sobering thought.

He was a middle-aged man with a matching hairline and expression. All had been quiet for the last two hours, and Ricks was not gifted in the patience department. Everyone back at the office dreaded being assigned stakeout duty with him, as he often grew too impatient for the task within a few hours. Everyone except Rowe. He was a short and wide man with dark hair and a bright attitude. He seemed impervious to almost anything thrown at him. It was as if the guy was just grateful to be breathing. Nothing got him down. It made them the perfect partnership and had even changed Rick's attitude and impatience for the better.

"This is silly. Why didn't we just bring him into protective custody?" Ricks said.

"We would've missed our chance to get the guy who's targeting him," Rowe commented.

"What makes you think it's a guy?"

"Guy, as in *person*," Rowe added.

"Is that even a thing? I mean, if you . . .What the—" The screens flickered and died and then tried to reboot. The image warbled and then almost cleared just before it started again. It sent the two agents tapping equipment and trying to source the problem. It took almost five minutes of fiddling before they got worried.

"Try the radio," Ricks said.

Agent Rowe grabbed the radio and pressed the transmit button.

"L1, this is L2. Do you copy?" Rowe said, using their code words for the night.

Back at the SUV, Scott grabbed his gear—a small backpack and two black cylinders, each the size of a scuba tank. The neighborhood had long since gone to bed. He stayed down and out of sight as best he could, moving to the hedge along the front of Agent Strickman's house. The foliage next to the house made for a perfect hiding spot. Just above the hedge, a window led to his target's bedroom. The window was a modern affair with a proper lock and double panes of glass.

Scott crouched down as he held up a small dental mirror to inspect it closer. Agent Strickman had placed an additional screw-type lock to prevent the window from opening at all from the outside. Scott pulled a small handheld device out of his pack and placed it on the bottom corner of the glass. Pressing a small power button, the device whirred to life, making almost no sound. It was a small version of the SmartCleave IP-protected laser. Within thirty seconds a three-quarter-inch hole was perfectly cut through both panes of glass. He lowered the hi-tech device and pulled a homemade apparatus from the pack. It had two connecting valves that were coupled to a regulator via tubing. From there, a clear hose delivered the tank's contents.

It took a few seconds to attach it to both canisters and turn the valves. CO started to flow at a high but still quiet rate, thanks to the specialized regulator.

He placed the clear tube into the hole in the glass and checked his watch. By his estimation, it would take five minutes for the ratio in the room to reach 10,000 ppm of CO. At that point, Agent Strickman would lose consciousness and die within the following three minutes. It would take his "friends" back in the van at least double that time to just get out of the van. He would be long gone by then.

***

Codi was bored. She had been one of three agents staked out watching Joel's house. She had parked up the street in an older agency car with tinted windows. Two more agents were on the opposite corner in a "plumbing" van. Staring at the same thing hour after hour was no picnic. The good news was that she was not alone. If she happened to turn away for a second, her team would still be watching. Between the three of them, Joel was covered.

The night had turned cold, and she had been forced to lower her windows slightly to keep the car from fogging up. Luckily, she had brought a coat and rummaged in the back seat until she found it. As she spun back around, she thought she saw a shadow by Joel's house, but after a careful look through the binoculars, it seemed all clear. Deciding to check in with the van, she reached for her radio. It made a brief squawk followed by a short burst of static.

"L1, thi . . ."

Codi tried to respond.

"L2, do you copy. I say, you are breaking up. Please repeat."

***

Most people believe carbon monoxide was heavier than air and would build from the ground up when it filled a space. But the truth is, CO is just slightly lighter than air and it generally mixed in with the air, rather than creating a barrier. All Scott had to do was wait to let the colorless, odorless gas do its thing. Even with oxygen still in the room, all it had to do was reach a certain saturation point to be effective.

Once both canisters were empty, Scott took the two small circular pieces of glass he had cut out. They were the size of thick quarters. He added a ring of clear sealant around the edges and replaced them in the windowpane. The result was an almost perfect fix that would have authorities hard-pressed to find it, let alone determine when the repair had been made. He heard a soft beeping from the CO alarm down the hall, but a quick peek inside revealed that the body in the bed was already unconscious. His work was done. Gathering up his gear, he moved back across the lawn for his vehicle.

Now to make good on the slippery female FBI agent.

Joel woke to a slight sound by the window. His eyelids were so heavy he had a rough time focusing, like trying to move in water. Everything was slow. He tried to get up, but his head barely cleared the pillow before it crashed back down. Something was wrong. This was no wine buzz. Fingers reached for his phone, but they seemed numb, and he fumbled it to the floor. He tried waving at the camera, but his arms quickly became heavy and dropped to his side. The last thing he remembered before everything went black was a faint alarm sounding down the hallway. *Fire? No, something else . . .*

***

"L2, do you copy?" Codi said again.

A reply of a partial vowel and a static ring came back. Codi repeated her actions. Same result. She didn't want to spook their target, by going over and knocking on the van's door, so she tried her phone. It seemed to be working fine, but each time it tried to connect, she either got a half of a word reply or a *signal lost* notification. She tried a text. It went out, but after a minute, she still had no reply. Codi's sixth sense sparked to life. *Something's wrong.* Opening her car door, she stepped out, spying the van in the distance. All seemed quiet. She tried to look casual, as she strolled down the sidewalk. Just another neighbor who couldn't sleep, eyes scanning for trouble. All Codi got in return was a peaceful neighborhood.

Movement to her left caught her attention. A shadowy figure carrying two canisters was moving away from Joel's house.

"Stop right there. FBI!" she shouted as she reached for her gun.

Codi missed the days in the military where under the same circumstances, she could have just fired rather than give a warning. The man dropped his canisters and dove into the shadows.

Three quick pops that sounded like a soft clap followed. Codi dove instinctively as 9mm slugs hit the car she was behind. She returned fire. Her pistol was not silenced and within a few moments of return fire, the homes on the block started to light up like they'd just heard Santa and his reindeer on the roof. She tried her radio again. Still no luck.

Inside the van, Agents Rowe and Ricks were going crazy. They couldn't get any of their electronics to work properly. They would get a signal and start to connect, and then it would crash and start all over.

Agent Ricks thought that they were being jammed, but the fact that they could still hear pieces and snips of Codi's voice on the walkie-talkie had them confused. When gunfire broke out in the neighborhood everything changed. Both agents grabbed their AR-15s off the back rack and headed out the rear of the van. It took Agent Ricks a second to process that the rear doors were locked from the outside.

"We're locked in!"

Agent Rowe headed for the front. He slid the divider open and grabbed the driver's side door. The handle moved, but the door wouldn't budge. Agent Ricks tried the passenger side. Same result. They were locked inside.

"Windshield," Rowe said, pointing.

Both men used the butts of their rifles to smash the front windshield. Once it was sufficiently cracked they used their feet to kick it out. Ricks went first and slid across the hood toward the pavement.

Codi crouched low behind the parked car that had absorbed the bullets aimed at her. She tried to peek around the bumper, but Joel's yard across the street was empty. The suspect was either gone or hiding in darkness.

During her stint in the Marines, she had trained with night vision optics. What she wouldn't give for even a Gen1 version now. The shadows would be lit up like a Ferris wheel at night.

The sound of sirens in the distance offered additional support. She tried one last time to reach Ricks and Rowe on the radio and then gave up, dropping her walkie-talkie to the ground. She moved quickly to the next car keeping sheet metal between her and the armed suspect.

***

Scott had completed his mission. One Agent Strickman down. Now all he had to do was get away. He moved across the grass carrying the two tanks. His SUV was a few homes away on the other side of the street. An unknown FBI agent suddenly appeared from across the street, shouting demands. It was only due to his quick reaction that he was not caught. He dropped the two tanks and dove into the shadows of a large shrub next door. Taking a prone position he fired four quick shots at his pursuer. He then rolled back behind the bush and moved away. Several return shots hit the bush area where he had been just a few seconds before. Now, all he had to do was flank the shooter that was stationed across the street behind a row of parked cars. He checked his watch, Agent Strickman should be going into cardiac arrest within the next minute. He just needed to delay things a bit more. He moved like a cat, every step carefully planned as he worked his way up the street, away from his last position. Slow and steady, his weapon aimed and ready, keeping in the shadows. Once at the end of the street, he would cross and then come back for the shooter.

When he reached the fifth house up, he quickly crossed the street. He saw one of the FBI agents sliding on his stomach heels first out of the windshield of their van. The agent was so preoccupied with his actions he never saw Scott approach. Without a second thought, Scott put two bullets in the back of the agent's head, and before his partner inside the van could react, he fired a burst into the van as well.

Codi took a chance. It seemed like a lifetime since the man across the street had fired on her—most likely only twenty seconds. She sprinted for the front of Joel's house, up his driveway, and around the corner. She stopped and then quickly back-tracked, keeping low, to the front porch. She carefully peered around. The area was empty, except for two black tanks lying on the grass. She held her Sig Sauer P228 9mm steady as she dashed for the tanks. A quick inspection told her nothing. What were they for? What was going on? Her head swiveled the area—nothing. Her UNSUB had moved off.

Codi let her mind go back. She thought she had seen movement earlier by the house. The tanks must have held some kind of poison gas meant for Joel. A closer inspection and a turn of the valve told her they were both empty. The sudden tell-tale sound of suppressed gunfire caught her attention. It was coming from where the surveillance van was parked. Codi took off on a sprint but stopped. *Joel!*

She turned and fired three rounds into his bedroom window, shattering the glass. She prayed that would work and ran after her mother's killer.

Scott heard the distant sound of sirens approaching. He climbed into his vehicle, hit the ignition, and lit up the tires. Time to put some distance between him and the crime scene. As he fishtailed into the street, his headlights flashed on an agent locked into position with her gun aimed right at him. Recognition was almost instant. Special Agent Sanders. The FBI woman who had escaped his last hit. Time for a twofer. He hit the gas as he ducked below the exploding windshield.

Codi had run up the street, fearing the worst for her fellow agents. Scott's large black SUV swung out and headed her way. She took an offensive stance and aimed her weapon, firing at the mass of steel, and stitching bullets across the driver's windshield with pinpoint accuracy. At the last second her clip ran dry, and she was forced to dive out of the way. Once the vehicle zoomed past, she reloaded a fresh clip and sent another thirteen rounds into the rear of the vehicle and both rear tires. The SUV bounced off several parked cars and sped away on shredded tires.

Codi jumped back to her feet and ran for her car. By the time she had it started and flipped around to give chase, the SUV was nowhere in sight. She sped past sleepy intersections checking both ways as she crossed.

Instinctively, she grabbed for her radio to call in help and realized she had left it in the street. A brief glimpse to the right found the SUV turning down a side street. Codi flipped her car around, leaving a black rubber circle on the pavement, and gave chase. It took almost three minutes to close on the big vehicle. With its back tires shredded it was difficult to control. Sparks flew from the rims as the SUV skidded dangerously around corners.

Codi had no time to play. She slammed her car into the rear of the vehicle and cranked the wheel to the right. The SUV spun out and crashed into a parked car, its rear wheels spitting out sparks against the pavement, but going nowhere. Codi was out of her car and on the driver's side of the SUV in an instant. Training her gun at the driver's side, she caught her target exiting through the passenger's side. He was half in and half out. The UNSUB had one hand on the open door and held his gun loosely with the other. She had him dead to rights, and they both knew it. He looked at his weapon.

"Don't do it. I hate paperwork."

The man looked at her, resolute in his decision. "The people I work for don't accept failure. I'm already dead."

"Who do you work for? We can protect you."

He started to laugh and then tried his luck. He raised his gun and squeezed—

Codi shot him dead. Three quick rounds to the mid-torso. He dropped, his left arm catching on the door's window frame, leaving him hanging while his face twitched and his lips quivered.

***

Joel blinked his eyes open. His head felt heavy, and it fell back onto the pillow. Everything spun and moved in a blur. His hand felt warmth, and he turned toward it. There was a woman's hand holding his as the gurney moved outside. He looked again. It was his partner Codi. How did she get here? His mind was fuzzy. She smiled and said something to him that made no sense. With a sudden jolt he was lifted into a small room . . . no, it was an ambulance. *Ambulance! What's going on?* His world went dark again.

***

The Locust glided under the most iconic suspension bridge in America. It spans a one-mile gap between San Francisco Bay and the Pacific Ocean and is known as The Golden Gate. Captain Charlotte Combs called for minute adjustments to their course and speed as the ship moved through the tricky currents at the mouth of the bay. The mission to build a hidden lab onboard was nearing completion. They would need to take on supplies and finish stocking the rooms before the lab would be operational.

Their destination, once through customs, was a pier in Port Chicago off of Kinney Road. They would need to navigate north through San Pablo Bay, across the Carquinez Strait, and finally to Suisun Bay. Port Chicago is a rail staging and warehousing area, due north of Walnut Creek. It has access to the Pacific Ocean through a series of waterways starting with the Roe Island Channel.

It was the site of the Port Chicago Disaster in 1944, where munitions accidentally detonated while being loaded for the Pacific theater operations. The explosion killed 320 sailors and civilians and injured 390 others. Of the 320 dead, only fifty could be identified due to the intensity of the explosion. Most of the dead were African American sailors. The unsafe conditions inspired hundreds of servicemen to refuse to load any more munitions. It was known as the Port Chicago Mutiny. Many were convicted and sentenced to fifteen years of hard labor for their insubordination, a fate only slightly better than death.

Just to the east was a single-sided pier with road and rail access. There was one large gantry on station there and a large flat loading area. It was leased by Global Consolidated Logistics, a shell corporation with ties to several legitimate businesses.

With the help of a tug, *The Locust* slid up to the dock and moored. Captain Combs killed the engines and signaled for the offloading to begin. There were two hundred containers to be removed and sixty-eight new containers to be loaded, several holding important equipment for the lab. It would take the rest of the night and most of the next day, but once loaded and refueled, they would be back on their way. It was time for her to stretch her legs on land. She pulled out her phone and requested an UberX.

***

The light was blinding. It seemed to come from everywhere. Joel blinked it away, and finally, his pupils decreased to the correct size. He was in a hospital or clinic and tried to remember how he had arrived there. Reading at home in his bed was the last thing he remembered. He started to lean up, and pain hit him like a sledge on an anvil. His head started pounding and spinning. He nearly threw up right then and there.

"Oh good, you're awake."

Joel lay back down and cast his eyes toward the source of the voice. He spied the beautiful steel-blue eyes set against freckles and the auburn hair of Shannon Poole. He tried to smile, but it took too much effort.

She moved to his side and held his hand in a tender fashion. "You've experienced carbon monoxide poisoning, and you're going to need to lay low for a little bit. Expect a headache and weakness for the next couple of hours."

Joel processed her words—*check* and *check.*

"I'll be right here, and we'll get through this together."

Joel scanned the rest of the room to find Codi standing by the door looking on with concern.

"What happened?" he managed to squeak out.

Shannon went through the events of the night as she knew them. Codi had briefed her on the details and was just grateful her partner was going to be okay.

"... if Codi hadn't shot out your bedroom window, we might have lost you."

"Wait. You shot out my window?" Joel asked, tilting his head up.

Codi shrugged her shoulders. "It was the best plan at the moment."

Joel processed her words. "You could have shot me."

"It was a chance I was willing to take. And see, it worked out," Codi said with a casualness that had Joel feeling flummoxed, but he didn't have the energy to do much else.

Shannon re-fluffed his pillow.

"What about the R Brothers? Why were they not watching the video feeds?"

Codi and Shannon shared a look.

"What?" Joel asked.

"Agent Ricks didn't make it. Rowe is in intensive care. Looks like he'll pull through."

Joel was speechless.

The women stayed with Joel for a while until Codi said her goodbyes and left Shannon to take care of him.

Codi checked her phone. It was nearly three in the morning. She ordered an Uber to take her back to the car she'd been using during the stakeout.

Chapter Nine

C odi walked from FBI headquarters with her head low. Discharging your weapon required some serious paperwork and after-action reviews. Killing a suspect, even if it was a clean shooting, was a nightmare, second only to the death of an innocent. The closure provided in taking down the killer of her mother, Detective Jennings, and Special Agent Rowe was almost lost. Next time, she would consider taking a bullet to save the grief she'd been through over the past several days.

Codi had been scrutinized, cleared, and finally reinstated. She felt probed and prodded emotionally. It was time to unplug from the bureau. What she needed now was some quality sleep and a large plate of food. She was starving. The first glimmer of a smile appeared when she spotted Matt's car at the curbside, waiting to pick her up. She double-timed her step and reached for the passenger door.

The car started to move before she had the door fully closed. Codi leaned back and rubbed her temples. The further Matt drove from FBI headquarters, the more she could feel the tension subside comparably.

"Wanna talk about it?"

"Not really."

"Good. Hungry?"

"Starving."

Matt took a side street to dodge some of the Friday afternoon traffic. He headed east for the water.

After a long silence, Codi turned her head. "So how was your week?"

"Awesome. I started on something new. Can't talk about it yet, but I was working with this kid who has climbed just about every mountain you can think of. He even free-climbed some crazy rock face. I can't remember the name."

"You're working with a rock climber?" Codi asked.

"Yeah. He looks a lot like a Black Joel, only with muscles. Remember that Z-Man project I told you about?"

"Oh yeah, the gecko gloves."

"More like paddles, but yes."

Matt glanced over at Codi. Their eyes locked for the briefest moment. It was a face that he would never grow tired of looking at.

"He climbed all of our walls, with and without a pack and with and without rain. The technology is amazing. It works great under lab conditions, but the amount of upper body strength required makes it less practical."

"You need something to go on the climber's shoes."

"I'd tell you that you are correct, but then I'd have to kill you."

Codi shot a glance in his direction. "Did you ever stop to think that you're killing me by *not* telling?"

"I read somewhere that every good relationship requires the gift of mortality."

"What do you mean?" Codi asked.

"Each person has to give a little piece of themselves to the other."

"Like Christmas, you have to give to get?"

"Not quite," Matt responded.

Codi's lips turned upward. Matt had a way of reeling her back in. It wasn't what was being said but the heartfelt normalcy of their conversation she reveled in.

"Well, as long as we can both keep our national secrets safe, we'll be good."

"So, has Joel gotten over being used as bait?" Matt asked.

"I think so, but that was a one-and-done. He'll never go for it again."

Matt turned left onto the highway onramp.

"The best part was all the attention he got in the hospital," Codi added as she reclined her seat slightly.

"I'm guessing most of it from a certain redheaded Mountie?"

"Yeah. She was there and stayed with him till he was discharged."

"Good on him," Matt said as he hit his turn signal.

He suddenly realized how comfortable and natural he felt around Codi. She was the yin to his yang. He had never known anyone like her. They just seemed to mesh. In that instant, he knew she was the one for him. Not because some huge gong was sounding in his brain, but more like a soft pleasant glow had erupted, like a summertime sunset. He made up his mind. He would need to do the most difficult thing he had ever done—find the courage to propose. But not tonight.

"So . . . blue crabs and fritters?"

***

The Mantis was the sister ship of *The Locust*. She resembled the Panamax cargo carrier in every way, except she was painted a faded blue and white.

"Status?" the captain asked.

"All engines are powered down and we are securely moored."

"Okay. Keep security on until we are safely back in international waters. I need everyone alert until we get out of here."

"Aye, Captain."

Captain Vadim Semenova left the bridge to walk the deck. It was a habit born of paranoia. As a young boy growing up in Soviet Belarus, he had learned the hard way that no man could be trusted. The KGB, and then the BKGB, had a way of doing things that kept everyone living in fear. Pointing fingers had husbands distrusting wives and coworkers constantly looking over their shoulders. He quickly learned that you should assume your closest allies were preparing to betray you. That way, you were always prepared.

Semenova always did a double- and triple-check on everything personally. It had served him well over the years.

The air was crisp as Semenova stepped down the gangway and surveyed the Portland, Maine harbor. He loved the cold. It was the one thing that always reminded him of home. He walked the entire circumference of the ship, looking for anything out of order. His first mate, another Belarusian named Max Odo, was good, but one could never be too cautious. The containers rose up into the sky, stacked and locked together from the last voyage. They would be offloaded, and then the ship would be resupplied. He had a unique situation with this stop, and he wanted no trouble to come his way.

The wind picked up and blew an icy breath from the north. Semenova's beard was little defense. The captain was a man of habits. He liked things a certain way, and he liked his routine. He was almost always found in a black turtleneck and black beanie with the Belarusian Navy badge. He looked like a classic mall Santa with a round face, full white beard, and shaggy hair. He even had rosy cheeks, thanks to the burst capillaries on his face from years of too much vodka. But his brooding and OCD tendencies would never mix well with children. His perma-scowl was not just for show.

In 1980, Belarus won its independence from Soviet Russia. But Semenova had seen his glorious state dump one corrupt government for another. He had been a proud and decorated captain on a modified Kashin-class destroyer, but money for the navy ran out, and his ship sat in dry dock for repairs that would never happen. Semenova took the hint and moved to the private sector. The pay and hours were better, but his days of influence were gone. He was now nothing more than an outspoken, rarely seen captain of a rusting cargo hauler, going from port to port, moving cargo he had no interest in.

Two years ago, everything changed.

***

"I got something!"

"What, halitosis?" Codi said, jovially.

"Why? What have you heard?" Joel did a quick breath test by blowing into his hand and sniffing the air. "I brush my teeth and floss three times a day. Maybe it's the coffee? I do drink a lot."

Codi rolled her eyes at her quirky partner. "Joel, I'm kidding. What have you got?"

"Oh, got it—yeah."

Joel had taken a couple of days off to fully recover from his CO poisoning. It was exactly the same amount of time that Codi was going through her post-shooting gauntlet. They had met for breakfast and were both anxious to get back at it.

Codi tried to encourage Joel and get things back on track by giving him an uplifting smile and an open hand that said *go on.*

"I've been building a picture of our UNSUB."

"We still don't know his name?"

"I haven't got a hit back from AFIS [Automatic Fingerprint Identification System] yet."

"That's unusual. They're normally pretty fast."

"Yeah, but last week, they got hacked pretty good. It was a big deal. The NSA got involved, even Homeland."

"Sounds like a mess."

"Yeah, well, everything is still a bit screwed up. We should have something later today."

"Anything on IPS?"

"No facial recognition hits, so this guy is smart enough to have never been caught."

"And smart enough to almost kill both of us and get away with it."

Joel nodded, as memories of the recent past started to flood back. He shook them off and re-centered himself. He had a silent mantra for times like these: WWCD (What would Codi do?), and the usual answer was *she would kick 'em in the teeth and take names.* It helped.

He glanced over at his partner. "Anyway, I have built a partial picture based on what we have so far."

Codi leaned over in her chair to get a better look at Joel's screen.

"The SUV he used was rented out of Philly by a Jordon Kaiser. I got a hit out of Dallas for a film producer there. He has no known history of ever doing anything wrong. Not even a parking ticket."

"An alias."

"Exactly. The tanks were generic CO tanks. The serial numbers on the bottom were ground off, so nothing there. I have around thirty hits within a hundred-mile radius of stores that sell this type of gas. Two of them look promising.

"Okay. So road trip."

"Right. And the last piece I have is the local hotel where he stayed."

"How did you get that? A receipt in the vehicle?"

"No such luck. I hacked—" Joel looked around to see if any coworkers were nearby. He lowered his voice. "I borrowed some camera feeds and pieced his SUV's travels to my neighborhood."

Codi nodded with appreciation. "Good work, Joel, but you know since we are personally involved in this case, we cannot work it. We are the victims here, not the detectives. Brian has made it very clear to us that we need to drop it. The case has been handed off to two agents out of the main office." She looked up trying to remember their names. "Rodriguez and Shultz, I think. They have promised to feed me details as they get them."

Joel leaned closer to Codi and whispered. "We are not working the case. We are following up on the missing corpse case."

The light suddenly went on for Codi. She leaned in and gave Joel a big kiss. "Of course. Joel, you're a genius! Come on. Road trip, and I'm buying lunch."

The Duo Nomad is an unremarkable three-story red brick building sandwiched between two other similar structures on Pennsylvania Avenue in D.C. It is a hostel that specializes in small groups with many multi-bed rooms, like a dormitory. Codi and Joel walked up to the check-in desk, a small room just off the common area. A petite woman in her twenties with black hair in a pixie cut seemed unfazed by their approach. She wore a chambray camisole that revealed a partial canvas of tattoos that covered most of her body. A silver ring was in her nose and a pair of diamond dimple piercings were in her cheeks. On the desktop was a small placard that said *Hi, I'm Crispy.*

"Hi, I'm Special Agent—" Joel started before being interrupted by the woman.

"Yeah, yeah, Feds. I can see that. You two need a room for a few hours?"

"What? Us? *No!* We aren't like that. A couple, I mean—"

Joel was a mess, so Codi stepped in. "We were hoping you could help us out." Crispy sized them up.

"We would love to know what you remember about a guest you had staying here. Joel?"

Joel took the hint and showed her the picture of the UNSUB he had on his phone.

Crispy briefly glanced at the photo showing no emotion. "You got a warrant?" she asked.

"No, but we can get one. The truth is, we don't need a warrant to ask you a few questions," Joel said, trying to regain some control.

"And the truth is, I don't need to answer your questions without my attorney present."

"It's just a few questions about a guest, and there is a death involved, so we won't go away till we get the information. How difficult things get is up to you," Codi added.

Crispy considered her situation for a moment.

"Okay, ask. Can't say I'll answer."

"First of all, did you recognize the man on the phone?"

Joel showed her the picture again. Crispy ignored him and only looked at Codi.

"He stayed here three nights. Kept to himself and paid in cash."

She pulled out some paperwork, shuffled through it, and handed a page to Codi. The receipt had nothing new on it, including the name—Jordon Kaiser.

"What room did he stay in?"

"The cat scratch suite, but it has long since been cleaned and re-rented," Crispy answered.

"Any security footage?" Joel asked.

"Are you kidding me? This is a *hostel.* We protect our guests' rights."

Joel slammed the door as he sat in the passenger seat of their black Ford Taurus. He lowered his window with a huff. It was one of the many revolving cars the motor pool assigned. The last occupants had been smokers, and Codi and Joel were forced to drive with the windows open.

"I don't think she liked me," Joel said as Codi pulled from the curb.

"She's just a feminist. She doesn't like anyone with a penis."

Joel tried to process this information. "What kind of a name is Crispy, anyway?"

"It's probably a name she chose," Codi said.

"Crispy? Does she use it as a noun or an adjective? It sounds . . ." Joel tried to find the word.

"Crunchy, Crusty, Crispy. Sounds delicious, and now I know just what I want for lunch."

Codi hit the blinker and turned right.

Hot Lola's was one of Arlington's hot spots in the fried chicken game. Their chicken came in Too Hot, O.G. Hot, and Not Hot. Codi went for the Too Hot and was surprised as she pushed herself to her heat limit. It was everything she loved in fried chicken. Spicy, crunchy, crispy. Joel and Codi laughed as they made fun of the crispy goodness during their meal. It was a much-needed distraction after their last week.

After eating, they headed south to Springfield. Joel had made many phone calls previously and their next stop was the first of two possible stores identified as recently selling two tanks of CO to a customer.

The WeldingPlus storefront was part of an industrial complex that had a molding shop on the right and a tile store on the left. They shared a common parking lot and a large sign on the corner. Joel opened the glass door to the sound of an electronic alert. He walked past the shelves of welders and plasma cutters on his way to the front counter. Three men stood in line and two more were working behind the counter. Codi surveyed the shelf-filled retail space. An older man was price-comparing with his phone. Not a woman in the place. It seemed the polar opposite from their last experience.

"Hi, we are with the FBI, and I was wondering if we could speak with the owner?" Joel asked in a polite way while showing his badge.

"I'm the owner. Name's Garth. Whatcha need?" a gray-haired man behind the counter said.

"Is there a place we could talk? We have a few questions," Joel asked.

"I got nothing to hide. We can chat right here out in the open."

He was a tall imposing figure, maybe six-three. With shoulders that were just starting to droop from age, he had somehow managed to skip the gut that seemed omnipresent with older men. His body posture said, "Don't screw with me."

"Okay, here is fine with us," Codi said.

His customers and employee all suddenly seemed very interested. They moved forward and watched as Joel and Codi asked their questions.

Joel said, "I spoke to a Stan Barber who said you sold two tanks of CO gas on the seventh?"

"That's me," said a wiry employee wearing a WeldingPlus shirt.

Joel showed the group their suspect's picture, and Codi asked Garth and Stan about the man who purchased the two tanks. The picture didn't match the customer, who was a regular. All of the men watching the interaction agreed; it seemed weirdly unanimous. Codi and Joel left the shop empty-handed.

The next stop was a store up north called AirGas Welding Supplies in Bowie, Maryland. It took a good forty minutes to get there, and it was nearly three in the afternoon. The wind had picked up, and the last remaining fall leaves left on their journey toward earth. The gravel parking area crunched under their feet as they walked from their car to the store.

"Crispy parking lot," Joel commented.

"Stop it," Codi replied as she opened the door to the shop.

A single man stood behind the counter. When Joel identified themselves, he seemed surprised to find FBI agents in his store. "What can I do for you?" he said.

Joel repeated his questions and showed the man the suspect's picture.

"You must have talked with the boss cause this is all new to me. I'm not sure I can give you what you want. Hang on a sec," the man said.

He turned and left for the back of the store.

"Joel." Codi nodded toward the door and Joel immediately knew what to do. He moved for the front door. He would quickly get to the back of the shop in case they had a runner.

"Hey, Jack! Got a second?" the man called out the back door into the rear lot. "Need you up front."

Joel stopped and returned to the sales desk.

An enthusiastic man in his late forties with salt-and-pepper hair followed his employee into the store. He took off a hardhat and hung it on the back wall next to three others.

"This is Jack. He owns the place and can probably help you."

Joel went through his introductions again but was interrupted before he could finish.

"Yes! Okay, right, we talked yesterday, about 2:45 if I'm not mistaken, about a customer who bought two tanks of CO."

He turned and grabbed a paper off the back cabinet. "Yeah, got the paperwork right here."

As he returned to the sales counter, Joel showed him the picture on his phone.

"That's him, alright. As you can see he purchased two tanks of CO, a Fisherbrand Multistage regulator, and some three-quarter-inch tubing. Paid cash. See, right here."

He pointed to the name on the receipt. "The name's . . . Jordon Kaiser."

"This friggin Jordon Kaiser is starting to tick me off!" Codi said as she hit the accelerator and headed back for the city.

"I know, right?" Joel answered, quickly putting on his seatbelt.

They drove on in silence for a bit. The day had been a bust. It was all part of being a detective. Some days you moved a case along, and some days you spun in circles. Joel and Codi were both feeling dizzy.

Chapter Ten

CAFÉ ATTILA – WALNUT CREEK – 6:51 P.M.

The strip mall-style eatery was a quaint hole in the wall. With surprisingly great food. Pullin sat in the back, facing the exit. There was a small collection of walnut-stained tables and chairs padded with red cushions. It was rarely crowded for dinner, as lunch was its prime attraction with lines out the door every day. He watched as a tall woman with blood-red hair and a checkered top approached.

She smiled and acknowledged his presence with a nod, knowing that a hug or handshake would have him scrambling for his sanitizer. "Good to see you again, Mr. Ikaika."

"You as well, Charlotte. Please, call me Pullin."

Captain Combs knew he didn't mean it, and she would never make the mistake of addressing him by his first name.

"How are things on my ship?"

"Sir, for us to actually need to meet in person like this means something's up. We should get right to it and not banter back and forth like two adolescents. Oh, and your ship is good. We are ready."

"I agree. And thank you for that." Pullin paused for a second. "We have had a few things of interest happen in the last few days. One was the successful test of our little bug and its vaccine."

"That's great news," Captain Combs responded with true interest.

"Thank you. It is, and let's just say the way it spreads is like melted butter." He unfolded his cloth napkin and used it as a divider between his hands and the table. "The other was a breach within the inner circle. I am still assessing the level of damage, but the persons involved have been dealt with. I need to know you are still on board and ready."

Charlotte centered herself for a second and looked her boss right in the eyes. "I have never been more committed to anything in my life. Dr. Kamba has the lab up and running. We are expecting Dr. Sales tonight and have everything else we need in place. You give us the green light, and I'll execute as soon as possible."

Pullin nodded slowly, pleased with the woman's tenacity. This is why he had come here. To look her in the eye and judge her commitment. He felt a small sense of relief, knowing she had his back and was fully on board. "Excellent. I will send you the destinations, and please make sure Dr. Kamba gets everyone vaccinated immediately. Consider this your green light."

Charlotte's face lit up at the response. She nodded in approval.

"Are you hungry? Can I order for you?" Pullin asked.

"I hear the spaetzle is quite good here, and yes, I could eat."

***

"Thanks for picking me up."

"Sure."

Joel pulled his Prius out into traffic. A light mist had been coming down since midnight and the intermittent wipers pushed the small drops aside.

"Garrett Scott," Joel offered.

Codi listened as she pulled down the sun visor and used the mirror to finish putting on her mascara.

"AFIS finally came through on our UNSUB'S print. Whoever hacked them didn't realize AFIS had off-site redundancy. Once AFIS cleaned out the corrupt files, everything returned as though nothing had happened."

"What's his deal?" she asked.

"Danish emigrant. Spent a lot of time in their special forces, Jaeger Corps. Not much more."

"Moved to America to live the dream of killing cops," Codi said, in a sarcastic tone.

"So now what?" Joel asked as he turned left onto a less crowded street.

"I have a friend who might be able to help us," Codi said as she picked up her phone and dialed a number she hadn't called in years.

It rang twice before a voice cut in. "Give it to me."

"Hey, Cap," Codi said.

There was a second of silence before a partial recognition kicked in. "Codi?"

"I see you haven't forgotten me."

"No chance. You were one of my best. How the heck are you? A real shame what happened with BUD/S and all."

"That is long forgotten," Codi lied.

"Okay. So what brings you to my extension?"

Codi brought the last commanding officer she served under in the military up to date on her life. They shared pleasantries and old times.

She finally got around to the matter at hand.

"I have a Garrett Scott out of Jaeger Corps. Now that you're MILINT [Military Intelligence], I thought you could take a look for me. He leaves the military and goes off our radar till about two weeks ago when he tried to kill me and my partner."

"Let me see what I can find out. Happy to help out the FBI."

They finished the call with promises of a soon-to-happen get-together and hung up.

"So?" Joel asked.

Codi finished her beauty routine with a coat of neutral-colored lipstick. She popped her lips together to smooth it out and closed the sun visor. "If he can't track him down, I might know someone in the CIA who can. All we can do now is wait."

***

John Brown was a loner by nature. He didn't interact well with others and lived most of his life in his head. As a technical writer for several manufacturing companies, he was content to live away from society in his world of facts and figures. Had he ever happened to have a girl for the night, he would need to open his dating instruction manual and read page fifteen. *Insert tab A into slot B. Repeat as necessary.*

John was of average height and had average looks with light brown skin that gave him a permanent tan thanks to some unknown ancestor. An ancestor he would never know as an orphan raised in the foster program. His childhood had been a revolving set of foster parents generally overwhelmed by the task they had taken on.

John preferred to wear his brown hair shaggy and rarely put a comb through it. He was happiest when he was in his home at his desk writing while wearing comfortable sweats and no shoes. And since the advent of Postmates and Grubhub, he could now have all his meals delivered. It suited him perfectly.

Today, however, John had to go out. It was a challenge for him to clean up and get dressed. Once he picked the right shirt and pants combo, which took several tries, he closed his apartment door and headed for the street. He had a meeting with a potential new client and wanted to be on time. As he stepped out onto the street, a van door opened across from him. He barely registered the action, as a sudden jolt of electricity overloaded his nervous system. He went limp, and two sets of strong arms from out of nowhere enveloped him. They placed him in the back of the van and sped away. He could just make out the Eastern European accent of the passenger looking back at him.

"That makes a dozen. Let's head for the ship."

A black hood was placed over John's head. He felt a slight prick on his neck, and then everything went black.

***

Joel paced back and forth in the hallway between cubicles. He was a nervous wreck and needed a sounding board. A voice from the cubicle on the left broke his reverie.

"*Joel,* you're wearing out the carpet. Find a seat."

Joel looked around, suddenly embarrassed. He poked his head into his partner's cubicle. "Hey, Codi. Can I talk to you for a second?"

Codi spoke without taking her eyes off the memo she was typing. "I think that's what we are doing. What's on your mind?"

Joel entered her workspace and sat in the extra chair. He scratched at his head as he brewed up the courage to speak. "How do you know when you like, *like* someone?"

"Like, *like*?" Codi replied as she stopped typing and turned to face her partner.

"Yeah, like, *like* more than regular like."

"Okay, it is natural and normal to like, *like* a person. You can tell if you do by the way they make you feel when you're around them or if you find yourself thinking about them throughout your day."

Joel nodded in a very thoughtful way.

"So what's up?" Codi asked.

"Oh, nothing. I'm just asking for a friend."

"Joel. It's me."

"*Fine.* Shannon asked me to go withherthisweekendtomeetherparents." His final words were packed like sardines in his mouth.

"Ah, and you don't have the best parent/child rapport."

Joel's relationship with his parents had always been tenuous. They were both successful professionals who had never spent a lot of time with their son. As soon as he was old enough, it was off to boarding school with the occasional trip home for a visit. Christmas breaks were an awkward affair, with huge periods of silence between the three. His parents tended to show love for their son through their pocketbook, buying him things that he never really wanted.

Joel managed to find solace in information. He became an expert with computers, and his book knowledge was off the charts. But he would trade it all for one real "I love you" from either parent.

Codi leaned closer and softened her tone. "Joel, just because you have a strained relationship with your parents doesn't mean everyone does."

"What about you?" Joel countered.

"You're saying the two of us are more along the lines of the exception?"

"Sure we are," Joel said with a dose of sarcasm.

Codi paused to gather her thoughts. She then made eye contact with her partner. "I had a great child/parent relationship when I was little. It wasn't until tragedy struck that it blew up. You have always had a strained family dynamic. Yet here we are. It's just one of the many things that define us. And for me, no one thing is going to be that big of an anchor to hold me back."

"You're saying I should just let it go?"

"More like own it and move on. You have so much to offer, Joel. Not just in a relationship but to the world."

Joel sighed, trying to get his head around Codi's words. He spun his chair around letting his head go back.

"It's funny," she said.

"What is?" Joel asked, stopping his chair.

"Matt's got a weekend all planned for us as well, and he won't tell me what it is. I guess we'll both just have to play it by ear."

"Probably going to propose," Joel said with raised eyebrows.

"Not a chance!" Codi replied. She caught herself and calmed her voice. "Anyway, you just might be surprised. Besides, Canadians are friendly."

"So your argument is based on the generalization of an entire country?" Joel replied.

"Just give 'em a chance. It's one weekend."

"I guess if I've put up with you this long, I can handle a quiet weekend playing cards and watching Jeopardy."

"See? There you go."

***

"Keep. Your. Head. Over. Your. Toes!"

Joel wobbled, overcorrected, and leaned back. He lost all control and went down in a puff of white, flipping and rolling to an abrupt stop.

Lake Louise Ski Resort was located on Mt. Norquay, just southeast of Edmonton, Canada. It was still early in the season, and the slopes were not overly crowded. Dark clouds hung in the sky against majestic mountain peaks. There was a slight breeze from the east dropping giant snowflakes in a gentle cadence. The double-black-diamond run had been too much for a first-time snowboarder, and Joel paid the price.

Shannon glided up to the wreckage for an inspection.

The weekend had been full throttle from the moment they got off the plane. Shannon's sixty-year-old parents were doers, not talkers, and they lived an extremely active lifestyle.

Shannon brushed clumps of snow out of Joel's hair.

Her parents, both on snowboards, zoomed past.

"See ya back at the lodge for some fire chili," her father yelled.

Joel leaned on one very bruised elbow, with a grimace on his face.

"You okay?" she asked.

He lifted his goggles and wiped away the snow. "I think I just broke every bone in my body," he said, trying to move his neck.

"I'll call for a snow dog to bring us some brandy."

"Is that a real thing?" Joel asked, the pain clear on his face.

"You are . . . adorable," Shannon said as she kissed him.

"Your parents are not what I expected."

"They do love their sports. When you come back in the summer, they'll take us rock climbing, and we can do some white water rafting. Why? What did you think they would be like?"

"More like . . . Parcheesi and hot cocoa," Joel said.

Shannon elbowed him playfully. "Come on, let's get you down the mountain. Maybe we should try skiing instead of snowboarding." She helped Joel up.

"How about lodging. That sounds bold to me."

"Funny. We're just getting started."

A brief flash of fear crossed Joel's face. "By the way, what's fire chili?" he asked.

"It's a tradition. You'll love it," Shannon replied.

"It sounds hot. Is it really hot?"

"Joel!"

***

John Brown awoke. It took a moment for him to register his situation. He had been stripped down to his underwear and was in a Plexiglass box about the size of four phone booths put together. There was a buzzing in his ears. Flies. He was in a box with about five houseflies. He tried calling out but stopped when he realized he wasn't alone. There were other clear boxes just like his, all lined up next to each other . . . maybe a dozen or so.

His surroundings were mostly white, with tables filled with equipment around the room. *Was this a hospital? No, some kind of lab.*

A slender woman with blonde hair blinked and shook her head as she stood next to him. She was also wearing just her underwear and finally noticed John in the box next to her. Her hands started pounding on her cage, and John could hear muted calls for help. The cries transitioned to screams when she looked down. John's eyes followed hers. There were several cockroaches in her box. *Something's very wrong.*

***

Matt couldn't sit still. He had given this weekend a lot of thought. Codi was not given to fanciful circumstances. She was more of a "down-to-earth" kind of girl. Content and happy in her own skin, whether wearing a drop-dead cocktail dress or an oversized set of well-worn sweats. He needed to make this weekend the right combination of special, intimate, and romantic—all the things he was bad at.

He had briefly considered asking her at the Redskins game during the kisscam or skywriting it above the stadium. The bigger the plan, the farther away it was from what he thought she would want. He decided to go small and simple, like a beachside sunrise. But that didn't seem special enough.

The one thing he knew he got right was the ring. It was perfect. A nice-sized emerald-cut diamond with two smaller baguettes on either side. It said *wow* without being too big to get caught during a pistol reload.

Matt had done a deep dive, talking to friends and searching the internet. He picked and chose the things that he thought might work. Then he made a list. A list that changed at least thirty times. Once the list was perfected, he put the action items in order. Now, all he had to do was implement his plan. *Easy to say.*

Matt picked Codi up from her house at six. She had packed a weekend bag, per his instructions, and was smiling. *So far, so good.*

They drove south on 95 and then east on 64 toward Virginia Beach. Matt turned his green Explorer into the Chesapeake Bay Bridge Tunnel that led to

Cape Charles. He pulled up to their hotel and killed the engine with a flourish. He was a pile of jangling nerves. It took great effort to act normal on the outside. The ride over seemed filled with meaningless conversation, designed to distract him from his anxiety. He constantly reminded himself to slow down and breathe. Luckily, the weather was good and the scenery spectacular.

The North Hampton Hotel was a white Victorian-style building with gray, pitched roofs and a wraparound covered porch. It had the feel of a large B&B but had the services of a real hotel. The marketing team described it as a retro-chic beach hotel with historic, serene, and spectacular views of the Chesapeake Bay. Matt had done a lot of research, and this place fit his needs perfectly.

"We are already checked in, so sit tight. I'll just drop our bags with the doorman."

The doorman turned out to be a woman, and she was on it. Codi watched as Matt handed her their overnight bags and tipped her. He was wearing khaki pants that showed off his nice backside and a collared print shirt with small pink flamingoes all over it. The shirt was cut to match his V-shaped torso. Everything about his form, including what you couldn't see, was familiar to her, and a brief vision of him minus the clothes passed through her mind. It made her lips part and turn upward. The stress she was feeling melted away. She thought about all the good times that had led up to this point. It was true; she loved him dearly.

Matt spun the car around and headed for their next stop, The Oyster Farm Seafood Eatery. It was the only white linen-tableclothed restaurant in the area with great reviews. It sat down by the harbor with a collection of other restaurants and had a two-tone navy and teal wooden exterior with white trim and a tin roof. Plenty of windows looked across the moored boats and water.

Inside, it was contemporary with the right amount of beachy panache.

"Reservation for Campbell," Matt said, fingering the ring in his pocket.

They were taken to a quiet table in the corner, and Matt let Codi take the back chair with a view of the room.

"This is nice. What's the occasion?"

Ever since Joel had guessed that Matt was going to propose, Codi had been on high alert. But she had come to terms with that possibility and dismissed it. On the other hand, Matt had been acting a little kooky. She was starting to wonder if Joel knew something she didn't. Her mind spun with the reality. Could she . . . should she . . . did she want to? *Codi, get ahold of yourself.*

Matt was an amazing man, but . . . okay, no buts. Matt was an amazing man. She decided to just go with it.

"I just thought we deserved a nice weekend together. Wine?"

"Yes, please," she said with a bit too much energy. She paused and purposefully slowed her cadence. "That would be nice."

The meal was amazing and the service attentive. Codi had the flounder *francaise* and Matt, the Portuguese-style mussels. They made small talk, and eventually, the atmosphere took over, and the comfort they felt around each other returned.

Once back at the hotel, however, Matt started acting quirky again. He took Codi to their room. It was a nice suite with a small kitchen and living area. The room was decorated with white linens, hardwood floors, and blue and white paisley curtains. The furniture was modern and not too dark. There was a nice-sized patio with two chairs and a small table. Codi removed her blazer, and Matt led her outside. The moon was reflecting off the calm waters of the bay. The view was breathtaking. Codi spotted a bottle of champagne chilling in an ice bucket next to two glasses.

"I see you planned ahead."

Matt smiled and nodded. He needed to do something with his hands, so he held onto the railing with a vise grip. "It's beautiful out. Thought we should enjoy it," he said.

Codi's full hair was down across her shoulders, accentuating her smooth graceful neck. The white t-shirt she wore fit tight enough to show the swell of her breasts above her flat belly. Her taunt arms revealed hours of laps in the pool, and her slender hips gave way to just the right amount of a bubble butt. *Man, is she gorgeous,* Matt thought.

"It's also cold," she said. "Come over here and keep me warm."

Matt stepped to her and held her tight, not wanting the moment to end. It gave him a surge of strength that had him feeling more confident in his plan.

Codi ran her hands across his back under his shirt. A shot of electricity jolted him, sending an involuntary shiver through his body. Matt closed his eyes and realized other parts of his body were coming to life. He pulled Codi's wanting lips to his and let the feeling go where it would. Codi responded by exploring his mouth with her tongue, and they stayed like that for several minutes. Finally, the couple had to come up for air.

"I need to use the . . . bathroom," he said. "Be right back."

"I'll open the champagne," Codi called out as she picked up the bottle.

"Perfect." He gave her a self-conscious smile as he left.

Matt moved to the bedroom door, opened it, and then quickly closed it behind him, hyperventilating. Inside, the room was perfect, just how he had requested.

He had called ahead and given the concierge very specific directions, including a sample photo. Red rose petals were everywhere. They were used on the floor to write "I Love You" in cursive, and there was a solid heart on the white linen duvet. Under the heart in large petal letters was "Will You Marry Me." There were at least twenty candles, and the room smelled great—a mix of ocean-side breeze meets floral.

He pulled the ring case from his pocket and opened it. He cracked the door open and called out through the crack.

"Codi, can you come in here for a second?"

"Sounds like a ploy to get me into the bedroom," she playfully called back.

Matt moved into position next to the bed and took a knee. He held out the ring, as if in presentation mode. He then mustered his best *I love you* look.

Codi set the champagne down and moved for the bedroom door. Her cell buzzed, and she paused to check the number.

"Cap?" Codi said in a quiet voice.

"Hey, can you hear me? The connection is really weak. Sorry to call so late on a Friday, but I just got the information you requested and it's time-sensitive."

"It's okay," Codi lied.

She could just make out his words.

"I'm sending a file with everything. The main points are: Garrett Scott is a fixer for corporate. I have an ASWIT on a logistics company called Tranzglobal Logistics. They have some loosey-goosey leadership that is buried in several shell corporations. I'll let you run that lead down."

Codi grabbed her blazer and put it back on as she stepped back out onto the patio, hoping the signal would improve outside.

"They seem to base their operations from a ship registered out of Panama, probably to avoid taxes. Now, the timely thing is, that ship is in harbor in Portland right now."

"Oregon or Maine?" Codi asked.

"Maine. And she's scheduled to leave tomorrow. Where it goes from there is anybody's guess. I know it's not much to go on, but that's what I have for you."

"This is super helpful, Cap. I owe you."

Matt waited on one knee wondering what was taking so long. He called again. This time even louder.

"Codi, can you pop into the bedroom for a second?"

Out on the balcony, Codi was concentrating on her call. The connection was still weak so she had her phone pressed tight to her ear, with a finger in the other.

"No, no just helping out a fellow government agency," the captain said. "We are all on the same team."

"Well, I still owe you. And thanks, Cap."

"Take care of yourself, Codi. What am I saying? It's you! I suddenly feel sorry for the other guys," he said, laughing.

They said goodbye and hung up.

Matt decided something was amiss. He stood, moved to the door, and slipped to the other side. Codi was just stepping into the living room from outside. She gave him an uneasy smile.

"What's wrong? Didn't you hear me calling?" he asked.

"Matt, honey . . . I am sooo sorry, but I gotta leave."

"What? Now?" Matt answered, a bit panicked.

"Yes, now," Codi replied in a soft voice. "Let me grab my bag, and I can call an Uber."

She headed for the bedroom door, and Matt leaned back against it barring entry.

"*No!* I mean, I'll get it. And I'll drive you back. Not a problem. Now, you just wait right here. I'll grab the bags."

"What is going on, Matt?" Codi demanded.

"Nothing. It's just dinner. It didn't agree with me, and it's not pretty in there."

Codi seemed to buy his excuse and stepped back with a brief nod. Matt did a quick spin through the door closing it behind him. He grabbed the bedspread and pulled it over the petals on the floor, effectively hiding both messages and the rose heart. He quickly blew out the candles and grabbed the bags. *Stupid, stupid idea. What were you thinking!*

He exited the door with the luggage and slammed it behind him.

"Trust me, you do not want to go in there. Phew." He added to his message by waving one hand across his nose.

"Matt, baby, I promise to make this up to you."

He gave her a quick kiss. "I know you will."

They headed to Matt's Explorer and drove away from their romantic destination back to the city.

There was a good ten minutes of silence before Matt broke it. "Codi, look—"

"No, Matt. I am so sorry. I am grateful you are so understanding, but this is who I am and what I do."

"I know it is, and you're good at it. I wouldn't want it any other way. Unless you could have left Monday," he said, giving her a brief smile. It broke the tension and Codi leaned over and kissed the man she dearly loved.

She got on her phone and began to organize travel for her and her partner.

"Joel, I'm sorry, but we have a strong lead, and it's time-sensitive. You are going to have to cut your trip short."

"Oh, thank goodness!" he exclaimed.

It was not the response Codi was expecting. "Okay? I'm arranging a flight to pick you up at Edmonton International. I'll send you the file, and you can read it on the plane. I'll meet you in Portland as soon as you get there."

"Oregon or Maine?" he asked.

"Maine."

"Got it . . . and thanks."

Codi looked at her phone for a second before hanging up.

All the way home, Matt couldn't decide if he had been a giant idiot, dodged a bullet, or was just plain unlucky.

Chapter Eleven

J oel and Codi exited their rental and walked across the parking lot next to the harbor. The pavement was wet from earlier rain, and the temperature had turned cold. If any more rain came, it would come down as snow.

"Winter is coming," Joel said as he hiked up the collar of his suit coat.

"I'm not sure you can say that anymore without a trademark infringement," Codi said, referring to a popular HBO series.

"How about it's friggin' freezing?"

"That's legal," Codi said.

They walked in silence for a second.

"So did he do it?" Joel asked out the side of his mouth.

Codi glanced his way with a curious look.

"Propose?" he added.

"No, he didn't propose. It was just a nice weekend getaway until I had to up and leave. So I guess you were wrong."

"Hmmm."

"What do you mean, *hmm?*" Codi asked.

"Nothing. It just seemed like . . . he was gonna do it. That's all."

"Well, keep those thoughts to yourself. You had me totally freaked out. I think Matt was picking up on my fear, and even he was acting weird. It would have been a real rollercoaster weekend for sure. But he definitely wasn't planning to propose to me. I can promise you that.

"Okay, my bad," Joel said.

Codi shot him a look. "Yeah, it was."

"So you don't want to marry Matt?"

"*Joel,* that's not what I'm saying. Matt and I are . . . well, I do love him and . . . I would say yes if he asked me. He's just not ready for that step yet. Besides, we are fine just the way we are."

"Okay, as long as you're sure."

"Sure . . ." Codi ran her hand through her hair. "What about *your* weekend?"

"The opposite of a proposal. Shannon's parents are hardcore."

"What, no hot cocoa and Parcheesi?" Codi asked.

"I barely escaped with my life!"

They walked a few more steps with the conversation still fresh in their minds.

"I guess we're both right where we belong," Codi finished.

They met up with a state trooper waiting near the gangway to *The Mantis.* He introduced himself as Trooper Smith, and they followed him up the ramp to the main deck. He wore the classic broad, flat-brimmed blue hat that complemented his light blue uniform. An H&K .45 auto was in his black leather hip holster. His boots and holster were shiny and polished from lack of actual use. Trooper Smith walked a bit pigeon-toed as he clanked his way up the metal ramp. He was of average height with unusually broad shoulders. Codi's first impression was that the man took himself a bit too seriously, but there were worse traits.

"We get a lot of reports about the ships that come and go here," Trooper Smith said with a Boston accent. "Sometimes the USCG [US Coast Guard] takes them, and sometimes, we handle it. It's a symbiotic relationship. I mean, we're all on the same team, right?"

"That's what they say," Joel answered.

"Most of them turn out to be nothing. Though . . . we did get a call back in May—"

"Can I help you?"

A man stood at the top of the gangplank blocking the way. The last of the day's sun was hitting the horizon, silhouetting him in black and orange.

"I'm Trooper Smith, and these two are special agents from the FBI." He used the acronym like a dare.

"We are about to shove off, so why don't you do the same? Unless you want to go to Maracaibo," he said.

"We have a couple of questions for your captain," Codi said. "It won't take long. I'd hate to get the Coast Guard involved and delay your departure."

The man gave them a pensive stare, and then, a sudden strained smile hit his face. "I'm First Officer Max Odo. Come with me please, but make it quick."

The man was a tall and imposing human, about six-three. His face was clean-shaven with a strong jawline and deep-set dark eyes. He moved with a fluidity that was a result of a disciplined fitness regimen.

He quick-stepped his way toward a metal door on the superstructure's starboard side. He spoke rapid Russian into his radio and then placed it back on his belt. He led them down a narrow hallway and into a small room with tables and chairs. There was a small setup on a back side table with coffee and tea.

"Help yourself. The captain should be here shortly."

An armed man stepped into the room and took up station against the wall. Max turned as Captain Semenova stormed into the room, slinging Russian curses. He was about to degrade Max's mother when he saw the visitors and suddenly paused. His eyes scanned the three law enforcement officials without moving his head. He muttered something in Russian to Max and watched as he left the room. He then turned to his guests.

"I am Captain Vadim Semenova. How may I be of service?" he said with fake politeness.

He pointed to the table, inviting them all to sit. Trooper Smith sat and gestured to Joel and Codi. His confidence now gone with the bear of a man standing in front of him.

"Captain Semenova, we have a few questions we need to ask you," Joel said.

"I gathered that from your presence on my ship."

He called out in Russian, and the guard by the wall proceeded to get him a coffee.

Codi leaned forward and redirected. "We are following up on a homicide tied to a business called Tranzglobal Logistics. What can you tell us about them?"

"Nothing, really," Semenova said.

"We know it's the company behind your operations," Joel added.

"Yes. Here, and on many other ships around the globe, even some land-based logistics. But I am afraid you are mistaken. There is no possibility of any murder happening on this ship. We have been in port for two days and have been busy loading."

"Not on your ship, but a hired assassin, paid or sponsored through Tranzglobal," Joel pressed.

"That is interesting. You either have your facts mixed up or someone is doing bad business behind our backs. We are nothing more than you see." He waved a hand around the room. "An old ship plying cargo, trying to stay one step ahead of the crusher. It is, after all, the place all ships go in the end, if Davy Jones don't claim 'em first."

There was a sudden jerk to the ship and Joel looked around, uneasy.

"Not to worry, just pulling off from the dock. I have made arrangements to escort you back in the tug. You have your business to do, and I have mine; schedules must be kept."

"Can you at least give us the name of your boss?" Joel asked, suddenly eager to get off the ship.

The Santa-looking man chuckled. "I would be happy to do so, but I think I can do one better. I have a copy of the articles of incorporation in my safe along with some other documents that might be helpful."

He stood and excused himself with a, "Be right back."

Codi and Joel shared a look. The ship was moving. They had a very bad feeling.

Two men wearing all black, just like their guard, rushed into the room brandishing Russian full-auto AK-74s. The guard in the room shouted, "Drop weapons now!" in broken English.

Codi, Joel, and Trooper Smith had no choice. They pulled out their pistols and laid them on the table where they were collected.

"Now phones!"

They complied by sliding their cellphones onto the table and watched with a real sense of dread as they, too, were collected.

The guard used the barrel of his machinegun to communicate. *Back away from the table and lay on the floor.*

The agents were tied with their hands behind their backs.

Twenty minutes later, the first officer, Max, returned to the room. He spoke a quick snippet of Russian, and the men pulled the prisoners to their feet. One guard pulled out a knife. He moved to the prisoners, eyeing them like a cat with a half-dead mouse. He used his knife to cut the back of Codi's suit coat and pulled it off her shoulders.

"I never liked that coat anyway. It was too boxy for me," she commented.

He then sliced the back and sides of her blouse and yanked the pieces to the floor. Codi held her ground. She had been in situations like this before and was not about to let them see fear. How she acted from here on out was a choice.

The guard moved to Trooper Smith, removed his hat, and placed it on his own head. He did a quick model pose that brought laughter from the other two guards.

"He's gonna want that back," Codi said.

Her response was met with a rifle butt to her stomach that nearly cut her in half. Codi was left gasping on her knees, fighting against the pain.

The guard then repeated his actions until Joel and Trooper Smith were both stripped of their coats and shirts.

"Enough!" Max said as he stepped to the Americans.

"I tried to warn you, but you were determined to come aboard." He shook his head at the thought of what might have been. "I have a special place waiting for you. Unfortunately, there is only room for two. I guess we can play a little game to see who wins. Actually, I guess it would be who loses."

He pulled a small revolver from his right pocket. "Russian roulette. One of my favorite games."

The three captives were led outside onto the deck. The view had significantly changed since the three first arrived. A black tug could be seen heading back to the lights of the port, and the mainland was fading surprisingly fast. Codi, Joel, and Trooper Smith were lined up against the metal railing, facing their captors. The sodium vapor glow of the ship's lighting gave the scene a greenish-orange glow that cut through the dusk.

Cold wind scraped across bare skin as Codi did her best not to shiver. Max took the small .32 revolver and opened the cylinder. He removed all the cartridges, save one. He then closed it back up and spun the cylinder, pointing it from one prisoner to another, enjoying their various reactions. He moved forward and placed the tip of the gun against Joel's forehead. He waited and watched as the tall, thin man squinted his eyes and gritted his teeth, and then nothing more. He left the gun there for a good five seconds before squeezing the trigger. There was a metallic click from the gun and a flinch from Joel. Max gave an "oh well" gesture and moved to Codi, placing the pistol on her head. *This was fun.* He started pulling at the trigger. Codi gave him no response.

"Do me a favor, would you?" she asked so calmly that Max looked slightly perplexed.

He released the trigger.

"You need one of us gone, right?" she said.

He removed his pistol from her head and nodded, curious as to where this was going.

"I am responsible for these two, so let me decide who has to die."

Max smiled at the thought. *Let it play out,* he told himself. *It might be entertaining.* He could always start back up if things got boring.

"Okay, who dies?" Max asked.

The two guards had never wavered in keeping their guns trained on the prisoners, one still wearing the Trooper's hat.

Codi pushed off the rail and looked at the men on either side of her. Trooper Smith was a blubbering mess. Joel had fear in his eyes but was keeping it together. *Good for him.* She moved closer to Trooper Smith, who became even more hysterical. Something about a wife and kids. She moved back to Joel and before anybody knew what was happening, head-butted him in the forehead and followed through with a shove.

Joel went over the railing and into the air. There was a brief scream and then silence.

"There. Decision made," Codi said as she turned back to face her captives.

Two gunmen ran to the railing and fired their guns down at the water.

Max was suddenly very serious. He pulled his Glock, holding it steady on the two remaining prisoners. "Playtime's over. Down on your knees, both of you!"

After the gunmen finished shooting into the frothy water below, they dispatched both prisoners with a blow to the head from their rifle butts.

Blackness.

***

Joel tried to blink away the stars from Codi's head butt as he free fell toward the water. His hands were still tied behind his back, and he wobbled awkwardly through the air. He did the only thing that came to mind. He took a deep gulp of air, then curled up and tensed for impact. The fall was just over forty feet. The water felt like concrete. Joel let himself go deep and then opened his torso to come to a stop. He torqued his arms down and under his legs and feet, nearly dislocating both shoulders. His hands were still tied, but at least they were in front. He looked up as a rain of bullets hit the water all around him, backlit by the ship's deck lights. They quickly lost momentum and drifted past him. Just as his body was starting to feel the first signs of hypoxia, Joel kicked and pulled for the surface. It seemed too far to reach, and he was moving slowly due to his tied hands. His brain signaled for him to breathe, but Joel fought against it, knowing it would mean death. Every stroke burned, and his mind was losing the battle with his consciousness. *If only I can . . .* Finally, he gave in and took a breath.

The shadow of the ship pulled free as Joel breached the water, sucking in breaths like they would be his last. He had cleared the water just as his body's reflex took over. He used his feet to tread water as he pulled with his teeth at the knotted rope around his hands. One inch at a time, the knot loosened, and finally, his hands were free.

Joel took stock of his situation. The ship he had been knocked from moved off, leaving him alone in the ocean. He could just make out land in the distance outlined by the last glow in the sky. It was many miles away and, worst of all, he just realized how cold the water was. Joel guessed he had fifteen minutes before succumbing to hyperthermia and drowning.

He slipped off his shoes and pants, now wearing nothing but his underwear. He let the shoes drift downward. The pang of losing his favorite lace-ups was short-lived. Grabbing the legs of his slacks, he tied a knot at the bottom of each one. He then ducked under the frigid water and began the process of turning his pants into a buoyancy device. A large gulp of air, exhaled into the pants over and over, until they were inflated. Once wet, most pants and jeans will hold air and can be used as a floatation device. Joel slid the inflated legs under his arms and started to swim as his blue lips chattered in the cold.

He had heard the saying, "out of the frying pan and into the fire." What he wouldn't give right now for a little fire.

***

Codi leaned up and rubbed the back of her head. Something crawled across her face. She flicked at it instinctively and looked around. The large room was bright white with a medical feel to it. She was wearing only her underwear—a black lacy bra and skimpy matching panties. Had she known this was going to happen, she would have worn something a bit more conservative on her backside. Her cell was a four-foot-by-four-foot clear Lexan box, just slightly taller than she was. There were several other people in boxes just like hers, all lined up together in two rows with about a two-foot gap between each box. The boxes took up about a third of the room's space. The rest of the room consisted of tables and sophisticated lab equipment. Codi stood up on shaky legs, using the sides of the cell to support her. She counted fourteen people, each in a glass box like hers. They all appeared sullen and despondent. Codi banged against her cage to test its strength. She wasn't getting out. A couple of technicians with lab coats working the perimeter glanced over briefly and then went back to work. She tried calling out, but her voice seemed to bounce back off the Lexan.

Each box had two tubes attached to the top, a small ineffective drain on the bottom, and no apparent door. They were bolted at the bottom, and there was a locked double-door access port about the size of a breadbox, most likely for food. That's when she noticed the cockroaches in her box. She quickly used her bare feet to smash them. She looked over to the guest next to her, a middle-aged African American woman sitting with her head down.

"There's no getting out of here," the woman mumbled.

Codi dropped to her level, and the fortyish woman with many stretch marks looked over with glazed eyes. She could tell the woman had once been much heavier. She wore nothing but a thin camisole and purple panties and sat with her knees up against her chest.

"How long have you been here?" Codi asked.

"I had flies." She was shaking as she spoke. "You had cockroaches."

Codi looked down at the smashed bugs on her floor. She lifted her eyes to see the remains of several houseflies smeared on the other woman's glass."

"What's your name?"

"Wilma . . . Wilma Grossman."

"Where are you from?"

"Oakdale."

She started to cry at the thought of all that she had lost. Codi let her be and stood back up. She took a second look at her situation. There were numbers on each box, and she was fourteen; Wilma was twelve. Each cage had been loaded with, as best as she could tell, flies or cockroaches.

Three boxes over, number eleven, was Trooper Smith in his tighty-whities. He had finally stopped banging against his walls and screaming and had dropped into a ball onto the floor, looking morose. Codi noticed a small clear tube sticking three inches into her cube. It had a steel ball bearing on the end holding back whatever liquid was inside. She touched it with her finger. It came away wet. She sniffed—no odor. She put her tongue on the end of the tube and tested it. Water flowed across it into her mouth. It was a hamster-style water delivery system. She was—they all were—lab rats.

***

First Officer Max Odo entered the bridge greeting the warm air inside. He moved to a coffee pot and poured himself a cup. The two prisoners had been dealt with, and the ship was now secure. He'd taken two trips around the deck to confirm it personally.

"So what do you want to do about Pullin?"

Captain Semenova looked over at Max, carefully processing his words. "I say we tell him nothing."

"He needs to know that the Feds are on to him," Max said.

"Onto *us* and we have handled them. *The Mantis* will soon be lost in a vast ocean, and no one needs to be the wiser."

"If this ever gets back to him?"

The captain paused and stared out through the glass at the black water in the distance. It was a risk, and with a boss like Pullin, deception could be a dangerous game, even if they were doing it to protect him.

"Perhaps, you're right. Get an encrypted message to Pullin and tell him what happened. Then let's go dark. No more outgoing messages till we get close to the next port. It's time to make *The Mantis* a ghost ship."

Max nodded and headed for the radio room.

***

Dr. Kamba typed the last few strokes on her computer and called Kyber over.

"I just updated Dr. Mahl. We should start seeing the first results in the next three hours, maybe four, based on our two late arrivals."

Kyber nodded. Since their trip out from the main lab in Nevada to *The Mantis,* Dr. Kamba and he had been busy getting their new lab set up and running. Dr. Mahl had been doing the same on the sister ship, *The Locust,* out in California. The original plan was for the two ships to leave at the same time, but the order had come down for *The Mantis* to weigh anchor ASAP.

The moment they had their human trials in place, the captain weighed anchor, and not a moment too soon. Apparently, the FBI had stopped by to investigate. Now, it was a race to international waters, where they hoped to slip away into the vastness of the Atlantic Ocean. There would be no going back to the US as *The Mantis.* In fact, they would have to change the name before hitting the next port, just to be safe.

Dr. Kamba leaned against the table and turned to face Kyber. They had been training for this day, and she knew how much was riding on their success—the fate of the world. Most of the lab was in full operation, with just a few details still to be ironed out. The pens holding their test subjects were functioning brilliantly, and the addition of two more subjects had been an easy adjustment.

"With fourteen test subjects, we can now have seven separate steps instead of six. I'll do a run-up and set a schedule for who gets the vaccine at each stage. Have you given the order any thought?" she asked Kyber.

"Yeah. I was going to keep it simple. Odd numbers get the vaccine and evens, the placebo. We can track the progress of symptoms and organ failure on the evens, and stagger the vaccine injections on the odds for a better look at when the vaccine is most effective," Kyber answered.

"And when it stops working altogether," Dr. Kamba added.

"Right. Seven should give us a decent snapshot of how it will affect the general population and what the mortality rate will be." Kyber set his tablet down on the countertop.

"Good. The test we did in India had too many variables. Now, we can control everything. This should give us a very accurate timeline."

***

Captain Semenova set a course for 140 degrees south-southeast as they cleared the harbor. He made it plain and obvious. The arrival of the FBI had been an unwanted wrinkle in their plans. He sent an encrypted message off and paced the bridge as he processed what it might mean. They had gotten away clean, but only time would tell if that would last. *The Mantis* was a unique vessel with a few tricks up her sleeve. He would be ready for whatever or whoever came next.

At ten miles out, he gave a direction change that would hopefully confuse anyone trying to track them.

"Shut down the AIS," Captain Semenova ordered.

The AIS, automatic identification system, was a transponder-based system that all large commercial vessels over three hundred tons were required to employ. It sent out a signal that allowed their main office to track their progress and helped make other ships aware of their position to prevent mid-sea collisions.

"Transponder shut down, sir," Max replied.

"Set a course to sixty degrees northeast. Ahead three-quarters."

"Aye, sir, sixty degrees. Ahead three-quarters."

The ship turned northward, setting a course that would ultimately lead them to Dublin, the first of many stops on their Atlantic tour.

Semenova opened his chart of the Atlantic. He looked over the cities marked in red that he would be visiting and did a quick calculation in his head. Three months. It would take them three months to complete the journey. Dublin. Cardiff. Saint-Nazaire. Lisbon. Rabat. Dakar. Porto Novo. Cape Town. Buenos Aires. Rio de Janeiro. Maracaibo. Port-au-Prince. Havana. Miami. Charleston. Each stop required only a short stay, but the lasting effects would be immeasurable.

His orders after that were quite clear. Stay away from the infected zones for at least three months. They had loaded plenty of food and could make all the water they needed to survive any delays, but keeping morale up on such a long voyage would be a challenge.

***

Joel had all but completely given up. His legs were too cold to move, and his right arm was the only extremity left working. He clawed forward almost robot-like. Most of his blood had moved to his core in an effort to protect his vital organs. He had beat his estimate of fifteen minutes and was close to thirty since hitting the water. The sky had lost its purple hue as night fell. Joel looked at an approaching ship. It was a cabin cruiser on course for the port he had left. It was making about eighteen knots and would cross within twenty feet of Joel's position. Joel shifted up on his flotation device, trying to make himself tall in the water.

He screamed for all he was worth and waved his hands at the fast-moving boat. The skipper seemed to be focused on the water ahead, but for whatever reason, never saw Joel, as the ship passed without stopping.

Joel continued to scream until he had nothing left. The ship faded into the distance. He figured he had gone about four miles since being dropped into the ocean. The problem was he was spent, too cold to go on, and he still had at least five more miles before reaching land. Joel slumped back down. The near-miss had recharged him, and he would try a bit more. Five minutes later, he was worse off than he had been before. Now, none of his extremities worked; it was all he could do to hang on to his inflated pants. His eyes drooped as his body started to shut down.

Cold water has a way of sucking the warmth right out of you, and at forty degrees Fahrenheit, Joel was not long for this world. A clang moved through Joel's ears, but he didn't process it. A few minutes later, another. This time Joel lifted his head. A large sailboat was moving his way. Its navy blue hull was almost invisible on the dark water, but its white sails were up and full. Joel tried to lift his arms and call, but his body refused to cooperate. A hoarse whisper was all that came out, and his left hand wouldn't move at all.

The ship passed within a few feet of Joel, and he tried one last push to make himself scream—nothing. The ship moved on, and Joel gave up the last of his hope. He put his face down on his inflated pants. He would take a short nap.

"Honey, I think there's a body in the water. Look!"

"It's just a piece of driftwood, dear."

It was the last thing Joel heard before his world went black.

Chapter Twelve

THE MANTIS – NORTH ATLANTIC OCEAN – 2:31 P.M.

Codi was feeling the effects of something. She was starting to sweat—a fever. The others in the boxes were all having various reactions. Some were vomiting and convulsing; others were standing in their own diarrhea, shivering. A few just looked petrified, and a couple of them sat listlessly on the floor. Whatever she had, it was moving through the prisoners, and it was moving fast. Her stomach hurt, and she was getting a migraine. Wilma, in box number twelve next to her on the right, had been coughing for several hours and had vomited multiple times.

A young man in his early twenties was in box number thirteen right across from her, and he seemed to be fine, just totally freaked out by the events all around him. Codi had tried to get some information from him, including his name. He just ignored her and everyone else around him. He was chanting some song Codi didn't recognize as he withdrew more and more into himself. The situation was too intense for him to accept as reality.

***

John Brown did his best to ignore the woman in the cell across from him. He had left for a promising work appointment and ended up here. He recognized many of the machines set about the room. As a technical writer, he had done some medical device pamphlets. His guts felt on fire, and he was having difficulty concentrating. The horror of his situation was not lost on him. He had lived a solitary life, and now, he would die in the same fashion. His long-deceased Catholicism left him with nothing but guilt. It was a penance for choices made. God was punishing him because he had left no place for God in his life. Perhaps it was time to reevaluate.

***

A voice on a loudspeaker cut through Codi's thoughts.

"Hello. Who we are is not important. What matters is that each one of you has been carefully chosen to help us save the world. Congratulations. You have been exposed to a new virulent strain of typhus."

Codi looked over to see a tall Black woman wearing a lab coat and speaking into a microphone. She had a slight accent that struck Codi as Nigerian, Somalian, or maybe Kenyan.

"Each of you will be given a vaccine at various stages of your illness. It is important that we understand your symptoms as they progress. What we are specifically looking for is intestinal or abdominal pain. Headaches. Fever. Cough. Liquid in the lungs. Blood in your stool and severe diarrhea."

It sounded like a bad pharma commercial.

"If you choose to survive this ordeal, please be forthcoming. Otherwise, I will be forced to withhold your vaccine. Let me be clear on this point—without treatment, your chances of survival will drop to less than ten percent. That is all."

Codi and Wilma shared a scared expression.

"We're going to die in a box," Wilma said through tears. Her forehead was beaded with sweat, and she looked pale.

"Wilma, we have to stay strong. If we give up, you are right, we will die in a box."

Wilma looked up at Codi with a pleading hope in her eyes. Codi was hard-pressed to meet her stare, as she had nothing to give her next-door cellmate but words. The two women tried to fight against the hopelessness. Codi put her hand up against the glass. Wilma matched her action. There were two feet of space between the cages, but they could each feel the warmth given by the other.

Dr. Kamba flicked off the mic and moved to her coworker, Kyber. She said, "It looks like the flies and cockroaches spread the *Salmonella Typhi X* at the same rate. I see no obvious variant between patients at this point."

"Not unexpected but still good news," Kyber said.

They had given the superbug an *X* appendix to differentiate it from regular typhoid. The newly developed superbug version of the bacteria had an unusually high mortality rate and was immune to all known antibiotics, but worst of all, it could spread through particulate body fluids—sweat, saliva, and so on. The Musca domestica and the Periplaneta americana had both been exposed to the bacteria. Once placed in the cages, any contact with the patients would transfer the contagion to the patient. The insects could also spread the *Typhi X* from one to another even through breeding. It was a very nasty microorganism and should it ever get loose into the general public, it would create a plague-level event.

Dr. Kamba flipped through several pages filled with patient data. She was still trying to get used to the speed at which the infection spread through the human body. Every one of her test subjects was already struggling with symptoms.

"Start by giving P1 the vaccine and P2 the placebo," Dr. Kamba said. "We'll stagger the rest by six hours per set of pens. That should give us a first and last option along the timeline."

Kyber nodded in agreement and prepared two syringes. One with the vaccine and one with distilled water. He stepped over to P1 and asked the subject a few specific questions.

***

A constant beeping seemed to get louder as blackness turned to white. Joel looked around at his surroundings with slits for eyeballs. *Perfect, I'm back in a hospital. The second time in two weeks.* This time, like the last, he had no memory of how he'd gotten there. There was an IV in his arm and a pulse lead that connected to the beeping machine next to his bed. A heavy heated blanket covered his torso.

He was grateful just to be alive. He sat up and let the cobwebs clear. He reached out and took the chart hooked to the foot of his bed. He looked it over. Northern Light Mercy Hospital. His name was listed as John Doe, and he had all the expected symptoms of a man who had been exposed to extremely cold water for far too long.

The last thing he remembered was a sailboat going past him and his complete resignation to his situation. He had closed his eyes and said a final prayer. A dim sound had clouded his prayer. It was the whoosh and clang of rigging, as sails were dropped and the skipper did a jibe to turn back his way. They must have pulled him from the water. He pulled the heated blanket off and rotated his feet to the floor. That's when the memory of how it all started hit him like a jolt from a stun gun. *Codi!*

Joel pulled the IV from his arm and removed the lead to the machine, causing a steady beep to ensue. He wrapped a blanket around himself and headed for the hallway in search of a phone. Halfway to the door, a large male nurse entered his room.

"Oh, good, you're awake." He checked the time on his smartwatch. "Shoot. I missed the over and under by twenty minutes."

Joel paused, looking at the man. "You bet on when I would regain consciousness?"

"Hey, not a lot to do in this town. You should be flattered; no one bet on your demise." He reached out to help Joel. "Come on, let's get you back in bed. You need to rest."

"I need to make a call first. Can you help me out with that?" Joel gave him his most serious look.

The nurse acquiesced. "Okay, but make it short. You've been through a very traumatic exposure event, and until your core is able to self-regulate temperature, we need to keep you here for your own good."

Joel nodded his consent, and the nurse guided him to a phone at the nurse's station. He dialed a code and then handed it to Joel. Joel tapped in a number from memory and listened as it rang.

"Fescue," Joel's boss said.

"SSA Fescue, it's Joel."

"Joel! Where have you been?"

"We got shanghaied, and Codi threw me off the ship before they could shoot me."

The two nurses at the station stopped what they were doing to look at the John Doe with the crazy story. Joel suddenly felt uneasy and turned away from them.

There was a moment of silence on the phone as Brian waited for Joel to stop clowning around. Then he remembered that it was Joel, and he didn't have that skill set.

"Okay, slow down and tell me everything, starting with where you are."

Suddenly Joel felt lightheaded. The room started to spin, and blackness encroached around his periphery. His knees went weak, and the dark claimed him once again.

The phone dropped to the floor. And a tinny voice called out, "Joel? Joel, are you okay?"

***

Dr. Mahl pressed the green button to connect the encrypted video chat. Pullin Ikaika stared back at him, all business.

"How are things?" Pullin asked.

"We have most of our human trials identified and will start collecting them within the next hour or so. The lab is up and ready minus a few details. I'll have everything in place before morning. Captain Combs tells me *The Locust* should be ready to leave in the next forty-eight to fifty-six hours." Dr. Mahl stopped, waiting for a response. When one didn't come, he continued. "We're ready in the lab to start human trials. I'm estimating sixty percent of every human infected will die."

"That seems a bit conservative from our previous tests," Pullin said.

"Yes, it is, but it still falls within our estimates, and we are still limited on real-world feedback. We should reach critical mass on time and meet our culling minimums at the very least."

Pullin nodded at the information. "We had a visit from the authorities on *The Mantis. A couple of FBI agents.*"

This got a rise out of Dr. Mahl. "The FBI!"

"Not to worry, Doctor, they have volunteered to join our other test subjects." He leaned slightly closer making his face large on the screen. "But I wonder if we shouldn't press things a bit on your end. Try to get launched as soon as possible, even if you don't have a full contingent of *passengers*. The data supports your theories so far. I say we go ahead and move to deployment."

The news had Dr. Mahl processing his options. "There are still many things we don't know. I need to complete the human trials at the very least. We are introducing *Salmonella Typhi X* into a very divergent environment. There are too many variables," Dr. Mahl said, the panic in his voice rising.

Pullin spoke with a staccato cadence. "Do what you can while in route then flush the evidence. We can't delay any longer. Time is no longer on our side, Doctor."

Dr. Mahl paused to collect himself. He was a true believer in this operation, and he would do everything in his power to make it all come together. "Okay. You are right. Time is against us. We'll leave tomorrow with whatever number of test subjects we can collect."

"Thank you and best of luck, Doctor. The world is counting on you."

They shared a common nod and signed off.

Pullin held the phone, still trying to decide his next move. He had largely gone under the radar to this point, but cracks were starting to show. It was inevitable but disturbing. He stepped to the picture window and stared out at the lake. It was a pristine deep blue with sunlight dancing off the few ripples carried on a light breeze. He knew the world-class view hid an ugly underbelly—the pesticides, oils, and trash carried in the storm waters every time it rained. Poisons that killed wildlife and could make areas dangerous to swim in. It was nothing compared to most water sources near population centers. And once you got to the third-world countries, it was deplorable.

Money, in Pullin's mind, was only of value if you used it. Keeping it holed up in posh possessions and banks was not his style. He would make *his* money work for him. To make things better than he found them. Quite literally, he was going to give the planet a face-lift, and if he made a few billion along the way, then that would just allow him to do even more down the road. This would be his legacy. His give back. A chance to complete what he had started so long ago on Oahu. And now, he would take all the credit for it.

But as everyone knows, you can't make an omelet without breaking a few eggs, and right now, it was egg-breaking time.

First, he needed to buy some time and keep himself abreast of any blowback that might be coming from Portland. He dialed a number from memory and listened while it rang.

"Hello?"

"Senator Crandall, how are you?"

***

Dr. Mahl redialed the encrypted device. He was sprouting beads of sweat on his forehead. A unique buzzing was heard until the connection was made. Dr. Kamba's face on *The Mantis* appeared on the screen. She looked a bit tired, but otherwise, she seemed to be holding up.

"Hey," she said.

"How are things on your end?" Dr. Mahl asked, wiping his forehead with a rag.

Dr. Kamba could see that he was speaking from a lab that was identical to hers. Her colleague looked a bit rattled, but science can do that to you.

"We left port with fourteen test subjects," she said, with a small bit of pride.

This raised an eyebrow on Dr. Mahl's forehead. *Fourteen was two more than they had planned. It must include the two FBI agents Pullin had mentioned.*

"The delivery system worked just as envisioned. All subjects are showing some signs of infection. We have started the first round of vaccines and will document the trials every six hours."

"Good. We will be short on subjects on our side, as our exit date has moved up. Keep me apprised of your results, and give Dr. P the green light. We are moving into delivery," Dr. Mahl added, with a concerned look.

"But we haven't completed—"

Dr. Mahl raised his hand, stopping Dr. Kamba mid-sentence.

"I know, but leaks and government agents have now made time our biggest obstacle."

Dr. Kamba seemed to understand and promised to ramp things up on her end.

"Make sure to flush all the subjects once you're done."

"Of course, Doctor."

***

Dr. Pendergrass was an entomologist professor out of the University of Utah. He had spent many hours in the wilds pursuing his passion, and his college lab had become a second home. A short, rotund man with a seriously receding hairline, he wore round glasses and a curious expression. His partner, Dr. Sales, was much taller with thick salt-and-pepper hair. He had a narrow face with a loose skin jowl that swayed as he moved. He, too, wore round glasses that matched his partner's. It had earned them the moniker The Bug Boys while they were teaching.

The two professors had been instrumental in a new application for entomology. With grants and corporate support, they had built an entire division at the college—breeding insects for chemical and biological analysis to be used in the medical world. Like plants used as medicine, insects can hold the key to a myriad of commercially viable opportunities. Spider webs were being used to create smaller and stronger cordage. The proteins in insect venom can be used for therapeutic drugs and anti-inflammatories. Pheromones were just one of the many chemical compounds found in entomology.

All that had come crumbling down three years ago when an experiment in their lab had taken a turn. The Bug Boys were working with a pharmaceutical company to isolate the chemical pheromone responsible for violence in Africanized bees. There was talk of using it as an antidote for humans with violent behavior. A hive of killer bees was harvested and grown in the lab so that they had constant access to the source. It was contained in a glass box and had specially-designed holes that only let the workers out into the open. No queens would fit through, thereby eliminating the chance the hive would multiply and spread.

A careless cleaning woman bumped against the latch on the access door, leaving a gap. By the next morning, the bees had moved to the ceiling corner of the lab. Once disturbed by students going about their daily projects, they attacked, killing one assistant and sending three others to the hospital in critical condition. The Bug Boys defended the bees, saying they just did what was natural. But it had caused such an outcry across social media and the news that the two scientists were summarily dismissed. Their program was shut down, and the lab was converted into storage.

The two disgraced professors were unemployable and seemed to be carrying a grudge with no way to act on it. Dr. Pendergrass had no viable skills for the private sector. Dr. Sales was slightly better off, as his family owned a chain of shoe stores. He found himself on his knees shoving tennis shoes onto snot-nosed kids eight hours a day—a hard lesson at fifty years old. The two entomologists were destined to melt away into history as only a sad footnote.

It was the perfect storm for Pullin's operation, and he scooped them both up and put them back to work. He had rebuilt their lab and improved upon it, hiding them from the public eye and giving them a purpose. The Bug Boys could now move forward with pride and satisfaction. They had been working to develop gestation procedures that could be controlled and replicated. They were given a short timeline and a massive sample population. The lab on the bottom floor of Pullin's estate had been home for many months, but its contents had recently been moved, sending the doctors in two different directions.

Dr. Pendergrass opened the door and took a deep breath. He loved the smell of larvae. They gave off a musky earthy scent that had a primordial slant. He stepped inside and closed the door to one of his "ovens," as he liked to call them because they kept the inside temperature at a constant ninety-five degrees Fahrenheit with sixty percent humidity. The ovens were really just giant steel birthing incubators used to grow larvae into pupae. From there, adults would be born and infected. Inside the oven were many trays where larvae wiggled and wormed their way through carefully prepared rotting flesh. The smell would be overpowering to most, but to Dr. Pendergrass, it was all in a day's work. He ran his hands across the squirming white fly maggots as they followed but one mindset: eat. He was proud of his babies, and soon, they would take flight for a very important task.

He had three walk-in incubators that held Musca domestica, and across from those were three slightly larger incubators that held thousands of Periplaneta americana nymphs, all working their way through their molt cycles on their way to cockroach adulthood. The tanks each required two separate entry doors to prevent escapes. Each metal incubator would hold just over ten thousand adult insects. They were housed in the second main lab on *The Mantis,* just down the hall from the main lab containing the human test subjects. The Bug Boys had spent the last year perfecting the process and timing required, as the two species had different life cycles. Now, Dr. Pendergrass would be ready for delivery at just the right time.

Satisfied that everything was in order, he left to check the next incubator. Had he not already been vaccinated, Dr. Pendergrass would now be infected with *Typhi X* and would have a less than thirty percent chance of living. Each and every one of his babies carried the unique strain and were capable of passing it on to everything they touched or mated with. It would be a black swarm of death that could multiply and replenish as it went. He was sure his friend and colleague, Dr. Sales, was having the same success on the other ship.

***

Joel awoke to a full room. There were two agents from his office, Gordon Reyas and Anna Green, talking to each other. His boss, Brian, was speaking to someone on his cell in a hushed voice. Shannon and Matt were off in the corner.

As soon as they saw that Joel's eyes were open, Shannon rushed to his side with a hug and a kiss. "We thought we lost you. I was so worried."

Joel hugged her back. She felt warm and her hair smelled like peaches.

He sat up. He was feeling much better. "We've got to get to Codi . . . and *fast*," were his first words.

He began with the events that had led him there, starting with their meeting the captain on board *The Mantis*. The room listened with rapt attention as he described the events, including his last memory of a lone sailboat turning back in his direction as he lost consciousness. After he finished, there was a beat of silence before Brian asked the first question.

"What do you think was the reason why *The Mantis* needed only two of you?"

"I have no idea, but it can't be anything good," Joel replied.

"Codi knows how to take care of herself," Matt added with false bravado.

Brian passed out orders that had Reyas and Green out the door and on the case. A doctor entered and chased the rest away, defending Joel's need for rest. Brian took Matt out for a drink, and they left Shannon behind to keep an eye on Joel—again.

Once the doctor finished checking Joel's vitals, Shannon slid a chair up next to the bed. "This is getting to be a habit. I like you better when you're not in a hospital."

"Hey, we have a room to ourselves and a bed; what's the problem?"

"Rest, Joel. I'm here to make sure you get your rest," Shannon said with the tilt of her head.

Joel frowned at the obvious meaning in her words. Any libido he might have been feeling at having Shannon in the room to himself was gone.

***

Kyber swiped his tablet as he moved to the next pen in *The Mantis* lab and looked in on subject P8. He was a young man about his age. He had dark eyes and hair and a youthful face. *He could be a relative*, Kyber thought. Then, just as quickly, he dismissed the idea. He tapped the glass to get his attention.

"How are you feeling? Can you describe your symptoms?"

"I'll kill you when I get out of here."

"I take it you don't want the vaccine?" Kyber asked without emotion.

The man lowered his head and thought for a second. He looked up at Kyber with a death stare and spoke in a dull monotone. "I've crapped myself five times, and thank you for not giving us any toilet paper. I see blood every time now, and my guts are knotted and painful. It feels like acid is burning through me. I have a fever and my cube smells. I don't dare sit down in this filth, but I am too weak to stand much longer. Can I have the vaccine now?"

A knot formed in Kyber's throat. This was too much for him. He knew that the information they were collecting was critical to saving the world, but at what cost? If they lost all their humanity, the world would not be a better place. He turned and walked quickly for the exit.

Subject P8 called after him, "Hey! What about my shot! You promised!"

Kyber poured himself a cup of tea and sat at the gray table in the galley. He sipped at his drink with shaky hands, his mind a thousand miles away. He remembered meeting Pullin Ikaika for the first time. It had been a revelation. The man had shown him a world that was falling apart. A place where pollution and overcrowding were killing humanity. Where greed and the bottom line won out over the planet's safety. They had similar goals, only Pullin had the finances to make it happen. Not a pipe dream down the road but actively pursuing a viable plan.

Many people had claimed the same things over the years, but Pullin was the man with the plan. Dr. Mahl had shown Kyber how his research could help nature reset the clock and give humans a future they were currently destroying, and Pullin followed up with the logistics.

Kyber had listened and studied the facts. He did his own research to verify the things he had seen. When given the chance to join, he jumped in with both feet. Now, he just needed to remind himself what was at stake. A few disposable lives for the future of mankind?

"You okay?"

Kyber looked up to see Dr. Kamba approaching his table.

"Yeah. It's not always easy to remain objective when dealing with human subjects," he answered.

"It's the last step, Kyber. We just have to get through this and then we can focus on replicating the vaccine for the ones left."

Kyber nodded his agreement.

"But you're right. It is hard," she added.

Dr. Pendergrass stepped into the galley, and both Kyber and Dr. Kamba stood like they needed to get back to their lab.

"Hi, Doc," Kyber called out.

The man had a permanent smell to him that had everyone in the lab dodging his company.

"Hey, want to have some coffee with me?" Dr. Pendergrass asked.

"Sorry, can't. I got injections to do. Besides, I'm more of a tea guy," Kyber responded.

"Right," Dr. Pendergrass said, disappointed. "Let me know when you want to take that tour of my bug ovens!" He called out.

"Ah . . . sure."

***

Pullin looked at his computer for the hundredth time. He had planned and re-planned this operation. How the FBI got wind of his ship in Portland was disturbing. Especially after working so very hard to close up any gaps created by Edgar Fallman's betrayal. Had he put too much stock in Garrett Scott to take care of the agents he had assigned him to kill? With Scott dead, he might never know the truth. Had he slipped up or just met a superior force. Was there a light now shining back in his direction, and if so, how much did the authorities know or suspect. These were questions that required answers—and now.

Pullin stepped back from his screen and considered the conundrum. It was time to pull a few political strings. A simple plan formed in his mind. He left his office and stepped out into the common area. Several of his most trusted staff worked here. They wielded what power he doled out, keeping his companies healthy and current. As he stormed past, one look at Pullin's sour expression had everyone focused back on their work, each hoping not to garner his attention at the moment.

Working from Pullin's estate on Lake Tahoe was the best of both worlds. A sophisticated business placed in one of the most beautiful countries on earth, away from prying eyes. A place of solitude and hidden technology.

Most importantly, however, was his latest endeavor—HYRDA. In Pullin's eyes, it was the only hope for humanity, and it was currently in full motion. Whether he lived or died was irrelevant to the operation, as the wheels were already turning. It was now his job to keep authorities and attention away from HYDRA.

The thought of an actionable direction seemed to calm him as he stepped out onto the balcony overlooking Crystal Bay. The impossibly blue water set against the beauty of the first fall snow was lost on Pullin as he pulled a burner phone from his coat pocket and dialed.

"Hey," a voice answered.

"I need you on the East Coast."

"What about our next group of subjects?"

Pullin and Crispin had worked with the team to generate a list of candidates for the human trials during the next phase in the project. They had selected people that covered a wide demographic and who would not be missed. They also needed to be healthy and reasonably close to the ship's locale. It had taken some serious hacking and computation time to get it right, but they had narrowed the list to twenty people per ship. From there, based on variables, they would pull the first twelve. If there was a problem they would skip over one and go on to the next on the list.

Crispin had taken on the task of collecting the subjects and delivering them to the ships. Portland had gone off without a single problem. They delivered the first subjects in small groups of three and then placed them in a container, which they hoisted onboard the ship. Each subject was stripped of their street clothes and assigned a pen and a number. Twelve healthy candidates were selected, keeping two cells open in case one of the working cells failed, as this was their first round of human trials. Once all of the test subjects were onboard and he was satisfied, Crispin flew back to Northern California to start phase two.

He was sitting in a local diner drinking a chai with just a splash of cream. The Walnut Creek area of California was much more hi-tech and polished than Portland, Maine had been. Every home seemed to have a camera, and every street intersection as well. It required a higher level of action and competency to complete the collection process. He watched through the diner window as his team moved on an elderly woman who lived alone. She was the last subject in the first group of three. Crispin looked up from his phone. Across the street, one of his best men, Whiton, dressed in a delivery outfit, knocked on her door.

"They can handle it without you," came Pullin's voice through his phone, pulling him away from the scene across the street.

From what Pullin could gather without being too forward with his contacts, the FBI was investigating their missing agents but had little to go on. He would need someone to stay abreast of their progress in case they needed to redirect the focus of the case. Pullin stepped back inside and over to his bar. He poured himself a shot of DeLeon Leona Anejo Tequila. It was a smooth, sipping tequila that left a lingering euphoria with every sip. He had a decoy in place in both the Pacific and Atlantic operations, but it was too soon to panic and use it.

"What is it you need me to do on the East Coast?" Crispin asked, interrupting his thoughts.

"Keep an eye on the FBI's ongoing investigation. I don't want any surprises. I have a contact for you. He's embedded and can get you everything you'll need."

Pullin leaned against the bar.

"And if they get too close?" Crispin asked.

"Distract them or eliminate them. We need to buy ourselves more time. The next thirty to sixty days are critical." He took another sip of the caramel liquor. "Have your guys finish up. *The Locust* will take what you can get them in the next twelve hours. Just don't let your guys be noticed."

"Consider it done. We'll get as many as we can and finish things up here," Crispin said.

"Remember, Garrett Scott was good, and they put him in the ground."

Pullin ended the conversation by draining the rest of his shot glass and hitting the end button.

Chapter Thirteen

THE KING'S HEAD — PORTLAND, MAINE — 1:20 P.M.

A cute waitress set two poured beers next to a bowl of pretzels on a table-top. One was cloudy and dark and the other practically clear. Matt reached for the stout stein and took a tentative sip.

"You okay?" Brian asked.

"Not really. You'd think I'd be used to this by now," Matt said, taking a few pretzels but not eating them. He just moved them around in his hand, lost in thought.

"This is different."

Matt nodded with his head down.

The King's Head Pub was just off Commercial Street next to the harbor. It was an old redbrick building with exposed beams and natural wood, part of what was once an old dockside warehouse. It had fallen prey to the ever-crushing wave of modernization. Matt and Brian had taken up residence at a front corner table with a view across the water. Moored boats bobbed in a slow repeating cycle as gentle swells moved through the harbor. Dark clouds threatened a change in the weather.

"Don't worry, Matt. We'll find her. Besides, you know Codi. This seems to be her MO," Brian said, before taking a sip of his craft Pilsner. The calming words seemed to have no influence on Matt who was unusually uptight.

"Doesn't make it any easier sitting here hoping she'll be okay. It's the least effective scientific method I know. I mean, she was right here." He gestured with open hands. "And now, two days later . . . gone."

"What do you mean?" Brian asked.

"Nothing," Matt said, trying to bury his answer in a chug of beer.

Brian set his glass down and leaned forward. "Matt, we've been friends long enough that I know when you're holding back. Let it out. You'll feel better."

Brian sat back and let Matt take his time. He opened his hands as if to say *whenever you're ready, I'm here.*

"I almost made the biggest mistake of my life."

"How so?" Brian asked.

"I was all ready to propose to Codi. Had the ring and everything. It was going to be . . ." He paused, reflecting on the recent past's events. "The perfect moment. And like a switch being thrown, she got a call and was gone. She never even knew. Maybe I read the whole thing wrong between us. I need to hit the brakes and reevaluate."

"*No.* No. No. This is good, Matt. Congratulations. I think you two will be great together." Brian slapped his hand on the table for emphasis. "We are all slaves to the machine, and Codi isn't any different. How much is a choice we make. Sometimes, things happen that are out of our control. It doesn't mean anything . . . it just is. We both know that when lives are at stake, Codi puts everything else in her life on the backburner."

Matt nodded his agreement.

Brian continued. "I wouldn't read too much into a blown-up weekend, and honestly, 'the perfect moment' is overrated. It took me three tries to get my proposal right, and by the last one, it just sorta happened at my cousin's high school lacrosse game. Weak sauce I know, but it isn't any less important to Leila or me. In fact, it's one of the things that define our marriage."

"What do you mean?" Matt asked.

"Things rarely go as planned. Kids, family, spouse, sports, piano lessons, friends, work—the list is endless. There is always something. It's how we act to fix or overcome the problems that really define us. Honestly, Leila and I have been overcoming and adapting since day one, and I don't think we would have it any other way."

Matt's eyes drifted to the ceiling in thought.

"You just have to start the journey with a first step. It doesn't have to be a leap, and with Codi, it probably shouldn't be."

Matt considered Brian's words of encouragement. He had planned to table the idea of proposing to Codi. She was too special to lose, and he had felt like he almost lost her, but in truth, she was too special to *not* act and move forward. He nodded at his new resolve and leaned back in his seat, both hands wrapped around his beer.

"Ok, say you're right," Matt said. "How would you, with what you know about Codi, go about proposing? I'm afraid I'm all thumbs when it comes to romance . . . and mind you, this stays right here."

Brian took a large gulp of beer. He had managed to turn Matt back around but romance advice—*not his thing*. This would be like a snake trying to draw a straight line.

***

Codi doubled over. The pain in her abdomen was excruciating. After many hours of throwing up until her stomach was out of bile, she was dizzy with a pounding headache that now was affecting her vision. Trooper Smith was three cells over from her, and he had been shivering for at least a day. The passage of time was impossible to predict, especially in a constantly well-lit room with no windows. When you're sick, every second seems to go by slowly. She could only hope that her actions with Joel had saved him from the misery she and Trooper Smith were enduring. Two hours ago or so, the man in the lab coat had given both her and her neighbor a shot. He said it was a vaccine, but by the obvious results of the others, the cages with even numbers were getting screwed. Codi had watched as every few hours a round of shots were administered to each set of cages, slowly working their way toward her. Over time, the ones in the odd-numbered cages seemed to be getting better. But the evens were all on a fast track to death.

Eventually, Codi lost all interest in her surroundings as she became too sick to care. After all that she had done and overcome in life, she was going to end up as a dead lab rat. She squatted in her cage. Her legs were too tired to stand. Wilma in the cage next to her was lost to a rampant fever and was speaking gibberish.

Codi looked up to see Matt staring at her from just outside the glass. He was smiling. It took a moment for her to understand his words. "You can do this, Codi. Fight it." His strong chiseled face and piercing green eyes that opened to a very good soul were just what Codi had needed. A partner in life that had her back and her heart. He made her a better woman because she wanted to be, not the other way around. She would have to tell him so. Love . . . something she hadn't known since her father died, and with it came both fear and comfort. Matt reached for her. Codi lifted her hand to take his, but her fingers fell short against the glass wall. She mumbled a garbled sentence meant for him, as he slowly started to fade away. She panicked and called for him to stay.

A bang on the cell from her cellmate across from her caught her attention, and the vision vanished. The young man in thirteen was twitching, and then his body went rigid. His skin turned red and then paled, and he slowly stopped breathing. Codi leaned over to get a closer view. The man whose name she had finally pried out of him, John Brown, was dead. And he had been given what Codi guessed was the vaccine. It was a sobering thought of what was to come—a horrible death. *Please hurry up and take me,* she prayed.

Dr. Kamba had supervised the first two subjects' removal on *The Mantis* lab, P1 and P2. At forty-eight hours, P1 had been given the vaccine and P2, the placebo. P1 had quickly recovered and was despondent, but otherwise looked healthy. P2 had severe symptoms and would be dead within a few hours. Each was removed from their clear prisons, washed down, and carried and/or escorted out of the room.

They were laid on a gurney and given a shot that would put them to sleep. Once out, a second shot would be administered that would stop their hearts. The corpses were then autopsied very carefully. Dr. Kamba looked for intestinal perforation and to what level the bacteria ate its way into the patients' organs. For the subject with the vaccine, they looked for side effects and signs of healing, along with any possible lasting damage. Each patient displayed differently, as they either had more time with the infection or more time with the cure, and each step along the way gave key insights into the experiment.

When the dissection was finished, the bodies were taken to a small room with an incinerator where they would be disposed of.

Dr. Kamba was encouraged by the initial results. Just like the mice they had used before, the human specimens were reacting well to the vaccine.

The process continued in a weird sort of countdown in the lab. Each pair of test subjects were taken but never returned. The count slowly worked its way down to zero. Some patients lay dead in their cells; some were perfectly healthy.

Kyber entered the crematorium as Dr. Kamba was supervising the cremation of P9 and P10.

"We've got a small problem," he said.

Dr. Kamba looked over at her partner.

"P13 is dead. I initially thought he was just unconscious."

"And he was given the vaccine—"

"Four hours ago," Kyber said."

"TOD?"

"Maybe thirty minutes."

"Okay," Dr. Kamba said, "let's get him on a table and see what happened. Hopefully, it wasn't a reaction to the vaccine."

"Already done."

She sighed. "I guess we can go ahead and dispose of P14 and finish up with the last two, P11 and P12, at the next interval. I think we have everything we need from this round of testing. Might as well finish up so we can move to the next phase."

"Yes. I'd like to get this behind us and start producing the vaccine," Kyber said, as he headed for the door to finish things off.

"Oh, hang on a sec," Dr. Kamba said with a curious look on her face. "I just thought of something."

Kyber paused and half-turned to Dr. Kamba. She had her index finger pressed against her chin in contemplation.

"We are probably past the cut-off time, but what if we give P14 the vaccine? It will most likely be ineffective at this late stage, but it might give us something worthwhile in the autopsy. A sort of beyond-the-point-of-no-return response."

***

The Portland Police Department is a three-story modern redbrick affair with plenty of glass and extra parking. It is located on the corner of Franklin and Middle Street, in the northeast part of town. The inside is dressed in functional white paint and faux wood.

Special Agent Reyas and his partner Anna Green were given a room just off the detectives' bullpen on the second floor. It was clean and had several tables and chairs to work from. They were assigned two detectives, Havok and Press, to help where possible, and were given very little to go on.

Havok was a short no-nonsense man with a hooked nose and a sour demeanor. He was an energy drink fiend and had the jitters to go with it. Everything he wore was black, which seemed to match his personality.

Press was a chubby Hispanic with a positive attitude. Over the years, he had eaten a few too many donuts and his hairstyle seemed to match—a bald spot in the center with a ring of hair around it. He had a sharp intellect, which directly contradicted his fashion sense.

"Okay, let's put it all on the board," Anna said.

Gordon pulled out a red dry-erase pen and started to fill in the large whiteboard mounted on the east wall as Anna ticked off her thoughts.

"Codi and Trooper Smith went aboard *The Mantis* at approximately 4:00 p.m.. The ship left the harbor twenty minutes later and headed south, for . . . where did Joel say?"

Anna looked through the notes taken during Joel's bedside briefing. "Here it is, Maracaibo. Where is that?"

"Venezuela, I think," Gordon replied as he wrote the information on the board.

"Okay, so let's get the USCG up to speed and have them intercept *The Mantis* as soon as possible."

"On it," Detective Press called out as he headed to one of the room's phones.

Anna continued, "We know that the shipping company is held by a Panamanian company that was involved in renting the vehicle Garret Scott used during his attempted murder of Codi and Joel."

"And we have to assume that they are up to something illegal if they are willing to kidnap three officers of the law," Gordon added.

"Anything else?" Havok asked.

Nothing.

"Okay," Gordon said. "Let's get on the security footage at the harbor and see if we can pick up anything."

The knowns were few, but it was a start.

***

Brian shook out his umbrella and placed it in the holder. He moved down the patterned carpet, past onlookers and clinking utensils. He turned into a room on the left and shook hands with his boss. He removed his coat, placed it on the back of his chair, and sat down across the table from him. Director Lyon was a politically connected power dealer in Washington. He had enemies and allies, and he knew how to use both to his advantage. He ordered a single malt and gestured to Brian.

"I'll have an Arnold Palmer, please," he told the waiter.

"I'm glad you could make the time to meet for lunch. We don't do this often enough."

"Well, when the boss calls . . ." Brian said, lamely.

"I keep hearing good stuff about your division."

"Thank you. My team works very hard."

"I'm sure they do, but a team is only as good as its coach."

Brian nodded nonchalantly. Puffery was not his strong point.

"I have an opening coming up for an assistant director, and a man of your talents who can follow orders would fit the bill nicely."

"Thank you, Director Lyon. I am . . . well, I'm kinda taken aback by your generosity."

"Honestly, if you get the position, you will have earned it," he replied.

This statement made Brian feel uneasy.

Director Lyon took a sip from his leaded crystal glass.

"I'm a team player if that's what you're asking, sir," Brian said, not sure where the conversation was going.

"Good," Director Lyon said as he leaned back and examined his underling much like a person selecting the perfect steak in a grocery store.

"I get the idea you are in need of something," Brian probed, uneasy with his boss's scrutiny.

"Not me as much as someone much higher up the food chain. Someone who can make things happen or kill a person's career before it ever gets going."

The waiter arrived and took their lunch orders.

Le Diplomate was a 'must be seen at' lunch spot for Capitol Hillers. It had green tiled walls with plenty of windows, excellent lighting, and white veined-marble tabletops. It was an homage to French café culture and could house private parties of up to one hundred guests. Director Lyon had reserved one of the smaller private rooms for their lunch meeting. The conversation turned back to more generic topics. Once the food arrived, small talk completely ceased.

Director Lyon suddenly set his fork down and gazed up at Brian. Brian stopped mid-chew.

"I have decided to be straight with you."

Brian swallowed and wiped his mouth with his linen napkin.

"The case you are overseeing right now, the one with the ship."

"Yes?"

"It has some kind of political ramifications. I'm getting way too much interest from someone much higher up. I'll do my part to figure who and why, but I'll need you to do your part and cross every *t* and dot every *i*. Tread very carefully on this one, SSA Brian Fescue."

"I will, sir, and thank you for the heads-up."

"Oh, and I'll need daily updates from your agents," he threw the last words out like an aside.

Director Lyon gave him a brief nod and picked his fork back up. "So how's the family?"

***

The sixth test subject cried as she was locked into the clear Lexan cube on *The Locust's* lab. It was set up just like its sister ship, *The Mantis,* with fourteen cages for human testing. She was an older woman with shoulder-length mostly-gray hair and had been taken from her morning routine just as she returned home from walking her dog, Cupid. The small fluffy, white and black mixed-breed mutt just watched as the woman let out a single cry for help before being injected and carried out the back door into a waiting van. The men responsible were kind enough to leave the house door propped open so the dog had a chance at survival. The woman awoke to a blur of passing overhead lights as two men pushed her on a gurney down a white hallway.

They took her into a large room that looked very scientific. Resistance was futile, as they were much too strong for her. There were fourteen clear cubes all in a row in the middle of the room. She was bolted inside one with the number three printed on the side. She screamed and banged on her clear prison walls until she was too weak to continue. A quick look around told her she was not alone. Other people were being loaded into the cells around her.

Santos checked his watch. Time was up; six subjects would have to do. He loaded the even-numbered cells with infected flies and the odd numbers with infected cockroaches. There was some serious panicking and screaming for a few minutes, but eventually, everyone ran out of steam. He made a note on his tablet and started the countdown. Dr. Mahl pushed through the lab, his mind focused on a task.

"With only six test subjects we should give each one the vaccine every twenty-four hours," said his assistant, Santos. "This will give us a good idea of when it is most effective and when it is no longer viable over the six-day period."

Dr. Mahl paused to listen. Santos made good sense.

"Do it. But give them a full forty-eight hours before starting."

Santos nodded. "We should be getting the results from *The Mantis* shortly," he said. "I'll add their data to ours. They'll have the results on the placebo subjects."

"Sounds good."

Dr. Mahl pulled a granola bar from his pocket and ripped it open. "Santos, I am confident that what we have here will work as planned. My only concern is the unknown variables the real world might throw at us, and I don't think we will get that here in a lab with six subjects."

Santos nodded in understanding.

Dr. Mahl continued as he chewed. "We are out of time, so we might have to just go for it and see."

"Not very scientific of us," Santos replied.

"Exactly."

"I'm going to check on Dr. Sales and see how his bugs are coming." Santos turned and headed for the exit door.

The Locust had left the dock at noon and was just then steaming under the Golden Gate Bridge. It would take another hour to reach international waters, but they had experienced no problems so far. Captain Combs stood on the bridge imagining the great journey before them. During the next three months, *The Locust* would lay siege to many cities along her way, starting a pandemic without compunction. It would be glorious.

***

Codi lay folded in the bottom of her cell in *The Mantis* lab, her head against the glass. There was an inch of excrement mixed with vomit on the floor, mostly the chunks that hadn't drained, but she no longer cared. With her eyes at half-mast, she longed for death. It couldn't come soon enough.

She had watched as innocents had been hauled from their cages and never returned. Two men in biohazard suits would use a small drill motor to remove the bolts holding the clear cage to the floor. It was then lifted off and the subject was rinsed off and carried away. One thing for sure she knew—they were never coming back.

Every few hours, two more victims were taken away. And now that the young man in the cell across from her had died, she was one of only three left. Trooper Smith was turning the corner and had stopped shivering. Wilma next to her looked dead, and Codi was not far behind. Two men in bio suits moved for Trooper Smith's cage. This was it for him and there was nothing she could do to stop it.

The Trooper was washed down, pulled out, and placed on a gurney. The men used kind words like, let's get you out of here and someplace safe. Codi knew it was a ruse. She pressed her face to her cell wall and watched as they wheeled him out of the room, knowing she would never see him again.

She felt the vibration on her cage as the two men unscrewed the bolts. Once it was lifted off, a stream of water shed some of the horror she had worn for the last few days. They seemed to be in a sudden hurry, like a long-distance runner when they see the finish line. Codi was the last one, and then they would be finished with whatever it was they were up to. After the two men rinsed her off, one grabbed her under the arms and the other took her legs. She was a rubbery mess of infection and death. Her head lolled for the floor as a kaleidoscope of images blurred past her warped vision.

They laid her on a gurney and rolled her into a room off to the left and closed the door. Inside, Trooper Smith was lying next to Wilma, both on gurneys. He was being restrained, but Wilma was not moving. One of the men gave Trooper Smith a shot and watched as he stopped struggling. The two men in biohazard suits moved to do the same to Wilma. Codi looked around and realized what was happening. An autopsy saw was on the table with several nasty-looking tools. This was the end of the line.

She willed herself to act. Anything, something. They injected Wilma and her face lolled in Codi's direction. She seemed too calm, looking peaceful for the first time since they had met. The man with the needle moved back to the table to reload. The other man, not worrying about Codi, was using scissors to cut off the last remnants of underwear from the other two patients.

The man with the needle returned and placed it on her neck and started to push it in. Codi knew this was it—act now or never again. She had been slowly feeling better and better since she had been given the second injection. It must have been the vaccine. It was slow to work, but it was working. Her only plan was to play as dead as possible, which, based on her situation was easy. She grabbed the needle out of the man's hand, flipped it around, and buried it into his thigh before he knew what happened. With a forceful plunge, she injected him with the contents.

"Hey!" he screamed as the situation dawned on him as to what had just occurred.

The other man looked up as his partner started to wobble and dropped to the floor with a heavy thud. Before he could react, Codi got off the gurney and grabbed the cadaver saw from the table. It was a battery-powered Stryker model 812. Codi flipped the switch and a nasty whine began, as the front blade came to life. It was made to cut easily into bone with minimal damage to soft tissue. When used as a weapon, it was like a hunting knife on steroids.

Codi stayed between her target and the exit. He would not be leaving the room. The sudden action after days of being trapped in a cage had her breaking out in a sweat and breathing heavy. She was far from well but was living on adrenalin to finish the job. The man lunged at her with his scissors to test her skill. They were the blunt-tipped medical-style used by many EMTs. Codi was a bit slower than normal but good enough to leave him with a nice slice on his forearm. He dropped his scissors and pulled back to check his wound. A collection of deadly tools on the side table caught his attention. Codi leaned in that direction to counter his thoughts. He panicked and dove under Trooper Smith's gurney out of sight.

Codi crouched behind her gurney and started to push it with all her might. She shoved it so hard that it smacked into Wilma's and moved her gurney as well, accordion-folding all three and smashing them into her target hiding against the wall. A *humph* was heard as the impact of metal on bones could be heard. Trooper Smith's body rolled off his gurney, adding a second thud. The man climbed out from under the pile with a gash on his head and anger in his eyes. He flew at Codi with all his might, eager for payback.

Codi was no match for the healthy male. She had just used all her strength pushing the gurneys into a pile. She let her assailant come and used his momentum against him. She stepped out of his way at the last second, leaving a swath of cadaver saw in his midsection, just before she was knocked to the floor. The saw flew from her hand. The man reached for the doorknob to make his escape. He started to turn the knob, but his fingers grew weak and his body gradually sagged to the floor, leaving behind a smear of blood on the metal door. Codi had left her mark.

She lay on the cold floor for an unknown amount of time and then stood on unstable legs. Moving over to Wilma, she checked for a pulse—nothing. The kindly woman had died, and there was nothing Codi could do for her now but mourn. And that would have to wait.

Trooper Smith, on the other hand, was still breathing. He looked like he had just lain down on the floor to take a nap. He could also wait, and so could the man she had injected.

First, Codi needed to get control of her situation, and hiding in this room was not a strategic plan. Her mind was muddled. Every thought hurt, but the hope of freedom, no matter how unrealistic, pushed her forward.

***

Back on *The Locust*, Dr. Mahl was satisfied with the results they were getting. His first patient had recovered. This was exactly as expected. The woman's autopsy had shown unique isolation of the pathogen throughout all tissues.

He was still waiting for the results to come in from *The Mantis* that showed both sides of the progression: the placebo, which resulted in death by organ failure and the vaccine administered at various intervals. But nothing so far. Perhaps he would try a secured call later when he had more time. He had picked up an egg salad sandwich he was working his way through in an attempt to stop his stomach from growling.

Dr. Mahl had given the replication of the vaccine a lot of thought. It was the most important part of their plan. They had three industrial gene replicators on board, as did *The Mantis*.

Over the course of their three-month trip, they should each be able to produce twenty-five million doses, give or take. With the addition of the fifty million doses produced at the main lab back in Nevada, that would make one hundred million shots available. By the time the world's population had reset they would be dearly needed.

The replicators were built using Dr. Mahl's strict instructions. They used key proteins and biotics and a special synthesized nucleotide-polymerizing enzyme. Each machine then stripped the enzyme down to the molecular level and reconfigured the parts into a computer-controlled soup that, when incubated for forty-eight hours, became a viable vaccine. It was much like the hi-tech machines used to make smart televisions. You put silica sand and a few other base ingredients in on one side and a finished TV came out on the other.

Against a world in crisis, one hundred million doses would not be enough, but they would be worth their weight in platinum to those who could afford it. Certainly enough to abate the epidemic from many cities. Once on the other side, it would be a new world. One that was able to sustain its population and one where the power structure would look very different. Because, if scientists governed the world, logic and procedure would prevail.

Chapter Fourteen

The security video played, and all four officers watched. They could clearly see Joel, Codi, and Trooper Smith walk up the gangplank of *The Mantis*. The angle was obtuse, and the man they met at the top of the boat was unidentifiable other than white male, brown hair, shaved face. They scanned forward with no further coming or going. Twenty minutes later, the ship left port.

"Not much to go on," Gordon said.

The words hung in the air for a moment. The task force room at the Portland Police Department grew quiet.

"How is the Coast Guard fairing?" Anna asked, breaking the silence.

"*The Mantis* has turned off her AIS, so they're having trouble locating her. The satellite sweeps have not identified the ship yet, but USCG has multiple ships covering all major routes southward. We'll spot 'em," Gordon replied. The phone in his pocket rang. He looked at the ID and answered it on the third ring. "Boss."

"Hey, Gordon, can you put me on speaker?"

Gordon pressed the button and set the phone on the table. He said, "SSA Fescue, you also have Anna and detectives Havok and Press."

167

"Good. Just wanted to give you all a heads-up. This case has gone political. Somebody with some juice is asking for details of the investigation to be passed along. It came down from my boss, and he said the same thing to me, so I'm telling you. You are to watch yourselves. Everything by the book, as normal, moving forward. I'll need daily updates of your shared findings."

Gordon and Anna realized what this meant—a lot more work with fewer results.

"Do you understand?" Brian asked.

"Ah, sure," Gordon replied.

"We understand," Anna added forcefully.

"Good." With that, Brian hung up.

"Great. We just doubled our paperwork," Gordan said as he put his phone back in his pocket.

"I see bullcrap runs at every level," Detective Havok said.

"He was giving us a message," Anna stated.

"What?" Gordon replied.

"Send daily updates of our *shared* findings. He was telling us to not send anything that might compromise the case."

"*Whoa.* We need to tread very carefully from here on out," Gordon said, grasping the implication as the words left his mouth.

All three nodded in understanding.

***

Codi peeked out the door. The lab was empty. She stripped the unconscious man of his white biohazard suit and put it on. The hood attached to the full-face gas mask, which filtered contaminates down to .015 microns. She picked up the cadaver saw and selected a bone mallet from the table. It was an all-stainless steel hammer with a chiseled back and flat front. The handle ended in a large fishhook that was used for prying off the upper skull from the lower.

She stepped out into *The Mantis* lab like she owned the place. The first thing that hit her was the fourteen Lexan cages that stood in the middle of the room. They were all empty. It made her blood boil. The last few days had been a nightmare from beyond the grave. Codi had prayed for death, but against all expectations, the late shot she had received was working. Feeling two steps up from death on a scale of fifty, she moved to the next door and opened it slowly. Inside were several refrigerators with glass doors. They held many blood and tissue samples. A quick look around revealed nothing more. She turned to leave.

***

Kyber was sitting at his desk staring absently at the screen. It displayed a chart he had built showing the rate of infection and the rate of cure based on the time of injection, all set against the duration of symptoms. It might seem complex to some, but it was now their new bible for *Salmonella Typhi X*. Kyber tapped on the desk with his fingers. He had reached his limit. The last three subjects had been taken to autopsy, and it would soon be over. He knew the importance of the work they were doing, but the human subjects were too much. They had carelessly used, abused, and then tossed the lives of fourteen people, all for the chart on the screen right in front of him.

He would not see it go to waste. Kyber sent a copy of everything they had done to date, including details on the vaccine, through the cloud to his own personal email, as well as a second backup to Dr. Mahl on *The Locust*. He double-checked that everything copied over and then closed out the program. Deciding the best thing for him right now would be a stiff drink—or three—he switched off his computer and headed for the galley. Starting tomorrow, they would be working on generating as many doses of vaccine as possible. That was more to his liking.

After donning scrubs for the autopsies, Dr. Kamba left her office and headed for the lab. She spied Dr. Pendergrass as he left his room with the incubators and headed her way.

"When did you say we would make port," he called out.

"Six more days," Dr. Kamba replied.

Dr. Pendergrass did a quick calculation in his head. "Good. I'll be ready with the first batch, and then every five to seven days after that, we'll be able to offload."

"That should work out just right," Dr. Kamba replied. "We're wrapping up our trials, so we'll be starting the replication process and begin to stockpile."

"It's gonna be a brave new world," he said, looking to the ceiling, imagining.

"It sure is," Dr. Kamba called as she turned back to her lab.

She stepped inside just as one of her workers in a bio-suit was stepping out of the storage room. He was holding the cadaver saw, and it had blood on it. In an instant, Dr. Kamba knew something was wrong. The body stance, the way he moved, and the two tools he wielded like weapons. She turned and reached for a control panel on the wall. She just needed to type in three numbers and the lab would go on lockdown, alerting the security team on the boat. She pressed the first two buttons before having to stop and defend herself from the *patient* who had somehow gotten loose and was now wearing a full bio-suit! Dr. Kamba snatched a large flask off the shelf and broke off the bottom on the hardened tabletop. She held the narrow part of the tube in her hand and used the sharp, jagged end like a knife. The man behind the facemask flicked on the cadaver saw. It sent a chill down Dr. Kamba's spine, as she was very familiar with what that tool could do.

She moved away as her attacker circled, holding her weapon out in front of her, each conscious of the other's weapon. They moved like two choreographed dancers unwilling to change the distance between them.

Her attacker paused and ripped his hood and mask off. It was a woman. Patient fourteen. How had she gotten loose?

"You should be dead," Dr. Kamba said. "The vaccine was given to you too late."

"I guess you'll have to change your specs," Codi spat at her.

"Incredible. You must have a very strong immune system. I must cut you open and see what's going on in there."

"Take a number." Codi followed the statement with a lunge with the cadaver saw and Dr. Kamba instantly realized the danger she was in.

They parried back and forth, each skilled enough to not make a fatal mistake. With sharp objects, maintaining distance was critical. You needed to stay out of the blood circle that could disable you in the fight. A cut on the arm or leg was acceptable, but anything on the torso or head could take you out. They moved around the lab using the Lexan cells and anything else to help shield them from each other. Two cats, each waiting for the other to make a mistake before pouncing.

Codi was getting tired. She had used all her energy taking out the last guy and was definitely not herself. The saw felt heavy in her hand. Dr. Kamba swiped at her face and missed her eye by less than an inch. *Codi, focus!* She wiped the sweat from her face with the back of her hand. Dr. Kamba swung a metal tray at Codi, and she used the cadaver saw against it. The metal blade cut into and then jammed on the edge of the tray. Dr. Kamba flung it away. The saw went with it. Now Codi had only her bone mallet. She moved behind a table, away from her attacker.

Codi leaned her elbows on the tabletop, trying to conserve her energy and catch her breath. Dr. Kamba smiled and moved slowly around the table. She would make quick work of the weakened subject.

"Time to die." She raised her jagged flask and approached from the side. Codi looked down, trying to catch her breath. She was out of ideas and energy. She would let the woman come close and try for a lucky shot. She checked the contents on the tabletop, and a simple idea came to her. With all her remaining strength, Codi swiped her arm across the table in Dr. Kamba's direction. There were glassware, tools, and a laptop. They all suddenly flew at the tall woman. Dr. Kamba reacted by covering her face as the flying debris headed toward her. Codi followed right behind it with a jump and an Indian tomahawk-style blow with her mallet. She let out a yell and made contact with the woman's left temple. The steel hammer crushed bone and drove the beveled end into her target's brain.

There was a jerking reaction followed by a complete shutdown of all vital functions. Dr. Kamba was dead before the debris hit the ground. She dropped to the floor like a rubber ball, her head bouncing off the hard surface. There were a few gurgles before her body stilled. Her face held a permanent look of surprise. After all the woman had done to fourteen innocent lives, Codi could care less. She pried the hammer free and staggered away, heading for her next target, anger the only thing driving her on.

***

Crispin parked his car in the U-shaped drive at Fish Point. It was the beginning of a dreary day with an ice-cold mist blowing off of the ocean. Rolling gray waves seemed to come one after another without a break. He walked past an old cannon on display and over to a large blue and tan gazebo in Fort Allen Park. It was elevated to give visitors a view of the bay while sheltering them from rain or sun. The park was empty this time of morning except for a lone jogger willing to brave the bitter weather. A lone male was in the gazebo staring at the ocean with a pair of binoculars.

"I see you found your way here," the man said, without lowering his binoculars. Crispin didn't feel like he needed to reply to the rhetorical question, so he just put his hands in his coat pockets trying to stay warm.

The man was a chubby African American with a bald spot right in the middle of his head. Crispin could tell his contact was jittery. It was probably the first time he had ever done something like this.

"I like to come here for the birds," he said, "and the fishing can be pretty good too."

"Detective Press, you are being well paid. How 'bout we just get right to it," Crispin said.

"Okay, sure." He almost lowered his binoculars but regrouped and continued. "We have looked at the security footage around the dock, and they know the three agents went on board *The Mantis* but never came off. The USCG is looking for them as we speak. They are tracking all routes to Maracaibo and other South American destinations. *The Mantis* has turned off their AIS, so we are not having any luck so far. Oh, and one of the FBI agents that went on board was found and rescued."

This last bit of information caught Crispin by surprise. Everything else seemed expected. "Interesting," he said. "Get me everything you can on the agent that was fished out of the sea. I want to know what he has said, or saw, or knows. Okay?"

"Of course."

Detective Press realized he was holding his breath and let it go in a slow controlled puff. "So when should we meet next?" he asked.

He waited for an answer, but when none came, he lowered his binoculars and looked. There was no one there.

***

Codi exited *The Mantis* lab into a white hallway. She guessed and turned right. There was a door with a large-handled lever. She rotated it up, opened the door, and stepped inside a large room. It was warm and muggy. It had a heavy earthy smell and a creepy vibe. Immediately, Codi was on alert. She stepped past a small desk and work area over to one of the six large metal tanks in the room. She opened the door to the one on the left. The smell overpowered her and she almost puked. She quickly put her hood and gasmask back on and continued in. There was a second door that would only open when the first one was closed, as a safety precaution. She followed the procedure clearly posted on the wall and stepped inside.

It was a nightmare. A small catwalk separated two honeycomb sides that were filled with thousands of cockroaches. Within seconds they were flying and crawling all over her. Even though she was safe in her suit, it was repulsive. She could feel them skittering across her arms, back, shoulders, and even her head. They made a faint crackling sound with each step against her bio-suit. She took a quick look around and saw everything she cared to. This must be where the cockroaches in her cell had come from, but why so many? Time to leave. Besides, she was starting to lose it; bugs weren't her thing. The door behind her opened. She spun as a man in nothing but a lab coat stepped inside.

"Hey! What are you doing in here? Your—"

As he spoke he realized the person in his incubator was holding a hammer. Something was wrong. He reached for a metal pole clipped to the wall that was used for cleaning. It was five feet long and made of aluminum. He held it two-handed like a spear ready to jab. Codi moved into a fighting stance, holding her hammer like a knife. Dr. Pendergrass jabbed at the intruder. Codi parried the pole away with a metallic clang. It was only a matter of time before he got lucky, as he had the advantage in distance. He could reach Codi, but she couldn't reach him, only the pole. The fight continued without a clear winner. Sparks flying off at every impact, the pole versus the hammer. With each thrust, Codi dodged or used her hammer to knock the pole away. The cockroaches seemed to sense something was wrong and took flight. The air filled with bugs, making it difficult for her to see her attacker.

Dr. Pendergrass suddenly stopped.

"No! My babies."

He had looked down and realized that Codi had been stepping on hundreds of cockroaches during their fight. There was a porridge of bug body parts and guts on the floor. He knelt down starting to cry, holding his hands out uselessly. "You've killed them."

Codi didn't wait. She threw the hammer with all her might. It flew true and straight, hitting the doctor in the chest. He was knocked back and the pole flew out of his hand. Codi stepped over and used her foot to knock him out. She picked up her hammer and exited the room, leaving the swarm behind. As she closed the first door a wind of strong insecticide spray flowed over her body, removing any loose bugs that had tried to hitchhike out. She opened the outer door and jammed a chair under it so it wouldn't close. Now the doctor would be trapped in the incubator, as the inner door would not open until the outer door was closed. The man was effectively a prisoner until she could come back later to fetch him.

Codi exited the room filled with the things of nightmares.

Chapter Fifteen

Codi moved back down the hallway away from bug central. She passed the door to *The Mantis's* main lab on the left and moved over to a door down on the right. Pulling her hood off and tossing it away, she took a large breath of air. It was too hot and claustrophobic to wear any longer. She was still running a fever, and the bio-suit was making her burn up. Pushing through the next door, she was hoping there were no more creepy-crawly surprises. She stepped into a white, modern, well-furnished kitchen and dining area. There were three tables with chairs and a small bar and island in the kitchen. The appliances were top notch, and it smelled like coffee.

Codi's taste buds immediately started to salivate. She moved to the island where she grabbed a breakfast bar and practically inhaled it. Next came a banana followed by an apple. She poured herself a cup of coffee from the pot that was steaming on the bar and stepped to the faucet where she poured some cold water into her coffee and guzzled it down. She refilled her cup with hot coffee, and now, she would savor it. As she turned to take in the rest of the room, a muffled flush was followed by a door opening. The man who had terrorized her for the last few days stepped into the room. He froze at the sight of her, watching in fear as she set her cup down and wrapped her hand around a hammer.

"Please . . . I am so sorry. I had no choice. If we are to save the world, a few sacrifices had to be made."

The man looked sincere, but after all the horrors he had inflicted on her, she would rather mash his brains in first and then listen.

"Save the world?" Codi asked in anger.

"Yes. I will show you. Please."

Codi held her hammer like a knife and finally nodded her approval. "Slowly. If you so much as twitch, I'll bury this hammer in your head."

The man nodded meekly and held his hands up like an inmate. He slowly walked for the exit door. Codi followed carefully behind, the food and coffee doing wonders for her energy. He led her back to the main lab and stepped over to his laptop. "May I?"

Codi nodded.

He entered his password. "There is going to be a major outbreak of a new antibiotic-resistant form of typhoid fever."

"A superbug?" Codi asked.

"Yes. But how did you kno—"

"Keep going," Codi ordered.

"We are all part of a team, put together to save humanity from the disease."

"Team? Are you with some government?" Codi asked.

"No. We . . . let me show you."

"That's enough. Hold it right there!"

Both Codi and Kyber turned at the suddenness of the voice behind them. It was the guard Codi had injected in the leg. He was standing ten feet away and holding a gun. *A gun? Where had he gotten that?* There was no way Codi could get to him before he fired. She opened her hands to her side and dropped her hammer. Kyber spun in his chair, and his arms shot to the sky.

"If things go badly, I have very specific instructions," said the guard.

The man had seen the carnage from the fight between Codi and Dr. Kamba. Her lifeless body lay on the floor with a small pool of blood around her head.

"And it looks like things have gone badly," he said. He pulled the trigger, shooting Kyber in the chest. The gun turned on Codi, freezing her in place. He reached over to a keypad on the wall beside him and entered several digits. The man re-aimed center mass at Codi's torso and squeezed the trigger. A thud came across his head, and the shot went wide. The shooter dropped to the floor with a gash on the back of his head. Trooper Smith stood buck-naked holding a bent microscope in his hands. His slight potbelly, hairy chest, and everything else on full display. He was still wobbly from his sedation, but he had timed his arrival perfectly.

An alarm sounded, and a calm voice followed. "Warning, lab will seal in thirty seconds."

Uh oh.

***

Captain Semenova sat in his swivel chair on the bridge, sipping a fresh cup of coffee. He gazed at the stacks of containers in front of him. It was a comforting sight. This was his domain and everything was running to perfection, just the way he liked it. A sudden beeping followed by a computerized voice pulled him from his thoughts.

"What the devil's going on?" Semenova bellowed.

"Sir, the lab's emergency closure procedure has been activated."

The captain stood and moved to look at the computer screen warning for himself.

"Okay, let's get someone down there to investigate. Scientists on a ship—I should have known better. And shut that alarm off!"

The alarm stopped as suddenly as it had started, making the bridge seem too quiet. Semenova listened over the radios as a security officer was dispatched to the lab. Now, all he could do was wait for the results and hope something very dangerous hadn't escaped.

Codi grabbed Trooper Smith by the hand and ran. There was one last door she had yet to try. She sprinted down the hallway pulling the loopy man that had just saved her life toward the end. They pushed through the door and into a small secure-looking room with no furniture or decorations. There was no exit, just a keypad and scanning unit mounted on the wall. Codi released Trooper Smith, and he slumped against the wall.

"I feel seasick."

"It's just the sedative wearing off. Come on," she said as she searched for a way out. "We need the code and someone who works here to use their hand on the scanner to get out." She paused to catch her breath. "Hopefully, the self-destruct doesn't include this room."

A beep alerted her, and the wall behind them started to slide open. She ducked behind it. An armed guard stepped inside. Naked Trooper Smith looked up and waved. "Hi."

"What's going on down—"

Trooper Smith leaned over and threw up.

"Warning, lab will seal in twenty seconds."

The guard stepped back, fearful of getting some crazy contagion on him, well aware that something nasty was going on in the lab.

Codi flew at the guard, grabbing his pistol in one hand and delivering a vicious blow to his head with her elbow. A shot fired off, just missing Trooper Smith. The guard staggered, but he held fast to his gun. Codi used her free hand to send another punch to his chin. She then dropped with all her weight, prying the gun away. Before he could recover, she pointed the gun his way.

He paused and raised his hands in surrender. Trooper Smith stood, feeling slightly better. He wiped his mouth with the back of his hand.

"Warning, lab will seal in ten seconds."

"We'll have those clothes," Codi said, pointing the gun in their captive's direction. "But first, let's step into the hallway."

The man dropped a few expletives Codi's way, as he stepped backward into the hallway. The sliding door behind them started to close. Trooper Smith had to scramble to get out in time. Once their captive was undressed and Trooper Smith redressed, Codi took his radio and handed it to her partner. She still wore the white bio-suit, and she was starting to seriously chafe, as it was meant to be worn with clothes under it. Codi quickly realized her worst fear—they were still on board the ship in the middle of the Atlantic.

***

Joel walked into the room. He was gaunt, and his eyes looked sunken behind his glasses. He had been through the icy depths of hell and come out the other side.

"Joel! What are you doing here? You should be resting," Gordon exclaimed at the sight of his fellow agent.

Anna stepped over and gave him a big hug. "So good to see you. Welcome back."

She knew Joel would not rest long with his partner in harm's way, so she introduced him to Detectives Havok and Press.

Gordon reached his hand out. "Never mind me. I'd do the same thing." As they shook hands, a big smile grew across Gordon's face. "You going to be alright?" he asked.

Joel nodded.

"Agent Strickman, I know they took your statement at the hospital," Detective Press said, "but it would be a real help if you could tell us everything you remember before going into the water."

"Okay."

Joel sat down and replayed everything he could remember from the time they went up the ramp until Codi pushed him over the railing. The agents in the room listened to every word. When Joel finished, there was a long moment of quiet.

"So what do we have?" Joel asked, breaking the silence.

The four agents joined in and brought Joel up to speed on the case.

"Has the Coast Guard picked up anything since they turned off their AIS?" Joel asked.

"Nothing yet," Gordon answered.

"What are the chances that Maracaibo was a ruse?" Joel asked.

"It's all we have to go on," Gordon replied. "The Atlantic is a big place with thousands of ships. If they are going in another direction, we just reduced our chances of catching them by eighty percent."

It was a sobering thought.

"We can expand the BOLO to more ports. If the ship does show up somewhere else, we'll get 'em," Anna said.

Joel nodded. "I've been thinking . . . this is more than just a simple smuggling operation."

"Why do you say that?" Detective Press asked.

"There is something going down on that ship. Something worth kidnapping a federal agent over." Joel paused to think for a second. "Detectives, are there any unsolved cases that have sprung up since *The Mantis* hit port?"

This was a new line of thinking. Detective Havok grabbed a phone and stabbed at the buttons. He spoke back and forth with his boss for a few moments and hung up. "We have eight new missing person cases that have been filed in the last two days," he said, looking at Joel.

This hit the room hard. No one spoke for a moment.

"I think they're taking people," Joel said. "This all started with the body-jacking of Typhoid Mary. Then the murders of Detective Jensen and Codi's mother, and the attempted murders of Codi and myself, all to stop us from investigating. It's all connected somehow."

"If it is, we're missing some pretty big chunks if we're going to put it together and have it make sense," Gordon said.

He was right. They were missing too many pieces, and Joel was seeing a connection that didn't exist. The phone on the desk rang. Detective Havok picked it up.

He listened for a second. "What is it? Seriously?" he said. "Okay, thanks."

He hung up the phone in slow motion.

"Make that nine, we just had another missing person report come in."

***

Codi held the gun on their prisoner as the three moved down the metal hallway in the bowels of *The Mantis*.

"We need to get to the radio room and get some help," Trooper Smith said.

With the tip of her gun, Codi prodded the guard dressed only in boxer shorts in front of her. "Which way to the radio room?"

"You'll never get there alive," he sneered.

"Let us worry about that. You just worry about answering my questions, or you'll never make it out of this hallway."

"Three levels up. D Deck, Room 201," he said.

"How many of you are there?" Codi asked, trying to decide if she believed him.

"Eight security and twelve crew," he said with a smirk.

Twenty in total, seven of them armed. The number seemed high, but Codi had been in worse situations. She had escaped from the lab, and now, it was time to get off this ship.

"Special Agent Sanders, what's the play here?" Trooper Smith whispered.

"Call me Codi, and we need to see what we're up against and find a way off this ship."

"Okay, which way?" Codi asked the prisoner.

"There's a set of stairs at the end of this hall," he said.

Codi shoved her gun in the man's back to move him along.

"Trooper Smith," she said, "do you have a first name?"

"Walther, like the pistol. What can I say, my dad loved guns. I got a brother named Colt and a little sister, Remington . . . Remi, for short. But everyone calls me Thor," he said.

Codi looked at him, questioning.

"Remi couldn't pronounce my name when she was just a tyke. It just stuck."

"Well, Thor, I had the perfect weapon for you earlier but had to drop it back in the lab. By the way, thank you for saving my life."

"Feeling's mutual."

She felt like she owed the man much more, but a simple thanks would have to do for now.

The prisoner said, "It's just up these stairs, I'll show you—"

"Hold it!" Codi commanded.

Their captive stopped.

"Relax," he said, "I was just going up the stairs."

Codi used her pistol to move him back to the hallway with Thor. "You two stay here. I'll take a look. Here." She handed the gun to Thor. "If he moves, shoot him."

"Right." Thor nodded and pointed the pistol at their captive.

Codi moved stealthily up the steps. She stayed low as she came to the top, not wanting to be seen.

Thor watched his charge like a hawk, not giving him an inch.

"You know you're in the middle of the Atlantic Ocean," the prisoner said. "There's no way off this boat."

"We could take a lifeboat," Thor said.

"The moment a lifeboat is released from its carriage, the bridge would get an alert and the captain would spin the ship around and run you over."

"Shut up," Thor ordered.

"I can help you survive this."

"How?"

"You give me the gun, and I'll take you both in and reason with the captain. We'll drop you at our next port of call. Our lab is finished. You two saw to that. That means we are all done here. Everyone on board will scatter the moment we hit land."

"Ryan, what's going on? What did you find?"

The squawk from the radio on Thor's belt distracted him for just a beat. He looked down. The guard, Ryan, leaped. He grabbed the gun, and the two men struggled, each unwilling to release their hold on the pistol. It was an ugly fight with head butts and knee jabs. Bodies were slammed against steel walls, and they finally ended up on the floor. Thor finally did a quick twist that rolled Ryan over on top of him and slammed his head into the base of the metal staircase. It was enough to push the gun lower, but it was still a wrestling match. This guy was tough.

Codi spied down the next hallway one floor up. It had many doors on both sides. A crew member walked away in the distance and exited a door at the far end on the right. Codi waited until he was long gone. She had turned to withdraw back down the steps when a gunshot echoed all around. Fearing the worst, she sprinted down to investigate.

Thor was standing in the hallway covered in blood, still holding the gun. The man they had captured was lying on the floor.

"Are you okay?" Codi asked.

"Yeah, most of this is not my mine," Thor said while wiping blood from his broken nose.

"What happened?"

"He moved."

***

In *The Locust* lab, Dr. Mahl looked over the downloaded files sent from Kyber on *The Mantis*. The chart was most impressive. Kyber had taken all the variables and their results and put them in a colorful graph that was not only easy to read but also showed impressive results. Results that were well within their projected requirements for success.

Dr. Kamba and her team were doing great work over on *The Mantis*. Given the nature of their subjects and the lack of outside influences, he predicted they would have close to ninety percent success rate on his expected findings. It was the variables out in the field he couldn't control, but operation HYDRA was too important not to push forward no matter the results.

This would be his crowning achievement, and in time, the world would come to appreciate and praise his efforts.

He turned his head back to Santos and called out, "We have the results from *The Mantis.*"

Santos stepped over to view the files. "Send me a copy."

"Done." He sent the files. "I now feel confident we can close up our operations here and focus on delivery and replication."

"You don't want to finish off the last two subjects? We only have twenty-four hours left."

"No. I think we have all we need. Get 'em cleaned up and out," Dr. Mahl replied.

Santos gave his boss a nod and moved to dispose of their last two living subjects. He would be glad to move to the next phase. He was tired of listening to them whine and moan. From here on, they were one hundred percent operational.

***

Codi knew they needed to find a hiding place and make a plan. They stuffed the dead man Thor had shot into a storage room and moved aft. Codi had taken the gun back from Thor, as he might be a bit too trigger-happy in her opinion. They moved up the stairs of *The Mantis*. The hallway one level up was lined with doors. It had the same green textured floor as the lower hallway and a single railing along the right wall to help navigate during rough weather. The hallway turned out to hold berths for the crew.

Codi and Thor ditched their outfits for clothes that fit much better. She tossed her underwear that had gone through hell and used a wet towel to clean off before redressing in a pair of jeans and a tee-shirt. She paused to look in a mirror and was shocked to see a ghost of her former self staring back. Her hair was stringy and dirty, she had lost a lot of weight, and her cappuccino eyes seemed dull and sunken in. In a word, she was a mess. The adrenalin that had first powered her through the lab had long dissipated, and she was running on sheer force of will. The battle that was raging inside her as the vaccine fought against the bacteria was tangible.

Thor slipped inside her room. Codi grabbed her gun and spun in his direction.

"Hey," he said.

"Sorry."

He was wearing brown dockers and a blue polo shirt with the ship's logo on it.

"We should finish clearing the rooms on this level. Stay close," Codi said.

They moved from room to room making sure all was clear. Once finished, they moved back to the stairwell that led to the next level. At the end of the hall was a door with a port window. Daylight was streaming through, and it called to them.

"We need to get off this ship," Codi whispered.

"If we take a lifeboat, an alarm will sound."

"Figures." Codi thought for a minute. "I say *The Mantis* is past due for a mutiny."

***

The report was due on Friday, but Matt was too despondent to care. He had gone back to D.C. and his job, hoping to distract himself from the thoughts that clung to him like flies on a donut. The EXACTO project had been moving well, and they had yet to find any major deficiencies with the self-guided bullets. They had tried wind, rain, even extreme dust, but the bullet found its mark each time. They would start on moving targets next week and extreme obstacles after that. Right now, he just had to finish this report.

Matt typed a few more words and then told himself he could pick it all up later. There had been no word from Codi or Brian, who had promised to keep him informed of any developments. Matt vacillated. He could go home and worry or stay here and get nothing done. He decided on a third option and headed for Maggie's down the street. He would use some quality alcohol to help him plan his next proposal. No sense in expecting a bad outcome when Codi was involved. She had a way of beating the odds, even with a perp's ripped-off arm. The thought brought a much-needed smile to his face. He grabbed his keys and left.

***

Pullin knew his days on the Lake Tahoe estate were numbered. As the world became chaotic, he would need to move operations to a more remote locale. He had planned for every conceivable contingent, but as with any war, no one could completely cover every variable.

One of Pullin's gifts was to make you believe that his vision of an operation was yours. He had a brilliance for spin-doctoring anything to make it look like you had thought it up. He had been especially good when it came to Dr. Mahl, and now the good doctor was off implementing Pullin's plan with full passion and conviction as if it had been his all along. His two captains were just as committed to the cause. That kind of dedication allowed Pullin to remain just distant enough, in case problems arose. He could pivot and reassess things from a safe objective position. He would be willing to sacrifice for the greater good, but only as a last resort.

He looked out at the blue, green, and white landscape of Lake Tahoe as he hit the plunger on one of his many sanitation stations. He rubbed his hands together, letting the ingredients do their thing. The view never seemed to disappoint, but he could see beyond the surface beauty and knew what lay below. Like a doctor with a new stage-four cancer patient. It was one of the reasons he set up offices here—beauty, perception, and personal motivation.

The Mantis was completing her human trials, and there had been no repercussions from the hijacked federal agent and state trooper—good news. Ever since *The Mantis* had switched off their AIS, she had gone dark with no outgoing communications. Pullin was hoping for an encrypted update soon but knew that if authorities were looking for her, it might not come until they were well and truly away from America.

On the Pacific side of the operation, *The Locust* was steaming to her first off-load. Within the next three days, phase one of HYDRA would be complete. He shook his head at the thought of all that had transpired to get things to this point. It was a massive undertaking, with many moving parts. Soon his benevolent plan would be a reality, but first, there needed to be a little suffering before all the good. He looked at the Korean stock market and placed a few orders. Nothing wrong with making another billion along the way, right? Shorting the markets when impending doom was completely unknown to the masses was an easy bet. He pictured the panic that would soon cover the globe. First, the hospitals would become overwhelmed and then the morgues. People would be afraid to leave their homes, but hunger would win out, and each time they ventured out, they would literally be risking their lives.

As things got worse, government-imposed lockdowns, martial law, and businesses closed for good. The economy would be destroyed and investing in companies, like Amazon, that could deliver to your home would be just one of the many wins he would reap along the way.

Once available, when the population numbers were right, the vaccine would be worth its weight in gold. And struggling governments, trying just to hold on, would do anything to get it and maintain their control. Pullin could use his money, power, and the vaccine to broker a place in the world where *he* was the one in control. And when the time was right, he would just give the vaccine away to the remaining struggling masses. They would grovel and thank him for his benevolence. He would stand upon a pedestal and look down at his adoring fans.

Chapter Sixteen

D etective Press whistled as he exited the station. He had a lot to be happy about. Two days ago, a courier had left a package with him that held fifteen thousand dollars in cash. He was letting his mind drift to the possibilities of how he would spend it. Leaking information about a case seemed harmless to him. He was not being asked to disrupt or divert things; he was just sharing what they learned. Tonight, he was meeting his bowling team. He would be the Big Man and buy a round for everyone. The thought put a smile on his face.

He hit the unlock button on his car remote. As he opened his door a shadow entered and sat in his passenger seat. Not a shadow but his contact. The man was dressed in all black, including gloves and a beanie. Detective Press eased into his seat and closed the door.

"You're putting us both at risk by being here in a police parking lot!" Press hissed.

"Relax and start the car. And turn up the heater. It's freezing out there."

Detective Press followed his commands.

"Now, drive away and try to look normal."

Press shook his head as he turned onto the street. He was not happy, but what choice did he have?

"Update," Crispin said.

Detective Press gripped the steering wheel until his hands turned white. He took a calming breath. "Agent Strickman, the one who got knocked off the boat? He's now part of our task force to find the two missing agents and *The Mantis*."

"I know. I've been watching him. What does he know?" Crispin asked.

Detective Press filled Crispin in on all the details, including the missing persons reports and the connection they believed *The Mantis* had to them. He ended with, "We have expanded the BOLO to every major port in the Atlantic."

"Hmm, looks like Agent Strickman has been a bit too busy. Might need to take him off the case."

"Take him off the case? What does that mean? Nobody said anything about *killing*. You can forget me helping anymore if that's where this is headed. I have done my part."

"Yes, and you have done a good job for us, Detective Press. Take a right up here and drop me off."

Press turned the car down a quiet street and pulled to the curb.

"I'll let you know if I need anything else," Crispin said.

"Just don't come to my place of work ever again, *understand?*"

Crispin exited the car and leaned inside to reply. "Perfectly."

He followed the word with three shots from a silenced H&K, closed the door, and walked away.

Press slumped in his seat. His car slowly moved down the mostly empty street. It gathered some speed until it bumped into the back of a pickup truck parked about a hundred feet ahead. There the car remained in gear with the engine running until a late-night dog walker noticed it three hours later.

***

Codi led Thor outside through a door to the aft deck of *The Mantis*. The *M* painted on the wall told her it was the main deck. There was a narrow passageway that led around the ship to the bow. No one was in sight, but that could change in a heartbeat. She could just make out the white superstructure rising mid-ship. Steel containers were stacked five high, rising to the sky, row upon row, heading to the bow. Two yellow onboard cranes had been stowed for travel, one aft and one forward. *The Mantis* used the onboard cranes for loading and offloading at smaller ports of call, giving her a broader reach than the bigger container ships.

The ship was divided like a layered cake. The bottom three levels were engineering, where the engine room, crankcase, steering, and workshops were housed, along with other equipment rooms and a myriad of pipes and venting. Next came the cargo bay followed by the main deck where the hull ended. That was where hundreds of containers continued upward. The superstructure mounted near the aft of the ship was a giant rectangle rising into the sky. It was divided from A Deck up to E Deck and was the main living and working space for the ship. At the very top level was the funnel deck that consisted of the bridge and other vital control areas. It also housed the captain's and first officer's cabins. Just in front of the superstructure, hidden below the containers, was the secret lab.

The perimeter walkway on Main Deck was a narrow, blue steel jungle of pipes, bins, and balusters. A cold ocean spray mixed with the ever-present oily surface made things very slippery. A three-rod railing protected passengers and workers from falling overboard. Cody led Thor along the railing as a simple plan began to blossom in her mind.

"How are you with mechanical things, Thor?"

"I can run a backhoe and repair my '67 Chevy. Does that count?"

"Perfect."

Thor climbed the steel rungs of the yellow-painted aft crane's superstructure, grateful he had no fear of heights. Once at the top, he entered a small steel and glass control room about the size of a small closet. The view was spectacular, but the height exaggerated the ship's movement, making it feel like a cheap carnival ride. Thor strapped himself into the padded chair and looked over the control panel. This was no backhoe. There were a lot of buttons and two joysticks. With words like "slew," "swing," and "boom," it was all a bit foreign to him. Thor took his time to make sure he got it right. He reached out and pressed a large green button. All the lights on the panel turned on.

"Okay, so far, so good," he mumbled to himself.

Meanwhile, Codi quickly moved toward the stern, looking for a place to hide. There was a giant metal spool of rope connected to a winch about twenty feet from the crane's base. She crouched down behind the spool and waited. Her mind flashed to her partner Joel for the briefest moment. He was a major germaphobe. He would never have survived the lab. She prayed that she had made the right choice in knocking him overboard. At the very least, drowning would be better than crapping yourself to death in a Lexan box. The thought hung heavy on her mind.

Thor grabbed the nearest joystick with his right hand. It was an industrial-strength controller with a black knob on top and a rubber cowling to keep moisture out. He gently pushed it forward. There was groaning and scraping, but nothing happened. He tried the other direction and got the same result.

"Okay, if first, you don't succeed . . . what?"

Thor looked over the control panel again. This time the words "carriage lock" caught his eye. He hit the disengage button, and the crane arm popped up several feet, shaking the whole boom. Thor grabbed onto his chair and waited for the ride to stop.

He then repeated his actions on the joystick, and the crane arm began to rise. He paused, making a mental note of the cause and reaction. He then moved the joystick down. The massive arm began to move back down.

"Okay, up and down. Check."

Thor grabbed the other joystick. With a few more attempts, he had the basics figured out. Up, down, left, right of the arm on one controller, and in, out and up, down on the cable with the other. He rubbed his hands together. It was showtime.

The wind off the Atlantic was cold, and it took only a moment before Codi was shivering. She heard the groaning and screeching of metal, but the crane didn't seem to move. She waited, anxiously watching until a loud pop, followed by the twang of overstretched cables, violently shook the entire crane from its mount. Codi held her breath.

The arm moved in several short directions. This brought a small smile to her face. Thor had figured it out.

She watched as the sheave block lowered from the tip of the crane. It was a large triangular chunk of steel with two pulleys and a hook. It was used to connect the load to the crane. Once the sheave block was lowered, the crane arm was raised up and stopped at a forty-five-degree angle. The crane then started to move left and then right in a timed pattern that soon had the sheave block pendulum-ing back and forth on the extended cable. With each swing, the crane's arm moved further left, guiding the large chunk of steel toward its target. It was like a giant medieval flail on the end of a chain.

"Sir, something's going on with the aft crane. I think it came loose," the navigator said, with his mouth agape.

Captain Semenova moved outside onto the flying bridge to get a look aft.

The bridge was at the top of the white superstructure just behind the foredeck about three-quarters from the bow. It sat just in front of the large blue funnel that expelled the exhaust from the entire ship. Inside the bridge was the ship's manual wheel and compass, but everything was run via electronics. The law required a man on watch at all times just in case, but the whole ship could run by itself. The sophisticated electronics made very subtle course corrections along the way to keep the ship heading in the right direction at maximum fuel efficiency.

The front windows of the bridge angled back and provided a magnificent view of the foredeck, forecastle, and ocean beyond. There were comfy chairs, each mounted on a swivel with cup holders for coffee. On both the port and starboard sides was a small outside platform called the flying bridge. It allowed for a view aft, especially needed during docking. There were thruster controls on both sides that could push the bow left or right when navigating tight spaces.

Captain Semenova saw the aft crane out of its mount with its sheave block swinging wildly back and forth.

"Get some men on that right away!" he screamed back into the bridge.

The second officer hit the general alarm and followed it up with an urgent message across the ship speakers.

"All available hands, I need you at the starboard aft crane. It has come loose. The ship is in imminent danger. I repeat . . ." He repeated the message and ran from the bridge.

Captain Semenova seemed mesmerized by the situation.

Max Odo entered the bridge a few minutes later.

"Captain."

Semenova held his focus out the port window, watching the loose crane, as he said, "We've had a crane come loose from its mounts. I believe it is just a mechanical failure but have your men readied, just in case it's something more."

"Aye, Captain. I'll be on channel one," Max said as he turned and left.

Codi watched as eight crewmen, followed by the second officer, who was barking orders, came running her way. She lowered herself and waited. Once they had gathered around the crane, Codi made her move.

She heard the first officer call out, "Paulo, get up there and stow that crane."

"Aye, sir."

"Paulo, stay right where you are!" Codi commanded.

The group all turned to the sound of her voice.

"Get down on your knees right now. I won't hesitate to shoot you."

In truth, Codi had no intention of killing unarmed crew members, but after all that she had been through, it wouldn't take much for her to change her mind. A couple of the men hesitated.

"I've got twelve bullets in here." She gestured to her pistol. "That's more than enough for the lot of you. Now get down on your knees!"

They slowly complied.

"Empty out your pockets on the deck. *Everything*," she called out.

They did. Wallets, phones, money clips, and a few keys.

"Now, in single-file, I want you to walk over to that lifeboat and get inside. Go on. Try anything funny, and you'll get a bullet in the back."

The men walked slowly over to the nearest lifeboat and climbed inside. It was a large orange fiberglass vessel attached to the side of *The Mantis*. Inside were bench seats with harness straps. Codi kept her distance from the last man, not giving them a chance to try anything foolish. Once they were all inside, she moved to the hatch.

"I'd put those seatbelts on if I were you. The landing's going to be a real bite."

The men, realizing her intentions, started to panic and quickly fastened themselves in place. Codi put two bullets in the emergency radio and slammed the hatch shut. She opened the emergency release panel and pressed the two red buttons labeled Emergency Release and Press and Hold. After five seconds, the green release light indicated, and Codi pressed it. A clanking sound was followed by a sudden and swift drop as the lifeboat fell from its perch into the sea. Codi heard muffled high-pitched screams followed by nothing.

She looked up as the crane's arm suddenly swung right, whipping the sheave block into the side of the wheelhouse. The steel surrounding the bridge crumpled like an off-brand soda can, as glass windows shattered and electronics fried.

Captain Semenova stayed on the flying bridge, watching the crane swing from side to side. He couldn't see what his men were up to, as the containers blocked his view of the deck, but there was no doubt that the crane was loose.

"Captain, lifeboat four just did an emergency launch!" the navigator called.

"What is going on!" He stormed back into the wheelhouse and stepped over to the control panel. Sure enough, the launch indicator light was on for lifeboat four.

He turned to go back out onto the flying bridge, grabbing his binoculars and radio to call his first officer and head of security, Max. As he stepped out onto the open deck of the flying bridge, he was greeted by a large chunk of steel. It made impact with the ship and the captain, obliterating them both in an instant. The captain was unable to register even an "Oh no!" before everything went black.

The navigator turned just as the sheave block continued its path through the bridge. He had no time to react and was masticated amid glass and shards of metal. Once the momentum of the sheave block stopped, it came to rest in the wheelhouse, impossibly tangled and jammed amongst the wreckage. What was left of the navigator twitched against the heavy steel weapon.

Codi watched as Thor climbed down from his perch and hit the deck with two feet. "Nice work," she said. "We're down eight crewmen."

"That just leaves four crew and a seven-person security team. Provided our source was telling the truth," he added.

"Exactly, and they'll be armed and ready," Codi said, out of the side of her mouth.

The enthusiasm on Thor's face died. "Right."

Max had just finished double-checking his clip on his Kimber Rapide Black Ice .45ACP. His security force had met in the repurposed rec room where they had armed themselves for an assault and waited for the captain's call. A sudden wrenching of steel against steel, with what sounded like a sonic boom, jolted them from the room. Trouble. Max tried to reach the captain on the radio as they double-timed it through the hallway on full alert. But there was no answer. Once on A Deck, Max sent three men up the side stairs to secure the bridge and find the captain. He and the other three men would clear the ship one deck at a time. He could see smoke coming from the bridge, but from his position, it was impossible to know what had happened.

He moved down the stairs to the forecastle so he could get a better perspective.

Codi and Thor headed for the mass of containers hoping to get lost in the metal jungle. The center of the ship had a stack that was lower than the rest. It would give them some degree of shelter until they could come up with their next plan. The only way anyone could see them would be to climb up here or by helicopter. Thor sat on the rough metal surface with his back to a container.

"Wow, that was something. I'm glad nobody started shooting. That control room was nothing but glass."

"We've been lucky so far." Codi took on a faraway look. The last few days had truly taken their toll. She tried to block the horrors from her mind and think of something more helpful. It didn't work. "What I wouldn't give for a hot shower and a three-day nap."

"I could go for some baby back ribs smothered in barbeque sauce and a gallon of Bud Light," Thor added.

"Okay, stop. That's just making my mouth water."

"Hey, that's a good sign. You must be feeling better." Thor turned and smiled at his new partner.

"A little, thanks," Codi replied. "And thanks again for your help back there."

"We just might survive this yet, if we can avoid getting shot."

"One thing at a time, Thor." Codi looked over to the man she had suffered and escaped with. "So what do you do for fun in Portland?"

"I'm a Pop Warner football coach. We're the Jaguars, named after the Jacksonville Jags. With the same colors and helmets. We've gone to the state playoffs a couple of times. I really love coaching kids."

A smile grew on Codi's lips. "Are you married?"

"I have an amazing wife, Anita, and a young daughter named Greta. She's got a heck of an arm for a five-year-old."

Once at the forecastle, Max had a clear view of the wheelhouse. It was smashed beyond recognition—as if a giant with a big hammer had whacked it from the side.

"Kramer, report!" he called through the radio.

"Max, it's rough up here. The bridge is destroyed with all hands," came the reply.

"The captain?" Max asked.

"I'm afraid so."

This hit Max hard. The man had been like a father figure to him. He had taken him under his wing and made a place for Max in this world. More importantly, he had given him a cause. A worthy endeavor with an altruistic purpose. It was now up to Max to set things right. "Hold what's left of the bridge. We'll clear the ship. See if you can raise the rest of the crew and have them report to you, except engineering. Tell them you're sending one of your guys there."

"Aye, aye."

Max moved his men left. He would do a quick circuit around the main deck, and then clear the inside and move his way up from there, eventually meeting up with the others on the bridge.

***

Dr. Pendergrass opened his eyes. The knot on his dome throbbed and made his head feel like warm soup. He lifted himself into a sitting position and waited for the room to stop spinning. The red glow of the incubator lights filled the space. He felt something and looked down. There were hundreds of cockroaches all over him climbing and crawling at will. Some on top of his clothes, some underneath.

He wiped away a grouping on his left arm and noticed some of his skin was missing. A quick flash of fear hit Dr. Pendergrass as he realized they had been consuming him while he was unconscious. He scampered to his feet shaking off as many bugs as he could and ran for the exit door. He stabbed at the green open button repeatedly, but nothing happened. *That stupid woman left the outer door ajar.* He was trapped.

Dr. Pendergrass turned with his back to the door and looked out at his creations. Thousands of cockroaches moved in his direction, hungry and ready for more, their sharp mandibles eager to rip and devour. Fists banged on the door, and he screamed for help, but none was forthcoming. He slowly slumped to the ground, his eyes alert and jittery. He was out-numbered ten thousand to one. For every one bug he smashed or flicked away, ten more replaced it. It was a useless gesture and he knew it. If any man knew what these guys were capable of, it was him. He hunkered into a fetal position trying to protect as much body as possible. At first, it seemed to be working, but the sounds of feasting clicks from hundreds of mandibles filled his ears. The first tear was followed by more until he was a sobbing mess.

***

Codi climbed up the two containers above her and peeked over the top. The wind blew her hair across her face. She could see the bridge a short way off a couple of floors above her. The destruction was palpable. Two armed guards could be seen standing amongst the wreckage. After a few more moments of careful surveillance, she climbed back down.

"What did you see?" Thor asked.

"Looks like two guards stationed on the bridge. A bridge that you did a fine job of destroying, by the way. I'm betting the others are looking for us. This may be the best odds we'll get before they all regroup."

Codi and Thor stealthily moved in and around the wall of containers, climbing like monkeys, while making their way to the end row before the foredeck, keeping just out of sight of the bridge guards. From there, they jumped across the small gap that separated them from the superstructure. They landed on a small, railed platform with the letter *D* on it.

"Okay. D Deck. We should be two levels below the bridge. Come on."

They moved up the first flight of stairs along the outside of the superstructure and paused on the next level, E.

Thor held just out of sight of the guard above him. He was unarmed and feeling very vulnerable. Codi moved off the railing and pulled herself up between the funnel and the superstructure. It was a three-foot gap. She used a chimney climb, where she placed her feet on one side of the gap and her back and hands on the other, slowly scooting her way upward. The trick was to keep pressure on both sides of the gap at all times. Inch by inch she moved up against the painted surface, blue on one side and white on the other.

Once past the bridge level, Codi continued up to the roof above it. The open space was filled with electronic dishes and several antennas. It was the very top of the ship, and the view . . . She didn't have time for that.

Like a cat, she tiptoed across the roof to the edge where the bridge had been destroyed, lowering herself past the ragged metal and peering over into the wreckage below. One guard stood near the one remaining flying bridge on the starboard wing, looking over the side for anything suspicious. The other guard stood just inside the open wound of the ship that was once the high-tech command center.

Very carefully, Codi lowered herself down onto the flying deck. She dropped low out of the sight of the guard inside, just up against the outside bulkhead, keeping her pistol ready for anything.

***

The main engine room, as usual, was warm and stuffy. It held two enormous V-12 diesel engines, a desalinization plant for fresh water, and two generators for electrical power. Klaus had been chief engineer for five years under Captain Semenova. He kept one of the cleanest engine rooms the captain had ever seen. Klaus had a passion for details, and even the smallest thing caught his attention. The sudden and extreme blast that shuddered through the ship put him on overdrive. He had no luck connecting with the bridge and was becoming seriously concerned.

"Pieter, go up top and see what's going on," he called over the engine noise.

His assistant engineer nodded and took to the metal stairs but stopped as Braedon, one of the security men trotted down.

"Braedon, what the devil's going on?"

"One of the cranes came loose and hit the bridge. We're going through the ship to make sure it wasn't sabotaged," Braedon replied.

Sabotage. The word hit Klaus like a bat to the ribs.

"How is that even possible?" he asked.

"Don't worry about it, Klaus. You keep things running down here, and I'll keep things safe. Once we get the all-clear, I'll take you up to see what needs fixin'."

Klaus nodded, now lost in the thought of a million possibilities.

***

Detective Havok rushed into the task force room out of breath, slamming the door behind him. He looked like he might scream or cry. Anna and Gordon looked up with concern.

"Somebody shot Press," he bellowed.

"Wait, what?" Joel asked, glancing over the top of his computer.

"They shot him down in his car on Spring Street. They're thinking it was someone he knew or let into his car. There are no holes in the car's glass." Havok tried to catch his breath. This sort of thing rarely happened in Portland.

"Do you think it's related to our case?" he asked.

"No, that would make no sense. Killing Press doesn't really affect what we're doing," Gordon replied. He quickly realized the callousness of his words and added. "Other than the emotional loss we're all feeling and the distraction it causes. There's no logic to that."

Havok nodded at the thought, still trying to center himself.

"They have assigned two detectives out of homicide to investigate. I'm to stay on our case," he said, clearly disappointed as he turned and left the room.

The three remaining agents sat in stunned silence.

"There's definitely more to this case than meets the eye," Joel said. "And no way his death was just a coincidence, after all we've seen so far. Come on, guys, am I right?"

Anna and Gordon had no reply.

***

Max and his men cleared the main deck of *The Mantis* and were halfway through A Deck. It was slow going, but everything on the ship appeared normal. There was no armed boarding party or evidence of one. Could this really just have been an accident? He didn't think so, but only time would tell. The secret door to the lab was still intact and they had heard no warning from anyone inside since it had been sealed. His desire to go inside, considering what they were doing in there, was low. That would be the last place they cleared. The idea of a crew member going rogue seemed to make the most sense, but who? He searched his memory of everyone he had hired and came up empty.

"Sir, nothing on A Deck," Omar reported.

Max nodded. They moved up the stairwell to B Deck.

***

Codi kept her gun aimed at the guard as he leaned over the railing surveying the area below him. A sudden sound of metal bouncing off metal caught his attention. The guard's ears and torso bent further, tracking the sound below. Before he could react, Codi moved in, grabbed his legs, and launched him up and over the railing. She ran back to the bridge, just as a scream was heard outside. The second guard spun in the direction of the scream, but Codi was on him in a flash. Before he could pull his gun, he was in her sights.

"Don't do it!" she called.

But he didn't listen. Driven to his core training, he grabbed for his MP5. Codi fired her weapon, but the first two bullets deflected off the machine gun he was trying to lift and shoot. The guard went down with a *humph*. He hit the deck and instinctively rolled left behind a destroyed electronics console. Codi followed him with a stitch of bullets, one hitting his arm and another his hip before he disappeared from view. She moved right to reacquire an angle, but the guard quickly popped up from behind the console and returned a three-round burst from his pistol, forcing Codi to dive for cover. Impact with her left knee on the steel floor radiated pain throughout her leg. The bullets made a cracking sound as they passed past her head, something she had heard too many times in her life. It was a sound most normal people would never know—hot lead breaking the sound barrier inches from your ears. It was followed by several ricochets as the bullets bounced off the steel surfaces of the ship. She winced at the shot of pain in her knee and her diminished hearing, but now was not the time for a wound inspection.

Codi peered out from behind the twisted wreckage. Her target was leaning out with half a head waiting for her to show. Two bullets hit and pinged off the steel just after she ducked back. That was close.

She lay down on the floor to get a small sliver of a view from under the twisted metal. She could just see the man's foot sticking out from cover. Rotating to her side and lining up one eye through the sight of her gun, she fired a single bullet into the man's foot, and then quickly hopped to her feet. The man hollered and reacted to the pain. His training was good, as he didn't leave the protection of his cover, but for the briefest instant, Codi had a shot. She didn't hesitate. The bullet went true and pierced his neck. He swung his gun back at her. She pulled her trigger again for good measure. *Click.* Her gun was empty. She had committed to a plan, and now, she was an open target for the man whose gun was pointed right at her. There was no time to duck or run. She could only watch as the man pulled the trigger with all his strength, only to be denied the kill shot. His neck wound was mortal, and it had grazed his spine just enough that he had no control of his extremities.

Codi watched as the man seemed to melt to the floor, hatred in his eyes for the woman who had bested him. She stepped over to verify the kill.

"Stupid."

Codi removed his weapons and his radio. A quick inspection told her his MP5 machine gun that had initially taken her first two shots was no longer functioning. She collected his pistol, a .45, whereas hers was a 9mm. She moved back through the wreckage to the flying bridge and called down to Thor. He came running up the last flight of steps with a worried look on his face.

When he saw Codi was unharmed, his shoulders slumped in relief. "I take it that worked?" he asked.

"Yeah. Nice toss and good timing."

Codi had given Thor two large bolts and instructed him to throw them onto the containers five minutes after she left. Without a watch, Thor had counted to sixty five times, reminding himself not to rush under the circumstances. The distraction was successful and for now, they owned the high ground.

"Unfortunately, we still only have one working pistol. Here." She tossed the guard's gun to Thor and placed her empty 9 mil back in her belt, just in case she managed to find some bullets down the road.

They looked around the bridge. It was mostly destroyed. Smoke still smoldered from two of the electronic cabinets but was swept away on the brisk wind through the now open jagged cavity. The crane cable clanged against the steel superstructure as the ship moved along.

The first thing Codi noticed was the entire steering controls and communications consoles were gone. The weird thing was a single padded swivel chair was still in place, mounted to the floor, the coffee in its cup holder still steaming.

"We need to get to the communications room and get a message out. What number did our prisoner say it was?" Codi asked.

"201, D Deck," Thor replied.

They walked through the door in the back of the destroyed wheelhouse and down the interior hallway, labeled the Funnel Deck. They checked each door they came to as they moved, just in case. They discovered the captain's cabin and the first mate's. They found the radio room. It was located just down the hall in room F-104, not D-201 like the guard had told them.

It was a small modern affair with a keyboard as a controller. A tower of electronics was mounted in a blue rack on the wall. The power was off, but it only took a moment for Codi to find the master switch and turn it all on. The problem was the password prompt that came up on the screen. No password: no radio, no communication. Even the marine radio was locked out. Codi and Thor looked around the room for a clue to the password, but none was forthcoming. They would need a live prisoner to get that information.

"I say we make a stand from up here. We can limit their options by making them come to us."

Thor nodded as the radio clipped on Codi's belt suddenly interrupted their conversation. "Kramer, what's your status up there? Was that gunfire?" said the voice.

Codi handed the radio to Thor. "Tell them we have a fire."

Thor nodded and pressed the transmit button. He jacked up his voice and scraped his fingernails across the radio's mic as he spoke. "Fire! We got fire and explosions!"

"We've got nothing down here," Max replied. "Be right there to help out."

Thor pressed the transmit button and just scrapped his fingernails across the mic this time and then released it.

"Okay," Codi said. "Get a good fire with smoke going in the wheelhouse. I'm going to jam the stairwell door so they have to come up the outside steps like we did."

Thor nodded and headed off to play pyro. The short hallway on the Funnel Deck had a steel door that led to a stairwell down through the middle of the ship.

It was the main thoroughfare for the officers and crew, as the outside stairway could be risky on a moving ship, especially in bad weather. Codi took a chair from the radio room and jammed it with a strong kick under the door lever so no one could enter from the stairwell.

Thor gathered a few charts and a lighter to set a small but smoky fire. He placed it on one of the smashed consoles and the flames grew. Soon a black plume was billowing out from the torn hole that was once the bridge.

Max clipped his radio back on his belt and moved with his men to the port side of A Deck. They could see black smoke rising from the gash in the ship. The stairs that led to the destroyed portside flying bride were a bent and mangled mess near the top where the sheave block had cut through on its way to the wheelhouse. That left the main stairwell inside the ship or the starboard side stairs on the other side of the ship. Max grabbed his radio and pressed the button.

"Braedon, are you in engineering?" Max asked.

"Copy that," came the reply.

"Any issues?"

"All clear down here, sir," he replied.

Finally some good news, he thought. "We got a fire in the bridge and could use your help. What's the status on the crew?" Max asked.

"I have Klaus and Peiter here with me in the engine room but have had no luck raising the rest of the crew," Braedon replied.

This was troubling to Max, and he pondered his very dangerous situation. He knew they were growing an especially nasty biological weapon onboard the ship. Had it somehow gotten loose and killed the crew? They had yet to clear the entire ship, but from what he had seen so far, there was no evidence of a boarding party or foul play, other than the crane. Had it come free all on its own or was there a saboteur onboard? Max had sent one of his best men into the lab and had not heard back from him since. Too many questions and not enough answers. First, they would need to get a handle on the fire and then go over every inch of this ship before he would be satisfied.

"Braedon, meet us at the bridge and bring Klaus," Max said.

"Copy that."

"And arm him," Max added.

"Understood."

Codi and Thor listened as Max called over the radio to a man stationed in engineering.

"That makes two coming up the stairwell, both armed," Codi said.

"And at least four or five, by my estimation, will be coming up the outside stairs we came up," Thor added.

"The two from engineering won't get through that door easily, so let's concentrate on the larger group for now. I'm guessing we have five minutes."

She paced about the clutter in the bridge, thinking for a beat, and then looked up at Thor who watched her movements with interest. He was still wearing the shirt with the ship's logo on it that they had taken from the crew quarters.

"I have an idea," she said, with raised eyebrows.

Codi filled Thor in on her plan. His interest quickly waned.

Chapter Seventeen

Max and his three men double-timed it around the superstructure to the outside stairs on the starboard side of *The Mantis*. They took the steps two at a time until they reached E Deck, one level below the bridge. He held them there for a second, listening for anything suspicious. With a quick motion of his hand, he sent two men up to investigate. With guns at the ready, they crept up the last flight of stairs. Once up on the flying bridge, they could see a man in a crew uniform inside the destroyed bridge trying to beat down flames with a blanket. There was no one else in sight.

"Don't just stand there," he yelled at them. "I could use some help in here!"

The guard waved at him and then leaned back over the railing and called down, "Max! All clear. The fire's real."

The two guards moved quickly into the bridge to help out.

A fire on a ship is a sailor's worst nightmare. It can quickly get out of control and take the ship to a watery grave.

The Mantis carried a sophisticated fire suppression system. In the lab and living quarters, a CO_2 automated system could be released both manually or automatically if a fire was detected. The ship also carried a heavy-duty main fire pump and an emergency backup fire pump, both capable of sending highly pressurized seawater to over thirty different fire hose stations and geared water cannons. Crew members were repeatedly drilled and trained on how and when to use them.

Max holstered his pistol and hurried up the stairs, his thoughts still on the fact that there could be a saboteur on board. It was an uneasy thought, as he had selected the crew and security force personally. The vetting process was thorough, and each hired crew member had expressed a genuine desire to help carry out their plan to completion, no matter the cost. These were dedicated men and women. How had he misjudged? Who had he misjudged?

Thor waited as long as he could, beating at the flames. His face was smudged black from the smoke, and he was coughing in earnest. He whipped his blanket repeatedly on the flames purposely having little effect on the growing inferno. The two guards quickly entered the bridge, eager to help out. As they got closer, they realized that the man in the crew shirt beating the flames was unfamiliar. Before they could respond, Thor pulled out the pistol he was concealing in the blanket and had them dead to rights. "That's far enough," he ordered.

Codi watched as two more men ran up the stairs, focused on helping with the fire and getting the ship back under control. She had stayed low on the roof waiting for the right moment. As the first two armed men passed and ran into the bridge, she stood strong on the roof above the bridge holding a nozzle connected by a hose to the fire pump on the floor below. She had pressurized it and used Thor's help to get the unwieldy thing on the roof. Codi waited until the men were on the flying deck before pulling the lever to release the flow.

High-pressure water shot out, knocking both men against the railing. It was a violent force that had Codi working overtime just to maintain her stance and aim. One man tried to pull his pistol, but she used the stream of water, capable of shooting over forty feet in the air to disarm and send him over the railing with a cry. With only one target left, she concentrated all her attention on the second man, effectively pinning him against the railing with the force. He managed to get one hand up in surrender.

Thor was surprised at how effective the water cannon had been. He watched as the two men were slammed back against the railing in a heartbeat. It was intense. The momentary distraction had not gone unnoticed, however, and one of the guards subtly moved behind his partner obscuring part of his body from Thor's view. He used the concealment to slowly pull his weapon and aim while keeping his other hand raised in surrender. He then tapped the barrel of his pistol on his partner's back as a signal for him to move. The man in front dropped to the floor.

Thor caught movement in his peripheral and spun back from the water cannon action outside. Impulsively, he pulled the trigger as gunfire returned in his direction. Two shots hit him center mass dropping him to the floor but not before he unloaded his weapon in the direction of the two guards.

The water hit Max like a mule kick. It knocked him back against the railing, pinning him there. Using both hands to protect his face from the water's extreme force, he barely heard Omar go over the railing with a muffled scream. He kept crouched down to prevent that from happening to him and raised an arm in surrender. The experience reminded him of being water-boarded during his military training, only this seemed much worse. He felt like he was being drowned while having a huge hand smash him. He couldn't catch a breath, and his eyes stung with saltwater. A few gunshots rang out from the bridge, and finally, the water abated, and he dropped to his hands and knees, gasping for air.

Codi watched as the man stopped fighting the high-pressure water. He curled defensively into a ball. She heard gunshots coming from the bridge and a flash of fear cut through her. She didn't have time to worry about what was going on inside and focused on what was right in front of her. Distractions got you killed. Codi pulled the lever to cut the water, leaving her target flopping on the deck, gasping. She grabbed her empty pistol and pointed it at the lone man.

"On your stomach—*now!*" She watched as the man complied and then slowly lowered herself from the roof to the deck, never taking her eyes off the man. "Now slide your weapons over to me."

The man glanced up at his usurper and realized she was deadly serious. He slowly unhooked his MP5 from the shoulder strap and slid it her way and then repeated the action with his pistol.

"Thor! Are you okay?" Codi called out as she collected the weapons.

"Sorta," came the reply.

She put the MP5 on her shoulder and racked the slide on the new pistol, tossing her own gun over the railing.

This action was not missed by the man on the ground who looked pained at having given up to an empty gun.

"Okay, on your feet, nice and easy."

He complied and they moved toward the bridge, Codi keeping her distance.

Max fingered a small throwing knife he kept on a wrist sheath, palming it into his right hand. When he was ordered to stand he rotated the blade away from the woman's view. The FBI patient escaping the lab was unexpected, but he would soon get to the bottom of this, and the ones responsible would pay dearly. He had been sure one of the crew had gone rogue, but thinking about it, an escaped patient made more sense. It was a scenario that finally had him letting go of the guilt he had heaped upon himself. Between the rest of the crew onboard and his remaining men, they would soon have the ship back in their hands.

He opened the door that led to the bridge, its glass window blown out by the earlier destruction. As the door hinged open, he turned with it and flung the blade with all his precision and might.

Codi kept a wary eye on her prisoner, maintaining at least five feet distance at all times. As he opened the door, she noticed him rotate and flick his arm. She dropped and returned fire. A knife swept past her head taking a chunk of skin and hair from her scalp. She hit the deck hard jarring her tailbone but was otherwise okay. The man in her charge was not, however, and now hung to the door trying to remain erect as his body began to fail him.

Codi slowly stood and moved closer to the man with her gun poised and ready, blood dripping down her forehead.

"What's the password for the radio room?" she asked.

His head wobbled slightly, and he tried to smile. "Our sister will finish what we have started. HYDRA will not fail," he said with a pained expression as he slowly dropped to the deck.

"The password!" she demanded.

His arm caught on the door handle, keeping his torso still upright, but there was no life left.

Codi kicked the man in frustration, then she checked his vitals. Nothing. She was getting nowhere capturing a live prisoner for the radio code.

Codi stepped into the wrecked bridge. There were two more bodies on the floor with several bullet holes leaking blood. Sitting against the wall was Thor, and he looked very pale.

Codi knelt, noticing two red dots on his chest slowly blooming. He had a raspy sound to his breathing.

"I think my lungs are filling with blood," Thor said.

"*Shh.* You're gonna be okay," Codi countered.

"You sure are a lousy detective," Thor whispered and then coughed uncontrollably.

"Hey, that's not nice."

"Okay, a lousy doctor," Thor countered.

"That's fair."

They both shared a pained smile, recognizing Thor was short for this life. Slowly drowning in your own blood was going to be a rough exit. Codi held him tight as he jerked, sputtered, and coughed up blood.

"Make sure you stop these guys and give my family my . . ." Thor finished on a whispered breath through crimson lips.

"I promise," Codi said softly while holding him tight.

She watched helplessly as he shuddered and jerked. Finally, his body came to rest. She continued to hold him close as she wept for the man who had helped save her. He deserved better.

Her tears turned to ice as Codi vowed to make good on her promise.

Based on the radio chatter they intercepted, Codi knew there were two armed men in the stairwell and one crew member still in the engine room. Beyond that, it was anyone's guess. She stood and left the bridge and the dead behind.

Moving down the hall, past the captain's room toward the metal door she had blocked, Codi pressed her ear to the cold steel and listened. Nothing. Carefully removing the chair from the doorknob, Codi slipped inside the stairwell. It was empty. *They would be heading back out to use the outside stairs*, she told herself and quickly moved down the stairs to come in from behind them. Codi realized the ship was now damaged enough, she could take one of the lifeboats and make her escape. They would never have the maneuverability to run her down.

She hurried down the stairs with a new mission in mind—to escape.

Her radio squawked to life.

"Code seventeen. All crew, I repeat, code seventeen."

It repeated one more time, and Codi had a sinking feeling. They undoubtedly had a workaround for when the radios were compromised. She could no longer count on eavesdropping on transmissions. With no idea what code seventeen represented, she prayed it wasn't a self-destruct signal.

Codi sprinted down the stairs, suddenly very wary of what might come next.

Braedon paused on the steps leading to the bridge. He could see First Officer Max Odo lying in a pool of his own blood. The bridge was destroyed, and a quick look identified several other bodies no longer among the living. He backtracked down the stairs and reached for his radio. Pressing the transmit button, he hesitated and then gave the signal that would alert anyone left living onboard to a set list of instructions.

There had been extensive "what-if" scenarios run by the officers, and he would not let them down even though they were dead. He steered the engineer, Klaus, to the back of the ship where they would wait five minutes before taking further action.

Peiter was all alone in the engine room. It was a massive space with two engines, each the size of a small locomotive. They were running cool and normal at about three-quarter speed. The hum in the room was unheard by him after so many years at sea, but the voice on the radio was as clear as a bell. They had been given the emergency code, and there was no doubt. He moved to a specialized control panel and followed the procedure. Using a preset code, he entered and pressed several buttons. One started a timer down from ten minutes.

Peiter turned to look at his magnificent beauties purring onward one more time, oblivious to their situation, and sprinted from the room.

Five minutes later, he was on board the aft port lifeboat, strapping himself in for a violent egress. Braedon set the timer and followed Klaus onto the lifeboat as well. There were only three of them left. Something had gone very wrong. The timer ticked down, and without warning, the securing clamps released, and the lifeboat fell into the sea.

Codi ran out into the sunlight as a clanking sound caught her attention. To her left, a lifeboat disengaged and fell into the sea. She ran to the railing where she could see three more falling away with it.

"No, no. *No!*" she called while sprinting to the other side of the boat.

There, the view was just the same. All the lifeboats had been released. A small flotilla of orange fiberglass bobbed away behind *The Mantis.* She stared listlessly at the railing as her planned escape floated and faded away. A dulled boom jarred the ship and shook Codi. She ran to the stairs to get a view of what was happening. The feeling of dread grew with every step upward. Serious black smoke spilled from several containers stacked in the middle of the ship. Codi's mind flashed to a makeshift raft she might assemble before the ship floundered. She had drowned on a previous case and been brought back to life by Matt. It was a fear she now harbored, and it began to rise in the back of her mind. She could remember the panic, the overwhelming instinct to breathe, and the cold polluted water filling her lungs. A complete shock to her system, as her body jerked, spasmed, and shut down. Never again, she had sworn.

The preset procedure began with clockwork precision. Small concentrated fireball explosives set throughout the lab ignited. The flames were allowed to burn and sear for exactly ten minutes, incinerating everything in their path. At ten minutes, the CO_2 fire suppression system kicked in and doused the flames, leaving the ship intact, but the lab was utterly destroyed. There would be no evidence left behind of what was being grown or done.

Codi watched helplessly as the smoke and flames poured out of the middle of the ship. Within a few moments, everything was all but gone. Eight containers were blackened, but the fire and smoke—no more. She let out an audible sigh of relief at the realization that the ship was *not* going to sink.

"They destroyed the lab," she muttered to herself, before stepping out onto the flying bridge. It held the only control panel left on the bridge. A small three-button device was mounted on a raised pedestal. She looked it over—Bow Thruster. There was a green turn switch that rotated and a black Port and Starboard push button. She turned the green switch, and it lit up, indicating power to the panel. This was good news. Codi knew that a bow thruster was used by larger ships to help them maneuver in tight quarters but didn't know much more. Her hope was to navigate the ship back to America by this means since both the ship's wheel and the electronic steering were both destroyed.

She looked up at the sun, which was streaming across the back of the ship—afternoon. They were heading east-ish, she surmised. Something from her military survival training kicked in, and she spied a harsh shadow across the deck from the pedestal. She remembered using a stick in the ground and the sun to determine direction in the wilderness. Codi pressed the starboard bow thruster button and held it in place.

A distant vibration from the hull was all that happened. No obvious movement or turning. She held the button down and waited. It took ten minutes before she noticed the slight change in the shadow's direction. The ship had started to turn.

Eventually, the large container ship came about, and Codi used the thruster to reset her course back to where she had come from, the shadow now 180 degrees from its original position. Satisfied that *The Mantis* was generally on course, she left the bridge in search of food and much-needed rest. Maybe even a hot shower.

***

Crispin listened to the silence on the other end of the line. He had just finished updating his boss on the latest developments. The case against *The Mantis* was progressing, including the fact that they were getting close to finding a connection to Pullin himself. They still had no idea where the ship was located, but many agencies were now actively looking for it.

One of the agents who had been taken on board managed to go overboard and was rescued, impossible as that might seem. The information he had spilled was out, and there was no putting it back in the bottle. The only thing left was to isolate themselves from *The Mantis* until circumstances changed.

Crispin could hear the wheels turning on the other end of the line as his boss processed the new development.

"Your decision not to kill Agent Strickman seems warranted since he has already spilled everything he knows. The damage *is* done," Pullin said, interrupting the silence. "No need to stir things up anymore. Besides, they can only guess at our intentions. Our main concern now will be to prevent the authorities from finding *The Mantis*. I have sent Captain Semenova orders to refit and rename her. The Mantis will be no longer."

"What was his reply?" Crispin asked.

"She is still dark, as per protocol, but I am sure they received the message and are working on her as we speak."

In truth, the silence from *The Mantis* bothered Pullin, and he feared for her success. The overdue update could mean several things, none of them good. He had a backup ship in place, but it would take at least four months to get her fitted and ready.

"Thoughts on my next move?" Crispin asked.

"Clean up your contact and take the next flight out. I want you by my side. I'll track the case from my D.C. connection."

"Already done."

***

Codi woke with a start. She was sitting at a table in *The Mantis* galley with her head on the surface. A small pool of drool was next to a mostly eaten turkey sandwich. She had fallen asleep while eating. That was a first. Her body felt punished and abused. Even moving her eyes hurt. The fever seemed to have abated, so at least she was over the main effects of the disease. Her hand tested the wound on her scalp. She would live, for now. The last few days had tried her multiple times, and she had come through, *still here and still fighting.*

Codi finished off the last of her sandwich and poured herself a cup of cold coffee from the coffeemaker. She made a mental note to brew a fresh pot soon as she guzzled the bitter liquid.

Stepping out into the hall, she made her way outside to the main deck. The sun was just starting to glow, the morning sky orange at the stern of the ship. She took that as a good sign. They were still heading west, and she had slept almost fourteen hours. On a table. No wonder everything hurt. She retraced her steps back to where she had launched the lifeboat with the crew the day before. Right where they had left them on the deck were their personal belongings. She collected up all the cell phones and headed up the stairs to the bridge. The room was already starting to smell of decomp. She took some time to move the bodies into the first officer's quarters and closed the door. It helped, but the two bodies that had been masticated were impossible to clean up all the way. There were pieces everywhere.

Codi stepped out onto the one working flying bridge where the ocean wind in her face cleared away the smell. She turned on each phone and found that all required either a password or facial recognition to open. One of the phones was an older model that allowed you to call 911 even if the phone was locked. She dialed, but there was no service. She placed the phone in her pocket and looked out at the spectacular view. Blue and gold water as far as the eye could see in every direction. It was a bit overwhelming.

Alone on a nine hundred-foot Panamax cargo ship in the middle of the Atlantic with no communications and only a bow thruster for steering. What could go wrong?

Chapter Eighteen

J oel moved his cursor to click on the next page and continued reading as he sipped a French roast.

"Somebody's up early," Gordon said as he entered the office adjacent to the detectives' bullpen.

"If you had a missing partner you would be too," Joel replied without looking up.

"Of course." Gordon felt chastised, but Joel was right, none of them should be sleeping until Codi came home. And with the mysterious murder of Detective Press, things were now messy.

The trail of *The Mantis* ownership through a Panamanian company, Tranz-global Logistics, had gone cold. There were at least three different shell companies leading to nowhere.

Joel pulled up the file on Garrett Scott, the man who had tried to kill him, and reread it. A fixer for corporate. He had worked for several companies, and Anna had run them all down, finding nothing worth adding to the file.

Whoever was pulling the strings was a very careful person.

Joel did an internet search of *The Mantis* and found nothing out of the ordinary. He clicked from "All" on his browser to "Images" and scrolled through the very few pictures of the ship that had been taken and posted. One, in particular, caught his eye. He zoomed in on the image. A group of five adults stood on the dock with the ship in the background. They were all posing with smiles on their faces. The name on the bow of the ship was out of focus, but with a little enhancement, Joel could make out the words MANTIS.

He fed the faces into the FBI's facial recognition program. Now, all he had to do was wait and see if he got a hit.

Detective Havok was next to enter the office. He looked like he had been up all night reviewing the files on *his* partner's death, which he had. The detectives in charge had no witnesses, no motive, and the only real evidence was that a 9mm pistol was used in the shooting. It was depressing. Police officer unsolved cases were the worst of the worst.

***

Land. It was just a ribbon on the horizon, but it was real. Codi put down the binoculars she had taken from the captain's cabin and considered her options. She was torn between dancing a jig and thanking God. This was great news, and she wondered if she was heading toward New England, Florida, or Mexico. The Mantis was moving at well over twenty miles an hour, and a ship that size didn't stop on a dime. She pulled the cellphone from her pocket and dialed 911. Still no signal. Her eyes surveyed the horizon as she waited. *Maybe another few miles.*

When she was just over five miles out or so, Codi set down the binoculars and headed for the engine room.

Eight flights of stairs brought her down to the engineering levels. As she opened the door to the engine room, the first thing that hit her was the heat and an ever-present hum. There were two huge engines running and several auxiliary systems. The harsh lighting bounced off the steel polished floor. It took Codi several minutes to find the control panel for the engines. It was a large pale-green console with dials and knobs. Some showed the RPMs, some the oil or coolant pressure. Codi looked everything over, eliminating the buttons and controls she wasn't looking for. In the middle of everything was a large red button labeled Emergency All-Stop. She slammed her hand down and the noise in the room gradually dropped in pitch and volume. The engines were off. Now, she just had to hope she didn't need to restart them as that seemed beyond her abilities. Satisfied that she had done all she could, Codi started back for the bridge.

With the engines shut down, the ship started to slow. At first imperceptibly, but more and more as they neared the coast. At about three miles out, Cody got a signal on the phone and dialed.

"911, what is your emergency?"

Codi had never been so excited to hear those words.

"This is FBI Special Agent Codi Sanders calling from the deck of the ocean-bound ship *The Mantis*. I have an emergency situation and need to be connected to 202 . . ."

Codi gave the operator the number for the FBI's Special Projects division. She listened while a series of beeps and clicks forwarded the call.

"Fescue."

"Brian, it's . . ."

"Codi? It's about time. Where are you? You okay?"

"Well, if you let me get a word in, I'll tell you," Codi said.

"Of course."

Codi filled her boss in on the situation. She had no idea where she was, but the land in front of her seemed to be growing by the second.

"Okay, keep this line open. I'll get a trace and send some help." He put her on hold and went to work. About five minutes later, Brian came back on the line. "It looks like you're about a mile out from Core Banks, also known as Harker Island, North Carolina, about sixty miles north of Wilmington."

"I have no way of controlling this ship, so I will either hit land or stop short," Codi said.

"I have Coast Guard and support all on the way. Hang tight," Brian said.

"Thank you, sir. Oh, and send an infectious disease doctor."

The pause on the line that followed was understandable.

Codi had missed returning the ship to her original departure city by seven states, but she had found America, and that was good enough for her. She could see Core Banks as the ship approached and was grateful there were no homes along the shore, as it now seemed obvious she would make landfall and a bit more. The ship was still doing at least ten miles an hour with less than a mile to go. Codi moved to the captain's cabin and threw the bed's mattress up against the bulkhead. She curled up against it waiting for the ship to impact land.

As the floor of the sea moved upward toward the shore, the reinforced bow of *The Mantis* plowed into the soft mud. The ship shuddered and slowed leaving a gash in the earth as she slammed her way up the shoreline. Codi was bucked and shaken as the ship fought against the physics of speed and mass versus soil composition and inclination, along with a few other factors. The ship moaned and creaked for several seconds until finally coming to a stop, leaning slightly to port.

Codi crawled back to her feet, eager to set foot on land. The bow of the ship had two reels of rope connected to electric winches. Releasing just enough rope from one of the windlasses, she climbed down to the sand below. She gathered herself and walked up the beach past the high-tide mark and plopped down in the sun-warmed sand. The massive ship, now motionless, towered over her. It took a few seconds for her to recognize the situation. She had been in automatic survival mode for so long, the gravity of the moment was just too overwhelming, and tears of joy fell without restraint. In spite of everything thrown at her in the last week, Codi had persevered and come out the other side, stronger and more determined than ever. Whoever did this would pay dearly.

***

The Locust tied to the dock, and the offloading of cargo began. It was nearly 10:00 p.m., but the harbor in Busan, South Korea never slept. It was the major Pacific artery for the country. After nearly eighty containers were removed, the process reversed. Sixty-eight different containers were replaced, bound for other destinations.

By 3:00 a.m., the work was complete and refueling and replenishing of the stores began. Once finished, *The Locust* sat dormant waiting for a morning exit with the tide.

Dr. Sales sat in the lab next to Dr. Mahl watching the screen in front of them. Container #AD125349 had been placed in a stack near customs for inspection.

Dr. Mahl activated a remote signal that opened thirty concealed vents in the container. A sonic repulsor turned on, and ten thousand cockroaches fled the container, all eager to do what they did best, scurry everywhere in search of food and shelter.

They waited twenty minutes and then reclosed the vents to hide the evidence of their actions. Next up was a shipside procedure. Dr. Mahl activated two panels in one of the containers on board that were part of their lab's camouflage. A couple of keystrokes and two powerful but gentle fans blew twenty thousand infected flies into the night air. The whole operation took less than thirty-five minutes. Their work here was done.

"I suggest you get back to your incubators, Dr. Sales," Dr. Mahl said. "Tokyo is only seven days away . . . and then Shanghai."

"It was glorious, wasn't it?"

"Yes. Now, we wait for hell on earth to consume South Korea," Dr. Mahl said, without emotion.

"I will be ready," Dr. Sales replied as he stood, excited to get back to his babies. For Dr. Sales, this was as close as he would ever come to having children, and he savored his responsibility.

***

The amount of infrastructure and equipment that was required to remove a beached container ship was staggering. Codi sat in the back of an ambulance watching as an IV filled her body back up with fluids and salt. Authorities from several agencies seemed to be running in every direction. Anyone who had ventured onto the ship was wearing a biohazard suit, but it was soon clear that any hazard of that type had all been extinguished with the destruction of the onboard hidden lab. A quick tour revealed that everything was blackened.

The doctor that was fussing over Codi was having a rough time of it, as her patient was more than a little annoyed. She had taken samples of skin and hair and drawn three vials of blood. The doctor wanted to take Codi to the hospital for testing. As usual, Codi had refused to go, but it took an intervention from the assistant director of the FBI's Special Projects to keep that from happening. Codi made a mental note that she would owe him one. After much back and forth, Codi was quarantined to her own apartment until the test results came back. This seemed to appease the medical staff as well as Codi. Matt had volunteered to take the risk of getting infected so he could be the caregiver for the next few days. As the ambulance pulled away and escorted her home, Codi had only one thing on her mind—Matt. After all that she had been through, she had missed him more than anything else. It had taken a near-death experience, but it was a truth held strongly in her mind.

***

Joel dropped off the rental as he, Anna, and Gordon headed for the terminal. The news of Codi's resurrection had been received with much elation. Trooper Smith's demise, not so much. Detective Havok could now focus on his partner's murder and seemed content to say goodbye to a case that had run its course in his small town. The flight back to D.C. was painless for a change, and all three agents were happy to be home. They would regroup and be back at it in the office the next day. Joel had mixed feelings about seeing his partner again. The last time he'd been with her, she shoved him over the railing of a container ship. It was an event that had nearly killed him, and he still didn't have all the information on Codi's actions since then. He needed a *why*, and it had better be something darn good.

Matt was so happy to have her back. He took a few days off to be by her side, disease or not. After two days of Grub Hub and binging Netflix, they were given the all-clear by the doctor. Codi had no signs of infection or typhus in her system. She was going to be fine. There was also no sign of the vaccine, and this had doctors puzzled. What kind of vaccine cured the disease but didn't work like a vaccine? Only more testing or access to more patients would determine that.

Matt had considered just blurting out his marriage proposal when he first saw Codi, as he had been extremely anxious during her hijacking. Having her back seemed like a dream, and he was going to make the most of it.

He had conceived and dismissed several new ways to go about proposing and was driving himself insane. Perhaps Brian had been right to just do it, no matter the place or time. He was sure that would fail with Codi. *Patience*, he reminded himself several times, as the week progressed.

Matt closed the bedroom door and walked back to the couch. Codi was sleeping soundly. He felt a mixture of relief at having her back and the pain his heart felt when he thought of her. This was a new sensation for him. As a scientist, he was a fairly non-emotional person. To have his heart flutter every time he was close to Codi was . . . He couldn't think of just one word to describe it, but it was driving him crazy. He had heard people talking about love. This must be it.

Sitting down with a plop, he pulled his laptop over and hit the On button. A moment later, he was looking at a web browser that was waiting for him to begin. He cleared his mind and typed a few letters: Romantic Engagement Stories.

The browser populated with hundreds of stories. Matt interlocked his fingers and reversed them away from his body. A few pops were heard as he did the simple stretch. Leaning forward, he dug into the information. The list was overwhelming and most of them cheesy. His favorite story was from a same-sex couple, but he wasn't sure if it was right for Codi. After forty minutes, Matt leaned back against the couch and rubbed his temples. It was a bust. *Maybe I should follow Brian's plan and just ask.* Codi was a captive audience after all. They had sent her home and told her to take the week off.

Simple. That was it. He would make all the things she loved for breakfast and then get down on one knee and profess his love for her. If he said the right things, it would be romantic. Now, all he had to do was figure out what to say. For this, he would need some advice.

"SSA Brian Fescue."

"Brian, it's Matt."

Matt proceeded to explain his dilemma to Codi's boss.

Brian listened to his friend, giving the occasional *Uh-huh* to let him know he was there. Matt seemed to be a bit all over the place, but Brian got the gist.

"Matt, I love you, man, and I wholeheartedly endorse this action, but I am not the best source for romantic dribblings. Listen to your heart. Speak from your heart. It will tell you what to say."

"My heart is broken. It just beats out of control every time I think about her."

"Well, there you go. Tell her that," Brian said.

"Seriously?"

"Yes."

"Okay, that actually makes sense. Thanks, Brian." Matt hung up before Brian could say more. He jumped to his feet and was out the door in a flash.

Matt woke early the next day and began the morning with two recipe books and a cup of fresh coffee. A bacon and egg soufflé was on the menu with fresh fruit and sourdough toast with fig jam. The trick was having everything ready when Codi awoke. She had been sleeping in the last few days, so that made it a bit of an unknown.

He put his ear to the bedroom door and listened. There was movement inside. Time to act. He tweaked the two dozen red roses on the table to perfection and pulled the soufflé out of the oven. Two slices of sourdough went into the toaster, and he crossed his fingers.

The door to the bedroom started to open, and Matt dropped to one knee with the ring in his hand. He cleared his throat just as the toaster went *ding*.

Codi stepped into the kitchen, not in her pajamas, but dressed for work. She was even wearing her gun.

"What are you doing down there?" she asked Matt.

Matt panicked. This was not part of his plan. She was supposed to have a slow, easy breakfast with all the foods she loved.

"Nothing. Just dropped a fork," he said weakly. "I made all your favorites." He added a hopeful ring to his words. He stood back up, pocketing the ring. He had a mortified look on his face and seemed to be unable to speak or move.

Codi stepped up and gave him a quick kiss. "This looks amazing, but something has come up at the office. I'm being recalled." She reached out and took a bite of the soufflé. "Hmm, this is really good. I'll take some with me. Amazing. I'll be home for dinner, and we can pick up where we left off. I gotta go. My Uber is here. Love the flowers, by the way."

Matt watched helplessly as Codi put some food on a paper plate and left the apartment.

"You're supposed to be taking a week off!" he called out lamely as he slowly dropped to a chair at the table. With head in hands, Matt pondered this turn of events. *This is going to be harder than I thought. Time for plan C, whatever that is.*

***

Codi was not happy with herself for lying to Matt, but by day four, she was feeling like her apartment walls were starting to close in. She would make it up to him tonight. He would understand. Besides, he had been acting a bit strange the last couple of days. Fresh air and a fresh perspective would do her more good than rest right now.

She had spoken to Joel, and he'd been a bit standoffish. The following day he had called again and seemed like his old self. Codi figured he must have finally gotten the report of what had happened on *The Mantis*, plus the lead in the case he was following seemed promising. There was nothing Codi wanted more right now than the person responsible for *The Mantis*, so anything Joel tracked down was good with her. Thirteen innocent lives lost that she knew of.

The sun finally won the war with the clouds as the city awoke to a gloriously warm fall day. Brian left his overcoat in his car as he walked to the office, hoping the good weather would last. A flash of brown hair caught his attention.

"Not so good at math, I see," SSA Brian Fescue said when he spotted his agent back before her required week off.

"Not my strong point," Codi replied with a smirk.

"Okay, just do me a favor and start back slow."

"That sounds just like me," Codi replied.

Brian shook his head and entered his office, his best intentions thwarted.

Joel was enjoying the collaboration of having his partner back. He kept asking her if there was anything she needed or wanted him to do until Codi's response was to be left alone. Eventually, he took the hint and shuffled back to his desk.

An email alert caught Joel's attention, and he opened it. His facial recognition search had hit on all but one of the faces in *The Mantis* photograph he had found.

Max Odo.

Captain Vadim Semenova.

Kyber Baqri.

Pullin Ikaika.

Unknown.

Behind each name was additional information, like place of birth, last known job, and so on, with the exception of one.

"Hey, Codi, you got a second?" Joel called to his partner across the hall.

"'Sup?" Codi said as she rolled her chair into Joel's cubicle.

"Any of these guys look familiar?"

Codi had a flash of panic shoot up her spine. Faces that she would never forget. She took a second to compose herself.

"Yeah, this one, Max, was the ship's first mate. He left me this nice scar before I . . . well, let's say, stopped him." She pointed to the scab in her hairline from the knife that had grazed her scalp.

Joel's mind flashed back to the man who had placed a gun against his head and pulled the trigger. "Thank goodness he's dead," he added.

Codi nodded in agreement and then looked at the next picture.

"That's the captain. I saw a few chunks of him up on the bridge."

Joel set the muffin he was chewing down with a disgusted look.

"This guy, Kyber, he tried to help me before a security guy shot him down in cold blood. Said they were a team trying to save humanity from a typhoid super-bug, or something like that. I don't fully remember, as I was a complete mess at the time with a raging fever."

She continued. "That guy, Pullin, I don't know, and the last one, 'unknown.' She ran the lab, Dr. Kamer or Kamba—something like that. Anyway, she tried to kill me with a broken glass flask, after infecting me with something very nasty. She sounded African to me. Not a hundred percent sure about her name, but I might be able to find out. Send me the file." The words brought added angst to Codi, remembering last week's drama.

"Does everyone you meet try to kill you?" Joel asked.

"Almost always, and if you're thinking about it, get in line," Codi responded.

The comment was followed by a chuckle from Joel, which helped lighten the mood in the room.

"So they're all dead but this guy here?" Joel asked.

"They're all dead." Codi pointed as she said, "Pullin Ikaika, who are you?"

"Let's find out," Joel answered.

"You find out. I have another angle I'm working on, and I'm going to find out who and what that woman was," Codi said as she wheeled out of Joel's office.

The report on *The Mantis* was preliminary, but it still had a lot of detail. Codi dug through it with mixed feelings, especially when there were reference photos.

The Mantis had been un-beached and was currently docked in Charleston. The FBI and USCG inspectors were going through everything on board with a fine-toothed comb. The lab was nothing but a burned-out hulk. The bridge, likewise. Nothing obvious seemed out of the ordinary on the rest of the ship. The one piece of interest was taken from the captain's cabin. It showed a plan for a three-month journey covering multiple ports of call all around the Atlantic. Whatever they were up to with the lab involved many stops in highly populated ports.

Codi leaned back in her chair and considered the information. With a flick of her wrist, she hit print to add the chart to the other evidence they were collecting. She was the only witness to what was going on in the lab, but she had been such a weakling during that time, she felt more useless than useful. Several other agents, including medical experts, had interviewed her before she'd been released from the scene and sent back to her home in D.C.

By afternoon, they had all moved to the conference room behind their cubicles. Agents Anna, Gordon, and Joel all watched as Codi sauntered in a few minutes late. They were glad to see her looking more like herself. Each gave her a hug before starting the meeting. Codi felt overwhelmed for a second, as she was still trying to get her mojo and emotions back from her "sea cruise."

"So what do we have?" Codi asked.

Anna stepped up to a whiteboard and started to fill it in as each person shared what they knew of the case. It was all the expected stuff like the Garrett Scott connection that led them to *The Mantis;* when and how Codi and Joel had been shanghaied; and the people missing from Portland. Codi paused here and took a few minutes to look at the missing persons. She was able to ID each one from the time spent in the glass cubicles with them as test rats. This tragically solved twelve missing persons cases in less than twenty minutes.

Joel waited until everything was on the board. It was a mishmash of evidence. He explained about the picture he had found and how Codi had helped him ID some of the persons and their roles. There were grainy pictures of the crew and security that had been identified, a few taken by investigators from the ship. Several *X*s represented the still unknowns. On the top right corner were several lines about a typhoid superbug with the words "cockroaches" and "flies" circled.

On the far left was the only picture of a living person.

"Pullin Ikaika," Joel read. "He's a Hawaiian-born power broker. A billionaire with companies in shipping, global logistics, financial and medical research."

"I know him," Anna said. "He's one of those ZPG guys."

Codi gave her a skewed glance.

"Zero population growth."

"I thought ZPG died out in the late eighties," Joel said, with his brow scrunched up.

"Since then the world has doubled in population," Anna said.

"Guess it didn't work," Codi added.

"Check this out." Joel spun his laptop around so all could see. "It's a lecture Pullin Ikaika gave at Stanford two years ago. Since then, he has fallen from the public eye."

"That's not easy to do these days," Gordon added.

Joel hit play. Pullin was standing at a glass lectern on a small stage. There was a large audience seated in a bowl-shaped lecture hall. He was dressed in all white, including his shoes. He spoke with passion and even banged his palm on the lectern a few times for emphasis.

We cannot sustain our current level of consumption. The amount of garbage alone will smother the planet at the rate we are going. World population has reached what I call a critical mass, and sustaining a sufficient food supply is already failing in many countries. In the past, the earth had a way of culling the masses. Floods, storms, plagues, even the lowly mosquito has helped. Man has also done his share with wars and genocide. But to what end? We are still at the breaking point. Something must be done, and done soon, if we are to avert global disaster, to stabilize our population at a sustainable level.

"Here's a piece from something more obscure, a fringe magazine interview," Joel said as he clicked another video.

I'm not looking to kill mankind or play God, but a good world plague that might drop, say, two billion mouths to feed would do it. Let nature select who lives and who dies and get us back to a population we can sustain.

"The ZPG people are now calling themselves Population Connection," Anna said, reading from their website. "They do a lot of world education on the subject and are the voice for population advocacy."

"Looks like Pullin feels they have gone too white-bread for him," Codi added.

"Yeah, and he sounds like more of a *minus* population growth guy now," Gordon said, sounding a bit uneasy.

"MPG, is that a thing?" asked Joel.

"It is if you kill enough people," Codi said.

The words hung heavy and true in the room.

Chapter Nineteen

THE FAINTING GOAT – WASHINGTON D.C.
– U STREET CORRIDOR – 8:59 P.M.

J oel pushed his food around the plate for the third time. He looked up at the most intense blue eyes that were staring back at him with concern.

"So is it the food or me?"

"What?"

"You've hardly touched your food tonight, and I am having to *pry* just about every word out of you," said Shannon.

"Oh my goodness. No, I've been so caught up in a case, and I guess I let my mind wander. So sorry," Joel lied, trying to cover his real emotions. In truth, he had been a bit afraid to see Shannon again after his near-death experience in Canada and complete failure with her parents. She had been a dream while he was incapacitated in the hospital, but since then, he had been giving them a lot of thought. He was sure he didn't measure up to her standards and felt embarrassed for being so incompetent around her parents.

He forced a weak smile on his face and gazed up at Shannon. Man, was she beautiful.

The Fainting Goat was a casual tavern-style eatery in the U Street corridor. It was filled with warm, wood tones and soft lighting. Shannon had convinced Joel to meet her there at 8:30 for a late dinner and chat. She hadn't seen him since he had left the hospital in Portland.

"Joel, if you're worried about what my parents think or how things went in Edmonton, I could care less. My dad is . . . let's just say he's different, and he has always used his active lifestyle to judge others. That's not who I am. I love my parents, but I'm not them. You are perfect just the way you are. I love you for your big brain and your kindness. Your willingness to rise or kneel when needed—that's a very rare quality, by the way—and your smile . . . I'd give it a ten." Shannon cocked her head, delivering her own thousand-watt smile.

"Really? You're saying I'm perfect?"

Shannon sat back, and her smile disappeared. "That was your takeaway? Perfect? Just forget it. It's strange how a man so smart can be so dumb. Come here." Shannon reached over the table and grabbed Joel with both hands around the face and kissed him for emphasis.

Joel's ears turned beet red, but the smile that grew on his face never wavered, the stress and concern all gone.

"Should we order dessert? I'm still hungry," he said.

***

Codi unlocked her front door and entered her apartment with a flare. She was excited to get back to Matt after a long first day back at work. The near threat they had avoided with *The Mantis* was still on her mind, but she vowed to drop it for the night. She had carefully planned their night's activities with payback-for-ditching-Matt in mind. Candlelight, soft music, and more were all on the top of her mind. Catching Pullin Ikaika and stringing him up by his balls was second, and she was determined not to get the two mixed up.

"Matt, I'm home!" she called. Codi picked up her phone to dial him and noticed the piece of paper folded on the table. She sat down with a sinking feeling and read the note.

Codi, you seemed to need your space this morning. I get that. I'm back home and hope to see you soon when you are ready. LMK Love, M

Codi lowered the note to the table and took a slow breath. She considered Ubering out to his house for the night, but the more she thought about it, the more she knew he was right. She did need some alone time. Matt knew her needs and had acted on his belief. It was just the right gesture, and Codi's heart filled at the thought. Her mind soon turned to action item number two, how to string Pullin Ikaika up by the balls.

***

Brian stepped out of the conference room and headed back to his office. He had tasked the team with compiling as much evidence as they could on Pullin Ikaika before they showed their hand. The man was politically connected and was probably the reason behind his lunch with the boss earlier. They would share evidence only when ready. From here on out, that information would have to be carefully controlled.

The team got to work. It was a slow and tedious process with many dead ends. By late morning the next day, they had compiled a significant amount of data on Pullin, but the only problem was that most of it was just that—data. Tranzglobal Logistics had been a dummy shell corporation mired in multiple shell companies, but after peeling back many layers and hours of research, Joel found the parent company, Pullin's Global Consolidated Logistics, GCL.

"This was a real logistics nightmare, no pun intended," Joel said. "I finally have a connection to Pullin and *The Mantis.*"

"Which means a connection to Garrett Scott," Gordon added.

"Right."

"What's with you and that corn-eating smile today?" Codi asked.

Joel suddenly felt self-conscience and tried to look serious.

"Let me guess," she said. "You had a date with Shannon last night."

Joel's tell was obvious to everyone in the room but Joel.

Cody relaxed and touched his forearm with affection. "Good for you."

A beat of silence filled the air.

"What made you choose me?" Joel asked.

"What?"

"You know, push me over the railing into the freezing ocean miles from shore."

"Ah. They were going to kill one of us, maybe all of us. I knew what you were capable of, Joel. If anyone was going to make it through, it was you. And I needed to make a decision before our kidnappers did it for us."

Joel's eyes lowered, remembering the trials he had faced in the open ocean.

"You are a remarkable man. Capable, strong, and very smart. I knew you'd find a way. And look, here you are."

"Were there really cockroaches?" Joel asked.

"Thousands."

"Thanks."

"For what?"

"For pushing me overboard."

Codi smiled. "You're welcome." She turned back to her computer and read from it.

"Here's all I've found so far on the good doctor, Dr. Kamba. A Kenyan-born thirty-seven-year-old doctor in infectiology and infectious diseases. Let's see . . . she was raised in Gatare where Rift Valley Fever decimated her village, including her parents. She went to live with her aunt in Nairobi and ended up immigrating to San Jose with her some twenty years ago. Got her degree at the University of California San Francisco. Worked for the CDC for a brief spell and then went into the private sector. The private sector is not good with sharing, so we don't really know what she has been up to since then." Codi finished reading and looked up.

Anna tried to summarize. "Pullin Ikaika's company owns the ship with an infectious diseases doctor working in a secret lab in international waters with human test subjects, flies, and cockroaches, all to help stop a typhoid superbug from decimating the planet."

"Doesn't sound like him, based on what we read yesterday," Gordon said.

"I agree. That summary alone is pretty frightening," Anna added.

"Or to help start," Codi said.

The other three agents all looked at her for clarification.

"They could be *creating* this superbug to distribute around the world."

The comment was scary and sobering.

"That actually sounds more like it," Gordon added.

Codi pulled up an image on her computer. "Look at this. It's a chart showing the voyage *The Mantis* was undertaking. All these destinations are major population centers. They were planning on releasing the sickness in each port."

"How were they planning on doing that?" Gordon asked.

"I did some research on classic Typhus," Joel said. "It can be carried and transmitted by flies."

"So this superbug, apparently, from what I saw," said Codi, "can be spread by both flies and cockroaches. That's why they were growing them by the thousands—to contaminate and release them into each city."

"And based on the recent outbreak in India it can be transferred from person to person by bodily fluids like a virus," Joel added.

"India . . . I wonder if that was a test run?" Codi's words hit everyone there equally.

"They weren't *saving* the world," Anna said. "They were bent on destroying it, using a highly communicable disease that has no known cure."

"HYDRA," Codi blurted out.

"What?"

"It's something the first officer said to me before he died." Codi tried to recall the moment as Anna wrote it on the evidence board in bold letters.

"'HYDRA will not fail,' he said. That must be what they're calling it. Wait. There was something more." She stood and started to pace. "'Our sister will finish what we have started. Hydra will not fail.' That's it!"

Joel typed for a few seconds.

"There is no information on Max Odo having a sister," Joel announced.

"Not *my* sister, *our* sister," Codi said.

No one had an immediate answer.

"Okay," Gordon said. "This is good. It checks all the boxes. Now, how do we prove it?"

His question was answered by silence.

***

Pullin answered his phone on the third ring. "Senator."

"Pullin, I have an update for you."

"Hang on a sec, will you?" Pullin put his phone on mute and called to his driver. "Pull over," he demanded.

The driver of his black Cadillac Escalade limo pulled to the side of the road. Pullin let himself out the back door and stepped away from the road. "What have you got?" he asked.

Senator Crandall filled him in on everything Director Lyon had shared about the case, including their next step.

Pullin listened to the details as he paced in the roadside gravel. Once the senator was finished, Pullin thanked him for his efforts, with an added promise to be one of his next big donors when he ran for office. He hung up before the senator could reply and held the phone in his hand for a few seconds while he considered the information.

A quick dial connected him with Crispin.

"Sir?"

"Change in plans. I need you to get to Japan and meet up with *The Mantis.*"

"Okay. I'll leave as soon as possible."

"Crispin, you'll need to take a team with you."

Pullin hit the red button to disconnect the call. Then, like many of his phones, he dropped it and smashed it with his heel.

He stepped back into the limo and called to the driver as he closed the door, "Take me back to the house. And step on it."

***

Three large black SUVs moved north along Highway 28. The broken view of the famous lake through the snow-frosted pines was breathtaking, but no one seemed to notice. Lake Tahoe was an almost black-blue against the cloudy skies. There was an air of extreme seriousness in the vehicles. Each federal agent wore a bulletproof vest and a warm coat with a yellow FBI logo clearly marked on it. Brian seemed to be in his element riding shotgun in the first vehicle. It was the first official FBI raid Codi and Joel had participated in. Most of their cold cases had taken them either out of the country or down a rabbit hole of paperwork. The full might of the FBI was either not needed or was too late in arriving.

Codi could tell this case was coming to a close. It was intuition, like a boxer who could sense a shift in the momentum of a fight. They had enough evidence to search and arrest Pullin and at least get him for aiding and abetting in the deaths of thirteen innocent lives. It might seem weak, but Codi was hoping he would, at the very least, resist arrest, and if all went well, they would hopefully collect and come away with more condemning evidence.

Black smoke rose up into the sky as they approached their destination. It was a signal that was not well received by the task force. As the first SUV pulled up to the entry gate, the driver hit his horn several times. A guard moved from the stone building and sauntered over to the driver's window.

"Can I help you?"

"Yes, I am FBI Special Agent Gordon Reyes, and we have a search warrant for the premises."

"May I see it?" the guard asked.

Gordon handed him the warrant, and the man looked it over.

"This allows you to search the home, offices, and garage structures and the surrounding grounds. Please refrain from going beyond this list or you can expect reprisals and lawsuits for an illegal search and seizure."

"Understood," Gordon said, already done with this wannabe cop.

The guard slowly moved back to the guardhouse and eventually hit the button to open the gate. He picked up his phone and dialed as the vehicles moved past.

"They don't know about the lab," the guard said as he gave a stern look to the black cars invading his domain.

"Understood. I can take it from here. Make sure no one else comes through that gate."

The SUVs blew past a mostly empty parking area and skidded to a stop on the immense looped driveway. Eight armed FBI agents exited and headed for the front door of the main house. The snow had left a recent frosting, and the stark white contrasted with the stone four-story mansion that stood before them. It was a Tudor affair with arched modern windows and a gray slate roof. Brian jogged up the steps to the inviting front porch that contrasted with the house in a more rustic way with bare wood beams. Two men emerged from the massive wood and glass pivot-door to greet them.

"I am Donald Fredricks, Mr. Ikaika's attorney, may I see the warrant?" one of the men asked.

Brian handed him the paperwork.

Codi whispered to her boss. "They knew we were coming."

"Looks that way," he replied, out the side of his mouth.

Donald inspected the warrant with care and then turned toward the inside of the house with a gesture of his outstretched arm and said, "After you."

"We also have an arrest warrant for Pullin Ikaika. We can take him into custody now, or he can remain with us during the search and then come with us once we are finished here."

"That is very kind of you, agents. I can assure you that Mr. Ikaika will cooperate fully. I'm sure he would appreciate getting as much work done as he can before you take him in for what I am sure will be a very brief period." Donald said the last part confidently.

"Agent Weathers," Brian said, "go with Mr. Ikaika's attorney here and keep tabs on his client until we are done."

Agent Weathers nodded, and the two men entered the house along with several other agents.

"You take the office. I got the fire," Codi said to Brian.

He nodded. Anna and Joel followed their boss, heading for the other building.

Codi jogged around to the backyard near the waterfront where a gardener was burning excess tree trimmings.

"Odd time to be burning brush," she called out.

The gardener looked startled at the voice and the obviously FBI agent walking in his direction. "It's the only time of year they let us do it," he said, nervously.

Codi moved closer and examined the flames. There was evidence of paperwork that had been burned along with the trimmings. The gardener looked away from Codi's gaze. A quick inspection told her they were too late. There was nothing left worth salvaging. Whatever they had thrown into the fire was now ash. She took a picture with her phone and left the fire to check out the garage.

Inside the main house, a few reams of paper were collected. Four of the agents who were brought along had accounting backgrounds. Ever since the FBI convicted Al Capone for tax evasion, paperwork and forensic accounting were at the heart of many cases. They began to sift through what might be of interest to their case.

Pullin eyed the federal agent sent to monitor him during the search. "Special Agent, can I get you some coffee? I'm in the middle of making a fresh pot."

"No thanks," Special Agent Weathers replied.

Pullin whistled as he poured himself a cup. He strolled over to a large window and gazed at the lake beyond. He seemed unfazed by the goings-on in his home as the view inspired him.

"I'm curious," Pullin said. "Where did the name *special* come from in your title? I mean, we have all heard of the term G-man, government agent, or FBI guy, but why *special?* I mean, I see nothing special about what you are doing here."

"It was a designation initially given to treasury agents in the 1800s. The FBI adopted the use of it in 1908 when the bureau was formed. It has to do with the authority to conduct investigations and make arrests. That's the designator for a special agent."

"I see," Pullin said as he let the room grow quiet.

Attached by only a covered walkway was the main business office for Pullin's various enterprises. It was mere steps away, a commuter's dream. Inside were multiple offices surrounding grouped cubicles. It was a three-story affair with a rec room, gym, showers, and gourmet kitchen. The entire building was mostly unoccupied, save for a few employees in some of the larger offices. It was a clear message—we knew you were coming.

Joel took the lead as they filtered through a mass of files and information, looking for the needle in a very large haystack. They collected hard drives and any paperwork they could find, but as a modern paperless office, it was scant pickings.

Beyond the office was a small building about the size of a one-car garage. It had a glass entry door, and you could see an elevator and a set of stairs beyond. Codi and Joel walked with their boss toward the entrance.

"Can I help you?" came a voice from behind them.

A quick look back revealed Pullin's attorney, Donald, walking their way.

"No, I got it," Codi replied as she reached for the glass door.

"That building is not listed on your search warrant, so you cannot go in there," he countered.

"What are you talking about?" Brian asked.

"Your warrant clearly states the main home, office, garage, and surrounding grounds."

"This is part of the office," Codi said.

"No. If you look closely, the office roof extends over this building but does not attach. It shares no connection to any of the other buildings. Therefore, it is a separate building and is not on your warrant. You have no legal right to enter."

"What's down there?" Joel asked.

The man just returned a false smile, nothing more.

"Screw this!" Codi said. "I nearly died because of your boss." She grabbed the door and pulled.

"Codi! We do this the right way or not at all," Brian cautioned. "We can amend the warrant in a few hours."

"I wouldn't bet on it," Donald said.

Codi held the door for a beat and then let go and walked to the nearest SUV. She was done here.

After nearly ten hours of searching and collecting, everything was loaded into a cube van that had been called in. They arrested Pullin, read him his Miranda rights, and left the estate just before the sun kissed the horizon in the west.

The FBI field office in Reno was small but functional. The team quickly overloaded the place, and several agents had standing room only. Extra coffee and donuts had been brought in, and the volume in the room seemed to grow as multiple conversations took hold.

Codi looked like she hadn't slept in twenty-four hours because she hadn't. The night was spent in a moldy hotel room with her mind going over every possibility on the case. Unable to turn it off, Codi finally got out of bed and made some instant coffee on the room's tiny kitchen countertop. She picked up the printed pictures taken of the home and offices during the search and perused them. Nothing seemed out of the ordinary. Pullin had known the FBI was coming to search and had most likely destroyed or erased much of anything incriminating. The hopeful feeling Codi had felt yesterday had turned to sour disappointment.

As she set down the stack of printed papers, something caught her eye. It wasn't much, but it might provide a small modicum of joy in Codi's otherwise foul mood. A hand sanitizer squirt bottle seemed to be in almost every room. She picked the stack back up and double-checked. Yep, every room.

The kitchen in the office was small but practical, and it took Codi only a minute to find what she was looking for—a can of cooking spray.

The office's only interrogation room was claustrophobic with a small table and four chairs. She carefully sprayed a thin coat of cooking spray in a small area on the opposite side of the table and then returned it to the kitchen.

She sat back and watched as Pullin and his attorney were led into the room before Joel and she followed. Pullin Ikaika sat smugly in a chair next to his ever-present attorney with his hands in his lap. The room had a camera and a hi-gain microphone. There was a one-way mirror and an overhead fluorescent light. The FBI had managed to arrest Pullin late enough the day before so that he'd been forced to spend the night in a cell. One small victory. The interview started promptly at 8:00 a.m. the next morning in an attempt to thwart any access the suspect might have to a friendly judge.

Codi began with a few simple questions.

They were all answered by Donald, the attorney, as Pullin just sat and watched the show.

"If you think my client is about to incriminate himself into whatever hunting expedition you two are running, you are mistaken," Donald said. "Whatever happened onboard *The Mantis* was Captain Semenova's doing, not ours. We used the ship strictly as a logistics goods transport and a tax incentive. The fact that it was part of our company was just for write-off purposes. It's a buyout leaseback, nothing more. The misguided and obviously regrettable actions that the captain took were not our doing and in no way reflect any part of anything we do."

"You're telling me you *lease The Mantis* to Captain Semenova and nothing more?" Joel said.

Codi had heard enough. She could see the joy in Pullin's eyes and his smug expression. The man was daring her to catch him. He believed himself above the law.

"This is ridiculous," she said. "Your client is dirty. He is responsible for the deaths of thirteen innocent lives. These people were kidnapped, tortured, and tested on. And after all that, they were thrown away like yesterday's trash."

Donald held his hand up subtly to stop his client from answering. "Look, agents," he said, "we can sit here and banter back and forth, but you will find no evidence of any kind that connects my client to the actions on *The Mantis.*"

"That's because you burned it all up!" Codi said.

"All you have is that one of my client's companies owns a ship. A ship that was leased to a captain that did some bad stuff. This would be like you trying to convict the company that rented a car to a man who perpetrated a crime. It's not going to happen," he said.

"You will not get away with this!" Codi started to lean in Pullin's direction, her arm cocked back and ready.

The door opened a crack and Brian called out, "Codi. Got a second?"

She didn't move, her anger still controlling her.

"Codi," Brian said again, in a calm voice.

She pushed her chair back, stood, and fumed out of the room.

There was a moment of awkward silence, and then Joel continued. "Okay, so explain to me about Garrett Scott, who I can prove was on your payroll and who tried to kill both me and my partner, and is suspected of killing Alice Sanders and Detective Jennings."

No answer was forthcoming. The air grew temporarily brittle with that stillness you get when someone is glaring. Joel took a deep breath and forged on. "Let me quote a video interview you gave." Joel read from a transcript.

I'm not looking to kill mankind or play God, but a good world plague that might drop, say, two billion mouths to feed would do it. Let nature select who lives and who dies and get us back to a population we can sustain.

"Agent. Anything you would like to bring into evidence must first—"

Pullin put his hand up to stop his attorney. He said, "Ah, my younger days. I was such an idealist, but I'm afraid my more practical self has won out. There is no way to save our planet based on our current course. I, along with you, will just ride it into the ground. Tragic, really." Pullin seemed truly sad as he laid his hands on the table.

It took a second, but his hands flew off as Pullin let out an audible gasp, inspecting a foreign substance that was now all over his hands. Fingers touched fingers as he tried to determine what the slimy substance was. His lips fell toward the floor as he started to lose his calm.

"Okay, how 'bout this," Joel said, unaware of Pullin's plight.

A beep interrupted the conversation and Pullin's attorney looked to his phone.

"We are done here, agent," he said as he slid his phone over for Joel to see a scanned picture of a document.

It was a judge's request for immediate release of the prisoner.

Joel paused, and then lifted his hands as if to say okay. "What's operation HYDRA?" he threw out as Pullin started to leave.

Pullin looked back and gave Joel a scowl that said: *Wouldn't you like to know*, before leaving the interview room. But his mind was on his contaminated hands.

"I know you're guilty, and we're going to bring you down!" Joel called out.

"Good luck with that, detective," Pullin threw back, trying to regain his edge.

"That's special agent!" Joel countered.

"Whatever." Pullin closed the door and dashed for a washroom.

***

Tokyo Bay was just starting to glow as the sun dropped out of the sky, now shining on the other side of the world. The lights from the Yokohama Red Brick Warehouse district were randomly turning on as the shadows of dusk flourished. *The Locust* passed under the Yokohama Bay Bridge, a white cable-stayed affair that was lit up for the night. A tug joined *The Locust* to guide her safely in. Captain Combs stepped to the flying bridge to watch the choreographed dance the ship would do before being tied to the dock. She never tired of it. As a woman in a traditionally man's position, Charlotte Combs had overcome more than most. It had taken vision and forward-thinking for Pullin to place her in this position, and she returned the act with full-blooded commitment to their plan. Not only would she see things through to the end, but she also believed it was the only option left to save a dying planet. Being part of the solution was a privilege.

Their first stop in Korea had gone off without a hitch. From there, they leisurely steamed in a broad arc to Yokohama, just outside of Tokyo. They needed to give Dr. Sales time for his next batch of bugs to mature. The cockroaches needed double the time of the flies, and the good doctor had put a system in place to stagger the growing process and still accomplish their goals on schedule.

After docking and offloading, *The Locust* took on an additional eighty-seven containers. They repeated the process, now perfected in Korea, and released the two waves of disease-carrying insects just after 3:00 a.m..

Refueling and resupply of stores took another two-and-a-half hours. First Officer Collins Eynaut then cleared customs and reported back to the bridge.

"We are good to depart, Captain. Crispin Gales, along with the extra men Pullin sent are all squared away in their cabins."

"Good. I hope we don't need them, but I will not make the same mistake Captain Semenova did. Have Crispin keep four men armed and on patrol at all times," ordered the captain.

"I'll let him know," Collins replied.

"And see to it that our tug gets alongside so we can shove off," she said.

A ship the size of *The Locust* required a tugboat to help her maneuver in the tight quarters of the dock area. The little boats were extremely powerful and could shove a ship that size with ease.

"Aye," Collins responded as he left the bridge with his radio in hand.

Next stop, Shanghai.

***

The news out of Busan, South Korea, was sketchy at first. Some kind of epidemic was spreading throughout the city. It was initially thought to be a flu of some sort, but authorities soon identified it as an unknown strain of Typhus. The sick and dying soon overwhelmed the hospitals, and the Korean government took steps to quarantine the city. They quickly realized that this strain of Typhus was not reacting to any known medications. It was their worst fear—a superbug.

As usual, the international news sensationalized the situation and people all over the planet were starting to feel dread. Within a few days, other cities in South

Korea started to see outbreaks, and more desperate attempts were implemented to stop the spread.

Public transportation was shut down. All flights in or out were canceled, and people were ordered to stay in their homes. Images of patients lined up outside hospitals and dropping dead in line filled the news. Soon, the whole world was living in fear of what had been coined the Korean Typhoid Superbug, or KTS. An infrared satellite image above the southern part of South Korea glowed brightly as every available crematorium, including a few bonfires, were working around the clock to burn the dead.

Chapter Twenty

The team sat quietly in the conference room after watching the latest news out of Korea. Anna was the first to speak. "I thought we had this case all figured out," she said.

"We did," Gordon returned.

"What do you think was in that other building on Pullin's estate?" Joel asked.

"Contraband, drugs, Snow Leopard pelts, the files we really wanted to see," Gordon replied.

"Maybe another lab, like on *The Mantis*," Codi added.

"Could be," Joel said.

"What we need is to get another warrant and go back and check out that underground building," Anna said.

"After the beat-down we just took on our last warrant, no judge will issue one without hard evidence. This guy is untouchable right now," Gordon said.

"What about Korea?" Anna asked.

"What about it?" Joel said.

"We can tie *The Mantis* to the superbug with what I went through on that ship. But that's not real evidence, just my word," Codi said.

"And we all saw how well we tied Pullin to *The Mantis*," Anna said, her helplessness growing.

"We know he put this whole thing together, but he's managed to keep his hands clean," Joel added.

"Didn't even spend twelve hours in custody," Gordon said, as he leaned back from the table.

"If we want to take Pullin down, we'll have to tie him to something solid," Joel said.

"I'll go for tying him to the bottom of his ship," Codi added, to a chorus of nodding heads.

Joel looked despondently at the evidence board. His eyes roamed the words and pictures for the hundredth time. There was something that tugged at the back of his mind. Something he was missing. Flies, cockroaches, Mantis, HYDRA, Semenova. He ran the information through his brain one more time. He paused remembering the story Codi had shared of the Lexan cells and the horrible infection she had battled. It made him suddenly shiver uncontrollably. Codi had done him a real favor by head-butting him into the ocean to drown. As a self-admitted germaphobe, he would never have survived the bugs. He popped back from his detoured thoughts. His eyes were staring at one word on the board—sister. *That's what was bugging him.* The man Codi had killed said, *our* sister *will finish what we have started.* Sister. A ship was called a *she*, and a she could have a sister.

"A sister ship!" Joel suddenly blurted out.

Everyone turned to Joel as if he had Tourette's. It took a second, but they quickly followed his thoughts and realized he could be right.

"Of course," Gordon added.

"Pullin had *two* ships," Codi said. "One to cover the Atlantic and one for the Pacific."

The clues dropped into place. The realization in the room grew and with it, a sickening dread.

Joel pushed his chair back, his voice thin. "This is how the world ends—one determined man with enough resources and followers to do his bidding."

***

Pullin found himself in a situation he had never been in before. Damage control. Sometimes, throwing money at a problem didn't solve anything. He needed to attack his issues one at a time. Eliminate it and move to the next.

He paced like a caged animal that hadn't been fed in a week. The FBI had raided his home. *How dare they.* He would make sure every single one of them paid for the incursion. He had carefully made a list of each agent's name who was part of the unfounded warrant. Two names seemed to boil his blood the most. Special Agent Sanders and Special Agent Strickman. They had both been marked for termination several weeks ago, and Garrett Scott had failed in his task. He now regretted letting Crispin off the hook for the failed killing of Agent Strickman in Maine a couple of weeks ago. He would not make the same mistake again. But first, he had to secure his side of the operation. Then he would send each and every one on his list a little present. A present only an entomologist would love.

He was pretty sure he was bulletproof, as he had carefully entrusted others to take charge and do his bidding, and all paperwork led to shell corporations. He just needed to make certain there would be no repercussions or a loose connection that could be traced back to him.

Pullin sat down and started a list, and tweaked the order several times before nodding at it with satisfaction. He flashed back to the table in the FBI's interview room. It had a sticky, slimy residue. Surely that had been intentional. His face turned red at the thought. Special Agent Codi Sanders. She would pay dearly. He would save her for last, take his time, and savor her slow demise. The thought soon had him back on track.

"Whiton. I think it's time to move the lab," Pullin said, as he entered the office.

Crispin's first lieutenant stood as Pullin entered the room. He was a broad-shouldered man with a can-do attitude and the loyalty of a rescued mutt. There was a large scar across his left cheek that said: *you should have seen the other guy.*

Pullin continued. "Given time, it is possible the FBI will be back with a warrant to search it. We have been several steps ahead of them, and I'd like to stay that way. I have a friend that has leased a building to one of my companies, a space that should work nicely. I'm guessing we are still under surveillance, right?"

"Yes. I saw a car parked out on the street with an *ImaFed* license plate," Whiton said, as he moved to his boss's side.

This brought a smile to Pullin's usually stern face.

"Let's ground-zero the lab here. We'll never be able to transport the equipment out without being seen. Transfer all the data and workers. Start fresh. I still want to have fifty thousand vaccinations within the next month."

"Wow, ground zero. That's gonna cost," Whiton said.

"I don't care about the cost. *Get it done!*" Pullin screamed.

"Sorry. I'll take care of it," he replied meekly and left for the lab.

Pullin stepped back over to a monitor on the wall and picked up the small black remote. He tuned into a foreign news source and turned up the volume. His body fidgeted with delight as he watched the death toll mount. It was hard to hold back the pride he felt at having a plan so detailed and perfect come to fruition. It was working. He was culling the planet, just like he had hoped. Making the world a better place for him and his followers. Soon, more countries would follow Korea, and he would watch from his tower, safe from it all as the world's population reset itself.

He checked the stocks he had shorted on the Korean market. They were plummeting. He would make an easy fifty million this week. But first, he needed to tie up a few loose ends.

It took nearly four hours to completely evacuate all of the lab's personnel and their personal effects. They were given three days off, after which equipment would start to arrive at the new lab's location. He had personally watched as all critical data was transferred and secured. Any samples that could be hand-carried were taken by key employees and the rest left to burn.

Whiton walked through the space looking at the millions of dollars in equipment he was about to write off. He paused by the wall and input the code to self-destruct the lab. A soft alarm with a warning began to count down. He hurried up the flight of stairs and out into the cold air. There was a rumble below followed by a plume of black smoke that poured up the stairway and out of the building. Incendiary charges placed throughout the facility melted and burned everything. After about ten minutes, the smoke dissipated as fire suppression kicked in. The lab was now a blackened crater.

***

Matt stared at his phone for the tenth time. He had become a bit of a mess. With two failed attempts to his name, he was starting to feel like he would never pull off his proposal. His eyes moved across several gadgets lying on the conference table that they had been testing for the DOD. The Z-Man Program (Gecko Gloves) testing was nearly complete and the EXACTO (Extreme Accuracy Tasked Ordnance) was looking promising. He was happy at his new job and liked the people around him. It had given him a fresh perspective and a new outlook. This was the type of place where he could prosper. If only he could stop thinking about Codi. She was on his mind way too often for a proper scientist to maintain his concentration. He considered a bold plan that would put this whole mess behind him: a text.

It was simple and efficient, just like Codi. He carefully crafted the words and then deleted them several times before deciding on a more abbreviated and text-appropriate message: *Codi I love U Will U marry me?*

His finger hovered over the send button and then he had a thought. He set the phone down and turned to his laptop and typed: *Is it appropriate to send a marriage proposal via text.*

The browser filled with responses.

He read through the list, some slamming the idea and some in favor. He did a quick calculation in his head. Eighty percent no, twenty percent yes. *Hmm.*

He opened a few of the links. "MissManners" used the term, *not recommended.* What did she know? "LoveLetters" wrote, *Lord, ya'll need to do better.* Okay.

He moved on to some of the sites in favor of it. "Sheknows" said, *getting a text proposal doesn't make it any less romantic.* Now we're talkin'.

Reading through some of the various messages that had been sent made Matt feel more confident of his idea. He modified a few words on his own text and hit the send button on his phone. A sudden sinking feeling took over, and he started to sweat.

***

The FBI conference room looked like a model of efficiency as everyone involved was focused on a single task. With the new direction in the case and the outbreak in Korea expanding, time was no longer on their side. Two cases had been reported in San Francisco, as a young Korean couple had escaped to Japan and made their way to the states, not knowing they were infected. The world was no longer safe.

Joel peeked up from his computer and announced. "Okay, it looks like between Global Consolidated Logistics and two other companies, Pullin has twenty-two different ships in service."

Anna stepped over to look at the screen. The room had gone stale with the smell of old pizza and stress. The harsh overhead lighting had everyone's eyes bloodshot and scratchy.

Joel hit the button and printed up the list.

"Do you have pictures of them?" Codi asked as her phone pinged.

"Let me see what I can find," Joel said.

Anna grabbed the printout. "I'll start a deep dive on the first eleven. Gordon, how 'bout if you take the rest?"

"On it," he replied.

Codi popped up the message screen and read the note from Matt.

Codi I love U and was hoping to see you tomorrow say 8:30 your place?

Codi smiled at the note and added a heart to the message as a reply.

Joel slowly found pictures of the ships in question. Codi scrutinized each one as they popped up.

"Not it."

When Joel pulled up a large blue and white container ship, Codi froze in her chair. "That's it."

Four sets of eyes moved for the screen. Joel zoomed in on the picture. *"The Locust,"* he said, reading the name off the stern.

"She fits the profile and looks a lot like *The Mantis,*" Joel replied.

"That's it. I know it is," Codi said, tapping the screen.

Joel did some more research. "Actually, I was wrong. *The Locust* is not 'a lot like' *The Mantis.* She's the sister ship to *The Mantis.* The same specs, even built at the same shipyard. Identical," Joel said as he compared the two ships.

"Told ya."

***

"Okay, this is unexpected. How did you know I was leaving now?" Joel glanced at his watch. It was a few minutes after nine. He had just come out the exit door of his office and was blind-sided by Shannon. She was wearing a hand-knit beanie and a buckskin leather coat. The streetlight made her hair extra red and highlighted her pale skin. He could see her breath as she spoke.

"I have a spy in your office," Shannon said, with a slight boast.

"Don't let my boss hear you say that."

"Working on something big, I take it?" Shannon asked.

"Yeah, and time is against us."

"Well, you're in luck. I picked up some green curry beef and tofu Pad Thai. My car is just across the street. Join me for dinner, and then you can get back at it."

Joel looked torn, knowing what was at stake in the world.

Shannon added, "Hey, you gotta eat, right?" hoping to convince him to join her.

Joel nodded and smiled. "Sure. I was going to do some work at home but . . ." He watched as Shannon sashayed over to her car in a very flirtatious manner. He was pulled to her like a magnet to iron, and before he knew it, he was sliding into the passenger seat of her car.

She rolled down the windows just a crack and turned on some soft rock.

"Just like high school," Joel said, with a crooked smile.

"I bet you had the girls wrapped around your fingers in high school."

"I was more of a fingers-on-the-keyboard sorta guy. Not a lot of dates."

Shannon opened the containers and Joel scooped out portions over rice. A couple of ice teas were fished out of the bottom of a grocery bag. Talk died as the two ate the savory meal. After a few minutes, Joel spoke through a mouthful. He used his chopsticks to aid in communication.

"So what made you, you know." He gestured to all the food.

"I was hungry. You were hungry. Just made sense."

"Really?"

"No, I missed you, silly. I hope the feeling is mutual," Shannon said, without looking over at him.

"*Hmm,*" Joel said, between chews. "I mean *yes,* it is. Totally mutual. It's all mutual all the time." He said the last part with a pained expression on his face. He hated it when words came out of his mouth without him thinking first.

Shannon stopped chewing and stared at him with her brows pinched.

Joel started to feel hot. His face flushed. He didn't know where to look or what to do.

"The curry is hot!" he exclaimed.

"You're loveable."

Joel paused and looked Shannon right in the eyes. He watched as she slipped a loose strand of hair behind her ear. She was stunning. "You know I think the world of you," he said, meekly.

"I know, Joel, and I feel the same way. I have regrets. Regrets for things I haven't done and regrets for things I have. But I want no regrets between us, okay?"

Joel nodded as Shannon leaned over and they shared a kiss. They held each other for a beat; it was glorious.

"Hope you saved room for dessert. I brought Ding Dongs."

***

Information on *The Locust* was dribbling in every few minutes. Gordon had retrieved a second whiteboard and Anna was filling it with everything they knew about the sister ship. It had docked in Busan, South Korea, seven days ago, and then Yokohama, Japan, yesterday. It gave them a clearer picture of how fast the superbug worked. The facts were lining up against Pullin Ikaika and they would soon take another run at him. Joel had made it his mission to get more hard evidence against him, and it was paying off.

The Locust had apparently turned off her AIS once she left Japan, as they could find no sign or signal from the ship.

"She's gone dark," Anna said in frustration.

"*The Mantis* did the same thing," Joel said.

"Must be their SOP [Standard Operating Procedure]," Codi added.

"We need to get a fix on that ship, or a lot more people are going to die," Anna said as she added more information to the whiteboard. "And warn Japan about what's coming."

"I think we have just expanded beyond our jurisdiction at Special Projects," Joel said.

"So now what?" Gordon asked. "Should we loop the counterterrorism division in?"

Codi didn't wait for anyone to answer. "Call the boss. We gotta stop that ship!"

***

Senator Crandall stared at his phone as if it might go rogue at any minute and attack him. He punched in the number twice and then hung it back up without sending. Finally making a decision, he pressed send.

The encrypted phone made a strange clicking sound and connected with a single ring. He didn't wait for the other party to answer. "We need to talk," he said. "I'm not sure I can be of service to you anymore. Things are getting a little hot."

Pullin Ikaika paused what he was doing and concentrated on the caller. "Senator Crandall, I understand your concerns, but we are nearly done."

"Well, that sums up perfectly why I'm calling because I'm done. No more."

"Have you ever been to Japan, Senator?" Pullin asked, in an almost whimsical tone.

"Sure, but what's that got to do with our situation?"

"Did you take the time to climb Mount Fuji?"

"Climb Mount—No! What are you babbling about?" The senator was getting impatient.

"Well, I did. It's an interesting experience. You start at the base where the trees and foliage are thick. Just about every day is filled with tourists who come to take pictures and buy souvenirs. A few of the more adventurous purchase wooden walking sticks for the trail ahead. It is a winding path that leads up to the top of the volcano. Every couple of thousand feet or so is a way station, or climbing hut, where you can rest, eat, and even spend the night. Of the few people that begin the journey, many take more than one day to reach the summit. As you reach each station along the trail, they will brand the station's name and elevation onto your stick. Something permanent that will mark your passage."

The senator rubbed his temples as he tried to follow the conversation.

"The eighth and last station is known as the Goraikoukan Hut. It's the last stop before the trail narrows and leads to the summit at over twelve thousand feet. It's also the least visited of all the stations. Do you know why?"

"No. But I'm sure you're going to tell me."

"It's because many travelers give up before getting there. The last five hundred feet is through a cinder cone field that slips backward with every step you take while you struggle for oxygen. Only the most determined hikers make it to the summit and have that final brand on their hiking stick."

"What's your point?" The senator asked, hoping the story was over.

"My point is that we are at the last five hundred feet before the finish. It is time to dig deep and push on, not pull back. We both know how important the work is that we're doing, and once we are on the other side of this, things will look quite different, I assure you."

"If you think a stupid object lesson will change my mind, you're mistaken."

"Imagine, Senator, being one of the very few in D.C. politics that is immune. You'll be able to write your own ticket to the White House when this is over."

A brief moment of silence followed the comment.

"Fine. I'll do what I can, but from here on out, we are very much at arm's length from each other. I'm talking an arm's length the size of from here to China!" With that, the senator hung up, trying to get a small dose of self-control back.

As a member of the Senate Intelligence Committee, he wielded much power, but that seemed lost on his greatest benefactor. The senator had started as a runner at the capitol building in Harrisburg, Pennsylvania. That was his first taste of politics, and he liked the flavor. It took twelve years to make it all the way to Washington, but he flourished. Special interests were easy to manipulate and he excelled at the D.C. game. Since gaining the seat at the head of the intelligence committee, everything had changed. He no longer ran around with his hand out; people came to him. He got things done, made a difference. He was what this great country needed. It infuriated him how Pullin treated him but soon, even that would change. As POTUS, he would rule supreme.

Pullin, on the other hand, had his fill of groveling and paying his way through Washington. Money called loudly enough when you needed something, but a time was coming soon when career politicians would no longer exist.

***

Brian hurried up the stairs of the J. Edgar Hoover Building in D.C. The FBI headquarters is eight stories high on one side and eleven stories high on the other. It has three belowground levels and a parking structure. The buff-colored cast-concrete facade is broken by numerous square windows set within the walls. Inside is a warren of offices and meeting rooms, but Brian had only one destination in mind.

It had been one of those rare days when his wife Leila hadn't called with a problem or to ask for his advice about the kids. Though Brian was always busy at the office, he worked hard to make time for family. He believed strongly in being present, whether at work or home, and in his mind, a balanced home and work life made the best employee. It was one defining quality that had helped him win his bride as well as the respect of others. Each task or need was given a priority, and often, family issues were right at the top along with the fate of the world.

His mind flashed to one of his agents—Codi. He had encouraged her to find this balance, but she seemed to be her happiest working a case. The latest conversations with Matt had given him hope that a change might be coming. In his mind, an engaged Codi with a serious commitment would be a healthy thing.

He entered the building, cleared the security checkpoint, and stabbed at the elevator button to the top floor as his thoughts turned back to the matter at hand.

Director Lyon was a mix of concern and impatience with Brian's sudden need to meet with him. His hope that the case of the missing agents had been solved by their return with no suspects left alive on the ship was now in doubt. Apparently not. He had taken and deflected some heat after the arrest and subsequent release of Pullin Ikaika. What was next for his young SSA, and how would he need to maneuver to avoid backlash?

Brian entered the large office and laid a file on his boss's rosewood desk. He sat in an off-white upholstered chair and took a short breath. The bronze-tinted window painted an anemic shaft of sunlight on the carpeted floor. Director Lyon pulled the file toward him and opened the flap. It was exactly as he feared—*The Mantis*.

"I have an update that needs your personal attention," Brian said. He spelled out the current situation—what they knew and what they suspected. He backed it up with a lot of facts and some strong probabilities. Director Lyon's frustrated face slowly faded and then went slack.

He grabbed his phone. "Get me the secretary of state."

***

At 8:31 p.m., Codi inserted the key to her apartment and turned the lock, the call she had just received still heavy on her mind. The Korean Typhoid Superbug was showing no signs of slowing down. Multiple countries were reporting more and more cases. KTS was growing by the hour. With no known cure, it was a death sentence to almost all who were infected. The elderly or immune-compromised didn't last a week. Children seemed to have the best luck with a thirty percent chance of overcoming the sickness. It felt like the weight of the world was hanging on her shoulders.

Matt was sitting at the table with his backpack and computer, working on something. She stepped over and gave him a quick kiss and sat down next to him.

He picked up her hand and held it without speaking. Sometimes, a touch was all that was needed to make someone feel better. A hesitant smile grew on Codi's face.

"I know you're not supposed to talk about work," he said, "but it looks like it might do you some good."

Codi nodded.

"So let me guess, you gotta go save the world?" Matt said.

"Something like that."

"Well, from what I hear, the world needs saving, and there's no better person for the job, especially since you're immune and all. Oh, almost forgot. I have a gadget for you to field test," Matt said as he reached into his bag.

"What, am I dating Q now?" Codi asked.

It took Matt a second to make the connection between himself and the famous gadget man from the James Bond movies. "Okay, I could be your Q."

"And this is my *cue* to say you're irresistible," Codi said as a slight smile finally grew on her face.

Matt rolled his eyes. "See, I am good for you." He pulled out two paddles from his bag and set them in front of Codi. She picked one up skeptically.

"This is the Z-Man Program I told you about. I was thinking you might like to field test 'em."

Codi looked confused.

"The Gecko Gloves. You can climb just about anything without a rope or ladder. You never know, might come in handy."

Codi remembered the name as she slid her hands into the paddles, grabbing the handles and rotating them back and forth to get a good view.

"Nice, thanks. Don't know when I'll get a chance to use these, but I can't wait to try 'em out." She hesitated a beat. "Matt, there is something I've been thinking about and wanted to ask you."

"Oh, yeah? Me too," Matt said as he perked up at her words. This could be a perfect segue.

"You know that case I can't talk about?" Codi asked, setting down the gloves.

"Of course. It nearly got you killed and seems to have consumed most of your time since you got back."

"That's the one. Well, I was wondering . . . With what you know about molecular dispersion, is it possible someone has developed a weapon similar in technology to your device and is using it to infect South Korea?"

Matt thought back to his past and a technology he had helped develop. Sky-storm, a machine capable of molecularizing a vaccine and sending it through the air. The particles were so small, they could penetrate skin and other surfaces, inoculating patients from afar. The device had been stolen and used as a bio-weapon. It was a nightmare Matt had yet to forget.

"It's possible, but from what I've read, no."

"Why's that?" Codi asked.

"The way this disease is spreading, it started near the docks and has spiraled out from there. If they had flown over the city and dispersed the disease with a molecular weapon, we would have seen a much different progression. Like every-where all at once."

Codi nodded. "Got it. Thanks. What was it you wanted to ask me?"

Matt stammered for a second trying to get his nerve back up.

"You hungry? 'Cause I'm starving," Matt threw out lamely.

"Sure, I could eat."

The call came in at 3:00 a.m. Codi picked up the phone and whispered a "hello," hoping not to wake Matt. The words on the other end made her sit up in bed, suddenly wide awake.

***

Snow fell like giant dust motes, drifting back and forth on unseen air currents. Hoarfrost formed a lacy white ring around the edge of the gray-blue lake. It would soon be winter and with it, all the lifestyle changes that would follow.

Pullin strode with determination from his house to the office complex next door. He had picked up the H&K VP9SK from his drawer and slid it into his belt, covering it with his loose shirt.

A call a few moments ago from his bought-and-paid-for senator had him tense and edgy, but he still had time to take in the crisp alpine air. It immediately cleared his head. The senator had spoken as if others were nearby listening, using phrases like: "How is your other girl?" and "We are looking for her, and I think we are coming to visit soon."

The message was clear and explosive to Pullin. The powers that be were onto *The Locust*, and authorities would soon be coming.

It was time to shake things up and trim away the fat. From the very beginning, every contingent he could imagine had been carefully considered and planned for. He had put back-up scenarios into place and even had replacement personnel selected and on hold. But in spite of all this, Agent Sanders and the FBI had taken down *The Mantis*. They had raided his home. It was difficult to fathom. And now they had gotten wind of *The Locust*. But he would not make it so easy. Soon, half the world would have their hands full and the other half would be living in fear, all too busy to care about a cargo vessel and her next destination. He would then be free to follow more pressing matters. He just had to get past the next few days.

He texted a simple code into his phone and sent it off. Now it was time for a little housekeeping.

He stepped into the main office, leaned over, and whispered into the office manager's ear.

She looked at him with odd curiosity.

"Do it," Pullin said, reassuringly.

A page went over the entire building, and soon every employee was gathered to hear an important message from the boss.

"I want to thank you for all the hard work. We have done some amazing things together. But as of right now, you are all fired, effective immediately," Pullin announced. "I will make sure you each receive a full year's salary and a bonus for your trouble."

A murmur suddenly sprang from the group.

"You have twenty minutes to get your stuff and get out."

The confusion continued as complaints and shock carried through the crowd.

Pullin watched as the sheep, in his opinion, seemed incapable of taking their next step. He raised his pistol, firing three shots into the ceiling.

"Now!" he screamed.

The group scattered in fear, each running to his desk to grab whatever seemed most important, before heading for the door.

Pullin watched as his minions scurried around the office and then left for their cars, never to return. He looked out of the window to his house, one he had personally designed. It was a statement of power. The biggest estate on the Nevada side of the lake, where he could take advantage of the tax break. He had enjoyed his time here and would remember it fondly. One day, he would come back. Setting the gun down, his fingers opened and dialed his phone.

"Yes?"

"Whiton, change of plans. Forget rebuilding the lab. We need to take a little trip."

***

Ambassador Shinguya practically ran from the White House at 1600 Pennsylvania Avenue to his waiting limousine. He had been given a ticking time bomb, and there was much to do. A light bead of sweat formed on his forehead as he picked up the secure phone mounted between the back seats and dialed. A distant ring tone that reminded him of home filled his ear. He remembered reading about the last days in the United States before the attack on Pearl

Harbor. Ambassador Kichisaburo Nomura had played diplomat, working with Secretary of State Cordell Hull in an attempt to stop the impending war. This, while Japan's fleet was already steaming toward the Hawaiian Islands. Nomura had smiled and given his word to the Americans, working tirelessly for a peace he knew would never come. The man had a spine made of steel. Even the day before the attack, he had continued negotiations as if nothing was wrong, all the time knowing things would never be the same for the two mighty countries. The call clicked through, jarring him from his thoughts. He would now do his best to save his beloved country.

"Prime Minister Kyoto's office."

"This is ambassador Shinguya. I need to speak with the prime minister. It's a matter of national security."

Within forty-eight hours, Yokohama was under siege with over a thousand cases of the now much-feared Korean Typhoid Superbug. The modicum of advance notice had authorities and hospitals ready and operating at full effect. The sick were immediately quarantined, and though there was no known cure, not all died. The Japanese efficiency with which authorities had surrounded the sick had done wonders toward mitigating the spread of the disease, saving thousands in the process. In spite of it all, by week's end, the Korean Typhoid Superbug had spread through much of the city. The Japanese people were seeing outbreaks slowly spread around the country. People had been ordered to shelter in place. Each afraid of friends and neighbors and the death sentence they might be carrying. Manufacturing and commerce ground to a halt as the country of Japan fought the disaster.

***

Captain Combs lowered her binoculars and looked down at the mercenaries working out on the bow. They had rolled several drums together and were lashing them to the deck. Her security force had doubled in size since Yokohama, including Pullin's right-hand man, Crispin Gales. He was a serious man with a never-ending agenda. He walked, talked, and thought military. She hoped he and his men were overkill and would not be needed.

The short walk back into the wheelhouse from the port side flying bridge turned her mind back to her duties. She placed her binoculars on a notched stand that held them in place even during high seas and used her fingers to tame her windblown hair. A quick glance at her navigator and first mate brought her a feeling of confidence. Both men were extremely loyal to her and their mission. She couldn't be prouder to have them by her side and knew they would use their remarkable skills to see things through to the end.

The bridge on *The Locust* was a marvel of technology that allowed total control of the ship from one location. It could weather the worst of seas and keep the ship on course while doing so. It could even counter swells to keep work in the lab steady during rough seas.

Captain Combs was wearing her usual white shirt with epaulets and navy pants. *The Locust* logo on her breast was matched by an unseen tattoo of the same. Her short unnaturally red hair with matching lipstick was her trademark. She was a woman in a man's world—fifty percent male and one hundred percent female. She bore no angry feminist grudges toward the male gender but was content to know she was smarter and better at her job than most men. Best of all, her crew felt the same way.

They had left Yokohama without incident, steaming for the Hawaiian Islands. According to their plan, they would never return to another port as *The Locust*. It was time to make some changes, both physical and legal. *The Locust* had left San Francisco with several sets of ownership and shipping manifest documents, all verifiable under scrutiny. She could literally leave one port as *The Locust* and return several days later as a completely different ship. Not just in name and legality, but in outside appearance as well. Cranes could be disassembled, superstructure changed, and paint applied. The crew had trained until they had the refit procedure down to less than forty-eight hours.

"First Officer Eynaut, it is time to go dark," Captain Combs said while looking out the bridge windows.

"Aye, Captain. I'll oversee the disconnecting and transferring of our AIS with *The Freedom*," Collins Eynaut replied.

"We'll also need to initiate operation refit," she added.

Collins parroted the command and left the bridge to disengage the ship's automatic identification system. The next task was to refit and rename *The Locust*.

They had planned for five facelifts of the ship over the course of their journey, and this would be the first.

"Navigator," Captain Combs said, "once the AIS is off, adjust our course to arc us back around to arrive in Shanghai in the next seven days."

"Aye, Captain."

Chapter Twenty-One

C odi sat at the makeshift command center, a table bolted to the floor of the C-17. The air at forty thousand feet was a bit rough, and the cabin bucked and vibrated every few minutes. Sitting around the black table-top with laptops and pooled lighting was the recently organized task force. A strong shaft of sunlight cut across the space, coming from the porthole window in the port exit door, but it did nothing to thwart the cold inside the cabin.

On emergency orders of the president, Codi and Joel had been flown to San Diego in a stripped-down military aircraft. They had been escorted to the back ramp of a C-17 Globemaster transport jet and introduced to the players on board. The pilot had called back for takeoff, and everyone buckled into the red webbed seats that lined the fuselage. Joel gripped his laptop like he might never see it again as the military airliner raced down the runway and up into the sky. Once the C-17 leveled off, the real work began. They were fighting against time and everyone knew what was at stake.

Naval Special Warfare's Development Group was responsible for the Navy's SEAL operations. And the CIA's Special Operations Group, known as SOG, was used for the most covert of all operations. From time to time, the two task forces would join to complete the more difficult missions, often creating conflict over operational command.

The quickly thrown together joint task force, code-named Clear Water, was made up of six guys from SEAL Team One out of Coronado and three members from the CIA's Special Operations Group. The OIC, officer in charge, was a man named Colonel Gilbert who had been rushed in from JSOC, Joint Special Operations Command, in an attempt to make everyone play nice. He was in his mid-fifties, and his black hair had yet to turn gray. He stood with a military bearing and had a stern face that hid his emotions. He was a recent widower who had turned his full attention to his career, no longer bound by any relationship other than the military. His respect for the SEAL teams was based on a similar background, having come up through the Green Berets with the army. The SOG guys he could take or leave, as they were generally less disciplined and often overzealous when the bullets began to fly.

Since everyone in the room wore black, it was hard to tell their rank or what branch of the military they came from, but his experience was carried on every word he spoke and the way he carried himself.

Joel and the intelligence officer, IO, a young man named Morales had set up their laptops next to each other. They had been instructed to work together to keep the task force up to date at all times. Morales was a tech genius the CIA had scooped up and trained. He had made his way into the exclusive SOG where he had been the difference between success and failure on several missions. His ability to access facts and data was unparalleled. He was in his early thirties and had high and tight red curly hair with matching bloodshot eyes, his affinity for Red Bull always on display. If he could have hooked up an IV, he would have.

Colonel Gilbert made the introductions. There was SEAL Team One, which consisted of Master Chief Dawson, Petty Officers Crab, Adams, Thran, and Ramirez. They also had two members of the SWCC, Special Warfare Combat Craft, to coxswain the rafts.

SOG had provided three of their men whom the colonel called Snap, Crackle, and Pop, in part to keep their anonymity, but also in honor of the sound their foes would make once they engaged. This got a chuckle out of the group, which helped lighten the mood—slightly. Once all the introductions were made, a plan started to form up. It was a rush job, which meant anything could happen or go wrong.

***

Special Agent Gordon Reyas stomped his feet to remove the excess snow on his shoes as he and his partner, Anna Green, entered the Reno FBI field office. They were met with two cups of coffee and anxious stares. The task force was assembled, consisting of two black Ford Explorers with federal plates and a total of eight agents, all ready to act. Joel had sent them enough connecting evidence to get a second search warrant to cover everything this time at Pullin Ikaika's residence. It had taken much too long to get, and they were all hoping this wasn't just a giant waste of time and resources. They also had a more bulletproof arrest warrant for the man himself, one that held many charges. There would not be a repeat of the last time. Pullin Ikaika was going to jail for a long time.

The snow along the shore of Lake Tahoe was here to stay for the winter. It was the time when tourists dropped water skiing for snow skiing and the local resorts were busy. Cars lined up, all wearing ski racks. As the task force pulled into the estate's driveway, they were met with an open gate. No guard on duty. The driver continued in, following the cleared blacktop to the main house. Once parked, the agents filed out of the SUVs, weapons at the ready. Gordon moved up the steps to the main entrance with purpose as other agents moved to surround the house.

The front door opened, and an older woman with fake blonde hair and overly stretched skin stepped out. She was unaware of what was going on, and as she looked up she nearly panicked at the sight of eight armed agents in tactical clothes. Anna couldn't tell if the look of surprise on the woman's face was permanent or not, but it never seemed to fade.

"Oh, dear!" the woman exclaimed, almost dropping the papers she was holding.

"We have a warrant to search the premises and arrest Pullin Ikaika."

She stared at the agents as her mind tried to put some logic into the situation. "Well, I don't know who that is, but I just got the listing to sell this estate. There's no one here. Feel free to see for yourselves," she said, with mock bravery through over-puffed lips that barely moved.

Twenty minutes later they had nothing. The underground lab had been destroyed and the home was empty, just as the realtor had said. Pullin Ikaika was in the wind.

***

The main operations center was in the basement of the Central Intelligence Agency, just outside D.C. It was filled with focused personnel, all working to provide support for the team in the air. This was a top priority mission. The room was set up for technology with a huge multiscreen display that covered two walls and a host of technicians working from hi-tech stations, all connected to the C-17 task force via satellite. Several views were of the inside of the transport jet.

As a courtesy, SSA Brain Fescue was included to represent the FBI's side of things, especially considering how they had uncovered the plot in the first place. Two hours into the mission, Brian's boss, Director Lyon arrived. He was followed shortly after by Senator Crandall, head of the intelligence committee, who took a seat in the back of the room. It was becoming a power struggle, and Brian just hoped the mission didn't suffer fools. He listened to the chatter coming in from the C-17, trying to tune out the conversations going on around the room.

"*The Locust* has turned off her AIS and changed course," IO Morales said. "She left Yokohama three days ago steaming for the Hawaiian Islands. We have several satellites in the area but no sightings yet."

Onboard the C-17, Joel raised his hand.

"Son, just say what's on your mind, we're not in school here," Colonel Gilbert said while gesturing for Joel to get on with it.

Joel, realizing his hand was still up, slowly dropped it. "I don't think they are heading for Hawaii. If you look at the time it took them to go from Busan, South Korea, to Yokohama, Japan . . ." Joel spun his laptop around, showing a map of the northwest section of the Pacific Ocean. The same screen popped up back at the DIA [Defense Intelligence Agency], along with an image of the task force, as he spoke. "It takes roughly a day and a half to travel from Busan to Yokohama by cargo vessel. Why did *The Locust* take seven days to make the journey?" Joel posed the question to the group.

"They had engine trouble?" Chief Petty Officer Ramirez said.

Ramirez was part of SEAL Team One under the leadership of Master Chief Dawson. It was a tight-knit unit that could practically read each other's minds.

"I don't think so," Joel replied.

"Bugs," Codi said. "They had to have growing time to let the next batch of insects mature."

Joel pointed his finger in Codi's direction to let her know she was on track with his thinking. He took the same finger and drew an arc that showed a seven-day journey to Yokohama. He said, "I think they made a big arc out into the ocean and back. It took them out of the shipping lanes and off the radar. Plus, it gave them the time needed to restock and infect their inventory. They're doing the same now before hitting their next port." Joel finished and leaned back to wait for a response.

"We should concentrate our satellites in this area," Chief Dawson said while pointing to a space in the ocean east of the tip of Japan.

"Where do you think their next target will be?" OIC Gilbert asked.

"I'm guessing Shanghai, Taipei, or Hong Kong," Joel replied.

"That's my guess as well," IO Morales added.

"Guessing? So not Hawaii?" Colonel Gilbert asked, with a flat expression.

"Sir, I agree with Chief Dawson," IO Morales said. "We should re-task the satellites to cover the area. It makes sense."

The OIC paused to look at his two intelligence men, one a civilian. He slowly nodded his head. "Okay. But if we get this wrong, and they hit Honolulu, we'll have a lot of deaths on our heads."

"If we let them land anywhere, the same applies," Chief Dawson added.

The C-17 itself seemed to agree, as it shuddered over a patch of rough air.

IO Morales got to work, his fingers literally flying across his keyboard. Even Joel was impressed with the kid's skills.

"Okay, next up, let's talk about once we find *The Locust,*" the colonel said. "Operation Clear Water and how we are going to operate to stop her." He paused to make sure everyone was following. "Chief Dawson, you will be in charge of the ground operations. Split your men into two groups, including the SOG guys."

Dawson nodded his reply.

"According to intelligence, this ship has a vaccine on board. That is our first priority, but we will have to neutralize whatever threat is onboard in order to get to it. The next priority is to stop, take, or scuttle the ship. Make no mistake about what the risk is here. Humanity is starting to die a horrible death and we can stop it. The ROE on this mission is to consider every crew member aboard that boat a threat. Am I clear?"

General agreement confirmed the colonel's "Rules of Engagement."

The colonel added, "So if there was ever a time to shoot first and ask questions later, this is it."

The room nodded in unison. Even the participants back in the DIA nodded.

"Where does this intelligence come from, sir?" Chief Dawson asked.

"Boots on the ground. It is why we have civilians on board. Special Agent Sanders here was aboard the sister ship, *The Mantis.* I'm sending her along since she knows more about the ship than any of us put together. But Agent Sanders, I'll let that be your call. In the meantime, give us everything you can. Even the smallest detail could make a difference."

Codi swallowed hard. She had been torn ever since her boss had sent her and Joel flying west at just over the speed of sound. He had promised her that the job would be an advisory role only. Her mixed feelings toward male special operators being what they were, she had managed to just keep the contempt out of her expression.

Memories of her failed BUD/S training and the men that had betrayed her trust started to take over her mind. The anger she had felt in the past was returning. Ever since meeting the special operators on board, she was feeling unsure and shocked at the level of emotion that had boiled up just under the surface. *Get it together, Codi. These aren't those men.*

She took a deep cleansing breath and unrolled a set of schematics from *The Mantis,* with several areas marked in red. There was even a hand-drawn box that showed where the lab was situated. She took the time to go over every detail of what she had seen and done from her time on the bridge to the engine room. The lab was hazier in her recollection, but she managed a fair description including the bug farm. The special operators listened with rapt attention, asking questions along the way.

"I have to say," Chief Dawson said, "we have no way of knowing how many men they have on board. After your takedown of *The Mantis,* they might have reinforced *The Locust.*"

"That's what I would do," Codi replied, matching his stare.

"I, as well," he said. "Based on the short time we have and the general lack of intelligence, except what you have given us, Agent Sanders, this is a real tough mission with way too many unknowns. We are probably walking into some kind of a trap."

"You are correct," said the colonel. "It could be a trap, but that cannot be helped. Our job is to do the hard stuff, and our number one priority is to obtain the vaccine in the lab—no matter the costs. The second priority is to stop *The Locust* from further distribution of her cargo. If that means sinking her, so be it. The CIA and JSOC have made it clear—as soon as we can get to her, we board her," the colonel said, with confidence that echoed back to the room in D.C.

"And if she has already crossed into Chinese waters?" Chief Dawson asked, looking up at the colonel.

The room fell unusually quiet, as all eyes were on Colonel Gilbert.

"We'll have to abort. I'm not starting a war with China by violating their sovereignty. But that can't happen. Understood?" He looked everyone over to make sure they were getting the message.

The tension in the room was palpable. It would only go up from there.

"Sir, I think you should see this." IO Morales pulled up a map of the suspected area.

The ocean was lit up with ship icons like an overdressed Christmas tree. There were easily five thousand ships between Japan and China alone. And those were just the ships over three hundred tons that required AIS transponders. Icons of ships filled the screen going in all different directions, each with its own AIS identifier. Finding *The Locust* was like finding the proverbial needle in a haystack.

A sudden ping came from Morales's computer, and he spun his laptop back around as his fingers pounded the keys. "*The Locust* has turned her AIS back on."

Everyone leaned over as he zoomed in on the section of the ocean the ping was coming from.

"She's still on course for Hawaii," Morales said, with an air of disbelief.

"Get ahold of the pilot. We need to course-correct," the colonel yelled.

"Hold on a second, boss," Joel said. "Do you have some way of getting a live feed of the ship?"

"It's *colonel*, not boss, and what are you thinking, Agent Strickman? Make it quick!"

"I've been doing some thinking about the AIS system."

"Son, just get to the point. We don't have a lot of time here. And somebody get this plane on an intercept course!"

A man in a flight suit jogged to a phone attached to the fuselage while IO Morales called out the new coordinates.

"Now, what was it you were trying to tell us?" The colonel glared at Joel.

"Right. What is AIS but just an electronic box, and electronics can be hacked and modified," Joel offered.

"True, but without the box in a physical ship moving on a course, we wouldn't be getting this kind of reading," countered IO Morales.

"Can you get me a live satellite feed of the ship?" Joel asked again.

"Just a sec." Information Officer Morales typed furiously, re-tasking a bird that was in the area as over-watch.

A moment later, a chunk of the ocean appeared on his screen. Several clicks revealed a lone ship steaming under its own power.

"Can you zoom in?"

The picture resolved to a cargo ship set against blue water with a rooster tail of white froth trailing behind.

Codi leaned in close for a good look. "It's not her," she said.

"Are you sure?" the colonel asked.

"Yes. Close but not quite," she replied.

IO Morales did a quick hull comparison with an overlay from *The Mantis*.

He electronically slid the semitransparent image over a live image of the ship and lined them up. One was wider and longer than the other.

"She's right, this ship is a hundred feet shorter and configured differently."

This information hit the room hard. *The Locust* was still in the wind.

***

Crispin watched as his men on *The Locust* finished final checks on their weapons. He had passed out Teflon-coated bullets capable of piercing body armor. The men had happily reloaded their guns with the blue-tipped armament. They were good soldiers who had a lot of experience and had proven themselves loyal. Some believed in the mission and others the cash, but each would do his duty to protect the ship. The room they were in had been converted from a rec room with a ping pong table to a ready room filled with the latest weapons Crispin had been able to acquire.

There were full-auto Tavor SAR Flattop B16s. The compact and reliable Israeli bullpup rifle was made for its maneuverability in tight spaces. They also had three British LAW rockets and a hand-held Chinese HJ-12 Red Arrow with its set-it-and-forget-it guidance system capable of bringing down a jet or a helicopter. The only slightly older weapon mounted to the ship was a French Malafon IIB—a rocket-assisted torpedo that was fired off a pedestal on the deck of the ship. It was carefully concealed behind a movable panel on the last aft container.

A coded message had reached the captain ten minutes ago, and she had relayed the information to Crispin. US operators were going to make a run at them. This is why he was on board, and it was what he lived for. He would show them a thing or two.

"We are expecting uninvited guests sometime before we reach the safety of Chinese waters," Crispin said.

"*Safety* of Chinese waters? Never thought I'd hear those words," replied First Officer Collins.

A few of the mercenaries laughed.

"The captain has ordered flank speed, which will give them a window between now and the next three hours or so. We have the element of surprise along with overwhelming superiority. They won't try to take us in any grand fashion. They will come at us with a covert boarding party of some sort. For this, we are well protected. These guys will try to use stealth and skill against us, but we'll be ready." Crispin looked around the room to the faces of the men he was proud to work with. They were some of the very best. "Collins, how are we situated?" he asked as he checked his pistol.

"We have placed the drums just as instructed. Port and starboard on the aft deck, and likewise, at mid-ship on the main deck. They are all connected to your phone's app through the ship's WiFi," Collins replied.

"Good. Sparks?"

A young heavily tattooed Frenchman, Sparks, who had been glued to his laptop attached to two larger displays, spoke without ever taking his eyes off the screen. "We have cameras up and operating covering 360 degrees with both infrared and night vision." He tapped on the screens that had multiple pictures of the ship and its surrounding area. "We may not see them coming until they are close, but we will be ready and know their every move from about a half-mile out in any direction."

Crispin said, "If they act like SEALS, we can expect them to board with grappling hooks here, here, or here." He pointed out three key access points he had identified on a blueprint of *The Locust's* deck. "Once we are certain of the entry position, we will move in, hold our ground, and on my command, engage. Sparks, as soon as you are sure of the total number of the attacking force and their position, I'll need you to join in. I want to show these operatives a real blitzbok," he said, referring to the nickname of the speedy attack shown by the South African Springboks rugby team. He didn't wait for an answer. "Everything clear?"

His question was answered with a collection of nodding heads and "yeses."

"Good. Once we are in Chinese waters, the first round is on me, lads."

***

"Special Agent Sanders, have you got a second?"

The OIC, Colonel Gilbert stepped out of earshot of the group, and Codi followed his lead.

The sun that had been streaming through the jet's porthole was now nothing but a pink glow as night approached. The C-17 Globemaster had raced the sun across the world and lost.

"Sir?" Codi said.

"I just wanted to say I have seen your file and made the effort to contact a few of my friends. You see, I like to know who I'm getting involved with before dancing with the devil," the colonel stated.

"So do I, sir, but I haven't even had time for a decent cup of coffee since I got the call-up." She returned his steely gaze with one of her own.

"I know what you mean. I just wanted to say how impressed I am with the work you have been doing. I believe, as do several other officers, that you got a raw deal at BUD/S."

His statement caught Codi off-guard and sent a jolt up her spine. She fought hard to keep her face from reddening.

"There is nothing I can do about that now, sir," she said, flatly.

"No, there isn't. But you are here for a reason, and it's my job to get the most out of my personnel. I just want that reason, *your* reason to be a benefit for the team. So whatever resentment you might still be harboring toward the boys that wear the trident, I'll need you to check that right now. Because nothing less than one hundred percent will do out there. I'm taking a big risk sending you in, and I'd say the odds are good you'll never survive the HALO jump. But the guys who are pulling my strings on this one say you will be invaluable down there. So don't let me down."

"You might be surprised, sir," Codi replied.

"I hope I am, Special Agent Sanders."

Codi held his gaze for a moment longer and then gave him a curt nod.

The colonel seemed appeased. He returned the subtlest of nods and then left Codi to head back to the table in the middle of C-17's fuselage.

Codi watched him go as her eyes scanned the confident faces of SEAL Team One. These weren't the same men who had conspired against her, but they were of the same mindset. If this mission was to succeed, she would have to be all in. The colonel was right—time to play nice. But trust, that would have to be earned.

"IO Morales, have you identified the ship?" the colonel asked as he stepped next to the man.

"It's *The Freedom* out of Jamaica, sir."

"Can you pull up her AIS information?"

"What are you thinking?" Joel asked, suddenly curious.

"I'm thinking *The Locust* is traveling through some of the busiest water on the planet," the colonel replied.

"She would need to have her AIS up and running or risk a collision," Joel added.

"Exactly."

"A switch!" Codi said.

"Right. It wouldn't be that difficult for them to hack an individual box, and we'd be off chasing the wrong boat," Joel said.

IO Morales worked his keyboard for a few moments. "Gotcha." He spun his laptop around.

The Freedom's AIS signal was on a ship right where Joel had suspected it would be, completing its arc from Yokohama back to China.

"ID that ship," the colonel demanded.

A moment later, Morales had an image up. He again slid an electronic transparency of *The Mantis's* hull over the image. "It matches *The Locust* in size, sir. There are a few differences from when she left Japan. The funnel is black not red, and the name on the stern is Freedom. Otherwise, it's the same ship."

"They're trying to disguise her," Codi said.

"Possibly. How sure are you this is *The Locust?*" the colonel asked Morales.

"Ninety?" IO Morales said, with an open hand gesture.

"I'm *sure* it's her," Codi added, staring closely at the satellite image.

He nodded slowly to himself, making a decision. "Get this plane spun around—*now!*" The colonel was beside himself with the zigzagging they had done through the air, all wasted time.

"Sir, there's something else," Morales added, not sure if he should say more. "She's three hours from Chinese waters."

"This just keeps getting better. How long to catch her?" the colonel asked as he checked his watch.

Morales did some quick calculations. "At our current speed . . . two and a half, including boat time to target."

"That's cutting it really close," Chief Dawson added.

"Tell the pilot to give us all he's got," OIC Colonel Gilbert called as he grabbed his satellite phone and dialed.

Codi moved over to Joel and leaned close. "Things are about to get real, and I need to have someone watching our backs that isn't also playing politics."

Joel looked up at her, realizing the situation. "Of course, always."

The two shared a smile, knowing it might well be their last.

"Oh, and Shannon is a great find, try to make it work," she added.

"You okay, Codi?" Joel asked, wondering about her sudden train of thought.

"Yeah, just realized life is too short for regrets so make your best choice and go for it."

Joel was about to tell her that was exactly what Shannon had told him.

"Agent Sanders!"

Codi looked over at Chief Dawson.

"I'd like you to take us through *The Locust's* blueprints one more time."

***

Nighttime. The bottom of the sea was alive with organisms. Some too small to see, others larger than a house. It can be an eerie place, as the moans and wails of the living communicate. The SSN-843 *Red Tide* cut through the liquid space ahead. Its mighty propulsor pushing thousands of gallons aside. The Virginia Class submarine was the pride of the Navy. With the latest updates in warfare platforms and technology, it was a distinction that separated it from all other subs.

Captain Torres looked at the dispatch handed to him by the ET-Comm.

"New orders, sir?" the XO, executive officer, asked.

"Yes, and they are very specific," he said as he handed the paper to his right-hand man.

The XO read the words, and his eyes slowly drifted up to the captain's. "These are for real?"

"I have no reason to doubt them. Nav, come to two-seven-five. Make our depth three hundred and ahead flank speed."

The navigator paused for the briefest of moments before repeating the order and making the changes. This was a command he had seldom heard. Going flank speed above the sea's thermocline was a risky proposition.

The captain reached for the microphone on the wall, considering his next words carefully.

"All hands, this is the captain speaking. We are now on the hunt for a verified target. Action stations. This is not a drill."

The red glow of the bridge seemed to increase with his words as sailors moved and reorganized themselves for the fight ahead. Captain Torres replaced the mic and watched the carefully orchestrated choreography of his men. They were efficient and calm. It was a good sign. Drills and training were one thing, but nothing prepared you for the real thing like the real thing. This would be good for all of them.

Most of the sub's sailors wore blue coveralls with the boat's logo on them and their names embroidered across their right pocket. A couple wore coats to keep warm and several had watch caps, a courtesy afforded only to submarine crews, a ballcap of their choosing, each as unique as the individual onboard.

For the first time in many weeks, he noticed the ozone smell of the air and the tiny creaks in the steel, as the behemoth tube changed course and sped up. Captain Torres never liked going this fast. Even the latest technology in the sub would not make them silent at flank speed, and being so close to Chinese waters, it was an invitation to collect visitors of the wrong kind. The slight cavitation of the shroud-covered propellers at full speed would be like a mating call to enemy subs.

"ST, drag an array and stay alert. I don't want any visitors coming up our rear end."

The sonar technician turned his Florida Gators watch cap backward as he refocused on his equipment. "Yes, sir." He released a small antenna array that would drag behind the boat, giving him another ear pointing behind them.

*****

Brian and his boss, Director Lyons, listened as the director of the CIA SOG and Colonel Gilbert discussed the current situation over the secure connection in the operations room back in D.C. Senator Crandall leaned himself in their direction, intent on listening in. The older gray-haired man with the bulbous nose had been sitting in the back of the room watching the proceedings like a vulture eying fresh roadkill. His slight paunch belly fought against his custom-tailored pinstriped shirt.

The operations center at the CIA was straight out of *Star Wars*. Just behind the technician stations was an oval table that had a state-of-the-art touchscreen as a surface. The image could be cloned to either of the even larger screens on the wall so everyone in the room could stay current on the mission. The ambient lighting was muted to give the screens prominence without being too dark. The screens on the walls could hold multiple images or one large view, depending on the complexity of the mission.

"What's the word coming out of China?" The SOG director called out.

"Nothing so far. I think they are still unaware of the threat, but that could change by the second, especially if they get wind of our operation," said one of the techs at his station.

"Japan has been hit hard, and even though they got an early warning, their infrastructure is becoming overwhelmed," the SOG director added.

"If this thing spreads, we will all be in real trouble. No known cure and a high mortality rate. It's the perfect killing machine," said Director Lyon, trying to be part of the not-so-subtle power play going on in the room.

The director of the SOG paused and turned to Director Lyons. He hit the mute button on the speakerphone and said, "Director Lyons, you and your team are here as a courtesy. Try not to get involved."

Brian watched as his boss's ears turned bright red. Checkmate. He had just lost the power play.

The SOG director unmuted the call and turned his back on the FBI director. He continued. "We must consider obtaining the vaccine at all costs."

"Even a war with China?" Senator Crandall piped up.

"No. I won't have that on my conscience. All known covert costs," he clarified.

"And if China gets wind of this, they'll take the ship and the vaccine for themselves," the colonel said over the phone.

"Not acceptable. I have sent a message to TACON in Honolulu, ordering in a Virginia Class sub as a failsafe. She was patrolling in the area and is now doing flank speed in pursuit. We can't let the Chinese get ahold of this ship. If we are not able to secure it and turn her around or at least stop her before she crosses into Chinese waters, she will go to the bottom."

"Sir," the colonel said, "that gives my operators only a small window at best to accomplish their mission."

"Your point, Colonel?"

"It's a big ask, Director."

"That's what they are trained to do, Colonel, the big ask."

The senator nodded as he listened to the conversation with a solemn expression.

The large screen on the right wall showed a zoomed-in section of the ocean. A blue icon showed *The Locust* steaming in a direct line for Shanghai. It was just a little ways from a dotted line that represented China's territorial waters. A yellow icon representing the C-17 Globemaster was closing in at forty thousand feet, and a red icon showed the Virginia Class sub coming up from the south at three hundred meters below the surface. They were both closing on the target. It was a race. The senator glanced at his watch—one hour to go.

***

Inside the C-17, the task force reviewed their plan for the tenth time. Every detail they could imagine was crammed into the operation. They accounted for the unknown and covered many "what ifs." With so much on the line and too little known, it was a best guess scenario.

The OIC Colonel Gilbert hung up his sat phone and stepped back to the table. "Okay, it looks like CIA is running the show now. We have been instructed to board and take *The Locust* before she crosses into Chinese waters. There is worry that the Chinese are alert to what's going on and are en route to intercept and take the vaccine for themselves."

The room seemed to pause as each person considered the colonel's words.

"I don't have to tell you what that might mean. One of the more deadly diseases in their hands with the only known vaccine. At the very least, it would be extortion to the rest of the world."

"What do you want us to do if we get there too late?" Chief Petty Officer Ramirez asked.

"Under no circumstances are we to enter Chinese waters. If you are too late getting on board, this mission is scrubbed. But, son, the military didn't spend millions in training for you to fail, so that's not an option," the colonel said.

"Understood, sir."

Chapter Twenty-Two

The lights in the cabin turned red as a ten-minute warning was passed around. Nine highly trained operators and one FBI special agent loaded up. They each donned MC-4 Ram air parachutes and gear bags. It would be a water landing, so flippers were strapped to their calves. Codi had done many jumps in her military career and had even tried sky surfing for a time when she had been at her most self-destructive stage after dropping out of BUD/S. The closest she had ever come to a HALO jump was when she had once considered not opening her chute and letting gravity do the rest.

She slipped the mask over her head and tried to breathe normally as the oxygen-rich mixture filled her lungs. The HALO—or High Altitude, Low Open maneuverer—was a specialty of the special forces. It allowed them to exit a plane at forty thousand feet undetected, drop through the air, and release their parachute at the last minute.

Codi willed herself to calm and let her mind flash back to her military days. She flicked her eyes in Joel's direction and got a thumbs-up in reply. The team lined up in two rows behind the two combat rubber raiding crafts, or CRRCs. They were prepped and moved on guide rails toward the exit ramp. Each boat contained two fifty-five-horsepower engines with a pump-jet propulsor. The two SWCC coxswains were first in line right behind the boats. They would board and drive the CRRCs to pick up their passengers and ultimately head for and overtake *The Locust.*

The five-minute warning indicator had everyone on edge. It meant they now had less than thirty minutes before they would have to scrub the mission.

Joel stepped to the back of the cargo space and watched as his partner did an idiot check on her gear, then the man's next to her, while he did the same to her. She seemed to mix in flawlessly with some of the world's best operators. *She was right at home.*

The jump master began the JMPI, or personal inspection of all the gear, one operator at a time. Once done, he started the countdown procedure.

"Move to the rear."

"Stand by."

The ramp at the tail of the jet slowly lowered and the fuselage became a wind tunnel. Joel grabbed a pipe on the wall and hung on as bitterly cold air circled through the cabin with a vengeance. Tonight, there would be no "do-overs."

"On the green!" the jump master called out.

The moment the green light flared, the men started moving the two crafts down the ramp.

"Five, four, three, two, one!" the jumpmaster shouted. "Go! Go! Go!"

Once their chutes filled with air, the CRRCs were jerked out of the plane. The quad parachutes deployed, and they immediately started to drift toward the sea. The rest of the operators followed behind, exiting into the air two at a time. Codi was in the last group. She stepped off the ramp leaning headfirst into the air.

It was a cold moonless night when the familiar feeling of freefalling took hold. She moved her arms back along her sides and tilted her head down. In no time, she reached terminal velocity, shooting down at over 120 mph. There was no feeling like it in the world.

The cold mechanical breathing in her facemask competed with the rushing of air. She kept her eyes on the man in front of her via a small red LED that blinked on the back of his helmet. He was nothing but a shadow in the dark sky. She flipped on her AN/PVS-31NODs, and the world around her lit up in a light cyan detailed view, compliments of the white phosphor technology. An occasional glance at her Zebra WT600 wearable computer, called a Dytter, gave her speed, distance, and elevation.

At twelve hundred feet, the alarm sounded letting each operator know it was time to pull their ripcord. Codi followed protocol. A sudden, violent jerk slowed her fall almost immediately as the canopy deployed and filled. She grabbed onto the toggles attached to the steering lines and flew herself into position behind the line of operators that was forming in the sky, each following the other at a safe distance.

The black liquid ink of the sea below was now glowing brightly, but it was still deceptive, and it seemed to rise up quickly as the group dropped. Hitting the water too hard would be like hitting concrete, so knowing when to flare your chute to prevent that was almost impossible at night without using your altimeter. Trust in your equipment, Codi's instructor had told her time and time again. She glanced at the numbers that were dropping at a steady but fast rate. Two hundred feet, then one hundred, fifty feet. At fifty feet, she pulled both toggles and bent her knees slightly. The salty water hit hard but parted as her body dove under.

Codi disconnected her chute and let it drift away and down. Pushing for the surface, aided by her auto-inflate MSV vest, she breached the water and jerked her fins free. They were designed to fit over her shoes, and she strapped them on with a pull. Immediately, she was able to move more freely through the water with her heavy gear pack and rifle. She removed her oxygen mask but left her helmet on. It took a second to find her team, but soon, they were moving as one, heading toward two boats that were now closing on their position. The pick-up went flawlessly, and the two SEAL coxswains spun the rafts and had them on target and heading toward The Locust some five miles away. The sea was mostly calm with the occasional swell that sent the small rafts into the air.

Codi clung to the straps on the gunwale of the CRRC. Across from her was Chief Dawson along with POs Crab and Adams. The other boat held the three SOG guys, Snap, Crackle, and Pop, along with Ramirez and Thran.

"HAVOC, this is Alpha one, on mission. I repeat, on mission," Dawson said into his radio.

A reply from the team inside the C-17 followed.

Chief Dawson turned his attention to Codi. He reached down and turned his radio off and leaned over. "First of all, I just want to be clear," Chief Dawson yelled over the engine noise. "Having a civilian on this mission was not our call. I respect what you have done and provided us with, Agent Sanders, but I expect you to do your absolute best to stay out of our way. That means you stay on the boat. If and when we get control, then you can come aboard. But under no circumstances before that. Am I clear?"

"That's not the plan, and you know it," Codi replied.

"Screw the plan. We're here now, and I'm in charge; you're not coming with us. If you have a problem with that, I'll personally throw you over the side right now."

Chief Dawson stared daggers at Codi, and she returned the favor.

"Are we clear?"

"I'd like to see you try, but, yeah, I hear you," Codi said.

Chief Dawson, feeling like he got the answer he wanted, turned and looked forward, never to put his eyes back in Codi's direction. He reached up and clicked his radio back on.

Codi let her anger build. It was guys like this that had derailed her SEAL career. If she could have gotten away with shooting him right then and there, she might have tried, but all that really mattered was the mission. Thousands of lives depended on their success. She would not be that person. She would swallow her pride and let the operators operate. Besides, having already taken down *The Mantis* was enough.

***

The ready room on *The Locust* had become malodourous as the tense minutes ticked by waiting for the enemy to appear. It was as though time was standing still, and Crispin was starting to lose his patience.

"All clear," came a squawk from the radios as his lookouts checked in.

Crispin pulled the mag out of his weapon and checked it for the third time in ten minutes.

"Two boats coming in from our rear starboard side," Sparks announced.

"Finally. What's the count?" Crispin asked, leaning over his shoulder to see the screen.

"Eight . . . no, nine operators and two drivers," he replied, keeping his eyes on the monitors.

A small smile grew on Crispin's face. "Okay, you know what to do. Let's get to our posts. Sparks, let me know the minute you see their ingress route."

"On it," he replied.

The rest of the men loaded up their gear and left the room with Crispin on their heels.

Sparks watched as two raiding craft moved to the starboard side of the ship. They soon were mirroring *The Locust's* pace as they moved closer to the hull.

"Starboard side, aft three-quarters," he fed into the radios.

"Copy on the move," came the reply.

***

The dark hull with sodium vapor deck lighting slowly grew in size. When they were just a half-mile away, Chief Dawson checked in with command.

"HAVOC, this is Alpha One. We're passing Tiger."

"Roger that. Tiger," came the response everyone could hear through their earpieces.

The check-in initiated the next step in the plan. Petty Officer Crab launched a small drone, sending it up and over the aft section of the ship. He selected an icon on the smart screen attached to his arm and soon the autonomous drone hovered over the selected section of the ship.

After carefully watching the deck for any sign of movement or defenses, PO Crab gave the all-clear.

Back onboard the C-17, the remaining task force watched the footage from a bird's eye view. The signal was fed back to the CIA and JSOC command centers as well.

No words were spoken as the operators pulled up, and then moved alongside the ship's hull. Once there, the two boat drivers kept the pace and distance constant to *The Locust*. POs Crab and Adams each grabbed for their gear bags.

The REBS launcher looked like a small old-school bazooka with a coffee can attached to the barrel. It was capable of launching rope or small ladders with a grappling hook over great distances, perfect for entering a building from the top, or in this case, a ship. It used compressed gas that helped keep it quiet and was compact enough to carry on a mission.

"Command, this is Alpha one. We are initiating Opossum."

"Roger that, Opossum. Be aware we are *T* minus ten before we have to abort," came the reply.

"Copy five by five."

With only ten minutes left, Chief Dawson gave the signal, and they fired the rubber-coated grapples up and over the railing and onto the deck. The second boat mirrored the action. Soon, four small cable ladders stretched their way up the hull to the deck some fifty feet above. The moment they were secure, Chief Dawson and Adams took to the ladders. From the other boat, Snap and Crackle did the same. It took about one minute for them to clear the railing at the top.

A moment of silence followed that seemed to last an eternity before the radio squelched back to life.

"Alpha One set. Alpha Two, go for ascent," came the announcement in the earpieces.

The next two operators began their climb.

Inside the C-17, the support team listened and watched the drone's video feed as four operatives climbed onto the aft deck. They huddled in a group behind a stack of three fifty-five-gallon drums lashed to the railing before calling in the remainder of the force. As the next four operatives climbed, two men made for cover, moving forward across the deck. The next two would leapfrog around them as soon as the last operatives made it on board.

Joel looked at the clock that was counting down the time before *The Locust* crossed into Chinese waters—six minutes and fifty-six seconds and counting. It would take a miracle to get there in time.

Codi looked up as the next four men left the rafts behind. She was alone with the two drivers holding the course alongside the steel hull of the massive ship. In anticipation of what might come next, she tightened her gear bag straps on her shoulders. A sudden explosion on the deck caught everyone by surprise. A large chunk of Chief Dawson flew past Codi and the SEAL driver, splashing in the dark water next to them. A few seconds later, automatic fire could be heard up on the ship.

***

The SSN-843 *Red Tide* was an exceptionally quiet boat. She had a special coating that absorbed both inside noise and outside pings, making her one of the most difficult subs to detect. The coating also allowed her to slip through the water like a wet bar of soap through fingers.

"Weps, load tubes two and three, stand by for a firing solution, and let's get a radio buoy up."

"Aye, Captain."

"Time to target?" the captain asked.

"We have only an approximate as the target has not been locked onto yet, sir," the weapons officer answered.

"What's your approximate?"

"Fifteen minutes, give or take thirty seconds."

Captain Torres nodded his reply and moved to the center of the control room. It was slightly bigger than a one-car garage. The ceiling was covered in pipes and cables, the floor a faux-wood composite that dampened footsteps while still maintaining traction. Along the walls was a collection of monitors and interactive keyboards that controlled the entire ship. It was all fly-by-wire. Gone were the days of hydraulic valves and periscopes. In the center of the room was the electronic chart table, a sturdy touch-screen surface that displayed charts and targeting information.

The captain watched as the icon of the *Red Tide* closed on the suspected target.

"Sir, I have confirmed the target. We are fourteen minutes and forty-eight seconds out."

The suspected target icon updated on the screen to a solid red and shifted slightly in its positioning.

It was now just a matter of time.

***

Crispin waited and watched as four heavily armed operators climbed onto the deck. They took cover behind the drums he had ordered placed there. Just as he had anticipated, they were following his script to the word. It would be a massacre.

"No one shoot till I give the order," he whispered into his radio. "I want them all on board first."

Four more men came over the railing and joined the group.

"Just one more to go, and then we'll deal with the two drivers."

Before the final operators climbed onto the deck, two more men from the group suddenly sprinted across the deck and took up position by the containers.

"Dammit, where's the last one?" Crispin said into his mic. "Engage," he said, not wanting to wait any longer as more of them might scatter. He pressed the virtual button on his smartphone and the drums exploded, sending some of America's best operators everywhere.

The four operators by the containers dove for cover and opened fire. A brief firefight ensued with bullets flying in both directions.

"Collins, take two men and try to get around them," Crispin ordered.

The first mate nodded and moved out to the right with Sparks on his heels.

Crispin turned to one of his other men. "Once they're done, let's light up their transpo."

"On it, boss," the man said while he grabbed two LAWs rockets and ran to the left.

***

Codi listened as the firefight up on the deck diminished. The comms in her ear were filled with dread as the remaining operators tried to fill HAVOC in on what was happening.

"Down, we say again, Alpha One down. Alpha Two down. Crackle and Pop down. Taking heavy fire."

The noise of automatic fire drowned out his voice, and then there was nothing but static.

"Abort, abort mission," came the cry from HAVOC over the radios.

A few seconds later, a man Codi recognized splashed into the water right next to her boat. He was shot through with bullets. Another operator hit a few beats after that. Codi didn't wait. She jumped from the raft onto the cable ladder leading up to the deck above.

"Agent Sanders! We are ordered to abort! Get back on the boat!" the coxswain yelled.

Before the man could finish, a small rocket-propelled charge smashed into the raft blowing it out of the water. Codi held to the ladder for dear life as it flopped and banged from the concussion of the explosion. Her earpiece smashed against the steel, ringing her head in the process and busting her radio. The blast bleached the rhodopsin from the rods of her eyes and she was temporarily blinded. She could smell burned hair and was sure she had lost a chunk to the giant fireball that erupted. The second raft spun around and headed away from the ship. It managed to get about a hundred yards before a second rocket caught up and obliterated it as well.

Joel was dumbfounded by the turn of events. The orders to abort seemed to fall on deaf ears as there was no one left to reply. Only the C-17 seemed to listen, as the bumpy ride smoothed for a second. The men at the table were stunned. Stunned at the thought of the consequences of this failed mission. The military was famous for passing down blame. There would be repercussions, reassignments, and loss of rank. The colonel sat heavily in a chair by the command table, his fingers rubbing his temples.

"We don't know they are all dead," Joel added weakly, fearing the worst for his partner.

"IO, confirm," Colonel Gilbert added.

IO Morales pulled up the last footage from the drone before the repeater station on the raiding craft that was sending them picture went dark.

They all watched in horror as eight operatives climbed the side of *The Locust*. Most took cover behind some oil drums lashed to the deck. Four others took cover over by the container stack. Codi remained on the raft.

"Why is she staying behind?" the colonel asked no one in particular.

The explosion flashed the drone's camera sensor, and it took a couple of seconds before the view returned. Gunfire from two directions was clear, as was the complete annihilation of the operatives next to the drums. In a few moments, the two operatives by the containers were surrounded and dispatched. They had managed to take down two of the ship's mercenaries, but that was it.

Joel watched the raft below. He could see Codi standing in the bow looking up to the gunfire above. A man with a tube over his shoulder ran to the railing and pointed it at the raft below. They all watched as Codi jumped to the cable ladder dangling against the hull just before a tongue of fire left the tube and headed for the raft. There was another explosion that blinded the camera. This time, no image returned.

Colonel Gilbert stood on shaky feet and dialed a preset number on his sat phone. "Operations."

"Send in the sub," Colonel Gilbert said.

There was a brief pause, and then, "I understand," came the reply.

***

Codi clung to the ladder, stunned at the events that had just transpired. She helplessly watched as more lifeless bodies were thrown into the ocean, some her fellow operators, some who looked like they must have come from the ship. She slowly started to climb the ladder not sure what her next move might be.

The farthest back ladder suddenly crashed into the ocean, then the next one after it. She realized what was happening. They were discarding the ladders, and when they got to hers, she would be in big trouble. Looping an arm around a rung she grabbed her tactical backpack and started to dig through the contents. She pulled two plates with handgrips out of the bag, the Gecko Gloves Matt had given her to test. Her left hand grabbed the handle of one.

The ladder right next to hers fell, splashing into the dark sea below. Her ladder was next. In a last-ditch effort, Codi jumped from her ladder and grabbed the handle of the other paddle aiming both for the hull, just as the ladder she had just been standing on fell away behind her. The paddles made contact with the steel. To her surprise, the Gecko Gloves gripped the surface and held, leaving her dangling against the hull ten feet above the water. She was attached to the boat like a poor man's barnacle, her feet slipping to gain purchase on the wet surface.

Codi used her upper body strength to slowly make her way up the hull, twelve inches at a time, the Gecko Gloves doing their job. Each holding firm in two directions. She could lift them with ease, but once adhered to the hull, they would not slide down. It was grueling work, and her arms and hands were soon at their breaking point. Halfway up the hull, an inspiration born of suffering hit. She hooked the strap of her M4A1 rifle over the handle of one and hung from it. That allowed one arm at a time to drop, rest, and reacquire circulation. She repeated this method several more times as she made her way up the hull until she hung just under the railing of the aft deck. Even with her rest-climb-rest technique of scaling the hull, her arms were totally spent. The sand was tumbling through the hourglass. She would not be able to hang on much longer.

Crispin was eager to clean up and get back out of the cold. He glanced out to the empty horizon. Taking down some of the US military's best was a rush, the kind of thrill that would happen only once in a lifetime. Ordering his men to hose off the aft deck and chuck the bodies of the dead overboard, he turned to see to the wounded. One of his operators had taken a bullet in the shoulder and was back in the ready room getting first aid. They would have to wait until they made port to get the bullet out and fully patch him up. Sparks was on surveillance again and had nothing to report. They had crossed into Chinese territorial waters a couple of minutes ago. That would be the end of any further American assaults.

He had lost three men, which considering the opposition, was excellent. Eight highly trained operators had tried to sneak onto the ship, and he had dispatched them all with relative ease. This was something he should celebrate. During his days in the South African Special Forces, known as the Recces, he had received some of the most difficult training on the planet. Only about eight percent of those selected passed the training. Some years, no one passed at all. Crispin had finished the training and gone on to excel as an operator. He had used his skills to propel him into the high-paying world of civilian life. Since joining Pullin Ikaika, he had learned that there was more to life than killing for money. He could kill for the good of the planet, and that is exactly what he had just done. He turned and headed back to the ready room as the last of the gore washed over the side of *The Locust*.

Codi peeked over the edge of the deck. She was hanging a good fifty feet above the water below. She could see three men finish throwing the last body overboard. One of them had a fire hose and started to flush the blood, body parts, and other debris into the sea. The water was coming her way. There was no chance she could get over the railing and under cover without being seen, and her arms were close to failing and dropping her into the ocean. She took a chance and slipped the rifle sling around the pole of the railing, and then used the quick disconnect to attach it back to the stock. Putting both arms and part of her torso over the gun, she hung like a bad trapeze artist, waiting to see if it would hold her weight. Cold water shot across the deck and poured over her as she hung just a few feet below the deck. It was freezing, and soon Codi added shivering to her predicament.

She waited a good five minutes until the water stopped and the voices faded away. She could tell the men were amped up after their victorious gun battle. Shaking from cold and weakness, she slithered onto the deck. A quick jog into the darkness next to the stacked containers and she dropped to a prone position. Her watch told her she was more than six minutes into Chinese waters. The mission had failed.

Crispin and his men moved back to the ready room as he checked in with Captain Combs on the bridge.

"We are in the clear. All boarders repelled with extreme prejudice."

"Good to hear, Crispin. We are now in Chinese territorial waters," the captain added.

A muted cheer rose up from the mercenaries.

"That should be the end of the Americans for a while," Crispin replied.

Sparks did a quick scan of the images on the monitor. Nothing out of the ordinary was on the screen. "Still nothing to report," he said.

"That's it, boys. Drinks are on me." Crispin pulled a bottle of Hakkiesdraad Mampoer out of his gear bag and handed it to one of the men, who opened it and took a drink. The South African fiery moonshine-like clear liquor burned all the way down. "No way the US risks going to war with the Chinese over us. Nice work." Sparks spun in his chair anticipating his turn.

Codi lay on the deck of the ship waiting for her strength to return. She knew time was running out, but going into battle too weak to effectively wield your weapon was a death sentence.

What made her an extraordinary agent was her capability to change from moment to moment and self-correct to the reality around her. She was an expert at adapting and overcoming. No matter what transpired, no matter what was thrown at her between here and the finish line, Codi would adapt and overcome. Success was the only option.

Slow is smooth. Smooth is fast. The SEAL mantra played through her mind. She pulled herself up and jogged, keeping low and in the shadows along the deck. The first door on the port side was familiar to her. She pulled it open to reveal a hallway that looked exactly like *The Mantis*. Codi moved along the hallway with its many doors to the crew's quarters on both sides. Dropping down the first set of steps to the lower level, she followed the hallway with the handrails to the sliding panel that had disguised the entrance to the secret lab on *The Mantis*. A shot of fear blasted her body, remembering the horrors she had faced not so long ago. The cage, the sickness, her fellow prisoners, all flashed past. It made her want to run and hide, to just put it all behind her, but she somehow managed to hold her ground.

Footsteps coming down the stairs behind her had Codi spinning and dashing to meet the intruder.

A young man with a beard and glasses, wearing a lab coat appeared. Codi shoved him against the wall and jabbed her rifle in his ribs. His eyes shot up in fright.

"I got thirty seconds to clear your lab. You can either help me, or I'll kill you right here and use your severed hand to go inside myself. So what's it gonna be?" Codi reinforced her statement with another sharp jab from her weapon.

"Help?" The man said meekly.

"Okay, good decision. Let's get inside and quickly."

She pushed him ahead of her, and they jogged to the secret panel. He turned the fire extinguisher, and the panel slid to the side. Codi ripped the extinguisher from the wall. A shot of sparks followed. She then placed it on the ground preventing the door from reclosing all the way. Once inside the small room beyond, the man used his hand and a code to enter the lab.

"What's your name?" she asked.

"Santos," the man said in a quivering voice.

"Okay, Santos, you're doing good. Keep this up, and you'll live to tell your grandkids. Now, how many people are in this lab?"

"Three . . . no four," he replied.

"Names."

"There's Doctor Erwin Mahl, Doctor Sales, myself, and two lab assistants, Carmine and Henry."

"That's five, not four," Codi said raising her gun to his head.

"Sorry . . . Car, Carmine, is on break. Sh—she's in her cabin," Santos stuttered.

"And Doctor Erwin Mahl is in charge? Codi asked.

"Of the lab, yes."

"Okay, I believe you. I want you to use the PA and call them all into the kitchen. Is that possible?"

Santos nodded his head.

"No funny business, understand?" Codi demanded.

Santos reached for the intercom panel on the wall, stabbing at the button.

"This is Sa—Santos. Anyone that can hear my voice, please meet in the kitchen for an important announcement."

Codi pushed him down the hall to the first door on the left and followed him into the kitchen.

"Take a seat at the bar and relax." Codi reinforced her demand with the point of her gun. "I know there is a code system on this ship. I want you to tell me everything you know about it." She backed up behind the door waiting for the other three lab members to arrive.

Santos looked down for a beat before reciting the ship's code system. "Code one over the radios means there is a seriously injured person. It is usually followed by a location, like code one, galley. Code three is an all-call for engineering, so it would be something like code three backup pumps. Code five—"

"Okay, hold on. Start with code seventeen."

Codi remembered the code that had come over the radio on *The Mantis*. She had been sure it was a self-destruct for the entire ship but had been lucky, as it only destroyed the lab. The code, however, did have the rest of the crew abandoning ship.

A brief flash crossed Santos's eyes; he was amazed at the level of detail this woman knew about their operation.

"Code seventeen is an immediate abandon ship with a lab self-destruct. We are given like twenty seconds to clear out of here before all our work is sealed and incinerated."

"Is there a code where you abandon ship and don't destroy the lab?"

"No. But I guess you could use code nine," he said, hopefully.

"What's code nine?" Codi asked.

"Lab containment leak. Abandon all hands with immediate effect."

Codi nodded to herself. "Okay, that could work. What else happens on code nine?"

"The lab is instantly sealed. Anyone left inside would be trapped."

Codi paused for a second as a plan started to firm up in her mind. The door to the lab's galley opened and a short middle-aged man with bronze skin, white hair, and a boney figure entered. He was wearing a white lab coat and a sour expression.

"What's going on—"

Codi pushed the man as he was speaking and pointed her gun at him.

"What are you doing? You are interrupting important work. We are literally trying to save the world here," he spat.

"How? By destroying half the population?" Codi countered.

Dr. Mahl hesitated, taken aback by Codi's words. He folded his arms and a small smile danced to life. "Half would be just about right," he said.

"Take a seat. Let me guess, Doctor Erwin Mahl."

Erwin shot daggers at his assistant, Santos, as he sat next to him.

As each one of the lab personnel entered the room, Codi quickly took control, and soon, everyone was hovering around the bar like the prisoners they were.

"Everyone up and move. Out the door and to the left, then last door on the left."

She used her rifle to herd the small group to their destination. Once in the room, Codi almost lost all resolve. The familiar warm, muggy earthy smell was overpowering. Visions of horror flashed past her eyes. Cockroaches. She would never be able to see one again without it affecting her. Even her dreams had not been safe from the horrifying memory.

"Into the tank," was all she could squeak out. Her mind was going on overdrive to keep her on task when all she wanted to do was turn and run.

Dr. Sales opened the door and stepped up; the rest followed.

"I'm going to give you ten seconds to all get into the chamber. Or I can finish you off right where you stand."

The group, suddenly energized, quickly closed the first door and then opened the inner door and entered the incubator. The moment Codi heard the clank of the inner door closing she opened the outer door, cautious of any betrayal. The space was empty. All four of the scientists were now locked away in the incubator. She jammed the outer door open and ran from the lab and all its terrors.

Chapter Twenty-Three

C aptain Combs paced the bridge back and forth as she processed their situation. There was no way they could leave China after docking with the possibility the US would warn China about them. Perhaps their operation on *The Locust* was coming to a close. She felt confident that they could still dock and release their payload, but they would need to do a serious refit and name change before exiting Chinese waters. They had planned for this, but having commandos breach their decks so soon into the operation was very unnerving. How had they tracked *The Locust?* They should have been boarding a ship nearing the Hawaiian Islands. Somehow, the US government was onto their deception, or there was a leak in the operation.

"You can take us back down to cruising speed," she ordered the navigator. "No need bringing any more attention to ourselves from the Chinese."

The navigator typed in the speed change, and the ship's vibration calmed.

***

Captain Torres drummed his fingers on the smart table display. He had been watching the SSN-843 *Red Tide* slowly close on the target, *The Locust*. The Navy's current Mk 48 ADCAP torpedoes had a range of twenty-four miles. Their target was moving away at twenty-six knots, and they were doing thirty-eight knots. This meant a closing speed of only twelve knots. It was like watching two old men in walkers do a hundred-meter dash—slow and painful. He closed his eyes and tried to will his boat to move faster, but he could do nothing as *The Locust* passed into Chinese waters. He would not dare to enter Chinese territory at flank speed. That would be the end of his men and the *Red Tide*.

He picked up the communications mic, "Enge, can you give us any more?"

"We're at one hundred and ten percent now, sir," the engineering officer replied. "If I boost us any more, we'll be risking a reactor scram, and that will cost us twenty minutes minimum."

"Got it," Captain Torres said in frustration as he hung up the mic. He wiped a small drip of perspiration from his brow. "XO, take us up to ninety and fly the antenna."

His orders were repeated by the executive officer, and the boat started to angle up. Some of the men in the control room grabbed something to hold onto while others just angled their bodies to compensate, like standing on a tilted balance board.

Once at depth, the antenna was reeled out. It had a small wing shape on the tip that pulled the wire close to the surface.

"ET-Comm, send this message immediately." The captain handed the communications officer a note. "Weps, get me a firing solution."

The SSN-843 *Red Tide* was an electronic marvel. It took but a few seconds for the computers and technicians to do the task.

"I have a solution, Captain," the weapons officer said.

"How soon can we fire?"

"Five miles, and that's if she maintains her course, sir, but that will put us at the limit of our range."

"I'm not going into Chinese waters without authorization. We'll fire that torpedo the second we close the gap."

"Aye, sir."

"Captain, I have a reply," the communications officer said as he handed a message to Torres.

The captain read the contents and then wadded it up and tossed it on the floor. It was not what he was expecting.

"Everything alright, Captain?" the communications officer asked.

"*No!* Weps, how close?"

"Three minutes."

"Weps, what's the variance on the Mk-48's range?" the captain asked.

"They're pretty accurate, sir. Plus or minus a half-mile, I'd say," the weapons officer replied.

Captain Torres paused for a second, considering all the angles. He looked at the chart that showed him less than a half-mile from Chinese waters. This was as close as he was willing to go. "Open outer door and launch tube one."

The weapons officer followed procedure. "Tube one launched. Running true and hot."

"XO, take us back down, two hundred and fifty meters. Course 0-9-1 and drop our speed to twenty-eight knots. I'm sick of cavitating across the whole Pacific Ocean. And get the antenna back in."

The control room buzzed with activity as the captain's orders were carried out. Soon, the craft was angling back down into the depths, away from Chinese territorial waters.

***

The Mk-48 torpedo felt no pain or fear. It wasn't concerned as it passed from international waters into Chinese territorial waters. It just did what the programming in its small brain said. The swashplate piston engine fueled by Otto fuel II, a liquid monopropellant fuel, spun twin contra-rotating propellers. Its sophisticated guidance system constantly evaluated and adjusted its attack options. A thin wire, attached to its mother like an umbilical cord, gave its brain reassurance and updates along the way. Once the target was acquired, its active/passive sonar would guide the high explosive warhead to its destination. Somewhere twenty-two miles ahead was a large metal signature that, once near, would signal a circuit to close, and an immediate irreversible reaction would take place that would destroy the torpedo and sink the ship.

***

Codi stepped out of the small security room and pulled the fire extinguisher, allowing the panel to close behind her. She padded up the stairs and made her way to the internal staircase that connected the bottom of the superstructure to the top, where the bridge was. Once there, she debated on which way to go and what would come next. With an imaginary coin toss, she decided to go down. Three flights later, she came to a small T-shaped room with three steel ship's hatches. She slid her rifle strap back onto her shoulder and pulled the Sig Sauer P226 from its holster. A handgun would be better for the coming conditions.

She spun the wheel with the label Engine Room and was met by a warm wash of air. It had an oily, damp quality. Codi quickly stepped inside. There was a steel walkway along the wall, like a viewing platform. In the middle was a set of open stairs that led down to the main floor below. She dropped down the steel steps to the main room. The engine noise permeated everything, making conversation difficult. She stepped up to a man in overalls looking over some gauges through black-framed glasses. He never heard her approach and was totally surprised to see a woman holding a gun in his face. His hands shot up into the air.

"How did you get in here?" he asked.

"I'll be asking the questions. How many men are down here?" Codi asked.

The man scratched his head as he pondered the answer. "Right now . . . just me and Crawley."

"Where's Crawley?" she demanded.

"He was over by engine one, checking the zerks."

It meant nothing to Codi. "Okay, let's go find him. You first."

The engineer moved toward engine one with his hands in the air. Codi kept her head on a swivel not wanting to be blindsided. The ship had two engines. Each the size of a small locomotive, and the closer they got, the louder it became.

Crawley was on his last zerk fitting, and it was the hardest one to reach. Each time he placed the grease gun on a fitting and pumped, he was quickly rewarded with pressure, meaning everything was in good order. The last fitting was in a tight spot, and he had to climb under the engine to reach it. As he stretched his arms out, the grease gun slipped from his hands and clanged on the deck. He twisted to retrieve it and in doing so noticed movement. A woman was holding a gun on the night engineer and heading his way. *Something's wrong here!* He slipped deeper under the engine and crawled out on the other side.

Crawley picked up a large spanner used for tightening only the largest bolts and worked his way back around the other way. He heard his name being called a couple of times but dismissed them. A quick peek under the engine gave him the position of the woman based on the legs he could see. Dipping back under the engine, he was intent on crawling out behind them and using his wrench to end the threat.

He stood slowly behind the woman and leaped, raising the spanner and swinging it for her skull with all his might.

Codi had followed the night engineer to engine one and the two had started to make their way around it. Her captive tried calling out to Crawley a few times, but there had been no response. He suddenly stopped and turned back to face her.

"Maybe he's in the head."

He had a shiftiness that told Codi he was lying. As he adjusted his glasses, Codi noticed a slight reflection of movement behind her in the man's lenses. Instinctively, she dropped to the floor, twisting as she fell. A quick reflex pull of the trigger, and a man swinging a giant wrench buckled and fell, dead before he hit the floor. Codi quickly spun the gun back at her prisoner who was reaching for the wrench. He stopped and returned his hands to the in-the-air position.

"Is he dead," he said with genuine concern in his voice.

"No thanks to you, yes he is, and *you* will be, too, if you try a stunt like that. Understand?"

He shook his head vigorously.

"No?" Codi queried.

"I mean yes! I won't do that." He quickly changed his shaking to nodding.

Codi prodded him quickly back to the control panel.

"Can I control the ship from here?" Codi asked.

"I suppose I can override the bridge if we go to manual."

"What do I have to do to initiate code nine?" Codi demanded.

He dropped his hands. "Code nine? You can't be serious."

Codi pulled back the hammer on her pistol.

His hands returned to the air. "Okay, okay. It's all automated. All I have to do is type a set of numbers into the system."

"Do it! And make no mistake, if you try anything funny, I'll end you right here."

She watched as he input in a series of numbers into the system and hit enter.

An alarm tone went off followed by: *Code nine, code nine, abandon ship, abandon ship.*

It repeated every few seconds.

"Good. Now take us to manual," she ordered.

"Give me a second. I have to think about how to do this," he said while rubbing his hands together nervously.

***

"We are about at the end of our wire, sir," the weps officer said.

The Mk-48 torpedo was pushing the distance limit of the guide-by-wire communications between the torpedo and the sub for target updates. It helped avoid jamming and decoys along the route, but the length of the wire was not endless. It was time to set it and forget it.

"Update target information and cut the umbilical," said the captain. "What's our time to target?"

"Five minutes, and we have a solid lock, Captain."

"Sir, we have company!" the sonar engineer called. "I've picked up a Yaun-Class sub bearing one two zero, closing to our position."

"Put it on the screen and classify her as target two."

A second icon appeared on the smart table overlaying the map. It was still a ways off, but there was no doubt as to its course.

The Type 039A Yaun-Class diesel-electric boat had air-independent propulsion, which allowed it to run the diesel engines for long periods of time underwater without having the snorkel up to provide air to the engines. Its design made it much quieter than the nuclear-powered *Red Tide* when running on electric because its batteries were silent, whereas a nuclear submarine had to maintain its circulating pumps at all times to keep the reactor from overheating and melting down. The big disadvantage was range. A nuclear boat could go around the world several times whereas the Yaun Class would have to surface every time it ran out of fuel. They were generally used for coastal defense.

The captain looked at the map for a few seconds longer.

"XO, take us deep and put some distance between us and target two."

The executive officer barked a series of orders, and soon the *Red Tide* was changing course and diving for the bottom of the sea.

"Nothing like a torpedo in the water to attract attention," the captain muttered.

***

Crispin burst onto the bridge as Captain Combs was just getting ready to exit.

"What are you doing?" he demanded.

"Code nine. We are done here," the captain replied.

"Do you think it's possible there is more here than meets the eye?"

"Why, what do you know, Crispin?"

"Nothing yet, but I don't believe in coincidences."

"Captain," the first officer called out, "the system is off-line. I have no control of the ship."

"Try restarting," the captain demanded, her frustration growing.

"Doing that now, but I'm getting an error message."

She grabbed a radio and hit the transmit button. "Engineering, did you initiate the code nine?"

There was a delay before a response came.

"No, Captain, it came from the lab, something about a contaminate that leaked or got loose."

Captain Combs looked to Crispin for a second and then back to her first officer.

Crispin said, "Captain, why would the lab alert engineering about a disaster and not us? I'm telling you, something is not right about this."

Captain Combs looked at her radio, her head slowly nodding. She lifted it and pressed the transmit button. "Doctor Mahl, do you copy? Does anyone in the lab copy? This is Captain Combs."

A scratchy desperate voice that sounded a lot like a high-pitched Doctor Erwin Mahl with a slight Indian accent cried back. "We've had an unexpected containment leak. Seal the lab! It's eating my skin. Heaven help—" The voice cut out mid-sentence.

Captain Combs and Crispin shared a look of shock. Crispin's jaw hung loose for all to see.

"Collins, abandon ship with immediate effect and make sure everyone makes it off safely."

"Aye, Captain."

"Crispin, come with me," Captain Combs said as she reached into a drawer and pulled out a pistol and racked a bullet into the chamber.

"What? We should get off this ship!" Crispin said.

"Doctor Mahl would have known that code nine seals the lab. He would *not* have requested that action. Something doesn't feel right, but I'm not willing to risk the crew's lives on a hunch."

***

"Command, this is Clear Water. What are your instructions?" Colonel Gilbert spoke the words as though he was afraid of the answer.

The C-17 had been circling a section of air over the original target's location. Since things had gone down the toilet, it had taken a few moments for the task force to recover.

"Are you reporting a complete loss?" the colonel asked.

"That is correct, sir."

A moment of static filled the colonel's ear. "Stand down and return to base. We'll take it from here."

"What are you talking about?" Joel shouted. "We can't just leave!"

The colonel just managed to get his hand on the phone's microphone to cut out the civilian's outburst.

"Everything okay, colonel?" the voice over the phone asked.

"Yes. We are returning to base," he said as he disconnected the call.

He turned to Joel. "Another outburst like that, and I'll have you restrained and gagged."

"We can't just leave them," Joel pleaded.

"Leave what, son. They're gone . . . all of them. Make your peace and then get back to work. We're done here." He called out, "Get this jet back to base." He then turned to the information officer. "IO, pull up the satellite feed on *The Locust's* last position. I want to watch as she goes down in flames."

Joel laid his head down on the table. His heart was smashed for his partner. He knew she would fight through this feeling, but he didn't have the strength. He tried to channel Codi and snap out of his funk, but all he got was tears. Tears he was now forced to keep to himself.

***

Codi nodded to her prisoner, who had passed his first acting test as a voice artist over the radio.

"Nice work. Now, let's get this ship turned around," she said.

"Give me a minute. They are trying to reboot the system." He continued to type on his keyboard until a final flourish left him with nothing but a black screen.

"Come on, come on . . . Okay. We are no longer a smart ship."

"So how do we turn her?" Codi asked.

"See that black dial? It will divert hydraulics and move the rudder. If we crank it ninety degrees, it should take about five minutes for the ship to do a one-eighty. Then we will need to reset it back to the neutral position, or we'll just go around in a big circle."

"What do you mean, it *should* take about five minutes?"

"I've never done this before. It's a best-guess sorta thing. Plus, we're a bit blind down here with the whole system down."

"Okay, I'll start the countdown. Let's do it," Codi commanded, with a nod of her head.

He reached for the black knob with the pointer built-in as bullets pinged off the steel of the light-green control console, smashing dials and ricocheting rounds dangerously around the room. The slugs found their way to the night engineer, and he dropped to the floor, leaving a bloody trail behind, his hand having never turned the dial.

Codi crashed to the floor almost instantly, a bullet grazing her arm, as she disappeared from the shooter's view.

Crispin had been the first one to enter the engine room. From the observation deck, he immediately appraised the situation—one engineer held at gunpoint by a female dressed in all black. She must have been part of the boarding party. Somehow, she had gotten past their assault and slipped aboard. Without preamble, he fired a volley in her direction. Captain Combs quickly joined in and the number of bullets on target doubled.

Crispin took the stairs three at a time as his partner covered his actions. He moved behind a set of fire pumps and signaled for the captain to follow.

Codi could feel the warm sensation of blood flowing down her arm. She would need to deal with it. But not now. She reached up and found the dial with her hand and turned it what she thought was ninety degrees, about a quarter turn. A silent countdown from five minutes began in her head.

Scooting past the fallen engineer, she peeked her head around the corner of the control console. A tall red-haired woman in a captain's shirt could be seen moving down the stairs. Codi flipped her rifle off her shoulder and did a quick snapshot. The bullet hit the woman's thigh, causing her to torque left and flip over the stair railing. A short scream was followed by a sickening crunch as human flesh hit steel floor.

Crispin heard the scream but was too busy trying to find his target to investigate. He would have to assume he was now alone. The view through his scope was blocked by equipment. He continued to move right as he attempted to flank the woman, hoping for a glimpse of her.

***

Collins watched as the last man crawled up into the orange and white fiberglass shell. "What about the rest of engineering?" a crew member asked.

"They're on their own," Collins replied as he hit the button on the console that would release the lifeboat after a thirty-second delay.

Scampering up inside, he secured the hatch behind him and found a seat. He strapped on the four-point harness just before a loud *clank* was followed by a sudden drop. It was straight out of an amusement park. The lifeboat free-fell toward the water fifty feet below. The sudden impact held no amusement as the entire boat dove under the water coming to a jarring stop. With whip-lash effect, the lifeboat popped back out of the ocean like a cork in a tub. The crew was shaken but okay as *The Locust* moved away leaving them behind. Collins unbuckled himself and moved to the controls, aiming the craft for the nearest coast.

***

The SSN-843 *Red Tide* traveled along one mile on the other side of the invis-ible border that defined Chinese territorial waters. She stayed low and quiet as her crew tracked the outbound torpedo's progress.

"XO, let's get a slot buoy ready; I need to send a message. Weps, update."

"Thirty seconds to contact. Still running true and hot."

"Good. We just might get out of this yet." He quickly typed a message on the smart table, and with a flick of his hand sent it to the communications engineer. "E-Comm, send that, and Sonar, keep a close watch on target two."

***

The Mk-48 torpedo had been given a set of coordinates to aim for, including a depth. Once it was within five miles of the target, the sonar locked on and spun up the last series of protocols. At one mile, the brain turned off the passive sonar and used active pinging only. It engaged a metal detector with pulse induction that would trigger the circuit to ignite the high explosive once a large metallic reading of 85 kHz or larger was obtained. The explosion would occur inches before impact with the ship, creating a plasma event that literally melted through the hull as it exploded.

At three-quarters of a mile away, active pinging told the brain it had detected a course correction of the ship. It was turning away. The brain recalculated the new position and adjusted for it. The torpedo moved slightly to the right, reac-quiring its target with ease. At eight hundred meters, all safeties were removed, and the metal detector took over. At first, it had a weak signal of 23 kHz, but the closer it moved, the signal strength increased. To 65 kHz, and then 74 kHz, as it closed on the ship, waiting for the signal strength to reach 85 kHz.

At two hundred meters, the signal had increased to 80 kHz. Then, just as if someone had flipped a switch, the swashplate piston engine died. Its explosive monopropellant fuel had run out. The torpedo continued on but lost speed as it went, the detector still climbing. To 83 kHz, 84 kHz, but that was all it would ever get to, as the metal projectile passed beneath the hull by a mere twenty feet. The brain, knowing it had failed to reach the target, reinstalled the safeties on the warhead. It then began a series of actions to engage in a complete shutdown. Finally reaching its crush depth on its way to the ocean floor, the tube structure failed and collapsed. No explosion.

***

At three hundred meters, the SSN-843 *Red Tide* matched its surroundings perfectly. Everything was black. It moved through the water like a wraith, waiting to share death with those around it.

"Captain, the target is turning," the sonar technician announced.

"Target one or two, son?"

"Target one is turning. It looks like they are heading back out into international waters."

"What about the torpedo?"

"It seems to have missed. I no longer hear it."

"It probably ran out of fuel," the weps officer said as he checked the countdown numbers on his screen.

"XO, bring us back up to ninety, nice and quiet, and let's get the antenna out again. Reload tube one and prepare to open tube two's door. I want to close the distance and end this ship without getting caught with my pants down by the Chinese. Get me a firing solution on target one, and do the same for target two, just in case they do something stupid."

The men on the *Red Tide* moved into action, each eager to complete the mission and get as far away as possible from the approaching Chinese sub. The sub was inferior to the technologies built into a Virginia-Class submarine, but in war, anything could happen.

***

What Codi would never know is that her actions to turn the ship clockwise instead of counterclockwise had been the difference that had saved her life and the ship's. The extra thousand yards it put between the hull and the closing torpedo had extended the weapon beyond its range. Had she turned the ship in the other direction, she would have shortened the range and met a violent watery death.

The danger, however, was far from over. A highly-trained operative was hunting her. She fired off a few bullets in the general direction of her assailant, hoping to keep him pinned down. The countdown in her head was somewhere around four minutes, thirty-eight seconds.

Close enough, she said to herself. She returned the dial to its neutral position and sprinted away, back toward engine one. She climbed underneath it and dropped to a prone position waiting for any sign of movement to follow. A beat later, she was inundated with hot lead as bullets pinged against the metal kill box she had hidden herself in. *Stupid!*

As she rolled out from under the engine, away from the source of the gunfire, Codi saw a red blob moving in her direction. The captain was still alive. She was a bloody mess. Starting with a partially caved-in head and a useless leg that was dragging behind her, she was slithering in Codi's direction, gripping her gun with her good hand.

Codi was blown away at the determination of the woman to keep fighting when already dead. What kind of zealots worked for Pullin Ikaika? It was truly shocking. She pointed her pistol at Codi and pulled the trigger repeatedly. Her caved-in skull, bleeding brain, and shaking hand made her aim wild, and bullets splashed all over the place. None, however, hit Codi.

After the captain had emptied her gun, her finger continued to pull the trigger, to a clicking backbeat. Finally, her head dropped to the floor and all was quiet. Codi made her way up to the top of engine one. There was a small metal ladder that led to a catwalk giving access to the top of the engine for maintenance.

She stayed prone, hoping her assailant would continue to look below for her.

Crispin stayed down behind a pressure pump, using his scope to survey the room. A little luck revealed the woman hiding under the steel engine on the left. He had emptied a full mag into the tight quarters. She had rolled out of sight just before a pistol fired rapidly over by the stairs. Captain Combs must still be alive. This was good news. He continued to move right in an attempt to corner his prey. With Combs on the left, the woman had nowhere to run. He wiped the sweat from his eyes as he moved. The engine room's hot muggy temperature was unbearable. He ducked behind a large generator that was humming. Through the circle view of his scope, he covered every nook and cranny as he eliminated possible hiding spots. Her luck would soon run out.

***

The sonar officer tilted his head as he listened to a change in ratio-to-target feedback. The screen confirmed what his highly-trained ears had detected. "*The Locust* has come about, sir, and is within firing distance," he said to the captain.

"Good. Flood tube one. Open outer door and get me a firing solution. And keep tube two warm and ready for target two."

"Aye, sir."

"I have a solution to target one, sir," Weps called out.

"Range to target?" the captain asked.

"Eighteen miles."

"Fire tube one."

A loud whooshing sound followed.

"Tube one away, running hot and straight," came the reply from Weps.

The crew listened as the torpedo's high-pitched scream moved away from the ship. They had finally dealt with *The Locust*. Now, they would have to reposition as quickly as possible to help make themselves less of a sitting duck for the Yaun-Class sub.

"XO, take us down to one-fifty and change course to 0-1-7. Let's put some distance between us and the Chinese."

The sub dove and moved right, leaving behind the place in the water where they had launched the torpedo.

Captain Torres listened to the countdown as the sonar operator tracked the outbound torpedo. In no time, they were ten miles and closing. *The Locust* was unaware, but she had turned herself into a world of hurt.

***

The C-17 seemed too quiet as they headed to the Antonio B. Won Pat International Airport in Guam. After losing the entire squad of operators, no one felt like talking. It was like a football team riding the bus home after a shellacking by their rivals.

"Sir, *The Locust* has turned around, and it looks like a lifeboat has launched," the information officer said, just loud enough for everyone to hear.

"What? Show me," the colonel said as he moved back to the table.

The IO spun his laptop with the satellite image of the ship on it.

Joel looked over to the screen, his eyes still red. Sure enough, *The Locust* was heading back toward international waters.

"What do you think it means?" IO Morales asked.

The colonel had no response. Nobody did.

"It can only mean one thing," Joel piped up. "Codi. She's alive."

"Let's not get ahead of ourselves," the colonel said as he sat back down at the table.

"I'm telling you, she has a way of beating the odds and coming out the other side like no one else. You gotta believe me. Codi is alive," Joel demanded, his voice rising as he spoke.

The colonel tapped his knuckles on the table for a second as he thought. It was true, no one had seen her killed. Was it possible? "IO, bring up the footage just before we lost the signal."

Morales did. He slowed the frame rate down to one frame at a time, clicking through the action. He froze the image just before the second raft blew up. Something was there on the side of the ship. He zoomed in and cleared up the grain. A fuzzy image of Codi hanging onto the cable ladder could be seen.

"See!" Joel exclaimed.

Colonel Gilbert grabbed and dialed his sat phone.

"Command."

"This is Clear Water. We have a development. The ship has turned."

"We are aware of that and are following it now."

"We think one of our operators is still in play."

"You think one man survived to take on the whole ship?"

"No, sir. One woman."

***

From her spot on the catwalk above the engine, Codi noticed movement behind one of the two large generators mounted to the left of the room. They were each the size of a Volkswagen Beetle. She concentrated and soon identified the barrel of a rifle next to one of the pipes. Being on top of the engine was like hanging in a polluted sauna. The exhaust was routed out of the room, but residual oil and diesel superheated by the engine made the air unbreathable. Codi pulled her shirt up over her nose trying to fight it. Focusing her sights on the dark space behind the rife, she calmed her breathing and waited for the drop on her eyebrow to fall and clear. She pulled the trigger.

A rewarding *ugh* followed as the rifle clattered to the floor. Codi quickly jumped up and leaped from the catwalk to the upper walkway and moved counterclockwise around to the entrance door, the engine noise masking her actions. She waited as the man down below picked up his rifle and moved toward the engine where she had just been hiding. She could see he was hit, but it seemed to have no effect on him.

"Drop your weapon," she screamed while keeping a bead on the man below. He seemed to disregard her and spun his rifle back up in her direction. Codi didn't hesitate. She sent a three-round burst his way. The man shuddered and dropped to the floor, his weapon skittering away, a crimson pool spreading across his chest.

Codi slumped to the floor. She tried to catch her breath and calm her raging mind. She took a second to cut a strip from her sleeve and wrap it on her wound. With a little help from her teeth, she tied a knot that would apply pressure and hold the strip in place. She stood on shaky legs and made her way back down to the engine room. A quick look at the control console found the button Codi had hit on *The Mantis*—Emergency All-Stop. She hit it and turned to leave, never planning on coming back.

***

"Five miles from impact, sir. The ship is slowing. She's a sitting duck now."

"What's going on with the Yaun Class?" Captain Torres asked.

"They appear to be staying on their side of the water. Probably just watching everything play out," the sonar tech replied.

"Let me know if there is any change."

"Aye, sir."

The room had gotten warm, and coats and sweaters had long since been abandoned. A slight bead of sweat grew on the captain's brow.

The torpedo continued to do its mission as it closed on the slowing *Locust*. Everyone on board now listened intently to the action as it played out. This was an extremely rare thing for a sub to really fire a torpedo with the full intention of sinking another vessel.

"Three minutes to target. Should I cut the umbilical?"

"Sir, I have a flash message from COMSUBPAC." The ET-Comm practically tripped trying to get the paper into his captain's hand.

A quick read changed everything for the mission.

"You're sure this is from COMSUB PAC Command?"

"Yes, sir."

"Sixty seconds from impact. Sir, I need to cut the cable."

"Weps, don't cut the cable! Deactivate torpedo. I say again, deactivate torpedo."

There was a brief moment of silence as the weapons officer typed frantically on his keyboard. The time to impact continued to count down. Thirty, twenty, ten . . .

"Torpedo deactivated, sir."

***

A cool breeze on the bridge's flying wing pushed Codi's hair to the side. She soaked up the salty tang of the ocean as she lifted an ice-cold bottle of Sapporo taken from the galley on her way here. While there, she had found a mirror and taken the time to inspect her burnt hair. She would need a new hairstyle while it grew back out.

The ship had slowed to a stop somewhere in the middle of the Pacific Ocean. They were either in Chinese waters or just outside of them, she figured, but truly had no idea. The bottle of beer was half-empty, and she could have kicked herself for not having grabbed two. If she had the energy, she would go back down and get another. Maybe later.

A sudden clunk of metal hitting metal underwater caught her attention. Codi looked over the railing to the water below. There was a faint white line of bubbles drawing a line right to the hull of *The Locust*. She immediately knew what it was. A torpedo had just hit the hull but hadn't detonated. Time seemed to stand still as she processed her current situation. She wasn't sure what to do next.

A strong boil of bubbles filled the ocean just off the starboard bow. It was followed by a mast and then the sail of a submarine. Codi gripped the railing wondering if it was Chinese. She would know in a second, and there was nothing she could do about it anyway.

A few seconds later a voice called out on a megaphone from the top of the sail.

"This is the SSN-843 *Red Tide*. We are commandeering this vessel. Cease all activity and prepare to be boarded."

The message was repeated one more time, and Codi, still leaning on the flying bridge's railing, released a sigh she had been holding. She lifted her beer up in a toasting gesture to the men on the sub. "Knock yourself out, boys," she said, to no one in particular with a growing smile. Her thoughts turned to Matt. She needed to make a call.

Within a few moments, a raft filled with armed sailors was powering over to the hull of *The Locust*. The threat was over.

EPILOGUE

Codi walked from the airport into the freezing rain. She was irate. The last ninety-six hours had been hellish. It started with a long ride on a submarine. She was transferred to the USS *Paul Hamilton,* an Arleigh Burke Class destroyer, and debriefed for twelve hours solid. From there, a helicopter took her to Guam where she was booked on a flight back to D.C. While waiting for her flight, she had found a place to get her burnt-chunk hairstyle fixed. She now had a bob cut, which would have to do while it grew back out. Matt and Codi had spoken several times over the phone, and she was looking forward to spending a few days with him once she was back in D.C.

On the flight home, she had received a message that ripped away what little confidence for the mission she still carried. The team sent to open the sealed lab on *The Locust* had set off the self-destruct, killing three more men and everyone Codi had left inside the incubator. Worst of all, the vaccine was gone, burned away with all of the accompanying details and documentation—a total loss.

Everything she and her team had worked so hard to do was now up in smoke, and the pile of bodies was growing. Pullin Ikaika had disappeared and authorities had no clue as to his whereabouts.

The blood and tissue samples they had taken from Codi gave no indication of how to make more of the vaccine. It was a worst-case scenario. What they had learned from Codi's samples was that the vaccine was not so much a vaccine as it was a compound that modified the body to become asymptomatic to the Korean

Typhoid Superbug. It allowed one's body to isolate the bug until slowly, over time, it died out. You experienced no symptoms during that time, but you were still contagious for several days. It meant that even if they had a vaccine, the disease would continue to grow until the shots got ahead of the infected. That would take time, but if they had managed to get the vaccine, they would eventually get ahead of it. But now, there was little hope of a solution.

The initial plan had been for each country to be given the means to replicate the cure and take care of their own citizens. The outcome, now, was much different—World War Three against an unseen enemy. Time, strict quarantines, and a little luck would be required if the planet's population was going to survive.

There had been rushes on stores and pharmacies as panicked citizens tried to get their share of food and supplies. Fights broke out and riots were not far behind. Soon, it would be vigilante justice in the streets as a bankrupt government failed its citizens.

It seemed obvious to Codi that the number-one seller was toilet paper. In fact, most stores were sold out of all paper products. Facemasks of any kind and sanitizer were next on the top ten. Given a little forethought, she should have invested in them.

The Uber driver pulled to the curb and Codi got in. She rode in silence, playing back in her mind the events of the last few weeks. Rain pelted the roof of the car as it pulled in front of her apartment.

A quick and meaningless "Thank you," was followed by a jog inside the building. She added a tip to the Uber app on her phone as she dropped her luggage and plopped down on her couch. A lightning flash filled the room, illuminating her foul mood.

Codi tried to get on the other side of it, but the failed mission with the loss of more lives was still too heavy on her mind. She had felt tremendous guilt for her mother's death, but the death of military operators was just tragic.

The men who questioned her during her debriefing seemed satisfied with the results of her actions and even spoke accolades regarding her daring feat to take *The Locust* on all by herself. She had stopped them from delivering another deadly dose of Typhoid superbug-infected insects on China and saved the ship from falling into Chinese hands. It was a win-win. She should be celebrating. But the bitter taste in her mouth dominated everything.

Codi disagreed with their conclusion and decided to let her dark feelings run their course. She could rethink everything once on the other side. Tomorrow, it was off to stay at Matt's house for an overdue stay. Nothing good would come from wallowing in misery for too long. The first vibration on her phone she didn't hear. The next four she disregarded, and her phone went to VM. When it started ringing again, she called out, "Siri answer the call and put it on speaker."

"Codi . . . Codi are you there?"

She recognized her partner's mood. He got a bit manic when he spent the entire day hopped up on caffeine and information. It was especially bad when he found a thread to pull or a clue that started to unravel.

A heavy sigh was followed by a meek answer. "Yes, Joel."

"Hey, I think I might have something. How soon can you get to the office?"

"Joel, it's 10:00 p.m.," she replied, flatly.

"Well, technically, 10:06, but it's important!"

"All right, hang onto your jockstrap. I'll get there as soon as I can."

"I don't wear a jo—never mind. You know what? I'll pick you up. Be there in ten."

Codi hung up. She was torn between going or just lying there and pretending the call had never happened. Another bolt of lightning flashed through the room. It seemed to be telling her to get up. Codi leaned forward and moved, robot-like, to the front door. Collecting up her gear, including her gun and badge, she left the comfort of her couch behind. So much for drowning herself in sorrow.

***

Senator Crandall pressed the built-in button on his sun visor and watched in his rearview mirror as his garage door closed, separating the cold rain outside from the dry inside. A hard light from a single bulb automatically illuminated his immaculate three-car garage, all decorated in white. His black Gucci loafers clicked on the finished concrete, avoiding the small pool of rainwater dripping from his car. He slammed the car door and headed for the door into the kitchen. The senator instinctively placed his keys in a small bowl by the door and reached for the light switch.

Nothing happened. The bulb was out or maybe a fuse had blown.

"Terrific," he mumbled to himself.

Before the garage door completely closed, leaving him in darkness, the senator flicked his smartphone light to life. A harsh beam illuminated the way ahead as he moved for the living room, hoping that a light switch there might work. As he reached for the switch, the cold feeling of steel on the skin of his neck stopped him mid-flick. He dropped his cell and froze, unsure what to do, the phone's light now pointing at the ceiling. A hand reached over and flicked the room to life. Pullin Ikaika was sitting, smiling, in the senator's favorite chair, a blue suede recliner with a matching footstool.

"Senator!" Pullin called out. "Come on in. Have a seat. Good to see you again."

Senator Crandall moved over carefully, away from the gun, and sat on the ivory couch across from the billionaire.

"You remember my man, Whiton."

The senator glanced back at a man dressed in all black holding a pistol pointed at him. He had a large scar across his cheek and a crooked smirk. A sinking feeling began to overwhelm him.

"What is the meaning of this? I have done everything you asked," he said with artificial bravado.

"Yes, I know. And for that, I am most grateful," Pullin replied, keeping his face placid.

"So back to my first question, what is the meaning of this?"

"I would have thought the meaning clear, Senator. Things have not gone as planned. I have a list, and I like to start at the top of my lists. I'm doing a little housecleaning."

The words shook the senator. His mind raced with wild possibilities. "You know I can still be of great value to you."

The senator's words were met with a smile that never reached Pullin's eyes. Eyes that pinched together with criticism. The senator knew immediately what was at stake. "You can't kill a United States senator and get away with it," he said, in a desperate plea.

"Who said anything about getting away with it? Sending a message only works if it is clearly understood," Pullin said as he pulled out his Galesi .22 pocket pistol, now sporting a small silencer.

The senator's eyes flicked back and forth between the gun and the man who now, literally, held his fate in his hands.

"Is that some sort of joke?" the senator said, gesturing to the small almost toy-like gun in Pullin's hand.

"For me, yes."

The small-caliber round was nearly silent as the first bullet tore into the top of the senator's right foot. It immediately had him writhing on the floor, crying out. The second bullet to the gut had the screaming down to a whimper. Better. Now, he could take his time.

***

Joel's wipers worked overtime as he drove through the relatively deserted streets. He had a jittery look and feel about him, like a man running on too much caffeine.

"Okay, please tell me I didn't get my hair wet for nothing," Codi demanded.

"Nice hairstyle, by the way."

"Thanks. I call it 'the bomb,'" Codi said as she ran her fingers through the short hair she was still trying to get used to after the bomb on the raft had burned a huge chunk away.

"Joel?"

"Oh, something has been bugging me. I just couldn't let it all go. What with Pullin disappearing and no luck with the vaccine, I just—"

"To the point, please."

"I've been looking for connections. Connections that might be of value to this case."

Codi looked over at Joel, slightly less irritated. But surely this could have waited until morning.

"Senator Crandall and Pullin Ikaika seem to have one," he continued as he turned left.

Codi looked at him with narrowed eyes, trying to follow his thinking.

The Prius seemed at its limit fording the flooded intersections, but somehow, like its occupants, it bravely slogged on.

"Hear me out. Not only is Pullin a big contributor to the senator's campaign, but the senator's been getting calls that ping to a cell tower near Pullin's house in Lake Tahoe."

"Weak, but okay," Codi said.

Joel cleared his throat. "Pullin has been ahead of us at every turn."

"Speaking of which, you were supposed to make a right turn back there," Codi said, using her head to point the way.

"We're not going to the office," Joel replied.

He now had Codi's full attention. He turned left and moved up a slight incline as he entered Logan Circle, one of the more affluent neighborhoods in D.C.

"Like I said, he's been ahead of us, and we need to warn the senator who he's dealing with."

Codi's shoulders slumped. "And we didn't just *call* him, say, tomorrow during business hours, because?"

Her phone vibrated, and she sent the caller to VM without looking.

"We need to look in his eyes when we tell him. For all we know, he and Pullin are in on this together, and if they are, time matters. There are people out there dying, Codi."

"I'm well aware, Joel, but Senator Crandall? Head of the intelligence committee? Slow down. This is a guy who can make you and your career disappear. We need to be very careful here," Codi warned.

"That's why I'm bringing you."

"Great," Codi said weakly.

They pulled to the curb and spied the house across the street. Through the pouring rain and occasional lightning strike, they could see a large modern home set back from the street. It was made of gray stone and lots of glass, glowing with a warm interior light. A cobbled driveway led to the entrance some eighty feet back from the sidewalk.

Codi's phone vibrated again, and this time, she looked at the caller ID. Matt. She vacillated.

"Aren't you going to answer that?" Joel asked.

"Not right now. I need my head in the game. So remember, if Matt's mad at me, it was your fault."

"*My* fault? I . . ." Joel stammered.

"Come on. Let's get this over with. I need to get home and brood for a bit before I head over to Matt's," Codi said as she opened her door and ran for the cover of the front portico with Joel following right behind her.

They stayed on the covered porch for a second shaking off the excess water. Joel flicked his sodden shoes like an unhinged dancer.

"Next time you get a bright idea, bring an umbrella," Codi said as she flicked the excess moisture from her hair with her fingers.

Once they felt somewhat presentable, Joel reached for the doorbell. Codi grabbed his hand and pulled it back. "Did you hear that?"

"No, what?"

"I don't know. Raised voices, maybe a moan. I think I recognize one of them. It's too loud out here in the rain to be sure. Follow me," she said as she sprinted to the right. Joel followed her over the locked gate and into the backyard. The backyard was large with a pool, an entertaining area, and a small pool house in the back. They crept up to a glowing window, staying low and out of sight. Through the raindrops and smeared glass, they could make out three men. One was on the floor writhing—Senator Crandall. The other two stood over him. Codi immediately recognized one of them as Pullin Ikaika.

"Call this in," Codi hissed as she sprinted for the window.

Joel pulled his phone and his gun out, not sure which he would need first.

She fired three shots at the man who had caused so much horror to the world. The bullets shattered the glass just before Codi dove through and rolled to a stop behind a couch. The three projectiles continued on, slightly deflected by impact with the windowpane. Two just missed the target, while the third only grazed him.

Pullin dropped as the first bullets flew. One left a slight tear in his shoulder—nothing to worry about now. He quickly crawled behind an upholstered chair in the corner of the room, leaving the wounded and dying senator behind. He held up his mini pistol, ready to defend himself.

Before Joel could do anything, the man standing next to Pullin opened fire in his direction. Joel dropped flat and rolled left, hoping to find cover. He shimmied behind a concrete mermaid that was spouting water into a small pool nearby. Bullets riddled the statue, and chips flew in all directions. Joel tried to make himself conform to the curved shape of the mermaid. Twice, certain female body parts saved him from taking a hit. He tried to dial 911, but a bullet took the phone clean out of his fingers after just 91. After the initial fusillade of bullets, Joel pointed his pistol back and blindly returned fire.

Codi quickly crawled right, hopeful Joel could distract the first shooter so she could get to the second. As she came around the couch, another volley of bullets backed her up. Shots from outside the home poured into the room, and the man targeting her switched back to Joel. Codi returned fire, but the man was well protected behind a large marble column.

Gunplay from all three directions continued, the flash of gunfire matching the occasional lightning flash. Behind the column, Codi heard the tell-tale click of an empty clip. She moved quickly out from behind her riddled couch, pistol in front of her. The man she had been targeting ran from the column and jumped for the destroyed window Codi had smashed through earlier. She took careful aim and pulled the trigger. The bullet caught the man in the leg as he left the room in flight, much like a superman takeoff. Codi pulled the trigger for a second shot, but she was also out of ammunition.

Whiton felt the hit to his leg as he cleared the window frame and rolled to a painful stop on the soggy grass outside.

"Hold it right there. FBI!" Joel called out as he moved from behind his destroyed mermaid. He held his weapon on the suspect as his hand shook from a mixture of adrenaline and caffeine. The man's form was barely illuminated by the room's warm glow. A large flash of lightning displayed the man's scarred, angry face as he turned to look at Joel. As the flash died, so did the power in the house, and everything in the neighborhood suddenly went dark. Joel sensed more than saw movement. He fired his gun in the direction of it, the muzzle flash from his gun just lighting his suspect who was a few feet ahead of his shots. Joel readjusted and fired several more shots. This time he was rewarded with a *humph* before a large splash sounded. Joel ran to the edge of the pool trying to locate a body in the dark water.

Codi crawled to the senator and checked his vitals. The only light in the room came from the flashlight app of a smartphone lying on the floor by the doorway. The senator still had a weak pulse. She turned slowly in the room looking for

Pullin. Two shoes could be seen under a chair in the corner. Codi stood and placed her empty weapon back in her holster.

"Pullin Ikaika, you are under arrest for the attempted murder of a United States senator, among other things," she said.

The man in the corner stood to face his accuser. "You!" He hip fired his last remaining bullet, which he had been saving for the senator's eye, in anger at Codi, the federal agent who had been a horrible thorn in his side and had ruined his carefully planned operation.

She had nowhere to go, so Codi stood stock still. The small projectile buzzed past her face by mere millimeters. The shock wave the bullet created, caused her right eye to convulse and sting, leaving it tearing and burning.

Pullin pulled the trigger on the small gun several more times without effect. He tossed it aside, wiping the gunshot residue from his hands.

"That's gonna cost you," Codi said.

Pullin stepped out from behind his chair and ripped his shirt off, revealing a bronzed fit form in the shadows. His torso and arms were covered with Hawaiian tribal tattoos that grew more visible as he stepped closer. He took a stance with his feet wide apart and began a chant, soft at first, but it grew in volume. He rhythmically moved his arms in a masculine fashion, beating his chest and legs, thrusting them into the air. A threat against all who would dare challenge him. Codi recognized the chant as a *haka*, a challenge performed by Pacific Islanders to intimidate their foes before a battle. Pullin finished with a growl, stuck his tongue all the way out, and made a slashing motion across his throat.

"You should rent yourself out for luaus and bar mitzvahs," Codi said with no fear in her voice.

Pullin's face turned red, and he charged. A huge wild beast determined to decimate its adversary.

***

"I think something's wrong."

Brian looked at his watch, now regretting his offer to Matt to call him anytime he needed to talk. He took a deep breath and calmed his voice. He and his wife, Leila, had been sharing a late-night glass of wine and decompressing from the day. He had shared a few minor details of the debacle at the CIA and how he was sure that the alleged crap that always rolls downhill might be coming his way.

He stood and stepped away as he spoke.

"Why do you say that," Brian asked Matt.

"Codi's not answering her phone, so I did a 'find her phone' search," Matt replied.

"That doesn't work with the phones we use at the FBI, Matt. She probably has it turned off for the night after all her travels.

"Normally, I would agree, but 'find my girlfriend's FBI phone,' does work if you happen to work for DARPA, and right now, it has her at 221 Q street NW in Logan Circle."

Brian started typing in the address, feeling another headache coming on.

"It's Senator Crandall's residence," Matt said. "And don't bother calling. She's not answering," Matt added.

Brian flashed back to the senator and the operations room at the CIA. He hated coincidences, and this was a big one. "Okay," he said to Matt, "but understand I have a procedure I am required to follow. I'll have a patrol car check it out and report back."

"A patrol car? Don't patronize me, Brian. This is Codi we're talking about. Something is going down in Logan Circle, and I'm heading there now."

"What! No, no! I need you to stand down, do you hear me?"

Matt didn't respond.

Brian checked his phone to see if it was still connected. "Hello?" Brian dropped a rare swear word for him and hit end. He stood motionless for a beat as he tried to regain his emotions.

It was decision time. Brian had to step up or step down. Failure could mean his career. But the right choice was not clear.

Leila stepped next to her husband. "What is it?" she asked.

"I'm not totally sure, but the protocol for a situation like this is to—"

"Screw procedure," Leila interrupted her husband. "Honey, you need to follow your gut. It's what got you where you are today."

Brian knew she was right. Consequences or not, he needed to protect his team.

***

Joel got down on his hands and knees and felt for the side of the pool. He could just make out the dark water in the gloom. Somewhere, there was a killer either dead or waiting for him in the pool. He had heard the splash over the sound of the heavy rain. Considering his next move carefully, the only thing that came to mind was, WWCD, What Would Codi Do? She would finish it.

He considered taking off his good shoes before getting in the water, but he could tell they were already ruined. Joel circled the pool unable to make out a body. If the man was dying he needed to hurry, but going in was the last thing he wanted to do. His mind flashed with the man drowning and flailing as he tried to get a visual. Nothing. Joel took a deep breath and slipped into the inky liquid. He moved in a search pattern back and forth, his gun held out of the water right in front of him like a white cane on a newly blinded man. He had a sudden unexpected flashback to the scene from *Jaws,* where Matt Hooper sees a bloated head pop out right before his eyes and practically levitates out of the water.

Joel's hand shook with fear and trepidation as he moved methodically through the blackness, back and forth like a lawnmower, his hearing useless in the downpour. *Joel, focus. Find the suspect and drag him to the side.* He sensed movement slightly ahead and to the right. He spun his gun in that direction, nearly pulling the trigger as a reflex. A flash of lightning illuminated the pool, giving it a temporary blue glow. Right in front of Joel was his target. The man lunged for Joel with both hands and a scream. Joel let out a squeal as he pulled the trigger multiple times, ending the suspect just as everything went dark again. Joel turned and fled the water, vowing never to go swimming at night again.

***

Codi lowered her stance as Pullin charged. He was filled with anger and had no respect for the five-foot-eight, 120-pound brunette. When he was inches from colliding with her, Codi fell backward and raised her feet up making contact with Pullin's stomach. When she hit the floor, she used her legs to launch her assailant up and over her. Pullin crashed into the edge of the couch with a *clunk*. He flipped over and scrambled back to his feet. This time, he was more careful. Taking a fighting stance, he closed on Codi. She raised her hands like a boxer and parried a few of Pullin's best shots. They traded punches and kicks, Codi getting the worst of the volleys. At six foot three and 230 pounds, Pullin was formidable, a beast against a beauty.

He tried throwing a few decorative items from around the room at his foe, including a floor lamp. Codi dodged just out of the way as each flew at her.

Pullin was getting impatient and tried a few haymakers, designed to end the fight. Codi ducked and weaved trying not to let them make full contact, but even a glancing blow was painful. She quickly realized that she could not stand in and trade blows with this man. It would be a guaranteed loss. She needed to try something else—and fast.

Her ears were ringing and her vision was a bit blurry from too many hits to her head. An idea born of desperation came to her. Codi dashed forward into Pullin's arms. He reached out to take hold of her and end the fight by squeezing the breath out of the weaker combatant. Codi watched as powerful arms enveloped her torso. She let gravity take her, kicking both feet down and forward, launching her out of his grasp and down between Pullin's legs. She followed with a hammer fist to his groin, and then flipped over and sprang to her feet. She was now behind him.

Before he could recover from the genital impact, Codi sprang back up and encircled her arms around his neck. She leaned back and tightened her grip. Pullin thrashed like a madman punching and slamming her into walls and doorframes. Codi's head took repeated blows against the drywall, but she hung on, knowing to let go now would be the end of her.

Riding the wild monster for all he was worth, Codi tightened her grip until she could feel him getting weaker. Eventually, Pullin dropped to his knees and finally fell over, unconscious. Codi continued to hold tight around his neck for a good ten more seconds before she dismounted and stood over the man who had tried multiple times to kill her. She considered ending things right here and now. No one would care either way, but she was an FBI agent and for once in her life, she was going to follow that through. Pulling a set of zip ties from her pocket, she hog-tied Pullin's feet and hands. She wanted to find Joel and see if he needed help, but her head was spinning and throbbing too much. She tried to stand but wobbled and collapsed in a heap on the floor.

Joel stumbled back into the dimly lit living room, soaking wet. He could see two human forms on the floor and worried for his partner. He heard sirens approaching in the distance. The largest of the forms started to moan and move. Joel grabbed his pistol and leveled it. He would take no chances.

"FBI. You're under arrest!" he yelled.

"Joel, he's already arrested, but you can read him his rights if you'd like, once he's fully conscious." Codi leaned up on one elbow as she spoke. She didn't dare try to stand, as the room spun from the simple exertion, so she stayed on the floor leaning up on one elbow.

Joel moved over to her and sat down.

***

Matt raced through the wet streets. Luckily, traffic was light. No one in his right mind would be out tonight. Between the fear of the spreading sickness and the horrible weather, D.C. had basically self-quarantined. He could see several emergency response vehicles parked by Senator Crandall's home. He pulled to the curb and ran up the driveway.

"Codi!" he called repeatedly as he neared the house.

Brian intercepted him just as a body bag was being hauled out of the house. Matt's eyes bulged.

"It's okay. She's okay," Brian said.

Matt's eyes scanned the people, all working the crime scene and trying to stay dry. He spied Codi sitting next to Joel on the steps leading up to the porch. A pop-up tent was over them, shedding some of the rain. An EMT was shining a small flashlight across Codi's eyes and asking her questions. Matt sprinted to her side. Joel let him take his place and patted him on the shoulders as he sat.

"She's going to be fine, just a concussion," Joel said.

"I was so worried," Matt said as he looked her up and down.

Codi had a distant stare that slowly focused in on the man next to her.

"You were?" she replied as the EMT put a final bandage in place.

"You need to take her to the hospital and get her checked out," the EMT said to Matt. "Head trauma is no joke."

"I will," Matt said as the EMT moved away. "Yeah, I know I shouldn't worry, but I couldn't help myself," he said to Codi.

Codi gave Matt a smile and leaned against him as he put his arm around her. She was a soaking mess with no make-up and a rat's nest for hair. She had cotton holding back a bloody nose and several butterfly strips holding cut skin together, but she had never looked more beautiful to him. He held her tight, and the two just sat there as emergency personnel moved past trying to do their jobs. A second gurney came out of the house. This one with Senator Crandall. He was unconscious, but they had stabilized him enough to travel and were rushing him to an awaiting ambulance.

Codi glanced up into Matt's eyes. "Matt, I've been giving us a lot of thought."

"You have?" he said.

"Yes, and I think we should get married."

"Like now?" Matt asked.

"No, not now. We should set a date, and do it like normal people do."

"So—"

"So, Matt, will you marry me?"

He was stunned. His mind spun in several directions at once. "No, no, *no!"* Matt pulled away and moved back, completely beside himself.

Codi was perplexed. Had she overstepped? "So you don't want to marry me?"

"Yes! I mean, no! This can't be happening. I'm supposed to ask you. I tried to ask you two . . . three times!"

"You did?" Codi looked confused.

"Yeah, and it got all fouled up. Hang on." Matt put both hands up in the air. "Stop. Rewind." Matt ran away.

Codi watched him go, mystified by the male psyche.

She watched as Matt paced back and forth using his hands as if talking to himself. The rain continued to pour, uncaring of Matt's predicament. Suddenly, he spun back around and ran past Codi as if she wasn't there.

"Joel, Brian, I need a favor. Anybody got a ring I can borrow?' Matt asked.

Joel and Brian were over by the front door talking to an investigator. Joel looked up, helpless. "I don't wear rings."

Brian followed suit looking at his desperate friend. "I haven't been able to take this ring off for a couple of years. I think it shrank. Sorry, Matt."

Two officers escorted Pullin Ikaika out past them. He had a sour look on his face, and the sight of Joel on the porch got his anger back up. He started fighting against the cops, swearing and threatening Joel. A third officer stepped in, and they shuffled the suspect into the back of a waiting cruiser. Once the door shut, the scene calmed considerably.

A distracted Matt suddenly remembered his mission. "Okay," he said to Joel and Brian, "empty your pockets. There's got to be something I can use."

Joel pulled out two zip ties he always carried when in the field. Matt snatched one up in an instant. He began bending it and slipped the tab through the slot, ratcheting it down into a small circle.

"Knife?" Matt asked.

Brian pulled a SOG Flash II Tanto from his belt and flicked it open. Matt cut the excess strap off and held up a small black plastic circle with a bump on it.

"Perfect. Thanks!" Matt ran off, leaving the two agents now more curious than ever as they watched him with rapt attention.

Matt approached slowly and confidently. He got down on one knee and looked up at Codi, water dripping down his face. He held up the plastic ring. "Codi, will you do me the honor of being my wife?"

"I take it you feel better now?" Codi asked, looking down at his pleading eyes.

"Yes," he replied with a smile.

"That's all I wanted Matt, was a *yes*," Codi said, smiling.

"Wait. What?"

"Relax, Matt, we're engaged."

Codi cocked her head, as Matt processed the situation. Had she tricked him or was he overthinking things?

Codi grabbed him with both arms and pulled him tight. She kissed him like they might never see each other again. It was the culmination of so many emotions, and it felt great. This was the magic each had yearned for. Something stronger than both of them.

Brian and Joel watched from the doorway. Matt had finally done it, and they couldn't have been happier for both of them.

Codi pulled back from the long kiss. She looked her fiancée in the eyes as she whispered in his ear, "You know I have a serious concussion. I probably won't remember any of this tomorrow."

Matt paused for a second and held her with both hands. "That's okay, I'll use a real ring, and we can do this all over again. I'll never get tired of it, or of you."

Codi prayed she would remember this moment forever.

***

Fifty-five hours later, Codi stepped into Joel's office looking more like herself, aside from the new hairstyle, the bandages, and the black eyes.

"Congratulations on your engagement," Joel said. "Here. Colombian dark roast with a hint of cinnamon." He handed Codi a cup of coffee as she sat in the chair next to him. He had both screens filled with information as multiple sources and newsfeeds tracked the evolution of the Korean Typhoid Superbug. "How's your head, by the way?"

"I've had a headache for the last two days and a couple of dizzy spells, but if I take it easy, things should be back to normal soon," Codi deadpanned as she sipped from her cup.

Joel updated his partner. "Pullin has refused to give any information or assistance toward the cure, even with the promise of a reduced sentence. Seems he's happy to take the blame and let things play out."

"It was, after all, his plan and dream to 'save the planet.'" She said the last part with a heavy dose of sarcasm.

"He's probably thinking humanity will eventually thank him for being brave enough to take action when no one else would," Joel added.

"In my mind, he'll go down as the biggest mass murderer in history."

The international fear of KTS spread much quicker than the actual sickness. In an effort to slow it down, most of the world's population was bunkered in their homes. Social media continually recycled the story, and humanity seemed to feed on crazy. It didn't help that the list of symptoms read like a bad horror movie.

Now immune, Codi had donated blood and other samples multiple times in hopes of giving the CDC a leg up on finding a cure. So far, nothing had worked.

It was truly an aggressive disease with its own agenda. Whatever they had injected her with was not a vaccine, in the medical sense, but something more.

The US had effectively gone on lockdown. People were asked to work from home and stay put. Schools and communities were closed, even restaurants could only serve to-go orders. The list of job exceptions was small, but the FBI was on it and every agent was doing double shifts.

"I'm trying to get motivated to write my AAR [after-action report], but with all that's happening, it seems so trivial," Codi said.

"And even though we stopped *The Mantis* and *The Locust,* the planet is still taking a major hit," Joel added.

"Yeah. It feels like a failure to me."

Joel nodded his head in agreement.

Codi stood and let out a sigh as she turned to go to her office.

A ping on Joel's computer stopped her, and she turned back to see what it was. "Hmm."

"Hmm, what?" Codi asked.

"I set up a search program to track down all emails and phone numbers connected with anyone aboard *The Mantis* or *The Locust,* even that guy who tried to kill us."

"Garrett Scott?" Codi said.

"Yeah, him. I gave it ten key words to search for, like HYDRA, typhoid, vaccine, and cure. Looks like something hit."

Codi sat back down next to her partner as Joel pounded on his keyboard.

"So how are things with Shannon?"

Joel stopped typing. "Good?"

Codi waited for more.

"I've never dated anyone that has their act together like she does. It's . . . fascinating and terrifying all at the same time. But for whatever reason, she seems to still like me. So it's good."

"Good," Codi replied.

Joel nodded and went back to his keyboard.

"Soo . . .it looks like one of the lab techs, Kyber, on *The Mantis* backed up a bunch of files to the cloud on his home email." Joel opened the files.

It was everything they had been looking for—a complete breakdown of the disease and detailed notes on how the cure was made.

Codi and Joel looked stunned as they perused the files. They had the cure.

***

Codi stepped up onto the porch of the gray home with black trim. It had a peaked roof and sat on a large lot covered in grass and trees. The modern all-glass front door was open, but she knocked anyway. A woman dressed in black with bloodshot eyes and a haggard look came to the door. She had been crying.

"Mrs. Smith?" Codi said.

"Yes?" the woman replied.

"I'm Special Agent Sanders with the FBI. I was wondering if I could come in?"

"I guess. And please, call me Anita."

She stepped back to allow Codi to enter. There were several family members in the home and a half-eaten lunch spread on the table.

"I'm sorry to bother you, but I feel strongly that you should know the truth about your husband."

Codi was welcomed and introduced. She met Remi, Colt, and Greta, along with other family members. After pausing a beat, Codi held out a small polished case and handed it to Anita.

"Thor was an American hero," Codi said. "He saved my life and helped save thousands of others."

"Please have a seat. Can I get you something to drink?" Anita said.

"No thanks."

The room was quaint with comfortable furniture set on a polished wood floor. Codi sat at the end of a long forest-green couch. She told them the approved version of her time with Thor on *The Mantis* and the things he had done amid overwhelming odds.

After a long pause, Anita stood and left the room. She returned with a photo album and sat next to Codi. They spent some time going through Thor's life in pictures. After some time, Anita lifted the box Codi had given her and opened it. Inside was a gold medal with a star set over an olive wreath. At the top was engraved VALOR.

"It's the Medal of Valor, our country's highest civilian honor," Codi said in reverence.

"He was always my hero," Anita whispered as tears rolled down her face.

Codi stayed another twenty minutes listening to stories of the man's life and how he had impacted his community. She then politely excused herself and left the home. The long ordeal was finally over. Coming here was the bookend that closed it all for her.

She did her best to file it all away and clear her mind for what would come next—plan a wedding. *Argh.*

ACKNOWLEDGMENTS

I 'd like to start out the acknowledgments with a special thank you to the most important people on my list—you, the readers. Thank you not only for reading and enjoying my novels but most of all, for the wonderful word-of-mouth promotion. There is no greater honor you can pay me than to recommend one of my books.

With deep appreciation to all those who encouraged me to write, and especially those who did not, I thank you. I also wanted to thank the following contributors for their efforts in doling out their opinions and helping to keep my punctuation honest: Jeff Klem, Kristin Woodruff, Natalie Call, Carol Avellino, Geena Dougherty, Bryce Kaleo Clark, and Wade Lillywhite. And a thank you to a host of family and friends who suffered through early drafts and were kind enough to share their thoughts, to my lovely wife Leesa, who is my first reader and best critic, and my editors, Cathy Hull and Cortney Donelson.

A special thanks to my publisher, Morgan James Publishing, and the entire team that helped make this all possible, as writing is only half the total equation.

As many concepts as possible are based on actual or historical details. Special thanks to the original action hero—my dad, Dr. Paul Loefke.

IF YOU LIKED THIS BOOK

Thank you so much for taking the time to read this novel. Hope you enjoyed the ride. I would greatly appreciate it if you would take a moment to leave a review. An honest review helps me write better stories. Positive reviews help others find the book and ultimately increase book sales, which helps generate more books in the series.

It only takes a moment, but it means everything. Thanks in advance.

Brent

ABOUT THE AUTHOR

Writer and director Brent Ladd has been a part of the Hollywood scene for almost three decades. His work has garnered awards and accolades from all over the globe. Brent has been involved in the creation and completion of hundreds of commercials for clients large and small. He is an avid beach volleyball player and an adventurer at heart. He currently resides in Irvine, California with his wife and children.

Brent found his way into novel writing when his son, Brady, showed little interest in reading. He wrote his first book, making Brady the main character—*The Adventures of Brady Ladd.* Enjoying that experience, Brent went on to concept and complete his first novel, *Terminal Pulse, A Codi Sanders Thriller,* the first in a series, and followed it up with *Blind Target.* The third book, *Cold Quarry,* takes the characters down another rabbit hole, and *Time 2 Die* stretches them to the limit.

Brent is a fan of a plot-driven story with strong, intelligent characters. So if you're looking for a fast-paced escape, check out the Codi Sanders series. You can also find out more about his next book and when it will be available by visiting his website: BrentLaddBooks.com.

INTERESTING FACTS

For more facts go to my website and see as well as read these details.
brentladdbooks.com

Mary Mullins AKA Typhoid Mary

Mary was a real person whom many consider to be the biggest single mass murderer of the turn of the century. Though she never purposely killed anyone, she has been connected to anywhere from five to fifty deaths. Working as a cook, she left her mark on anyone that was unlucky enough to eat what she had prepared. Mary was the first person to be identified as an asymptomatic carrier, meaning she felt no symptoms but could still transmit the disease. Her story in the book is all based on facts with a few embellishments by the author.

During her twenty-five-year confinement, four hundred other healthy carriers of typhoid were identified in New York, but no one was forcibly detained or victimized like Mary was. In her own words: "I am an innocent human being. I have committed no crime, and I am treated like an outcast—a criminal. It is unjust, outrageous, uncivilized. It seems incredible that in a Christian community, a defenseless woman can be treated in this manner."

History has two versions of Mary's burial. Some say she was autopsied and cremated, while others claim she was hurried off the island and buried. I obviously used the second version for this book.

Typhoid Superbug

Recently, the world saw yet another evolution of the typhoid strain. In November 2016, doctors in Sindh, Pakistan observed cases of a novel H58 *S. Typhi* strain that was resistant to not only the three first-line antibiotics and fluoroquinolones but also a third-generation cephalosporin called ceftriaxone. This new strain is classified as an *extensively* drug-resistant (XDR) typhoid. Scientists warn that a superbug version is real. They have had several outbreaks across the globe. Infectious disease experts say they expect more and more cases in the coming months and years because the bacterial gene behind it is likely far more widespread than previously believed. The danger we face is real and currently, there are no known cures for the disease.

Secret Ship Lab

There have been several reports of companies using labs aboard ships in international waters to avoid prosecution. As it stands now, a ship in international waters is bound only to the country's laws of the flag it is flying. There are a few exceptions, such as drugs, arms, and human smuggling. But creating a new strain of bacteria is not covered in the exceptions. So technically, what Pullin Ikaika was doing onboard the ship in international waters was not illegal.

Chicago Tylenol Murders

The Chicago Tylenol Murders were a series of poisoning deaths occurring in the Chicago area in 1982. The victims had all taken the medication, which had been laced with potassium cyanide. A total of seven people died, with several more due to copycat crimes.

No suspect was ever charged or convicted of the poisonings. New York City resident James William Lewis was convicted of extortion for sending a ransom letter to Johnson & Johnson, but no evidence connecting him to the original murders was ever found. To date, no person has been convicted of the crime.

The incident led to reforms in the packaging of over-the-counter medication and federal anti-tampering laws. The actions of Johnson & Johnson to reduce deaths and warn the public of poisoning risks have been widely praised as an exemplary public relations response to a terrible crisis.

Asymptomatic Patients

The cells in Mary Mallon did something very unique. They created a protein that invaded the body's macrophages, the Pac-Man gobblers of foreign pathogens. The macrophages took the bacterium *Salmonella enterica serovar Typhi* and encapsulated it, turning the pathogen into a hospitable anti-inflammatory state and harmless to the body, overall. Once there, it slowly withered and died. Patients, in general, who are asymptomatic are hard to identify, as they show no symptoms. The problem is that they can still pass on the sickness.

Supermax Communication

The prison scene in the book where inmates used thread from a blanket to "fish" by casting notes out to other inmates is real and taken from a tour given to reporters at a supermax facility. Inmates were not allowed to talk or shake hands, so it was one way they were able to communicate with each other. Of course, it was limited by their casting skills and the length of thread they had.

DARPA – Z Man Program

The Z-Man project is a real DARPA gadget. It has been tested and refined, using the abilities of the Tokay gecko as a guide. "Geckoskin" was one output of the Z-Man Program. It was a synthetically fabricated, reversible adhesive with the ability to climb surfaces of various materials and roughness, including smooth surfaces like glass. Geckoskin initially was a stiff fabric impregnated with an elastomer that was able to maximize compliance with the surface while reducing compliance in the load direction, thus increasing adhesion. A proof-of-concept demonstration showed that a sixteen-square-inch sheet of Geckoskin adhering to a vertical glass wall could support a static load of up to 660 pounds.

A free ebook edition is available with the purchase of this book.

To claim your free ebook edition:

1. Visit MorganJamesBOGO.com
2. Sign your name CLEARLY in the space
3. Complete the form and submit a photo of the entire copyright page
4. You or your friend can download the ebook to your preferred device

Morgan James
BOGO™

A **FREE** ebook edition is available for you or a friend with the purchase of this print book.

CLEARLY SIGN YOUR NAME ABOVE

Instructions to claim your free ebook edition:
1. Visit MorganJamesBOGO.com
2. Sign your name CLEARLY in the space above
3. Complete the form and submit a photo of this entire page
4. You or your friend can download the ebook to your preferred device

Print & Digital Together Forever.

Snap a photo

Free ebook

Read anywhere

CPSIA information can be obtained
at www.ICGtesting.com
Printed in the USA
JSHW040316160422
25022JS00001B/56

9 781631 958489